A Death in Panama

by

Ronald A. Williams

DORRANCE PUBLISHING CO., INC.
PITTSBURGH, PENNSYLVANIA 15222

ISBN: 978-1-4349-0732-5
Printed in the United States of America

First Printing

For information or to order additional books, please write:
Dorrance Publishing Co., Inc.
701 Smithfield St.
Pittsburgh, Pennsylvania 15222
U.S.A.
1-800-788-7654
www.dorrancebookstore.com

Prologue

I

The large black cars had been arriving at uneven intervals since morning. Now, six sat parked in the circular driveway at the rear of the house. From the edge of the driveway, the land sloped southward toward the swiftly flowing brook hidden in the embrace of the forest of pine trees, where it could be heard gurgling during the night.

As each car pulled in, a gigantic chauffeur emerged and, swinging his gaze in a full circle behind the dark glasses, sniffed out the horizon, searching for patterns of difference that might contain the possibility of threat. Satisfied that the environment was harmless, at least for the moment, only then did each help an old, wizened man from the rear seat. Age had reduced nature's attempts at individuality, and each man, dressed in a dark suit of a vintage consistent with his age, seemed much the same. Leaning heavily on the arms of his chauffeur, each moved haltingly up the short walk to the rear of the house.

Inside, it was freezing, and though no sound could be heard, it was easy to guess that the air conditioner was going full blast. Though it was now late summer, everyone in the house wore a sweater, and each man hunched against the blast of cold air, leaning a little more closely into the bulk of his chauffeur. They were shown to the room at the front of the house on the first floor, and once they were settled into the comfortably overstuffed chairs that sat in a semi-circle around the center of the room, the chauffeurs left, and the door closed solidly behind them.

There were now six men, five of whom sat in the chairs that were evenly spaced around the room. This had clearly been an office, but one of grand proportions. The shelves on three sides of the room were still stocked with hundreds of books, and the grand, dark-varnished, mahogany desk on the fourth side seemed to have settled into the floorboards. The space, intimidating in the best of times, gave off a sense of perverse power, a sense made ironic by the presence of the sixth man in the room. He lay on a hospital bed, his mouth agape, his eyes staring deep into some place beyond the ceiling. The air smelled of death, and the five, so close to their own ends, seemed frozen, staring with rheumy eyes at the figure, waiting for something. They had been summoned by the dying man, and they had come from up and down the east coast to hear his last words. Each man carried within him the fear of the past, and now one man—Blackett —sat pulling nervously at the white handkerchief he held in his talon-like fingers. The center of the handkerchief was already showing signs of fraying.

On the hospital bed, the figure breathed shallowly, the gurgle of death loud in its throat. The mouth moved without coordination, a sound escaping the terrible body. The men leaned forward, trying to hear if anything articulate would come from this man who had controlled their lives. The six were as close as fear makes men. Long ago, in the gray mists of time, they had acted together as a most efficient cadre, and those acts were now their bond. The room stank of the antiseptic smell of the hospital, but these men did not know, their olfactory senses having long been dulled by age and experience.

Ten years ago, the man on the bed had been diagnosed with lung cancer and given less than a year to live — if he changed his life. He had essentially told the doctors to go to hell and had, if anything, increased his smoking in an exhibition of contempt for their concern. He had no family that he accepted, and almost all his contemporaries were dead. His estate lay far away from any neighbors, serviced by a phalanx of servants, most of whom had never seen the old man. They were very well paid, and they did their jobs well. Each had been carefully selected by a member of the dying man's law firm and was more than just a servant.

The old man was an inveterate smoker of Cuban cigars. No one asked how the man continued to receive Cuban cigars after all these years, but they had learned that there were few things beyond his reach.

Now in his ninety-fifth year, he was dying, the cancer having redesigned his body, creating newer, sharper angles that left shadows in the spaces once inhabited by flesh and muscle. The white blanket covering him gave evidence of the planes and acute angles that were now the geometry of his existence. The cancer, which he had allowed to be treated for a short six-week period ten years ago before ending it with the words, "I am going to die anyway," had spread to every part of his chest, and each man in the room knew that the pain must be intense. The dying man had taken himself off the morphine, and the face, skeletal now, had fixed itself into a grimace of determination, a visible statement of the will that fought the pain the tumors wrought. As they constantly subdivided, taking up more and more of the healthy space in his body, the will that had pushed this man all his life had fixed itself in the preservation of consciousness. He had long ago ceased to care about his body, and his extraordinary will maintained his life though he should have been dead a decade ago. The ferocity of that will frightened the men, who were themselves of no small influence, for they remembered its exercise in circumstances much different from these they now experienced.

They had not come out of affection for this man. Fear had brought them here, fear and a dimly understood guilt about the nature of their lives—lives largely created by the man who lay dying on the bed before them. They had come because he had the power to destroy them, and though this was paramount in their minds, they knew too that his power went much beyond that. In the twisted chambers of his mind lay the secrets of many governments, but most importantly, in this man's tortured but brutally controlled mind were the secrets of Panama. It was this word, Panama, that had been brought to them last night, along with the message to come to Gordon Heights, far out on Long Island, to the home of the dying man. They had not spoken to him or one another in half a century, but this word had made the death visit an imperative, and each had pulled his old bones from the comfort of his grand, ancient home and left immediately.

Now, they watched and waited, waited for this man, halfway to eternity, to tell them why he had summoned them. They did not speak but sat immobile and silent, their shoulders hunched against the cold and the fear. On the bed, the body moved slightly, and they all tensed, watching in stony silence as the head, completely bald and now unnaturally large, turned with millimetric slowness until it rested on its side, and the vacuous eyes lay on Blackett, who at once felt a tremble within him. Gradually, the eyes seemed to pull back from some place that the body could see beyond the here and now, and a feral brightness came into them. Blackett felt certain that the eyes were controlling his faltering heartbeat, and he breathed heavily, forcing the air into his lungs, exciting his heart so that it would continue to beat. The dying man still had the power.

Exhausted with the effort of moving the ponderous head, the body lay still for a long time, dead to the world, except for the eyes, which bored into Blackett. The lower corner of the mouth gradually became wet with spittle as the man re- laxed in his struggle with the blasted body, and a line joined the mouth to the sunken pillow. As if aware that the man was ready to speak, the old men stood slowly and shuffled to the side of the bed where the head faced them. He seemed to be gathering himself, willing his dissipated energies into this final act. When he spoke, the old men knew the danger they feared was indeed here.

The dying man spoke slowly and haltingly for a short time, ending with one word: "Culebra." He then fell back, eyes staring, the mouth once more agape.

Each of the old men felt the grave move closer. Culebra. *El lugar de muerte*, the locals had called it. The place of death. It was clear this was the reason for the summons to Gordon Heights, and they soon left, each lost in the mists of his per- sonal hell as the memories of the place called Culebra gave life to his terror. Soon, the driveway was empty, and the cus- tomary tranquillity of the estate returned. Inside, the body lay unmoving, but the face had relaxed, the earlier fierce de- termination at last at rest. And on the face was a bitter smile. He knew he had not yet breathed his last.

II

It was hot. In the distance, Rupert Barnes could see the mist in the mountains looming over Panama City. The balcony on which he sat was thirty stories high, and the city lay sprawled below, with the people, small in the distance, going about their tasks. He smiled. Panama had changed. In fact, this was another world from the one he had left sixty years before. Then, it had been a hellhole, a place of danger, disease, and death. He turned his wheelchair slightly, aware of the heat but ignoring it and thinking of the mountains that still contained the secrets of that time when the land was changing hands and loyalties.

His gray suit of fine, though aged, cloth must have once been form-fitting, and the lines that had been cut into the suit still showed; but, as the man had aged, the suit had fallen in on the shrinking body, and it now hung loosely. His face was craggy and very brown, leathery almost. It was the face of a white man who had been born and lived in the tropics. In spite of his age, the eyes that looked out on the city were hard and fixed, giving evidence of a will that had sustained the man all his life. His body had weakened over time, but the pitted, age-spotted face had the lines of experience, and in the eyes, if one cared to look more deeply, was the twinkle of a man who was not immune to humor.

He looked out at the canal, where a ship was moving slowly behind a tugboat whose stern was practically submerged as the great diesel engines moved the ship along this wonder of modern engineering. He felt a surge of pride at the thought of the role he had played in the creation of the canal and, as the ship slipped noiselessly by, the old man closed his eyes, seeing clearly what this place had been seventy years ago.

The ship that had brought the men from all over the West Indies had last stopped at Jamaica, and when the strong, very black men had boarded, Barnes had kept apart from them, preferring to be either alone or with the hundreds of men from Barbados who had found their nationality among the puking that the surging waters of the Caribbean had induced. By the time they had reached Kingston, they had been transformed from villagers into nationals, and though the villages still had a hold on them, the question, "Where you from?" gradually came to be answered, "Barbados" instead of "BellePlaine," "Carrington's Village," or "Mount Standfast." They had arrived in Panama as full-fledged Barbadians, or Bajans, as they were familiarly called. Even then, they had held themselves back, somehow aloof but without pretension, and this had continued through the time of the building of the canal. It was as if they had known of the tragedy that would occur here and their role in it and had therefore insulated themselves from it.

The most powerful memory he retained of his arrival in Panama was the two-way traffic. His ship, *The Endora*, had anchored offshore, and the men boarded the "lighters," the smaller boats that took them in turns to shore. The boats returning from the shore were also full, mostly of white men, their skin reddened by the sun and their eyes dulled from what he assumed was exhaustion. Some, however, looked terrified, their eyes darting around. Barnes thought it all rather strange. When the ship docked, he saw a line of white men standing impatiently, waiting to enter the boat that had been disgorging its passengers. Curious, he asked one of the men why they were leaving, but they ignored him, and sensitive to the possibility of embarrassment, he walked on with the newcomers.

The first thing he noticed was the smell. The stench assaulted the senses, seeming to rise out of the ground itself, filling the air with the sickly sweet, fetid stink of the swamp. A man from St. Vincent standing next to him cursed, "Jesus Christ. Why they don't clean up this place?"

Barnes shrugged, concentrating hard to keep down the liquid rising in his throat. The smell seemed a solid, living thing through which he was pushing his body, parting some cloying, clinging presence that threatened to close up his nostrils and throat and choke him to death. He kept moving, gradually allowing his mind to accept the smell.

The temperature was fiery hot, but it had obviously rained earlier. The streets had turned to mud, and the gutters, or, rather, the indeterminate edges of the road, were running with garbage and the occasional dead animal. He looked around at the other men whose feet, covered for the most part by homemade canvas shoes with soles of scrapped rubber, were now covered with mud. They were a motley crew with strange yet familiar accents, chosen from the islands that stretched north to south as a thin barrier reef to the Central American isthmus.

Looking back along the line, he saw the hard, leathery bodies that had worked always and were accustomed to hardship and deprivation. The faces that, on the ship, had been full of laughter and had lit up in response to the men's crude jokes, were closed and cautious, and the eyes had taken on that hooded look so they seemed less to see than to reflect the world. They were waiting to see what this land would bring. The promise had been of riches beyond anything they had ever seen. Ten years earlier, each had known someone who had returned from Panama with enough money to build a small home, and they were determined to do better now that the Americans were in charge. The bills posted in Bridgetown had read: "Get rich with America. Come join the Great Adventure of Panama." They had responded by the thousands, leaving the sugarcane, banana, and cocoa fields to head for the money in Panama—Yankee money: the best kind. The boats coming from the islands were crowded, too crowded to allow each man to have a berth, so they had laid at night on the open decks or in hastily erected tents when the weather turned foul. Barnes had slept in a tent one night but had vowed to remain out in the air rather than stay in that close, smelly space again. Now, walking through the clinging mud, the effluvium of the city stinging his senses, he thought of the open decks with something like affection.

In the line of men, he stood out. His eyes were alive with curiosity, and he stared at everything with a smile on his face. Though he was aware of the smells and the primitive nature of the city, he was also excited about the possibilities. Unlike the other men from Barbados, he had not come to Panama to escape poverty. Barnes was not sure he could put his reason into words, but the closest thing he could think of was purpose. Panama offered him the opportunity to escape the comfortable mediocrity of being the fourth oldest Barnes. The family was headed by his elder sister, Ruby, and this meant that he had to make his own way. He could have run one of the plantations, but there burned in him the need for something more. Management of the dry-goods store had never appealed to him, and he would have lost a fortune if Ruby had not kept an eye on things, always careful not to offend but firm in her advice. She smiled very little, and there was no mistaking her "advice." When questioned, her smile would disappear, and he would be left facing a visage reminiscent of the sphinx.

The old man smiled now, thinking of his sister who had died almost twenty years before. She had been a tyrant, and he had been glad to get out of Barbados and away from her. Panama had been his chance to prove he could make something of himself independent of the family. And he had done that. Even she would have to admit he had succeeded beyond her expectations. She had never said this, of course, but in the years after Panama, on the few occasions when they had written, she had treated him with a respect that had been absent in the days before he had left. He was the most successful of the Barneses, the one who had gone away and built a fortune on his own. His face twitched a little at the thought of that fortune. When he had received the message from the dying man in New York, the past had risen up to confront him, and that past, so carefully hidden in the recesses of his mind, had come in the form of a threat, a threat contained in a single word: Culebra. He had hidden from that past for almost fifty years. The actions performed in that place had faded to vagueness, carefully buried in the secret places that unpleasant memories die or live embalmed.

He had left for Panama the morning after the call from New York on the first U.S. Airways flight out of Philadelphia, where he had lived for the last thirty years. Why he had headed for Panama he could not explain, but with the word "Culebra" had come an uncontrollable urge to get back to the land that had started it all. He had not seen the other six men since 1946, but now the word "Culebra" was being whispered again, and the fear had returned. It would have been better if the dying man had left this world without feeling the need for redemption. He had called the seven together because, close to death as he was, his ears were still everywhere, and one of them had heard the word "Culebra." Now, the conspiracy of silence was threatened and, with it, the lives of very powerful men. By not attending the meeting, Barnes had cast suspicion on himself, but he did not care. He had not taken any pains to hide where he was going and would be found soon enough. There was no use worrying about that. Tomorrow, he would head inland to the place.

It is easy now that the boats can take you down the canal, he thought ruefully.

So different from when he had arrived a lifetime ago. Now, he needed to rest.

At eighty-eight, I am no longer as energetic as I used to be, he thought with a smile.

Pushing the wheels of his chair slowly, Barnes moved into the moist coolness of the air-conditioned room and within minutes, he was asleep.

III

The old woman moved slowly but confidently through the short passage of the wooden house, running her fingers along the uneven boards that made up the wall of the bedroom until they reached the space between the door and the wall. As her fingers reached the end of the wooden door, she paused, reaching her hand out again until it met the metal headrest of the old cast-iron bedstead. Inching along, turning left again, her leg brushing the side, she moved toward the foot of the bed. The room was a simple rectangle with a louvered window in one wall. This was open to allow the air to circulate, dissipating the stifling heat that lay trapped under the galvanized roof. She quickly ran a straightened finger under her throat, scraping away the perspiration and wiping it into the whitish apron she wore over her dress.

Her face was a study in contradictions. The skin, even after a lifetime in the sun, was light, close to what used to be called mulatto, and the features were, in the main, small and self-contained. Her nose, however, sat on these fine features with a flaring majesty, signaling the other part of her origin, and the wide nostrils were spread, as if smelling out the world. She reached up and, pinching the indefatigable nose between forefinger and thumb, pulled it upward and out. It was an involuntary action and the duplicate of a lifetime of such actions. The nose, more obedient to the dictates of nature and gravity, stubbornly returned to its original flare. The mouth had long lost its teeth, and since she had not put in her dentures, it lay fallen, hinting at spaces yet unseen. The eyes stared out at the world unblinking, and the laugh lines lacing the delicate skin around them attested to a life that, though hard, had been lived without bitterness.

The face was not smiling now. Instead, it carried the hint of a frown as she sat on the bed.

"I know dat I put them dere. But my old head so bad dat it look like I can't remember where I move them to."

The voice was quiet but heavy with the cadences of the island, though if anyone had told her she had an accent, she would have laughed, denying it with humor and a gentle suggestion of being flattered at being noticed. She had lived in the village most of her life, and though it had changed over time, it still contained the same sounds she had heard growing up at the turn of the century.

But even de sounds change when yuh come to t'ink 'bout it, she thought now.

Dependent as she was on her ears for contact with the world, she had been aware of the growing sharpness of the tones in the voices around her.

"People don't even talk to one another no more. Dey just tellin' people t'ings," she said aloud and then sucked her lips, impatient at her own dawdling.

"Now whe' I put dem papers?" she asked herself, standing up and running her fingers between the mattress and the bed springs. There was no expectation that she would find anything since she had checked there many times before. Frustrated, she sucked her lips again, an odd sound without her teeth, and sat heavily, her unseeing eyes staring in the direction of the wall. She tried to reorder her thoughts, seeking to remember the last time she had taken the papers out. Since she could not read anymore, having lost her sight close to fifteen years before, she took the letters out more rarely now, although she loved the touch of the paper. In her mind's eye, she saw him as he had been in 1904. Rupert Barnes had been something special, and though he was from that family, all the girls had liked him since he was not stuck up like the rest of the Barneses. He was the only one who would come down into the village to talk to the men and flirt with the girls. Always laughing, he never seemed to be worn down by the cares the other Barneses wore so obviously, particularly that one called Ruby who had run everything when she was alive and would not cut the poor people a break, even when the crop failed and they did not have any money to buy ground provisions from the Barnes plantation. When she died back in the sixties, people didn't even turn out for the funeral, and everybody said that they didn't know how somebody with so much money could be buried as cheaply as if she were one of the poor people. It only went to show that you would die the same way you lived. And Ruby Barnes had had no friends.

The old woman looked troubled again, her face a little lost now. She had to think where she had put the papers. Holding her head very still, she let her mind go back. The last time she could remember taking the papers out was when her grandson had come home from New York. He had stayed at a guesthouse, not wanting to live in the old house, though she had told him that it did not make sense to spend all that money at a hotel when she had a good bed he could sleep on for nothing. He had said that he didn't want to put her out, and she had protested that he wasn't putting her out. In fact, she would welcome the company, but he had wanted to stay at the hotel. It had been one day while he was in the island that she had been sitting on the bed, separating the sheets of paper and running her hands over them. She knew every word. Rupert Barnes had written the letters to her after he had gone to Panama.

Pregnant and unmarried, with no prospect of marrying him, she had hidden in her aunt's house, prey to the scorn of her mother who worked in the Barnes' fields as a picker and could not vent her anger publicly. Her mother had hated the Barneses with a virulence the old woman never understood, but she had reserved a special version of her venom for Rupert Barnes. To her, he was the worst of his kind, the serpent in the grass who whispered encouragement into the ears of the young girls, pretending friendliness when he wanted only one thing from them. Her mother warned her to stay away from the Barnes family, but she had made every opportunity to see Rupert, and, truth be told, she thought with a small chuckle, she had been as anxious to find out about him as he had been to find out about her. He had been seventeen then, and she had been one year younger when her bleeding stopped. She had known what it meant, but since she washed her own clothes, her mother had not known for some time. She was three months pregnant by the time her mother discovered her condition, and the woman had beaten her with a leather belt as her father mutely looked on. Even today, she bore the mark of that beating. It was only after her father had snatched the belt from her mother that the lashing had stopped, and she had stood, the blood dripping from the hem of her dress and making a small puddle between her feet. That beating had torn away the bonds between her and her mother and had linked her to the child.

Ruby Barnes, the witch, had sent Rupert away, but he had written to her for a long time, always with the promise of a return and though later she recognized the lie and the improbability of the promise, she had never given any other man much time. Rupert's son had died nine years earlier, but she had had no way of contacting the boy's father. The letters had stopped long ago, and word had come back that Rupert had married and had gotten rich overseas. She still remembered the coldness she had felt when his letters had turned dark, and she could hear the pain in the words that spoke of torture and death, betrayal and fear, instead of love. Soon after, he had disappeared and had not returned, not even for Ruby's funeral. His last letter, she knew, was dated December 18, 1912. He had been on his way from Panama to Cuba, and he was going to continue working for the Americans. That was the last she had heard from him, but she had always kept the letters.

"Now I done gone and lost dem like an ole fool," she said aloud.

Tears welled up in the sightless eyes. In those letters—written from 1905, when he had left Barbados, to 1912, when he had disappeared—Rupert Barnes had poured out his love for her, and she had felt so close to him as he talked about the hardships they were enduring in that country the Americans were developing.

She could remember no other instance when she had taken the papers out since the boy—her grandson—had walked in on her while she was "reading," as she still thought of it. *He must have moved them. But why would he do that?* Her heart quailed at the thought that the boy might have read her letters.

"Oh, my God," she said aloud, holding her hands tightly together. "Wha' if he start askin' questions 'bout wha in dem letters?"

She stopped, catching her breath, then laughed shyly, a little ashamed of herself. She was being foolish. The boy would not have read her letters nor taken them. She had just misplaced them and needed to sit down and think, that's all, and stop acting like the old fool she was. Brushing against the bed to orient herself, she retraced her steps, returning to the small verandah on the eastern side of the house where the breeze from the East Coast pushed away the heat. Passing through the small sitting room, she turned on the television before walking through the open door. On the television, two men were discussing the American President's proposed return of the canal to Panama.

IV

Jack Haight watched the buildings flit past his window as the American Airlines Boeing 757 rushed along the ground to the end of the runway. Panama City looked dry, although in the distance he could see the deep green of the rain forest painted against the solid flank of the mountains. He thought of the geological anomaly that was Panama, a country made up of the exposed spine of the American continents. The two giants were connected by this forty-mile wide spine, and in this, Panama's importance lay. Almost a hundred years ago, huge dreams had been constructed around this tiny strip of land, and it had all but destroyed the pride of a nation. The French had never been the same after Panama, as their arrogance had been flattened by the impenetrability of Culebra Cut. Haight could not help but admire these men though. In the last few weeks, he had read all he could about Panama and was still surprised how little was known about what the construction of the canal had meant in the formation of the United States.

He glanced at the boy who sat uncomfortably beside him in the leather seat. Dean Greaves was partially responsible for Haight's making this trip to Panama, having come to work for him on the recommendation of a friend in the

Business Department of Lehigh University. Haight had spent three years lecturing there but had left a year ago to manage Haight's Plastics and Paints, the business upon which his family's wealth was built. Haight's Plastics and Paints was expanding rapidly, particularly in overseas markets, and though his heart had never really warmed to running the business, he enjoyed the deal making. It had been he who had seen the possibilities in the overseas markets. The managers had politely listened to him when he outlined a strategy for overseas expansion in Africa, Asia, and Latin America, and they had politely pointed out that, while Asia might be viable, Latin America and Africa were economically depressed areas of the world with little disposable national income. He had persisted, knowing these continents, though short on money, were long on pride, and public works would soon be the order of the day. When the resistance in the company's management crystallized, he fired the president and simply ordered the overseas expansion policy be implemented. In the seventies, as the United States slipped into recession and the independence movement in the developing countries reached full flower, Haight's Plastics and Paints had been the beneficiary, and the company had grown dramatically. It was now the third largest paint company in the United States.

While the policy of expansion had worked well in Africa and Asia, it had been much less successful in Latin America, caught up as it was in the struggle to define itself. The whole continent, indeed the culture, was fighting a titanic battle with its past, struggling to enter the modern world. Its spirit was torn between the historic weight of medieval Spanish excess and what Haight thought of as American political entrepreneurship. The two halves of the South American self seemed stalemated, and the push back and forth stalled the development of the continent. Haight was certain that the forces of history stood firmly on the side of American entrepreneurship and that *latifundia* would lose. In fact, his development plan was predicated on the assumption of greater democracy, which, in his mind, meant a more distributed income. When this happened, newly freed people bought more, consumed more, and built more. It was this simple assumption that had taken Haight's Plastics and Paints to Africa and Asia, and he knew that the strategy would also succeed in Latin America.

The young man next to him had unwittingly started all this. When Haight got the call from Marcus Dennis, an old acquaintance and professor of Economics at Lehigh, he assumed Marcus was simply placing one of his students in a high-profile company. Haight smiled, thinking of the conversation. Marcus had been insistent that Haight read the student's senior thesis before making a decision, and Haight had laughed, responding that he had left the university to avoid reading senior theses. Marcus had not joined in his laughter, and Haight agreed to read the thesis. The young man had been researching the impact of the building of the canal on the political economy of Barbados, and while Haight found this interesting, it was in Dean's speculations that he had seen something more startling. Somehow, the boy had gotten the idea there was an inconsistency between the official figures for the tonnage of earth removed from Culebra Cut and the official depth of the canal, and he asserted that the bottom of the canal had to be many feet deeper than the official depth given in the Department of the Army's records.

Haight would have dismissed this as an undergraduate error except for one thing. The cost figures for the canal and the per-cubic-foot excavation costs were, according to the boy, also inconsistent with the total cost of the project. When Dean had calculated the depth using the per-cubic-foot figures, the canal turned out to be fifty feet shallower than if he used the total cost figures. These suggested a much deeper canal. It did not make any sense. Haight felt the boy had made a mistake. The funding for the canal was a matter of official record, and since the funding had come from Congress through the Department of the Army, the dollars had been thoroughly scrutinized. The depth of the canal at the cut at Culebra was also a matter of official record, so where could the boy's miscalculation have occurred? Since the total cost of the canal was also on record, Haight thought the per-cubit-foot costs the obvious culprit, and he had a somewhat startled accountant do an independent analysis. The official number had proven to be correct. The per-cubit-foot costs were considerably higher in the documents the man had checked. Still, Haight had been intrigued by the vigor of the boy's analysis and had re-read the thesis. Dean had not given the source of his cubic-foot figure, and since he had meticulously indicated his sources everywhere else, this stood out. Haight had called Marcus Dennis back.

"Marcus, what are you trying to foist on me? The political analysis is intriguing, but the calculations are pure speculation. I had someone here run some numbers, and it turns out your boy is wrong. What are you fellows in the Econ department doing these days? Still graduating students who can't read, write, or multiply?"

Marcus had laughed, replying, "So you noticed the numbers. It's good to know there's at least one political scientist who can add."

Haight, wondering why Marcus was so comfortable with a student whose calculations were so obviously incorrect, had asked, "What's going on?"

"I'm not sure. I rejected the paper you have, of course, and he has written another that is more acceptable though less interesting. He came up with this idea for the paper a few months ago and wouldn't back off when I told him that the calculations did not hold up. He claims he has some kind of proof the numbers are right."

"What proof?"

"Well, he's a little cagey about that. From what I can gather, he found some information when he was in

Barbados last spring. His family is originally from the island. He hasn't been too forthcoming about the documentation, and I think he changed his paper rather than have me question him too closely about it. Still, I feel sure he found something interesting, and it probably could make a good paper if the appropriate discipline were applied. He's a good student, in spite of the speculative nature of the paper you have."

Haight, intrigued, had asked, "Well, Marcus, what do you want from me?"

"Jack, I think this kid is good. As good as I have seen in a while. He shows an instinct for academic work, but he is interested in getting a job. I tried to talk him into staying on for graduate school. Even offered a full scholarship. If he's going to go to work, I would like to see him in an environment where his curiosity would be encouraged. That way, he won't be completely ruined by lucre."

Haight had laughed, knowing Marcus Dennis had inherited his money, and this gave him the freedom to be liberal.

The man had continued, "I also know you're interested in Latin America, Jack. In Dean, you have a head start."

"Does he speak Spanish?"

"Like a native," had been the immediate reply.

Haight thought for a long moment. Maybe there was something here. And Marcus was right. He was working on a way to get into the Latin American market more aggressively. The company had looked at Argentina and Chile but had returned to Central America. He was certain Nicaragua and El Salvador would get much worse before they got better, but maybe now was the time to begin the groundwork in the region. If this were true then everything pointed to Panama being the place to begin. El Presidente may be as corrupt as hell, but he did give American business free rein. Maybe Panama was not a bad place to start, he had thought.

But instead, he had said, "So what do I get in return for this favor, Marcus?"

Marcus had chuckled, answering, "Why, Jack, my undying loyalty, of course."

"When can you have him come over to see me? I have a meeting in New York next week. I could meet him then. And you can buy me dinner."

Marcus agreed at once, and the next Thursday they had dinner. Haight, impressed with the earnestness of the young man, had spoken little of the thesis, but he had left the dinner certain that the boy's research was thorough. Dean just gave that impression of competence, which Haight admired, recognizing it as the quality that marked his own personality. Having re-read the thesis, he had been again struck by the anomaly of the calculations. There was something else. The political analysis was incomplete, as if the young man had found out something he did not feel comfortable writing about, and this sense of mystery had completed Haight's analysis of the young man.

He had offered Dean a position in his office as Director of Latin American Operations, and it was one of the few times the young man had smiled since they both knew there were no Latin American operations. In the weeks since then, Dean had shown an aptitude for the ambiguity of his position and had begun the laborious process of compiling the economic data on Panama. The young man had a natural talent for searching things out, and Haight had taken the calculated risk that Dean wanted to find out something in Panama. This would make him work that much harder on the project. So far, Haight had been proven correct. The boy seemed never to sleep and had been soaking up all the information he could find on the country.

It was actually a call to an old colleague in the State Department that had changed what Haight had been thinking of as something interesting into what he was beginning to think of as a mystery. He had contacted Trevor

Cunningham, the assistant secretary of state for Latin American Affairs, to get a feel for the politics of Panama and had been surprised by the vagueness of the answers. Since leaving Harvard, Haight had spent most of his life in the State Department, and he recognized the telltale signs of avoidance. He had thought his questions perfectly straightforward, but Cunningham spent most of the time reshaping the questions, and Haight recognized the technique. Cunningham had been trying to extract information from him while shutting him out, so he had been forced to seek the information through less official channels that he had not used in the four years since his breakdown. Or whatever it had been. He had taken a leave of absence from the State Department when the pressure of the insanity in Vietnam had driven so many into their own vicarious madness. Unable to process the terrible information coming into the department, he had left, spending time at Lehigh, allowing his scarred mind to heal itself in the relative peace of academic life.

Tracking down information on Panama, he had been drawn to the young man's thesis again, and on the third reading, Haight identified what had bothered him earlier. Dean had given a full economic analysis of the great cut at Culebra, but he had totally ignored the political and logistical analyses. It was so obvious that Haight wondered why he had not noticed it before. Culebra was the center of the paper, but Dean, it seemed, had avoided a thorough analysis of it. Haight could not understand why. When he put this together with his call to the State Department, it added up to a mystery, and he did not invest millions of dollars in mysteries. This question would have to be answered before he would make a decision on Panama, and that meant he would have to do ground-level analysis.

As the plane pulled up to the gate, he wondered where this would lead. Panama was a good choice, he knew. It was stable—at least, as stable as any place in Latin America—and friendly to American capital. Still, he had to know why this boy next to him had weakened his thesis through such an obvious omission and why the State Department seemed so jumpy about answering simple questions about Panama. As the plane jerked to a stop, Haight looked full into the young man's open face, which always seemed friendly though not yet comfortably so. The eyes held Haight's attention, for they were impassive, and even as the boy smiled widely, Haight wondered what those eyes hid.

V

Dean Greaves felt the pressure in his arms as he pushed his body away from the floor. This was his daily regimen: one hundred push-ups, one hundred squats, and, when a bar was available, one hundred pull-ups. He ended the strength-training part of his workout with five hundred sit-ups. This was followed by a three-mile run and half an hour of calisthenics. Today, he would forego the run and calisthenics since he had stayed up most of the night reading after having dinner with Mr. Haight and the American cultural attaché. It was obvious the two men knew each other, and he was not surprised to find that Mr. Haight had been in the diplomatic corps before he left to run Haight's Plastics and Paints. Dean was still uncomfortable in Mr. Haight's company, though he recognized the man had given him a terrific opportunity. This, however, was a far cry from the flat in Brooklyn, and he was still unsure how to act. Haight did not seem to mind his discomfort, and the very fact that he paid no attention to Dean's occasional gawking at the riches that were now ever-present, had made Dean more comfortable.

There had not been a lot of time for gawking, however. Since Haight had hired him at Professor Dennis' urging,

Dean had been up to his ears in economic data, the number crunching and political reports keeping him up late most nights. It was amazing how much information Mr. Haight seemed capable of absorbing—and how quickly. Dean would spend two days analyzing some economic issue, and Mr. Haight would read the report and immediately pounce on the analysis, punching holes in the argument, forcing Dean to re-conceptualize. Dean had never seen anyone do this, not even the professors at school. It was as if the man's mind made links as he read, redrafting the paper in his head. Dean always left these sessions feeling drained and slightly stupid, but Mr. Haight always suggested that his work was useful and seemed genuinely satisfied with the information he was getting. Like last night, after the attaché had left, Mr. Haight had asked Dean, "Well, what do you make of that?"

"Make of what, sir?"

"Old Wayne Cimnieki there. What do you think of him?"

Dean was uncomfortable commenting on Mr. Haight's friend, but the man had been watching him closely, so he replied, "He seems fine. Friendly. You seem to have known each other for a long time."

Mr. Haight had grunted, nodding his head.

"Did you notice that he never asked why I was down here? Now, I wonder why that is?"

Dean felt silly since he had not attached any significance to this. In fact, he had not noticed. That, however, was Mr. Haight, always noticing everything and storing it for analysis.

Dean jumped to his feet, the perspiration dripping from his body. Glancing at his figure in the mirrors lining the walls of the fitness center in the hotel, he smiled with satisfaction. The muscles still rippled, the two months of sitting in front of a desk not yet having any effect. He had stopped competing just after his return from Barbados, where he had gone to see his aunt and to complete the research for his senior thesis during the spring break. He had finished out the season running at the Mid-Atlantic championships, but his heart was no longer in it after he read the letters taken from his aunt's house. Guilt overcame him as he thought of what he had done. He had not meant to take the letters, but seeing the large pile of yellowing sheets with the ungainly, fading black scrawl on them, he had been overcome with curiosity. His aunt had almost guiltily moved the papers, using her body to hide them, but in her haste, she had left one sheet in plain view, and he had said nothing when she asked him to wait for her outside. Before he left, Dean picked up the sheet.

Back in his hotel room, he had hurriedly read the page, and it gave him the idea for the thesis. His intention had been to write an analysis of the impact of Panamanian money on the island's economy, and most of the research for that had been completed. The page, however, had intrigued him. For one, it was surprising and slightly embarrassing to hear someone refer to his aunt in such passionate terms. More importantly though, the page had mentioned a "second floor" under some place called Culebra. He had no idea what that meant, but his curiosity had been sparked.

The next day, as the old lady slept outside on the verandah, he took the letters. It had seemed easy enough to return them once he had read them, but the world that emerged in the letters had been both frightening and intriguing. Something had happened in Panama, and while the letters were not explicit, it was clear it was something bad. The person who had written the letters was both afraid and torn by guilt about whatever had happened. Dean wondered about the "second floor," which sounded as if it was under the bottom of the canal. This caught Dean's attention and led to the speculative piece about the canal being fifty feet deeper than the official record. He had no proof of this except for the statement about the second floor, which the man—Rupert (there had been no last name)—had been involved in digging. This second floor had clearly been constructed separately and in secrecy.

He had expected Professor Dennis to dismiss the thesis because his attempt at making the numbers support his speculation was transparent. Still, the professor's interest had been evident, and Dean had not been surprised when the man asked him to meet with Mr. Haight. Also, as he had worked the numbers, he had had the feeling he was missing something, but he could not get the right combination of statistics to prove what the letter had asserted. In any case, it was an intriguing problem, and he would continue to work on it. Maybe when he saw Culebra, the speculation would make more sense.

The papers were at a friend's apartment in Washington, where he had been doing some of his research. Though the company was headquartered in Charleston, South Carolina, Mr. Haight had explained that it would be better if Dean stayed in Washington since most of the work he needed to do would be best handled from there. Dean had been happy to live in D.C. since it was close to New York, and he could take the train home to Brooklyn to see his mother.

Having had no opportunity to return the letters to his aunt, he had packed them in his suitcase. He had to figure out a way to return them without suspicion. They had been photocopied anyway, and he did not need the guilt.

Speaking of guilt, I should call Pam, he thought.

He had not spoken to her for three days, and she would be upset. Grabbing a towel from the pile near the desk, he walked out of the exercise room, toweling the perspiration from his neck.

CHAPTER ONE

WASHINGTON, D. C. 1904

Claudette Binai-Lemieux closed her eyes and rested her head on the soft cushions that formed the headrest of the carriage seats. Of course, she did not actually recline but sat straight up, her eyes shutting out the sensations of Washington. She had returned from the Senate chamber only a couple of hours before. For the last year, she had sat in the balcony, listening to the interminable speeches caused by the conflict in Congress over the building of the canal across the isthmus of Panama. It had been a year of hope and disappointment as the battle raged over the choice of the site, and her husband, who now sat beside her in the jolting carriage, had begun to show frustration at the indecision.

Looking at him now, she realized he had aged in the last year, fighting the battle at which he had become proficient but to which he had never grown accustomed. An Army engineer, he understood order and a chain of command, and Washington, it seemed, had neither. He had spent day after day testifying as to the efficacy of the Panama route, arguing its superiority over a path through Nicaragua. She had felt his anger but had not allowed herself to see the effects of the self-control until now, and that worried her. Never having been in the tropics, Claudette had read all that could be found on the area. Though there was not much that was useful, the glowing picture her husband portrayed of Panama did not conform to the experience of the French, whose failure in Panama was graphically demonstrated in the literature. They had failed because they could not control the ravages of the tropical diseases that seemed to find in Panama such a congenial home. Claudette Binai-Lemieux had said nothing of this to her husband, not wanting to add her fears to the list of concerns he already had.

He had won. Today, the Senate, with the not too subtle urging of the President, had finally voted for a Panama route. Her husband had been sitting on the main floor on the far side of the chamber. Except when testifying, he always sat there so that he could see her, and she knew he took comfort from her presence. When the vote was taken, he had been tense, his shoulders hunched in the unconscious way he had of facing aggression and which a lifetime in the military had not corrected. Though he would never think of exulting in victory, she had seen the shoulders drop, and he had leaned forward into the desk in what appeared to be a silent prayer.

Now, as he sat quietly beside her in the dusk, the sharp features and the pugnacious jaw that bespoke his determination were clearly outlined. Characteristically, he said little about the decision, and she could see he had already jumped to the next problem: actually building the canal.

Washington in October was already cool, and the leaves, having lost that blighted look of summer, were now lying still as if preparing themselves for their annual death. Claudette loved the fall, and this was particularly true in Washington, where the summers descended so oppressively, and nothing seemed to resist the humidity. Instinctively, she dabbed at her hair, which was pulled back into a large bun that emphasized the planes of her face. She had the delicate bones of the French from the Pyrenees; indeed, her father had come from that region of France in 1863, just in time, as he was fond of saying, to see "the final madness of the civil war." He had, for a man from the mountains, a most improbable occupation, for he had been a boat builder, and in the expanding economy of the United States, particularly with the growing emphasis on the navy, Marcel Binai had done well. He had reared his daughter to be American, though he remained unrepentantly French in sentiment, and this rubbed off on his daughter, who found her American sensibilities now assaulted by Gallic pride. The discussions about the canal were always tinged with a feeling of French failure, for they, as everyone pointed out, had been unable to complete the grand design, slinking home, torn apart by the diseases of the tropics and the insanity of the Dreyfuss affair. She desperately wanted her husband to succeed in this job. In her mind, it would vindicate France while glorifying America, for her husband, Charles Lemieux, was also French in descent, his family having come to eastern Canada in 1827 and to Connecticut forty years later.

Claudette reached over, resting her hand on her husband's, and he looked at her, his eyes crinkling with pleasure. With his wife, the stiff military bearing disappeared, and he became playful, more approachable. Charles knew she had sustained him during the long debate of the last three years and was certain he would have quit had she not been gently insistent that victory was bound to come. His eyes saw her now in the dusk, and he marveled again that she had chosen him. His love was palpable, changing the atmosphere of the carriage, filling it with a warmth that dissipated the chill of the autumn evening.

Claudette smiled and said, "You should be very proud, my dear."

His smile broadened, and he placed his other hand over his wife's.

"Proud? Proud of you, I am. Myself, I am tired, and the work has not yet begun. Panama will be a challenge."

"You are up to it. Your whole life has prepared you for this. The difference here is not one of type but of scale, don't you think?"

"Sometimes, my love, scale is everything," he replied with a suggestive laugh, and she joined him.

"You know what I mean, Charles."

"Yes," he responded, turning more serious, though a trace of the smile remained. "Panama is bigger than any project I have managed, but that in itself is not the difficulty. I believe the primary challenge is going to be labor. The French never adequately solved the labor problem. And this was not because they had too few men but because they could not keep them alive. The primary problem of Panama is not engineering but medicine. That is going to be our challenge, and our success will depend on it."

Claudette thought of his statement for a moment, then replied, "But you said nothing of this during the hearings, Charles. Why?"

"The Senate had no interest in it. Neither did the President. They do not desire a long struggle against disease, but, rather, a triumph over nature itself. The spirit of the age is for the conquest of nature through the brute force of engineering not the gradual experiments of medicine. I had to be an engineer for them to be comfortable. Yet, I do believe that a medical man would have been equally helpful as the commander of the project."

Claudette was always amazed at this quality in him, his ability to remove himself from his circumstances and to be hypercritical even to his detriment. *It must be his training as an engineer*, she thought.

"Have you selected a director for the hospital?"

"I have, actually, and if I'm given full freedom on this, he'll be the first member of my team."

"Who is it?"

"John McCormick. He was with us in Cuba and practically got rid of the yellow fever and malaria problem in less than a year. Of course, Panama is different. The environment is less contained than in the city of Havana, and much of it is still virgin land, so the swamps will create a danger that did not exist in Cuba, but if anyone can solve the problem, John McCormick can."

"Have you approached him about Panama? Will he come?"

"No, and I don't know. I haven't seen him for a couple of years, but he was obsessed with his theory of how to eliminate diseases that are endemic to the tropics. This is just the challenge that's likely to excite him. Anyway, that's what I'm counting on."

Claudette was thinking of what Charles had said as the carriage pulled up to a large, Georgian house that stood back from the cobblestone street through which they had been moving. This street was much narrower than the highway and ended in a turnabout. The carriage now stopped, and the driver's assistant, a young man of maybe fifteen, jumped down, placing a footstool next to the door before opening it. Charles Lemieux descended and, offering his hand to his wife, helped her down. As the carriage clattered off to its waiting place near the end of the street, Charles Lemieux pulled his frock coat down, squared his shoulders, and arranged the pugnacious jaw into its public position of military arrogance. Claudette smiled, watching her husband assume the public self again. He was not particularly tall, but the square, upright, military bearing made up in presence what he lacked in height, and that intimidating jaw completed the picture of indomitability. The coat was perfectly cut, dark gray, and showed his figure, which, at forty-five, was trim. He had labored over the selection of his dress tonight, she knew. This was his triumph, and though his appointment to lead the project was not in question, the difficulties of the politics of such an undertaking as Panama were going to be formidable. The impression he made tonight would go a long way in easing or making more difficult the innumerable demands he would have to make on Washington over the duration of the project, which was expected to last fifteen years. Taking his arm, Claudette felt a surge of pride, and she squeezed his rigid body briefly against hers, feeling the slight answering return of pressure.

A manservant answered the doorbell, and they were escorted into the large anteroom where their coats were taken, and a second servant led them into the reception room. The house seemed much larger now that they were inside, and Claudette could feel the rigidity returning to her husband's body. He did not like these affairs and often spoke disparagingly of them, but he knew their importance to the project, and nothing would get in the way of that.

The furnishings in the large, circular room were Victorian, stolidly elegant, and uniformly white. What caught Claudette's attention, though, was the stained-glass skylight from which a giant chandelier appeared to hang. Charles was also staring at it, since the delicacy of the glass seemed to defy what their senses were telling them: that it was supporting the chandelier, which appeared to be at least a hundred pounds. Claudette imagined that Charles was solving the engineering problem, but she was just struck by the beauty of the piece. The chandelier and the skylight formed a unit. The lights from the flickering chandelier reflected from the glass while the glass bounced the light back to the shimmering, golden surface of the chandelier which resembled a giant wine bowl, its reflected fire conjuring up images of some ancient bacchanalia. They had both stopped to stare when a strong, resonant voice said, "Quite the show-stopper, isn't she?"

They looked down, startled and a little embarrassed to have been discovered gawking like children. Lemieux was first to recover and said hastily, "Yes, it is. What's holding it up, Mr. Bryant?"

The short, polished man laughed softly before answering.

"I'll give you a while to figure it out, Colonel. You should find the engineering intriguing."

Then, turning to the woman with a slight bow, he said, "Forgive my manners, Mrs. Binai-Lemieux. Welcome to my home."

Claudette felt her heart bound in pleasure. So this was Edward Bryant. She knew of him, of course, but had never met him before. He had quietly supported Charles' position on the Panama route for the last three years, clearing the political dangers for him without ever meeting her husband. Edward Bryant was what was called "a power" in Washington. He did not just have power as in the ability to alter events by his intervention, rather, he was "a power," creating events by the fact of his existence. He had made a fortune in the railroads during the last quarter of the century and was spoken of with awe by even the magnates in the country. He had, however, retained his sense of adventure and was known to do pioneering work on his projects, forsaking the comforts his wealth brought to brave the wilds of the uncharted spaces where his projects usually started. There was a story told that he had found the first passage suitable for laying train tracks across the continental divide. He had set out alone at the beginning of winter and had gotten lost in a blinding snowstorm. Stalked through the winter by packs of hungry wolves, he had killed several of them, using their flesh for food when his stores ran out. When the ground had become too wet to light a fire, he had eaten the raw wolf meat. He had survived, coming out of the wastes of Wyoming almost not recognizably human. He had paid a price for this, though, and now walked with a pronounced limp, the result of having lost three toes on his left foot to frostbite that winter.

At sixty-five, he still had the tanned, lean look of an athlete. Claudette felt flattered and immediately chastised herself for being silly. She said in reply, "Not at all, Mr. Bryant.

We were admiring the chandelier and the skylight. You must know the impact it has."

"Indeed, I do," he responded, adding conspiratorially, "It is intended to take people's breath away. It gives me a chance to measure them while they are distracted."

Claudette joined the two men's laughter, recognizing the truth of the statement behind the banter and feeling a little cautious at the thought that this man could expose his purpose with such a sense of impunity.

"And how did we do, Mr. Bryant?" Claudette asked.

"The Colonel's capacities I already knew. It was yours that intrigued me, Mrs. Binai-Lemieux. I can see, sir, that you are well matched."

The three laughed as he allowed the pun to hang in the air unexplained. Charles Lemieux had continued to stare at the chandelier, and now he said, "Suspension wires. Probably triangulated from wall to wall."

Bryant chuckled, nodding as he did so.

"Very good, Colonel. Mrs. Binai-Lemieux, you see you have a brilliant husband. Did you also arrive at the correct conclusion?"

"Actually, Mr. Bryant, I was much too struck by the beauty of the chandelier to worry about how it was hung."

Bryant continued to laugh, nodding more vigorously.

"As well you should be. I can see you will keep your husband's excesses in check. You understand that method should never overwhelm purpose. Don't you agree, Colonel?"

"Sometimes, Mr. Bryant, it is difficult to see purpose without having identified a method."

"Spoken like an engineer."

They had by now left the reception area and had entered a large room full of people, some of whom Claudette recognized. As they entered, the whole gathering turned and started to applaud. She was surprised, and both she and Charles stopped. Bryant looked at them, smiling proprietarily.

When the applause died down, he said, "Ladies and gentlemen, I give you the conqueror of Panama, Colonel Charles Lemieux."

With this, the applause started up again. Claudette could see the tightness in Charles' jaws, and she reached out, touching his arm. He looked at her, and, seeing her smile, some of the anger went of him. He did not want this. The expectations were already high enough without this circus being created. Panama was going to be difficult, as the French had found out, and he would have preferred to work as most engineers did, in relative obscurity. This kind of thing simply made his job more difficult. As soon as he thought that, however, he felt ashamed. Edward Bryant's support had been constant during the last year; without it, it is possible the Panama route would not have been chosen. The New York interests that had supported the Nicaragua route were powerful and had influence all the way to the White House. The Southern politicians also preferred a Nicaraguan route since this had the potential of revitalizing the port of New Orleans and, by extension, the State of Louisiana. The deep South, just forty years away from the defeat of their way of life, was not insensitive to the implications of such a revival of trade. This unholy alliance of the South and Wall Street had threatened to provide an advantage to Nicaragua, since the railroads saw in the Nicaraguan route the opportunity for immense profits. They had almost won. It had been Edward Bryant's intervention three years before that turned the tide. He had used his not inconsiderable influence to neutralize the White House and had made sure that the commission looking into the route was not stacked with Nicaragua men.

Maybe he is entitled to a little pomp and ceremony, Charles Lemieux thought, relaxing visibly.

The room had quieted by this time, and they were all looking at him. He had had no idea he was supposed to speak and had prepared nothing. Now, however, he raised his glass.

"Ladies and gentlemen, to victory."

The toast was repeated, and they all drank. Charles Lemieux looked at the roomful of dignitaries, recognizing Secretary of State Hay and the Secretary of War, Taft. The president of Atlantic Railroad was standing in a corner, the usual sour smile on his face. These were men who could make or break the project, and Charles Lemieux knew Edward Bryant had purposely set him up for this. The man knew Panama would be composed of the unexpected, and he wanted to see how Lemieux would perform in these circumstances. He also knew the reality of building the canal, like the railroads he had built, would only be ostensibly about engineering. The primary problem would be politics, and if Charles Lemieux could not handle this, then the project was in the hands of the wrong man. He had neatly created a test for Lemieux and a celebration of his triumph all in one, and no one would be the wiser if Lemieux failed tonight. It was with this knowledge that Lemieux now spoke.

"Gentlemen, it is important to recognize that our victory lies in the future. For the moment, we have only struggle and danger to look forward to. It is a struggle, however, I enjoin with all my heart, and this is for one simple reason: In this endeavor, I have the support of the greatest nation on earth. To that, I give you the United States of America."

Charles Lemieux raised his glass, and the applause started again. Edward Bryant stood watching him, a wry smile on his face.

"Very good, Colonel. Now, let me introduce you around. I assume you have met the Secretary of War, Mr. Taft."

"We have met on occasion, but we do not know each other well."

"Then I think we must correct that. Taft is a coming man, Colonel. He has ambitions, and, more importantly, he will control your budget. Roosevelt is important, but, on this project, Taft will have the last word."

As he spoke, Bryant looked in the direction of a woman of stunning beauty, and she immediately glided over to where the three were standing. Claudette noticed that no one had approached them before, and it occurred to her that no one intruded on this man. Bryant introduced the young woman, and immediately Claudette found herself skillfully engaged in conversation with the newcomer and also being gently led away from her husband. She felt her anger rise but struggled to control it, recognizing that Charles needed these introductions. Still, she did not take kindly to being so casually excluded. It galled her, too, that Charles made no conciliatory gesture to her, accepting her exclusion as natural. The young woman was, however, speaking.

"Your husband is quite handsome, Mrs. Binai-Lemieux."

Claudette raised her eyebrows before responding. The comment seemed strangely forward for someone whom she had just met, but she supposed that times were changing, particularly for these young people. Claudette was herself thirty-nine, but the girl was certainly at least a decade younger than that, and she wondered about her relationship to Edward Bryant. The girl, however, had continued to speak.

"He is very fortunate to have Edward as a sponsor. That practically assures the success of his project."

Claudette looked at the young woman, then said, "His project?"

"Well, you know what I mean. He's going to be in charge of building the canal. That makes him responsible for everything. He's going to become the face of America, and it will be a handsome face, don't you think?"

Claudette was not sure what to make of the comments, but she was beginning to think she had seriously misjudged the girl. Young and beautiful, she appeared flighty, but Claudette was not sure of that anymore.

"My husband is an engineer, and an extraordinarily good one. I don't quite understand your fascination with his looks."

The young woman giggled, a tinkly sound that carried beneath it a deeper resonance that was not at all childish.

"Oh, please don't be offended, Mrs. Binai-Lemieux. I am sometimes too blunt. I only meant to say that he was selected not only for his engineering skill but because he will be the image of America, and it is important to have a handsome image."

"Why?" Claudette asked, genuinely perplexed.

"Oh, you will find out later tonight. Why do you think they are building this canal?"

"Well, that is pretty obvious. We need a way to link the east and west coasts, and using the rail overland or the sea around the tip of South America takes much too long. The canal shortens the trip and makes travel more convenient."

"All true, Mrs. Binai-Lemieux. But why would Edward, a railroad man, be so enthusiastic about a project that threatens to take profits away from his business?"

Claudette had never thought about it. She knew Edward Bryant to be a railroad magnate, but he had many other interests as well. She had simply assumed the canal would serve whatever interests he had, and she said this.

"It is true that Edward will probably make money from this venture, but I don't think that is his motivation at all. He is consumed by this project, but I have seen little evidence that he intends to make money from it. His motivation is different this time. There is something—let's call it glory—that seems to be infecting the conversations being held about the canal."

The young woman had been walking as she spoke, introducing Claudette to a number of women who now all seemed to have drifted away from the men. The room into which she had been steered was another stunning entrapment of space. The walls were a dark, pinkish Italian marble with cream-colored striations running in perfect symmetry from ceiling to floor. The space had been broken up into a series of alcoves that could be isolated by dropping the Romanesque curtains hanging from the ceiling. These appeared to be woven from gold thread and were pulled back and held in place by golden silk cords. Claudette wondered if any of the rooms in the house were identical. So far, from what she had seen, each one was idiosyncratic.

As they entered, the women congregated around them, offering their congratulations. Claudette knew she was being looked over and fully recognized she would be the talk of many a bedroom later that night. In this respect, Panama was bigger but not different. This had been the ritual since Charles gained some reputation for building major projects. He was a minor celebrity, his picture having been in the newspaper a number of times for dams and bridges he had built, but his reputation had been made through the railway he had pushed through the Northwest against all odds. This, she believed, had brought him to the attention of Edward Bryant, who had made his name in a similar fashion at an earlier time. Charles had received a congratulatory letter from the railroad czar when the last tie had been laid, along with a bottle of champagne. *He still has the unopened bottle at home*, she thought with a smile.

Claudette pulled her mind back to the women who surrounded her, making conversation.

"Well, what do you think, Mrs. Binai-Lemieux?"

"I'm sorry. I seem to have been daydreaming. Forgive me, but I didn't hear the question."

"Mrs. Horton was wondering what you thought of going to live in Panama, or 'that godforsaken place,' as she put it."

From the direction of her guide's eyes, it seemed the question had come from an older woman who, even in the warmth of the house, had kept on her boa. She was looking at Claudette speculatively, her eyes, surrounded by makeup, lost in the darkness of her mascara. Claudette knew her from her frequent appearances in the newspaper. She was a widow who dominated Washington opinion through her articles in support of women's rights.

"I wondered how you would fare in that climate, my dear. The tropics cannot be good for you. We die at an alarming rate in those places. That hemisphere of the globe seems to have been assigned to the darker-skinned people. We probably have no right to be there, and that is why we die off so quickly."

Everyone recognized the thrust of Emmaline Horton's comment. Her husband, the publisher of a Washington newspaper, had died of malaria while traveling in Africa. She had vowed never to leave the United States again, and this was a promise she had kept.

"Actually, Mrs. Horton," Claudette replied, "many more Negroes died in Panama than did the French when they made their attempt on the canal."

"Probably, my dear, but that was most likely due to carelessness, not their constitutional incapacity as is the case with our people."

"Not at all. I have been reading about the French phase of the attempt to dig the canal. Most of the Negroes died from malaria, which is a tropical disease. In fact, the French really didn't know how many Negroes died because so many of them lived in the jungle."

Claudette had not noticed, but the room had become rather quiet. She was ignorant of the protocol that allowed Emmaline Horton the unchallenged right to any opinion. The worthy Mrs. Horton had herself become somewhat accustomed to this status of seer and was at something of a loss as to how to put down this upstart. Not entirely certain of her facts, she resorted with great assurance to an opinion with which she was sure everyone would agree. Shuddering mightily, she said, "The jungle. The very word conjures up the horror of man's state."

The group of women laughed in relief, and Claudette, recognizing that the woman was seeking some agreement, responded, "That is the part I shall least like, I think. I lived with Charles in the northwestern mountains when he was building the railroad there, but jungle and heat seem so different, so primitive."

On this, they could all agree, and the conversation slid easily back into more conventional and familiar channels, Claudette all the while feeling a bit of a hypocrite since she disagreed with much of what was being said. Her thoughts drifted away from the voices of the women and turned to the place where she would be spending the next several years: Panama. Even the sound of the word was exotic, intriguing. She wondered what Charles was doing outside with the men and felt a fresh surge of pride in his selection. This would be the most important event of the century, and her breast swelled with the thought that they would be at the center of it.

Charles' career in the Army had been sterling before 1898, but everything changed in Cuba when Teddy Roosevelt noticed the captain whose construction ideas made the successful execution of the war possible. His career had sped up after that, and his promotion to colonel had come in fewer than four years. Claudette recognized that the man who was now President had much to do with this, grateful as he was for the swift victory that had created his legend in Cuba. The assignments that followed had given Charles ample opportunity to excel, and this he had done. After the construction of the dam in Colorado, he had been acclaimed as one of the great engineers in the country, perhaps even the world.

He had grown up with the figure of Ferdinand de Lessups as his guiding light, and she knew beneath the stolid military bearing, an ambition burned to be seen as superior to the man who had built the Suez Canal and who was still his hero. Panama provided an opportunity he could not have imagined in his wildest dreams, for De Lessups had failed in Panama, and this gave him the possibility of direct competition with his idol. Panama had broken the indefatigable De Lessups, and Charles was determined it would not break him. Claudette felt that in Charles' triumph would also lay De Lessups' and France's, and so her pride was both in her husband and in her culture. She had the utmost confidence in Charles' ability, but somewhere inside her lay a small area of doubt. Panama would be different from anything Charles had done before, and when all was said and done, the great De Lessups had failed.

Outside, the men had headed into the smoking room. There, Charles Lemieux found himself the center of a circle of congratulations and the recipient of various pledges of support. His attention, however, was caught primarily by two men: Secretary of State Hay and Secretary of War Taft. They had offered congratulations and had then retired to a secluded corner of the room and were now deep in conversation. Charles was, meanwhile, fielding questions of varying levels of intelligence and, while keeping the men in view, was constantly distracted by some comment. Still, all of these men supported the Panama route and, therefore, needed to be courted.

At the moment, Charles was answering a question posed by Augustine Walters, who owned Walters Shipping. The man had asked why the French had failed, and Charles was explaining.

"The French, sir, did a magnificent job of making the impossible possible. The dream of a path through the Americas from the Atlantic to the Pacific was the driving ambition of the Spanish from the time of Columbus, and the isthmus figured prominently in the imagination of the sixteenth century for precisely this reason. Yet, no nation had the imagination to reduce the scale of that task to an engineering possibility until the French."

The man to whom he spoke looked unhappy and doubtful.

"The French failed because they are French. Colonel Lemieux, great tasks can only be performed by great cultures, and while France may have been great once, it has lost that spark which inspires a nation. That is why they failed."

Charles Lemieux felt the anger rise in him, and though he did not recognize it as springing from his French roots and would have denied it had anyone suggested such a thing, he clearly objected to the bigotry inherent in the statement.

"I am not sure, Mr. Walters, that culture has much to do with it. What a nation achieves is done through the genius of its individuals, its commitment to freeing the individual's will, and its capacity to generate the wealth great enterprises demand."

"All of which, Colonel, goes to prove my point. Would you assert that the natives of Guinea or the Congo are equally prepared to engage in this endeavor? That we, the white race, are no better situated to lead this enterprise than the painted-faced savage? And you, Colonel, are you no more than some fellow who is placing stones together to create what he fondly believes to be art?"

Charles felt ill prepared for this argument, his faculty tending toward the concrete rather than the speculative. When faced with a problem, Lemieux's mind reduced it to pictures with levers, gears, and balances. Speculative philosophy always seemed simply an exercise in futility, convenient for those who had time for it, but lacking in value for the practical men who made the world a more convenient place to live. Yet, he knew this conversation was not inconsequential. This would have been obvious even if he could not see the calculating look with which Edward Bryant was regarding him. He had known from the moment he had been separated from Claudette there would be a test. He was sure his selection was complete, but there would be varying levels of freedom depending on how he handled himself. They needed his engineering skill, but there was a number of ways to extend or to limit his power in Panama.

Taft and Hay had given up their conversation and had walked over to join the group as Augustine Walters' voice had risen. Taking a shallow breath and smiling carefully, Lemieux responded.

"You have me at a disadvantage, sir. I am an engineer and, as such, know little of the eddies and tides of culture. But this I do know: Panama will be won by engineering skill, backbreaking labor, and the conquest of the tropics and all that it has to throw at us by way of disease in nature's many virulent forms. If our culture better prepares us for this, then, Mr. Walters, I will be a convert to your way of seeing things."

Lemieux ended with a broad smile, and Walters returned it with a slight bow. From the corner of his eye, Lemieux saw a look of understanding pass between Taft, Hay, and Bryant, and from the smile on Bryant's face, he felt certain he had passed the test.

Another man he had seen before but could not place was asking, "Colonel Lemieux, who will do your backbreaking labor? Surely not the Panamanians. This would seem to me one of your most serious problems. Augustine's concern with the value of culture notwithstanding, it seems to me the French failed because they could not sustain their labor force. Is this not true?"

"Yes and no. The problem was not the French's ability to attract workers. There was no shortage of workers. There were close to thirty thousand West Indians imported from the British islands. The Panamanians, to answer your question, were not at all interested in the work. The West Indians were, but they proved to be just as vulnerable as anyone else to the diseases of the Panamanian jungle. The French were unable to conquer the toxins of the tropics, and so they were defeated."

"But, Colonel, nothing has changed, so how will we fare any better than the French?"

Lemieux paused, judging whether it was time to discuss the health issues surrounding the assault on Panama. What he said tonight would be all over Capitol Hill tomorrow. He was now an authority, and the irony of this was he had never even set foot in Panama. His theories were largely based on engineering and health studies, his staple reading for the last four years. Still, he knew these men were all adventurers in their own right. Each man here was wealthy, and most had made his own money, so risk was not entirely foreign to them. If he impressed them, he would have support for the duration of the task in Panama, and so he said, "The major problem we will face in Panama will not be engineering or the lack of labor. Our primary problem will be maintaining the health of our workforce. The French tried but failed to do this, and it destroyed the enterprise. We will have to make sure this does not happen to us."

"And how do we ensure that, Colonel?"

"Before we attack the problem of digging the canal, we will have to conquer malaria and yellow fever. This, gentlemen, will be the secret to our success in Panama."

"And how will you attempt this assault on Panama's defenses, Colonel? Is there a plan?"

This had come from Edward Bryant, and Lemieux turned to him saying, "Not quite a plan yet, but a man."

"And who is this man?" asked a voice from behind Lemieux, who spun around, his surprise overcoming his need for dignity.

"John," he said excitedly, walking out of the circle of men who had been questioning him and rushing over to his friend, saying as he walked, "What are you doing here?"

"Mr. Bryant was kind enough to invite me. He said you would need me, sir. I, of course, would not be so presumptuous as to think that," John McCormick ended seriously, though Lemieux knew he must be laughing inside.

Lemieux turned, looking at Bryant with a new respect. The man had anticipated his request and had never made any mention of it. Bryant seemed to be enjoying Lemieux's surprised face and, chuckling, indicated that Lemieux should introduce his friend.

"Gentlemen, allow me to introduce Captain John McCormick, the conqueror of Cuba's diseases, and the one man I am absolutely certain I need to succeed in Panama."

The men in the room had no idea who John McCormick was, but they applauded, and McCormick bowed, an ironic smile on his face. Lemieux was just about to turn his attention back to McCormick when Bryant walked up and took his arm.

"There will be time enough for reunions, gentlemen. Now, I must take Colonel Lemieux away for a while."

With that, he shepherded the engineer out of the room, heading back into the recesses of the mansion. Lemieux walked quickly beside the man, his eyes catching glimpses of the treasures Bryant had accumulated from a lifetime of travel. Suddenly, the lighting changed, and the place became darker as they walked on to a terrace leading to a small bower that had obviously been imported from the tropics. The lush leaves, even in the semi-darkness, gave off a dull shine as the deep green intersected with the muted light from the gas lamps burning on the far end of the patio. Charles Lemieux was impressed. It seemed Edward Bryant was determined to prove he could reshape the world, and, so far, there was no reason to doubt this. The man stopped, looking into the gloom of the bower. Then, Lemieux saw a figure separate itself from the darkness and walk energetically toward them. He gasped in surprise, and Bryant chuckled. By this time, the figure had reached them.

"Good evening, Edward. Thanks for bringing the colonel out to see me."

"Not at all, Mr. President."

The President stuck a large hand out, grasping Lemieux's and pumping it vigorously.

"Congratulations, Colonel. It's good to see you again. Last time we were together, you were a captain."

Then, turning to Bryant, he added, "He pretty much won the war for me in Cuba, you know."

Bryant nodded slowly. Charles Lemieux, recovering from his surprise, said, "Good evening, Mr. President. I'm delighted to see you, too. I have appreciated your support over the years. The difference in rank you noted was due in no small part to your influence."

The President made a dismissive gesture, turning at the same time to Bryant.

"You see, he's already turning into a politician."

They both laughed.

The President took Lemieux's arm, and the three walked over to a marble bench set back in the bower.

"Colonel, I wanted to offer my congratulations but did not wish to steal your thunder, so I opted not to be officially present tonight. Edward was kind enough to arrange this meeting for me. I wanted to impress upon you the tremendous importance of this enterprise to the country. I am sure you recognize this, but indulge me for a moment."

President Roosevelt paused as if searching for the right words, though Lemieux knew the man was never at a loss for words.

"Charles, this is an historic moment. We are in a new century, a century that will—no, *must* belong to the United States. It is our destiny. Six years ago, you helped me break Spain's final hold on the Americas, and tomorrow you begin the step toward American ascendancy. Oh, there are practical reasons for the canal. Edward here could give you a thousand. But the symbolism of victory will stamp out the United States' role as the pre-eminent power in the world. If not us, then who? I see the potential for chaos if the United States does not fulfill its responsibility to humankind. Europe is exhausted, and, like most great animals in their death throes, their power only appears still to be present. Their thrashing around gives the appearance of purpose; their reflexive muscular contractions give the appearance of strength. The French failure at Panama and Britain's colonial drive into Africa and India in the last century are evidence of these thrashings. In their apparent triumphs, they have already sown the seeds of failure. The French's magnificent dream of a waterway from the Atlantic to the Pacific died at Suez, for they exhausted their national energies in that effort, though they did not recognize it. So, too, Britain believes itself an expanding power, but it is caught up in Europe's milieu and will soon fail. Who then will carry the civilizing burden? We will. The United States must, if the civilizing influence of our culture is to continue to expand. And if this is to be the case, we need two things to be clearly defined. The United States must have a defined sphere of influence. We must lay claim to what is ours, and those are the seas that rub our shores. The expanding power of our navy will ensure this. With Spain removed, we cannot allow another European power to enter our sphere of influence."

He paused for a moment, then continued, "France could not be allowed to finish the canal. We must. That, Charles, is the second thing we need: a symbol. Panama will establish the might of the United States and stake our claim as one of the great nations of the world."

The President smoothed his large, walrus-like mustache and paused for breath. He had been sitting, his body leaning forward urgently, and he now stood, pacing back and forth before the two seated men.

"You are at the outset of great things, Charles. Panama is more than just a commercial route, although that will have its value as well. Think of it for a moment. We're talking about the construction of a symbol that will stand in history with the Egyptian pyramids and the hanging gardens of Babylon. No modern culture has built on that scale. Not the

French, not the English, and certainly not the Spanish. No nation has had the will or the genius to build on this scale for millennia."

He now stopped pacing and, looking down on the two men, said quietly, "But the United States will. And you, Charles, are the man at the center of that history. I know you will succeed because America must."

With that, he abruptly said goodnight and walked off into the gloom. The two men sat quietly for a while, Lemieux thinking that he was truly fortunate to be selected for this task. He had never before thought of it in quite these global terms. This was a turning point. The United States was a power on the rise, and he was going to be central to that rise. Chest constricted with emotion, he looked over to Edward Bryant, whose face, partially obscured by the darkness, carried its characteristic smile. He was not surprised when the man's cool voice intoned, "Of course, it won't be worth a tinker's damn if it doesn't make any money."

CHAPTER TWO

WASHINGTON, D. C. 1904

Later that evening, Charles Lemieux watched his wife as she undressed. *She is truly beautiful*, he thought, remembering the day he met her. It had been cold, and he had been meeting a friend from Annapolis for dinner. Dressed in a white tunic and military slacks, he made quite a picture in the gray, long coat as he repeatedly stamped his feet to keep them warm. On the verge of abandoning his wait, a voice behind him said, "I am sure if you came in and sat next to the window, you would see whomever you are waiting for just as easily. And you wouldn't freeze to death."

He had turned, surprised by the young woman who stood in the half-opened door, smiling impishly. Recognizing the truth of the statement, he turned on his heel and walked into the restaurant. It had been full of college students, and he felt a little silly in the stiff military uniform as he had sat down with the two young women. They were both students at a finishing school for women in Virginia and were in Washington for dinner. From the beginning, Charles Lemieux had been struck by the shy, young woman with the girl who had invited him in, mesmerized by her quiet beauty as she sat across from him. She laughed easily and spoke about many subjects with a clarity he found enchanting. He had hoped the night would go on, and when the young women stood, saying their good-byes, he stumbled up, fighting his anxiety as he tried to ask the quiet young woman whether he would be able to see her again. Again, her friend had come to his rescue, asking if he came to Washington often. Relieved, he indicated that he lived and worked in Washington for the Army Corps of Engineers, and they agreed to meet in a week when the young women would next be in the city. As this went on for several weeks, it became more evident that Lemieux and Claudette were very attracted to each other, and, gradually, her friend would leave them alone. It was no surprise when they were married a year later. That was nineteen years ago.

Looking at his wife's body now, Lemieux felt the same passion he had struggled against when he met her, as the robe did nothing to disguise the shapeliness underneath. Not unaware of her effect on him, she smiled.

"You were quite the star tonight," she said with a slight lean of her head. "I am not sure how to handle a celebrity."

"A quandary easily solved, my dear. I am perfectly willing to instruct you."

She laughed, a clear, crystal sound, as she walked sinuously over to him.

"Such kindness," she responded, irony heavy in her voice.

Lemieux had been sitting on a chair next to the bed, and Claudette sat across from him. Looking at the bedroom, one of three rooms that constituted their apartment, she could not help but think of the opulence of the mansion she had just left. She said to Lemieux, "That was quite an affair tonight. You seem to have been well accepted."

"It did go well. It's all due to Mr. Bryant, though. For some reason, he seems to have taken to me and is willing to provide sponsorship. It's not even clear why or how I came to his attention. It is clear that he wants very much for me to be successful. When we left the room tonight, I found he had arranged for me to meet secretly with the President in the garden behind the mansion."

"The President was there tonight?" Claudette asked excitedly.

"Not officially, but we did meet privately."

"What did he say? He is supporting you, right? Did he say when you would leave for Panama? Did he—"

"Stop! Stop! He did not say much. Just a long speech about the importance of this enterprise to the United States and its role in the world and that I was now part of that history."

"That means he is supporting you, Charles. Not that I had any doubts, but this pretty much seals it, don't you think?"

"Well, it's not a bad sign."

"Not a bad sign?" Claudette laughed, throwing a pillow at him. "You had a secret meeting with the President of the United States who said you were part of his vision of America's future, and all you can say is, 'It's not a bad sign'? You are impossible, Charles."

He chuckled, nodding in assent. Despite his apparent calm, he was excited. Today had been a great triumph. Walking from the room, he soon returned with two glasses filled with champagne, one of which he handed to Claudette. Raising his glass high in a military salute, he said, "To me. To Panama. To victory."

With each toast his voice became louder and more comic, so that by the end he was the perfect picture of the dandy, a picture that did not agree with the aggressive jaw. Claudette collapsed on the bed, holding her glass gingerly to avoid spilling. Lemieux drank deeply and finished by wiping his moustache with the edge of his thumb. Claudette sipped lightly. Then, putting the glass down, she walked across the room to Lemieux and hugged him. He slung his arms loosely around her and said softly, "I love you very much."

She smiled and tightened her arms around him. After a while, she said, "Charles, have you thought about what this enterprise means? For you, I mean?"

"Not much. It's going to be a challenge, of course. Whatever they say about the French, what they did achieve was magnificent. I think the major problem is that De Lessups underestimated Panama. He—"

"No, Charles. I am thinking beyond the digging and construction of the canal. You are no longer simply a soldier. You have always approached your work with a soldier's gift of self-absorption and self-sacrifice, and those qualities I so admire in you will serve you well now. But until tonight, I didn't think of the magnitude of what you are attempting. The young woman who took me away from you and Mr. Bryant at the mansion kept talking about how attractive you were."

At this, Lemieux preened comically, and Claudette slapped his hand, narrowing her eyes.

Lemieux said, "That is Margaret Atherton, I found out. Her father is an ambassador. Her relationship with Mr. Bryant is undefined, to say the least."

"Well, whoever she is, she kept mentioning your good looks. I was becoming a little irritated until she pointed out that you are going to be America's image for the duration of the building of the canal. I just wonder if you have thought of that at all. This is going to be different from building the dam or the bridges or the railways. Important as they were, Panama is meant to be something bigger, and the fact that the President came secretly to see you only confirms that."

Lemieux untangled himself from his wife, walked to the other side of the room where the bay window looked out on the city of Washington, and pulled the blinds back. The streetlights had been put out, but the moonlight illuminated the night, making of the near darkness a romantic, silvery sheen with suggestive shadows that moved in the distance. He had avoided thinking of the project in the terms

Claudette just described because it always led to another question. Why was Bryant so interested in helping him become the commander of the canal? Under the terms of the treaty with Columbia, he would be the equivalent of a military governor; and while he had command experience—every major engineering project contained elements of running a small town—he was very fortunate to have been singled out for Bryant's support. He had been certain the job would go to Colonel Stevens, who had a much higher profile than he did, but Bryant had supported him from the beginning, and so his improbable dream was going to come true. Throughout all this, Bryant had said nothing to him—until tonight. Lemieux was still not certain he understood Bryant's interest.

He turned back to Claudette who stood where he had left her, watching his broad back block out the window.

"You are right, of course, darling. This is so much bigger than anything I've done that there really is no way to measure its scale. I am only now beginning to understand just how significant a political event it is. Throughout the struggle to get my idea of a Panama route across, I handled the political challenges, but even then, most of the demands were on my engineering skill. I had little time to think of what it would mean to actually run the operation. Tonight, as I stood there with all those powerful men, I realized just how important this canal is to America, and I'm ashamed to admit I had given this little thought before. I thought of the engineering challenges, the possibility of fame and, perhaps, fortune, and the men I would defeat if I were fortunate enough to be chosen, but not once did I think of it as an American statement to the world. As I listened to the President tonight, I suddenly became aware that this was something of a coming-out party for the United States, and I am going to be hosting that party."

His voice had become solemn as he spoke, and Claudette joined him at the window, grasping his hand as she did so.

"No one is better suited to this than you, Charles. The men backing you are not sentimentalists. They have selected you because they recognize your value to them. Men like the President and Mr. Bryant are right to think of the honor of the United States, and you will fulfill that desire for America's honor, but you will do it through the skill you bring as an organizer and an engineer."

Charles Lemieux looked at the lustrous, alabaster face of his wife and bent to kiss her in gratitude. They moved arm in arm toward the bed and soon turned the light off.

Later, Lemieux laid thinking of Edward Bryant and the comment he had made as the President left. Claudette had said that men like the President and Mr. Bryant would be concerned with the honor that would accrue to the United States, but Mr. Bryant's comment made Lemieux wonder. Anyway, it was not his responsibility to account for the morality or purpose of others. His wife's body was warming his, and he turned toward her, his hands reaching for the secret places of her, and she, laughing low in her throat, leaned into him.

CHAPTER THREE

WASHINGTON, D.C. 1904

At the mansion, Edward Bryant was not asleep. He sat on an architect's chair, staring at the maps that covered the four walls of the bare room. Each was a version of the map of the recently created Panama. His creation, he thought, although the President was fond of taking the credit. Bryant laughed as he thought of Roosevelt's last speech in Berkeley, California. He was reported by the press to have said, "I took Panama." Bryant shook his head. He would never understand politicians. Swiveling in the chair, he stared at a geological map covering one wall of the room. It showed a detailed crosscut of the soil and rock that had been removed from the cut. His eyes moved easily and familiarly over the drawing, extracting from it the secret everyone had missed. Midway through the cut, he had noticed the change in the soil structure. The composition was different, the strata more tightly bunched together. This map had been sent to him before it had been sent to France, and he had ordered that a second map with more uniform and less discolored strata be drawn for public consumption. The map that now lay encased in the Congres International d'Etudes du Canal

Interoceanique was a fake, although accurate in every detail except for the alterations he had ordered. He had seen that configuration of strata only once before, and that had been in California forty-five years before, when fortunes had been made. He thought how ironic it was that the gold rushers on their way to California had traversed the very area he was certain was a gold mine, never suspecting they were passing what might prove to be a bigger find.

And good thing, too, for he had no intention of having a rush this time. This would make the money back he had lost in the French speculation on the canal. "La Debacle" had cost him a fortune. It had started out with such enthusiasm. De Lesseps had just completed the Suez Canal, the greatest engineering feat of the nineteenth century, and "the great engineer" had assured everyone that a canal at Panama was possible and achievable in a relatively short time. Bryant had seen the possibilities of the canal, and, when the shares had been placed on the market, he financed a French company to purchase twenty-five percent of the value of the shares at a cost of close to thirty-five million dollars, a considerable sum even for him, although his railroad in Panama had provided the collateral for some of that initial funding. A privately owned canal connecting the Pacific and the Atlantic would be lucrative, and he had no doubt the dividends would far exceed the initial investment. He had had no intention of allowing the canal to be publicly owned. Once the project was completed, he would have slowly purchased the shares until he had a stranglehold on the canal.

Thinking of this now, Bryant ground his teeth in frustration. Had Charles Lemieux seen the anger in the man's face, he would have had even more doubts about his benefactor's purposes. As De Lesseps had continued to pronounce victory and the work had fallen behind, Bryant had seen his money dribble away.

"A nation of politicians," he said angrily to himself, walking over to the geological map and running his hand over it affectionately. His influence had bought him the inside information, and, while not able to salvage his investment in full, he had gotten the geologist's map. The man had been in Bryant's pay from the beginning, providing Bryant with information on the geological feasibility of the project. It was obvious the man had known what the compressed lines on the geological map meant, though he had pretended ignorance. His bones now lay somewhere in the woods of Virginia. Bryant was convinced he had the only such map.

When the French left, he was faced with the challenge of reactivating the project while keeping his information secret. Getting the American government interested had been impossible under McKinley, and when the President had been shot in Buffalo, Bryant had shed no tears. With the "cowboy" in the White House, Panama was much more possible. And so it had proven. Roosevelt, after his initial flirtation with a Nicaragua route, was swayed by substantial contributions to his campaign coffers and had shifted to solid support of the Panama route. For three years, however, Bryant watched in frustration while Congress batted the idea around without being able to make a decision. He had been pleased when Charles Lemieux emerged as a champion of the Panama route, for he was the right sort of man, with an impeccable military record, a modest reputation for public works, and experience serving under Roosevelt in Cuba. Bryant let it be known he found Lemieux acceptable, and the President publicly supported the man.

Now, he had only to expedite the process of getting Lemieux on his way to Panama. He wished he was younger, but knew he was past that kind of risk now. It was not like the old days when he took every opportunity to forge a way into the wilderness. Lemieux would win the prize for him. With this reassuring thought, Edward Bryant made his way out of the room, double locking it behind him.

The guests had long gone, and the oversized mansion rang hollowly with his steps as he made his way up the spiral stairs toward the bedrooms. Within minutes, he was asleep. Outside, Washington was deadly still, but, in the early morning, this only emphasized the clopping of a single horse trudging through the street on the way home from some final late task.

CHAPTER FOUR

BARBADOS 1905

Ruthie Greaves walked slowly though assertively down the long road, at the end of which she could see the Barnes Great House. She was not looking forward to this meeting. Looking at the canes surrounding the house, she sighed, thinking of the work that had to be done to ensure the Barnes' crop would be successful in spite of the drought. The green stalks waved gaily in the slight breeze, for which Ruthie was thankful because the sun burned down from the cloudless sky with a remorselessness that was all but intentional. The white limestone road seemed to bounce the heat back up under her dress, and she tugged at her underclothes with some irritation as the sweat accumulated in her crotch. Ruthie pulled the straw hat determinedly down over her eyes and continued to place one foot in front of the other, the distant house seeming not to get any closer. This worried her because this was her half-hour break for midday "breakfast," and she did not want to get back to the fields late.

I don't want to have that black overseer put he mouth on me cause I would surely tell he something, she thought.

Thinking of her reason for going to the Barnes Great House, which was to see Ruby Barnes, she felt both anger and fear. The meeting last night had been heated, the voices, low and urgent in the night, sounding their desperation and their fear. There had been no rain for almost a year now, and the fields were dry. The village existed in a symbiotic relationship with the plantation, which provided work but could not survive without them. Their shillings kept them alive in the nascent economy of the colony, but their bodies were nurtured by the sweat of their brow and the small plots each one kept. In those plots, the ground provisions were grown, and these supplemented the meager earnings they got during the crop season. After the crop ended, there was little work, and they became totally dependent on the small plots for their sustenance. The drought changed all of those relationships, and as the villagers devoted more time to ensuring that the Barnes plantations prospered, they had to neglect their own land, increasingly becoming an appendage of the plantation and the wage system that retained the conditions of a generation before.

"Nuffin aint change. Nuffin aint change at all," Ruthie now mumbled to herself, thinking of the stories her grandmother told of slavery days.

As their plots crumbled in the torrid heat and they spent longer and longer hours in the Barnes' fields, hunger set in, living in the village "like a neighbour," as Miriam had said last night. Two days ago, Miriam's child had died, and Ruthie had gone over to her hut to help her prepare the child for burial. The frail thing on the dirty bedclothes made her heart quail, but she could not let Miriam see her cry because she knew the woman was hanging on by a thread, the brightness in her eyes not simply the product of hunger but of an incipient madness that lurked not far beneath the surface of each of them. People always died when that madness showed its face.

She had called the meeting at her hut the next evening more to give Miriam something to do than with any expectation that action would come from it, but the women had surprised her. As they sat on the floor around the kerosene oil lamp that cast lurid shadows against the walls and gave their faces a character they lacked in the daylight, Ruthie felt something different in the room. It was not quite anger, not quite defiance, but a quiet determination to see something, as yet undefined, through.

Miriam's child had died from starvation, and they had hugged her, each in turn rocking away the pain they all shared. Miriam had then surprised them.

"It goin' happen to wunna children, too, yuh kno'."

She had spoken into a long silence and her voice, in that setting, at that moment, sounded prophetic. These women, still not far removed from the worship of dead ancestors as their African forebears had taught them and which two hundred and fifty years of Anglican doctrine had not quite destroyed, shuddered silently, for they wondered what the dead child was saying to its mother. Unseen by Miriam, each had thrown imaginary dust over her shoulder to avoid any curse the child might send, but they also agreed with the bright-eyed woman. The drought was killing the village, and the men did not seem to mind. There were not many men around anyway. The ones who had any ambition had been leaving for months now, on their way to Panama.

Few of de ones who lef' worf anyting. Of course, dat don't apply to Deighton, she thought with a smile.

He had stayed because he could not stay away from her. He was a carpenter, and what little work there was, he got, and this kept them from the starvation that was alive in the village.

She wondered what had possessed her to accept what the women had asked her to do, for she was going to ask Ruby Barnes for two things. First, the women wanted food, and they could not pay for it, so they were asking Ruby Barnes to give it to them. They had made it clear they did not intend to go into debt for it. They were also asking for more time off to tend their plots since this would relieve their dependence on the Barnes' food. Last night, as they had sat around the lamp, it had all seemed perfectly reasonable; now, in the light of the midday sun, it seemed like madness. Ruthie knew Ruby Barnes, and there was not a generous bone in her body. Her father was supposed to have done a lot for the colored people a few years ago, but none of that had rubbed off on his daughter. She and Ruby were about the same age and had, in fact, grown up together, but Ruby seemed much older, as if her avarice had aged her. Ruthie was afraid of her but determined not to let it show.

She had been walking with her head down, allowing the long brim of the straw hat to keep the glare of the sun from her eyes, and looking up, she now saw how far the house was. Though still some way off, it no longer appeared to be in the distance, and she put her head back down and trudged stolidly on. She was dressed oddly, if one did not know her work, for in this heat she wore a long dress that went all the way to her ankles. It was loose fitting and had long sleeves kept tight around her wrists with a sharpened piece of wood stuck through the cloth. In spite of the heat, she knew it was important to protect herself from the sun, and the canes within which she worked all day could cut her body with their serrated edges. The heavy clothes were, therefore, a double protection. At the upper field since five o'clock that morning, she had waited until the overseer arrived to ask permission to work there since she could reach the Great House and get back in half an hour, and she knew she could not do it from the lower fields where she normally worked.

Dat black son-of-a-bitch sitting on his horse, lording it and looking me up and down, undressing me wid his eyes, pretending dis was a big decision, she thought angrily.

She had put him in his place before when he had come up to her and asked her a question. Ruthie did not take that from anyone, and she had loudly pointed out that she was a married woman, and if he did not know his place, she would tell Deighton and he would get a cut-ass. That had made the overseer an enemy since some of the women who had been nearby had heard, and the rest had been told, so whenever the overseer rode by, somebody always seemed to be talking about someone getting a cut-ass. So this morning, when the little, no-dick "good-fuh-nuttin" had sat on the horse, pondering, Ruthie had not been particularly worried. She knew he still harbored thoughts of getting her, so while he would show off his power, he would not deny her. In any case, she was not absolutely certain she did not wish to be denied. Then, she could blame not seeing Ruby Barnes on the overseer and not have to admit the fear she felt.

After a while, he had said sternly, "You kin wuk here today. Just mek sure dat you get back in time fuh afternoon wuk." He had paused, then added suggestively, "Course, I cud give you a ride. Then yuh won't have to walk all dat way to de house."

She had laughed and turned away, grinding her hips in an exaggerated "wine" as he sat on his horse, seething with anger but fully aware she was putting on a display just to show him what he could not get. She giggled. Men were so silly and so easily led. The ground had become smoother, and, looking up, Ruthie realized she had traversed the long carriageway and was now in the circle that fronted the house. Quickening her step and hoping no one had seen her moping along, she soon ascended the steps, but once there, she was not sure what to do. She had never been to the Great House before and was afraid to bang on the door.

She had just raised her hand to knock when a voice called out, "Wha you want at de front door?"

Ruthie spun around, her hand raised defensively, but it was only an old black man, and she quickly regained her composure.

"Wha it got to do wid you? I come to see Miss Barnes."

"Well, come down from dere an' go 'roun de back. You not suppose to be dere at de front door. You kno' dat, too."

Ruthie's eyes narrowed, but she trudged slowly down the front steps. The old man, whom she recognized as the watchman, waited for her and seemed about to take her arm, but she pulled away and strode ahead of him toward the back of the house, angry that she had been seen and denied by this foolish black man.

At the back of the house, he called out, "Miss Kirton, come an' help dis one. She say she here to see Miss Barnes."

From the bowels of what was evidently the kitchen, a fat woman with a kindly face appeared, and Ruthie lowered her head and said, "Good day, Miss Kirton. I come to see if I kin talk to Miss Barnes."

"Ruthie? You come to see Miss Barnes? She kno' dat you comin'?

"No, Miss Kirton."

"Well, come in out de hot sun. You want a glass uh water?"

Ruthie nodded, self-conscious now that she was actually in the house. The old woman handed her a cup of cool water, and Ruthie drank gratefully. The woman continued to watch her speculatively while she drank. Then, when Ruthie handed the cup back, she asked, "Wha' you come to talk to de mistress 'bout, Ruthie?"

"De other women ask me to talk to she 'bout de drought."

The old woman hesitated and then, nodding, walked off into the darkness of the house. The old man had remained outside, clearly curious about what would happen when the mistress came. Ruthie could hear voices in the depths of the house, and soon they were coming toward her. Ruby Barnes came into the kitchen first, and Ruthie was again struck by the carriage of the woman. She was thirty-eight, the same age as Ruthie, but looked over fifty, not so much because her body had aged but because of the gravity that afflicted her face. Ruby controlled the Barnes empire, which was made up of most of the southern part of the island and a variety of stores in Bridgetown, the capital. The weight of that control showed on her face, but Ruthie knew Ruby had not always been like this. When she had been younger, Ruby had come into the village and had played with the other girls, although even then she was always in charge. Ruthie looked at her now, and there was no recognition in the woman's eyes. In fact, what she saw further accented her fear, for there was something remote about the woman. It was rumored (and not denied by the Barneses) that somewhere in their past was black blood, but this was not evident in the family now. Ruby Barnes was white, though her skin showed a tan that was uncharacteristic for white women in the island since they stayed away from the sun.

"Yes?" she now said impatiently, but Ruthie continued to stare, not sure how to begin.

"Well, what can I do for you?"

Miss Kirton, the cook, seeing Ruthie was tongue-tied, tried to help by saying, "She come to ask you if you kin help out de people in de village because uh de drought."

"What do you mean, Mabel?" Ruby Barnes asked, turning to the cook, but before she could respond, Ruthie blurted, "A chile dead las' nite 'cause it aint had nuh food."

Ruby turned back to her slowly, eyebrows slightly raised.

"De women ask me to come an' talk tuh you 'bout de state uh de village. Children deading, Miss Barnes, 'cause dey aint got enough to eat."

Ruthie stopped, but the white woman stood waiting.

"Dey want tuh kno' if dey cud haf moe time off tuh wuk deir plots. Dat is de onliest way dat dey kin grow food enough to keep people alive."

"What are you asking me, young woman?"

Ruthie felt the anger rise in her chest, and, for a moment, she could not breathe. The cook must have seen this because she interrupted.

"It true, Mistress. Tings hard in de village, an' since de people got to be in de fields mornin', noon an' nite, dey aint got nuh time to grow anyting."

Ruthie was overcome with gratitude for the old woman and, having recovered, added, "Dat is true, Miss Barnes. De women want time to wuk deir plots, but dey want some help directly, too. Dey askin' if you cud give dem some food now."

"They don't want much, do they?" Ruby Barnes replied, a little anger coming through in her voice.

Ruthie was not sure where her courage was coming from, but she was feeling less afraid as the conversation went on.

"No, Miss Barnes. Dey not askin' fuh much. Dey goin' either let deir children dead or stop wukkin' in de fields an' stan' home an' mek sure deir children got someting tuh eat."

Something in Ruby Barnes' face changed ever so subtly. The even planes were gone, replaced by a visage where the bones seemed more evident than the flesh, and Ruthie took a step back. The voice, however, was unchanged.

"Do I detect a threat in that statement, Ruthie?"

"Well, at least yuh 'member who I is. Look, Miss Barnes, I aint come here to mek nuh noise, just to let you kno' wha de women ask me tuh say tuh you. I goin' hafta tell dem someting."

The two women stood facing each other, trapped in their roles, the conclusion so obvious to both of them. Finally, Ruby said without emphasis, "Tell them no. I will sell them provisions. Depending on the quality, it may be at a reduced rate, but I will not give away what I have earned. As for time off from the fields, again, no. The crop is at a very precarious point now, and the fields need all the hands I can get to ensure we keep them watered and clear of grass. I cannot afford it."

Ruthie was filling her lungs with air when Miss Kirton chimed in.

"Ruthie, you should go now. I goin' come by you house later."

Ruthie looked at the old woman, knowing she was trying to save her further humiliation, but she was unable to move. Ruby Barnes turned and walked from the room, her back rigid and contemptuous in its leave-taking. Ruthie felt the water well up in her eyes and fought it back as the kindly old woman came over, placing an arm around her shoulder.

"Don' worry, Ruthie. I goin' talk tuh she when she cool down. She aint as bad as she soun'. You go back tuh wuk now 'fore you get into trouble wid de overseer. You kno' dat won't serve no purpose at all. I goin' talk tuh you later."

Ruthie walked out of the kitchen and made her way slowly back to the front of the house. As she passed the front verandah, Rupert Barnes, Ruby's younger brother, was sitting there, a glass of lemonade in his hand.

She was about to walk by when he said, "Good day, Miss Ruthie. It's hot today."

She was surprised. The Barneses were never this friendly. Although, now that she thought about it, this one was always sauntering about the village as though he didn't have anything to do.

But I know dese Barneses. Dis one probably just smelling 'bout de village fuh something tuh ketch, she thought. There were many half-white, light-skinned people in the village, including Deighton, her husband, and the Barneses were never too far from that skin. What she did say was, "Good day, Mr. Barnes."

"Say hello to Audrey for me."

Ruthie almost stopped, surprised at the familiar reference to her daughter, and a little core of worry sprang to life in her heart. Nodding without looking around, she marched out of the circular driveway, entering the long, white road that led back to the fields and the disappointment of the women. She was not looking forward to seeing their faces when she told them their requests had been dismissed by

Ruby Barnes. Above, the sun had barely changed position in the sky, but the intensity of the heat had increased. Even the canes seemed beaten and stood limp now that the earlier breeze had disappeared. Nothing moved, and the long line of canes stretched away on both sides, disappearing in the distance and the haze of the heat waves made by the broiling sun. The road appeared to be dancing a jig in the undulating waves that formed in front of her.

Ruby is uh bitch. Pretendin' dat she din't know who I was, she thought.

The renewed anger came to Ruthie's chest in waves as she thought of all the things that could have been said to the white woman. She was upset with herself for not having thought of them. Walking along the cart-road, she could see the women who worked in the fields pulling the nut grass, down on their knees, searching out the green, innocent-looking killers of the canes. She knew from experience that their hands would be dark with the dust of the dry land, and their fingers would be bunched together, the muscles having adjusted to the action of squeezing and pulling the short grass from the ground where it clung with such strength.

Deir backs goin' be hurtin' tonight from all dat bending over, she thought as she approached.

Further away, another group of women were carrying on their backs heavy canisters with weed killer in them. These jobs were given to the strongest women in the village and would, only a year ago, have been the work of the men. Since these jobs were somewhat better paid than picking grass, the women had complained from time to time about being excluded. Well, they were not excluded now. Ever since the men had one by one gone off to Panama, the women had taken most of the jobs. The village was practically all women and children now.

Except fuh de ole men. Women doin' ev'ryting now.

An unusual look of softness came into the stern face, and she looked again at the women with the canisters whose right arms were pumping the lever on the side of the cans. They pointed the nozzle held in their left hands at the ground where the fiercely resistant nut grass clung to the soil. Though she could not see the spray from this distance, she imagined it hissing its way to the grass, covering it with the deadly whiteness. In a few days, the green leaves would turn brown, but the grass still had to be pulled out because the roots seemed to find ways of avoiding the poison.

Dis is a hard lan', she thought. *Fuh nearly t'ree hundred years, de white people try to mek somet'ing out of it, but dis Barbados don't listen tuh nobody.*

Looking around, she noticed, not for the first time, that most of the trees were gone. When she had been a child, most of the land had been covered with grass and woods. Now, wherever she looked there were the waving green stalks of the sugar cane, ignorant of their unconscious tyranny. She wondered now how something so graceful in its movement and sweet to the taste could be so destructive. Her mother had been born in the last days of slavery and had told stories of that time. Ruthie was glad those days were gone and almost did not wish to hear the stories. Yet, something about her mother's voice held her, as the women's bent bodies were holding her now.

She had not heard the horse approaching, so the harsh voice startled her. Looking around, she saw the overseer sitting comfortably astride the horse, his face stern. She despised the man but, in spite of herself, could not help noticing that his body was strong, tall, and straight. The voice dispelled any illusions, however.

"You already late and now standin' 'bout daydreamin'? You bettuh get you ass back to dat row ovuh dere an' start weedin'."

Ruthie was just about to say something when the overseer casually allowed his whip to drop to its full length, and she felt the muscles in her back involuntarily tighten. They stood like this for a second, and then Ruthie, fear clinging at the edges of her heart, stalked off to the sound of the overseer's quiet laughter. The women had not looked up, but it was evident from the tension in their bodies that they had heard the short exchange. They all knew the overseer was after Ruthie. They were afraid for her since she would not stand for his attentions as many of them had. He had not yet gone beyond the point Ruthie had defined as her limit, but they worried that some day he might, and then they were sure Ruthie would kill him. Now, they watched with their senses while she took her place in the line. Margie, who was working next to her, looked at Ruthie from the corner of her eye, and Ruthie shook her head slightly. Margie understood, and shoulders slumped as word passed to the women. As Ruthie joined in the rhythm of the line, there emerged a unity of purpose as the hoes rose in unison to some unspoken song they heard but did not voice.

CHAPTER FIVE

BARBADOS 1905

Rupert Barnes had watched the woman walk away from the Barnes Great House, noticing the uncanny resemblance, down to the cadence of her walk, between Ruthie and her daughter. He had been seeing Audrey for months now—secretly, of course. They met in the village late at night when everyone was asleep, and now he smiled at the thought of seeing her tonight. Why had her mother come to the house? It was unusual for the villagers to come up here and still more unusual for them to come during the middle of the day. With only a half-hour for lunch and in the current circumstances of the drought and the need to tend the fields every moment, that half-hour was jealously guarded. It must have been something important that led her to walk in the hot sun all the way from the fields to the house. Even in the carriage, the heat was oppressive. Rupert walked into the coolness of the stone house. The house had been built over a period of time beginning in the 1800s, and the coral stones – "soft stones," as they were called – dissipated the heat. The constant breeze descending from the east coast also helped to combat the heat, even in these oppressive days.

He walked through the house to the eastern verandah where Ruby sat, a ledger in her hand. He watched the bent neck from which the spinal bones protruded, noticing that the hair was turning gray. There was something vulnerable about her as she bent over the book of figures, trying to make a profit, as all their ancestors had, from this land. She was, as usual, simply attired in a long, khaki-colored dress. Rupert doubted anyone had ever seen her body. Ruby was bred to the plantation, and that was all she did and all that interested her. She had never forgiven her brothers for fighting her over leadership of the Barnes enterprises, and though Rupert still lived in the Great House, his three brothers had departed when their father left the entire estate to Ruby, who was the eldest. The Barnes' wealth had been accumulated through the very simple practice of primogeniture, but no woman had ever been firstborn. The boys had been certain her rights would be ignored, and they had waited for the old man to overlook her and pass the land to Mortimer, Rupert's eldest brother. The old man fooled them all by keeping the principle of leaving everything to the firstborn intact. It destroyed the family's unity, for they fought her in the courts, trying to split the land evenly among them. They lost, and she, in victory, proved as vicious as she had been cunning in the quest to retain her birthright. She banished them from the plantation, and though Rupert visited their homes from time to time, he had not seen the whole family together in many years. Too young to have been part of the conflict, he had remained at Sedges with Ruby, but she did not trust him, and he could not blame her.

Rupert had little interest in the plantations and even less in the stores that consolidated the wealth the plantations produced. Ruby saw his lack of interest as laziness, a fatal flaw to her mind; and while she had seen him through Lodge School and, less than a year ago, had given him control of one of the stores, she had no faith in him and practically ignored him except to point out his weaknesses. Rupert was ambivalent about her, admiring her instinct toward the practical and the success that had resulted but also despising the single-mindedness that produced that success.

Now, as he watched her secretly, seeing the exposed neck, that ambivalence was strong in him. He stepped on the boards of the verandah, and his older sister looked up, startled.

The face, he thought, *denies all possibility of vulnerability.*

It was a severe face, and the fact that she did nothing to adorn it and pulled her black, graying hair tightly back, allowed the full skeletal nature of the face to impress itself upon the onlooker.

She could have been beautiful, he thought, *if she cared enough to try.*

Even as she looked up, seeing him assessing her, the eyes narrowed, and she seemed to pull a cowl over them so that what had been open and dark brown only a second before was now opaque and unreachable. Rupert felt the familiar choking that always attended dealings with his sister, and he hesitated, wondering what had been the connection between this woman and him before the battle over the land soured her. Occasionally, Audrey would tell him stories her mother had told her about when his sister was young and had been fond of going into the village to play with the black girls there. The person she described bore no resemblance to the woman who now sat staring up at him.

"Well, are you going back to work, or is this another half-day's worth of effort?"

Rupert felt the gall rise in him at the address. This was Ruby's way of putting him off-balance, he knew, but it made no difference. He was on edge immediately and could feel no affection for this sister who seemed to find in her life one thing of value: the preservation of the Barnes estates. How could they have the same parents when he felt so remote from the history of the family? Ruby despised him for his laziness and what she thought of as his weakness, but he had no intention of being like her, obsessed with the preservation of these fields that had grown from the wilderness. For two and a half centuries his family had been in a battle with this land, and it still seemed the same. Every year brought the worry that the crop would fail and the great Barnes family would be ruined. It seemed to Rupert a pitiable way to live, devoid as it was of pleasure in achievement, although there was some pride in accomplishment. Ruby was a perfectly adjusted adjunct to history, a cog in a wheel of endeavor that stretched, unbroken, back to the first Portuguese ship that had sighted the island and named it "Los Barbados," or "the Bearded." Rupert was aware of the history that had collided here, and he was not at all certain he felt much pride in what had transpired. Ruby thought little of the history of this place. She was content to make the land work, to dedicate her soul not so much to its survival, as her ancestors had done, but to its subordination. She was successful at this.

Looking at her now, he felt the usual confusion, wanting to reach out to her but feeling unable to.

"Half a day it is, Ruby. We can afford to lose a little money, don't you think?"

She stared at him coldly, then said, "You can lose what you make, Rupert. That ought to limit you to just about nothing. That store isn't making any money as it is."

"Everything else is making money. We can afford to lose a little to the workers. They need more than we do. Things are difficult in the villages, Ruby."

"Things are difficult here, and your carelessness does not help. Have you looked at these lately?"

She shoved the books on her lap out to him angrily, and, enjoying her anger, he replied comfortably, "I never bother with the things. What's in them?"

Ruby sucked her teeth, a sound made by straining inhaled air through the teeth, and Rupert laughed, saying, "Careful, Ruby. Someone could mistake you for one of the villagers."

Ruby's eyes got even narrower. They both knew what he meant, and color was not a subject about which one joked. She turned away after a while, then said, "Did you want something from me, Rupert?"

"Actually, I noticed Miss Ruthie just left. What did she want?"

Ruby paused for a moment before answering.

"She said she was bringing a message from the women in the village, although I think it was her idea. She was always fast and never knew her place."

"What message, Ruby?"

"She said one of the children died last night, and that has the women up in arms. They are apparently demanding I give them food and reduce the number of hours they are in the fields so they can take care of their plots and grow food."

Ruby ended with a short, brutal snort. Rupert watched his sister carefully, trying to understand the motivation that made this woman who she was. He knew the villagers were starving, and he did not have the heart to deny them the goods they wanted when they came to the store without money. The men had gone off to Panama, but they had been sending back precious little to help these women, many of whom had children out of wedlock. Young as he was, Rupert understood the reasoning behind the decision. The men were worried that the women would squander their money. They particularly worried they would be supporting other men's children, as the women cavorted with whomever they liked while the men were away. As a result, they tended to send money to their mothers, who guarded it jealously, not even spending it on themselves; or they kept it with them in Panama, deluding themselves that they were saving it for the day of their return, when they would make it up to the women. In the meantime, the women and their children suffered. When they came to the shop asking that they be allowed to "trust" some item, he did not have the heart to say no to them, and that infuriated Ruby.

Their most serious argument, which almost drove him out of the house, had occurred a few months before, when he had given away a cartload of yams in the village. The drought had nearly destroyed the crop, and when the diggers had come with their straight irons to free the yams from their underground beds, they had discovered only "ends," the stringy residue of the underdeveloped tubers. Since the villagers had bought by the row, sight unseen, it was their loss if the yams were no good. Audrey had told him of it, and Rupert, ashamed of Ruby's behavior, had not only gone into the cool storage space where the best yams were kept and taken them to the village, but had also used the shop money to repay some of the women who had purchased the rows of yams. Ruby had erupted when she found out about "that act of stupidity," as she had called it, and they had had their first real fight. It had liberated him, though, and, subsequently, he had assumed a slightly sardonic tone with her. She had noticed this, the absence of his previous deference being so obvious.

"Whose child died?" Rupert now asked.

His sister shrugged, and he continued.

"Why can't we give them some food?"

Ruby did not answer, and he asked the question again. His sister turned slowly and looked speculatively at her brother.

"We can't afford to."

"Why not? We are not threatened. They are."

"How would you know, Rupert? You are ignorant of what goes on at the estates. Purposely so, I might add. You have shown no capacity for managing the store, as simple a task as that is. I'm not sure what you learned at that school, but it clearly was not responsibility. I am tired of your irresponsibility."

Rupert felt the insecurity inherent in his relationship with his sister return. She could always make him feel the fool with her attacks, and she knew this. He was in turmoil, trying desperately to retain his sardonic distance but feeling the old domination she exerted coming back.

In retaliation, he said angrily, "We are not talking about my irresponsibility but yours. Rather, Ruby, we are talking about your greed."

His sister stood, body rigid and arms held straight down at her sides.

"You insolent wretch. Get out. I will not be insulted in my own home."

"It is my home, too," the young man shouted back.

"No. You have done nothing to build it. You have done everything to tear it down. I have been working my hands to the bone to hold this place together while you and the other three have done nothing to help."

Her voice had risen to a shout, and Rupert recoiled in surprise, not accustomed to seeing his sister out of control. Still, he was not going to back down now, so he replied in like tone.

"You've shut everyone out with your ungodly obsession with this place. You don't want any help because you are afraid you may be called on to give some part of the fortune you're building."

Ruby, her outburst over, stood listless, looking almost ashamed that she had lost control.

"Fortune?" she said softly but with a quiet intensity that made her voice seem to be hissing. "If only you knew, boy, how many times I wish I could give it all up. Do you think it is easy to keep this enterprise going? That I wanted to sacrifice my life to this, to protecting you? Well, you are wrong, Rupert. You are wrong."

She moved past him into the house, but before she could get out of the room, he said, "Are you going to help the villagers this time, Ruby?"

The woman stopped, her back rigid, the lines of her dress pulled out of shape as a result. For a long time they stood like this, and then the sharp-boned woman walked off, not answering. Rupert stood and, not sure what to do, looked at the gardens, wondering what all this meant.

CHAPTER SIX

Barbados 1905

Ruby angrily strode from the room, heading upstairs to her boudoir. Approaching the stairs, she was hailed by Miss Kirton, and she stopped again, anticipating the purpose. The old woman walked over to her mistress.

"You and dat boy fightin' agin? I doan kno' wha de matter is wid de two uh wunna. An' you use to be so close, too."

Ruby was in no mood for reminiscing, and she asked shortly, "Is there something I can do for you, Kirton?"

"Yes, as a matter uh fac'. I did want to talk to you 'bout wha Ruthie say."

Ruby, beyond anger, just waited. It was as if everyone wanted to give her instructions today.

"I kno' dat it aint my bidness, but you goin hafta to do someting to help de village people. Now dat de men gone way to Panama, de women doin evryting demself, an' deir children suff'ring. You can't stand by an' let dis happen. You father wud not let dis happen. An' you can't let it happen neither."

54

Ruby looked at this woman who had been with her family for as long as she could remember and wondered what the old woman thought gave her the right to speak to her like this.

"Kirton, I suggest you get back to work. I will be taking dinner early this evening."

With this, she continued up the stairs, and the old woman waddled away, mumbling insolently to herself. Ruby entered her room and sat down heavily. The plantations were becoming more of a burden, and she was tired. She walked into the adjoining room and, poured water into a basin from the ewer. She dipped her hand in and pressed the cool water into her face, finally pressing the heels of her hands into her eyes. A headache had come from the heat and the stress, and she lay across the bed in her clothes, a most unusual action for her. None of them understood or liked her, but she knew it was important for her to succeed.

Her father had left her two responsibilities: raising the boy and making sure the estates continued to grow. He had known the three older boys were useless. They wanted wealth and power but lacked the capacity for hard work, and her father had recognized this. When he left the plantations to her, excluding the boys, she had been both shocked and elated, recognizing the opportunity that had been given her. Her brothers' reaction had surprised her. She had seen no indication before that they resented her, but immediately after their father's burial, the battle had begun. First, they tried to cajole her into giving up the plantations, promising to pay her well for them. When she refused, they offered to manage the plantations on her behalf. Again, she had refused, and then they had gone to the courts, arguing that, as a woman, she ought not to be allowed to handle the plantations since so much of the colony's wealth was dependent on the success of the Barnes' plantations, which, given their size, could determine the success of the colony's crop. The economy of the island, they contended, ought not to be left to "the peculiar instincts of a woman." She never quite got the meaning of that phrase, but it had been the talk of the island for weeks.

People had followed the trial with great interest, although with different intents. The rich, mostly white people, had watched with a feeling of embarrassment as the struggle, which most poor people spoke of secretly as the "avariciousness uh de w'ite people," seemed to air their private affairs for all to see. As a small though powerful minority, they had sought invisibility within an overwhelmingly black population, and most felt this exposure was bad for them. The crisis of confidence had begun a generation ago when slavery had officially, if not actually, been abolished, and the whites, from a position of power, had become aware of the masses of blacks around them now in a position, if not of power, at least of potential empowerment. This created a schism in the country in which assurance was replaced by uncertainty and intuitive power with racial arrogance. This trial was embarrassing because it mocked the illusion of solidarity the group had so carefully created and protected since 1838.

For the poor, it was pure theatre. They followed the trial with rapt attention, debating the merits of the case with an authority that would have been amusing had they not taken themselves so seriously. They laughed, as was their wont, at the "peculiar instincts of white people," speaking of them familiarly, as if they were, as a group, distant relatives of whom they were vaguely afraid and, more importantly, slightly ashamed. There was an odd familiarity in the relations of these two inhabitants of the island who saw each other over barricades that hid their selves. So, the poor, mostly black population laughed at the trial and the embarrassment of the whites.

Ruby cared little for the relations of the groups or the embarrassment of her group. The battle, as she saw it, was for her soul. She rejected the assumption that she was incapable of managing the plantations and particularly resented the fact that her father's wishes were being flouted by her miserable brothers, who cared for nothing except their comfort. In this, she was not entirely fair. Her brothers were no better than society had made them, and their greed fit very easily with their social philosophy. It was fortunate that the judge, an Englishman who had recently arrived on the island, turned out to be a strict constructionist who found no reason to invalidate the will her father had drawn. She won her case and asked all her brothers, with the exception of Rupert, who was too young, to leave. They would have done so in any case. She had seen them from afar since then, but they had not visited the plantation since nor had they spoken to her.

Rupert had been different. As a young boy, he had been always a pleasure, capable of love and affection, which she desperately needed. He had grown up almost as her son, and while he had never given her any reason to suspect him of betrayal, he maintained a good relationship with his brothers. She did not resent this and indeed encouraged it. He seemed to need company in ways she did not, and, rather than question it, she simply accepted it. She constantly tried to keep him from going into the village and fraternizing with the people, but he always flouted her direction on this point, escaping in the evenings to meet his friends there. She was certain he was cavorting with the girls in the village, and word got back to her that he was actually involved with someone (she did not know whom) and this irritated her to no end.

She was upset because, despite Rupert's generous nature, or maybe because of it, he had grown up to be a fool, with no sense of his social responsibility. He was inclined to see in acts of kindness the essence of affection, not realizing that these people had been managing their betters for all of their joint history.

Ruby turned on her side, staring out the window at a brittle, brazen sky that promised no relief from the pun-

ishing drought that had belittled the best efforts her hus-
bandry could produce. And that careless idiot outside
wanted to give away what she was trying to build. He understood nothing, thinking his friendliness was enough to
protect him against a world that respected only power and
wealth. He still needed to be protected, though he did not
know this and probably hated her now. One day, Rupert
would understand that the world was not a safe place, that
it behooved one to be on guard always. She would not give
away the family's wealth, and she would not allow the villagers' problems to supersede her own. They would have to
work until the estates were out of danger because if they did
not and the plantations failed, the impact would be much
worse.

She stood, intuitively dabbed her hair into place, and,
squaring her shoulders, walked out of the room. She strode
resolutely through the house, composing her face into something approaching a smile and willing her mind into com-
pliance. At the door to the verandah she stopped, breaking
stride abruptly and letting her breath out. Rupert was
nowhere to be seen. She walked swiftly to the rear of the
house, where the cook, sweating profusely, was banging pots
and pans, and Ruby groaned inaudibly, recognizing this was
being done for her benefit. Kirton was angry at having been
dismissed earlier, and Ruby knew from experience the insolence would be around for days unless she straightened it
out immediately. Walking past the old woman, she looked
into the yard for Rupert's horse, but it was not in sight.
Behind her, the cook said under her breath, "Everybody
leavin' de house. Place so dead, nuhbody can't be happy here
nuh more."

Ruby pretended not to hear, and the woman went on.

"Boy aint home but five minutes, an' first ting yuh know
one set uh row. Now, de boy ride 'way an' nuhbody aint kno'
when he comin' back."

Ruby smiled to herself, wondering at the old woman, who, without conceding her anger, was giving her the information she needed.

It is a curious relationship we have constructed on this island, she thought. *No doubt about it. They are so dependent on us for everything, and no matter the women's insolence and the men's irresponsibility, there is something innocent about them.*

She knew this was an illusion because of the occasional violence in the village, and she had once witnessed the deliberate cruelty of a beating one man had inflicted upon another. The beating had mesmerized her, and she had watched it from beginning to end, when the beaten man had fallen, his head bleeding from the cuts the stick had inflicted and his face swollen beyond recognition.

She had heard later that the fight had started innocently enough. Toggles Haynes, whose family lived at the base of the hills bordering the northern plantation, she had known since childhood. His family had never worked on the plantation, preferring to plant their provisions in the small plot her family had given to a member of the Haynes family some time in the past. They were an odd bunch, keeping to themselves and living a largely self-sufficient life. There were two brothers and three sisters living with the old parents who still went "into the ground" every morning to plant. The family raised chickens that they sold to the villagers, and although it was said they seemed to sell more chickens than anyone ever saw in their yard, no one accused them of anything, for the whole family, the girls included, were known for their violence.

Their land lay next to the plot owned by Cardinal, and, like the Hayneses, the Cardinals were thought to be better left alone. The conflict had started when the Haynes' chickens crossed over into Cardinal's land and destroyed his tomatoes by pecking holes in them. When Cardinal found out, he shouted across the dividing line at the silent house, insisting they had to pay him for the destruction their chicks had caused. There had been no answer, and in the days following, the Hayneses seemed to encourage their chickens to go and pick at everything in the man's land.

This had gone on for several weeks until, one morning, Toggles Haynes came out to find not a single chicken in the yard. He had called, clucking his tongue to attract the chicks, but nothing happened. Then, he noticed a single rooster, its red crown lying flat and its striking brown and black feathers now smudged with dust, staggering toward the yard. Cardinal had poisoned the chickens. Toggles had walked into the house, saying nothing to his still sleeping family, and had taken down, from the wooden shelf, his fighting stick. Back outside in the cool of the morning, he rubbed linseed oil into the dark, iron-like texture of the wallaba wood, and as the sun had come up, the stick gleamed evilly in the light. It was a long stick, over six and a half feet in length, and as he rubbed it, it was possible to hear him singing under his breath the hymn "Abide With Me" as if, like a hero of old, he was invoking some spirit, possibly Christian, to give him the strength to perform the task for which he was preparing.

The sun had long risen when Cardinal came to the ground, exhibiting some combination of insolence and guilt. Cutlass in his hand, he had casually swung the blade as he walked, neatly slicing the tops off the grass.

Toggles Haynes had stood up, placing the bottle of oil on the ground and then walking slowly toward the man who, though appearing to be working in his field, was tense and fully aware of Toggles. A few feet away, Toggles stopped, placing the stick next to his foot and holding it in the middle. Cardinal had straightened up, the cutlass hanging at his side. Each man was aware of the possibilities inherent in this act, and they stood as if now hesitant to begin. Cardinal looked as if he wanted to say something, possibly an apology, but Toggles had, at that moment, shifted the stick by kicking it with the inside of his foot, and, suddenly, it was in his other hand. He had moved into a crouch, his right hand closed tightly around the stick while the left loosely held it between the thumb, which pointed down toward the ground, and the fingers that curved above the stick. It was the classic opening position for stick fighting, and Cardinal, knowing Toggles' prowess with the stick and now afraid, had fallen into a crouch of his own, the cutlass held above his head and slightly to the right. People had appeared, standing in a silent line, watching the two men circle each other. No one thought to stop the fight, and the men had moved closer.

Suddenly, Cardinal charged, a little clumsily, and Toggles parried the blade easily, guiding it away from his body, using the man's charge to force him past. This exposed his back, and before Cardinal could recover, Toggles, changing his hold like lightning, gripped the stick with his left hand and, releasing the right grip, flipped the stick across his body, slamming its end into the man's kidney. Cardinal grunted and turned, the gleaming blade now held in front of him. The blow had eliminated all likelihood the fight would end without bloodshed, and the men had begun to fight in earnest. It was obvious that Toggles had the superior skill, but he still had to be cautious about the sharp blade that constantly threatened him. The men circled, not sharing any blows, each waiting for the opening that would end this struggle. Above, the sun shone innocently down, watching this battle with equanimity.

Suddenly, Cardinal turned and ran. Toggles, surprised, straightened up, dropping one end of his stick to the ground. Before he could recover, Cardinal stopped, grabbed a large stone, and threw it with unerring accuracy at Toggles. The stone exploded against his head, and immediately blood flowed down the front of his face, leaving a crimson stain against his shirt. Toggles looked confused for a moment and then unbuttoned his shirt and wrapped it around his head, staunching the flow of the blood. He finished by tying the ends together behind his head, and this had given him the look of a sixteenth-century brigand who had been in a protracted battle for some rich city.

Cardinal, on seeing the blood, had stood as if he recognized that some line had been crossed, and he watched as the bloody man crab-walked toward him, the fighting stick now held close to his left shoulder and the other tip pointing diagonally away from him toward the ground. Cardinal recognized the position. This was the deadly seventh position, employed when fighting was to be to the death. As the other man moved within reach, Cardinal swung the cutlass with all his might, but the stick flicked it easily away, and before he could pull his arm back, the stick had snaked out, cracking his wrist. As the cutlass had fallen, he had seen the stick coming in again, and then the stars exploded as it had connected with his head.

With the other man defenseless, the stick had been everywhere, and it became obvious that the fight, if it could be called such, was not intended just to be won. Cardinal's body lost its shape as the stick landed on every unprotected area, and the swelling had taken what had been familiar only a moment before and changed it. There had been cuts all over the man's body, and his clothes were practically torn off by the stick. Still, the beating had continued. There had been an inevitable quality to it, and the screams of the battered man had seemed surreal as the quiet onlookers watched without interference. There is a space between sanity and madness that the brave encounter. Many have said it is a quiet land where sounds die before they are born, and all things seem possible. It is a strange land that lacks a moral pole, and it is here, it is said, that murderers see the truth of their acts. It was this place that Toggles occupied, and Cardinal's death appeared to be only moments away. The people stood, apparently mesmerized by the act of violence.

Ruby had been standing on the brow of the hill, watching the slaughter and feeling sick to her stomach, yet unable to move. There had been, in spite of the initial revulsion, a hypnotic quality to the fight until it had turned into simple destruction. Then, she had run down the hill and across the yard toward the two men, one of whom had twirled the stick with such fluid destructiveness and the other who had been openly bawling, crawling around on his hands and knees begging the other man to stop. As she had run between them, Toggles abruptly walked away, and she looked down at the broken man, realizing she felt not sympathy but contempt.

There was something she feared in that violence, something that lay just beneath the surface that spoke of innocence and playfulness. She had been as much struck by the impassive acceptance in the faces of the people who had watched as by the beating itself. There was something she would never understand about these people. Ruby remembered the stories her grandfather told of the slaves he had owned before the English had stolen them. His constant advice had been not to trust them, particularly not to trust their laughter. Rupert wanted to ignore all this. The only thing standing between order and chaos in this land was the control she exerted. Left to their own devices, these people would revert to their natural primitive state. They needed authority to bring out the best in them, and this Rupert would never understand. She would not accept their laziness. They would work, and they would take care of their children as they had always done.

She strode from the kitchen and headed into the darkness of the inner house, never noticing the old woman's face, which was tight with sadness as she shook her head slowly, watching the straight-backed woman leave.

CHAPTER SEVEN

BARBADOS 1905

Audrey laid her head on Rupert's shoulder and closed her eyes, trying to absorb and accept what he had said to her. The cool night breeze played against the back of her thighs where her dress had been pulled up to her waist. He was inert beneath her, and she slowed her breathing to hear his heartbeat. It sounded loud and hollow in her ear, which was pressed firmly against his chest. Opening her eyes, she could see the whiteness of him in the darkness of the night, and moving her head softly against his chest, her mouth took in the saltiness of him. They had been coming to the top of the hill for months now, and so far it had been kept a secret. At least, she had not heard anyone in the village say anything. Rupert was so friendly with all the girls, it was easy to disguise his interest in her. It had only been a few months ago when he had asked her to meet him at the beach, and she had agreed. There were other girls along so it had the feeling of a picnic more than a rendezvous. Still, she understood that he had invited her separately from the others; while they had all swum and sat around and talked together, she knew he had wanted to be with her.

At first, she felt a little foolish thinking this because he had given no special indication beyond the invitation and was as close to the other girls. It was only when they were leaving and he quietly thanked her for coming that she realized his disinterest was a protection for her.

Rupert was different. She could not remember when they had begun to see each other at night, but it had evolved into a pattern. The nights they planned to meet, she sneaked out of the house and walked carefully along the track bordering her home to the "gap." Since her bedroom was next to her parents', this was not an easy task, and she would wait until her mother and father were snoring in unison before attempting to leave the house.

He waited for her down the "gap," under a breadfruit tree that, with its expansive branches and broad leaves, created a pocket of deeper darkness in the night. At first, they would just stand there and talk, whispering to avoid having their voices carry to the houses close by. She had always wondered about the sounds from her mother's bedroom, but when Rupert first touched her after some weeks, she had been surprised by the pleasure. It confused her when his hands made her heart beat faster and her breathing change. When alone, she had tried to duplicate the feeling, but it had not worked, and soon she had grown impatient with the touching. She wanted something more, something that also frightened her.

There is no telling how long this would have gone on if, one day at the beach, he had not said to her, "You are a virgin, aren't you?"

Audrey felt the challenge in the question and was surprised she felt no pride in her virginity. In fact, it was with a feeling of inadequacy that she responded, "I bound to be if you won' do nothin'."

Something changed then, and the darkness had come into his eyes. He recognized the challenge, and something male, terrifying, and ugly had come up in him. When he had spoken, there was a crack in his voice, as if the thought of what she suggested frightened him. Looking at him, she had seen for the first time the power of her body and the control it could exercise over men. He had seemed less assured after that, and she had grown into a position of power with him. It was her first such feeling, dominated as she was by her parents. Rupert had become a source of pride, and, though secret, the relationship sustained her in ways she dimly understood. It became a counterpoint to the dominance of her mother, whose voice ruled the village, and she fantasized about the possibility of being Rupert Barnes' wife. This always ended with a kind of imaginary blankness because she had no idea what such a life would mean except that she would be rich. She had never been inside the Great House, though she had walked by it from time to time on some errand, and had looked into the mysterious darkness with wonderment. Its size intimidated her, and the fact that the light did not penetrate the inside made the place mysterious and powerful in her mind. She created scenes in her head about life in the Great House and placed herself in the center of these scenes, being hostess to parties and dinners. In this, she was no different from the other girls, but the possession of Rupert gave her dreams solidity and allowed for the possibility of them coming true.

Audrey could still remember, in some deep recess of her mind, the sharp pain of her deflowering, but it had been accompanied by a strange sense of serenity she understood to be maturity. It had taken a long time, involving several tries, for her hymen to be completely broken, and she had bled each time. He seemed to be more in agony over this than she, and his tentative aggression had frustrated her for many nights. Several weeks ago, he had shown her his shoes and the dark spots on them and had told her this was her woman-blood, claiming he would keep the shoes forever. She had laughed, slapping at his shoulder, but had been deeply touched by the gesture, which was so personal and so sweet.

Audrey moved her lips against Rupert's chest, and he stirred, coming back to himself. He was always like this afterwards, more dead than alive, wanting to drift where she could not follow, and she would hold him to her, not letting him go away. Eventually, he would come back to her, the sweet sourness of his breath the indication that he had slept a little. Now, he moved his hands absentmindedly down the back of her thighs, and she felt herself quicken inside. He was not yet aware of what he was doing, she knew, and it would take her reaction to arouse him from this torpor. Not yet ready for that, she leaned on him, and he drifted away again.

She was afraid. Her period was ten days late. Earlier, her stomach had felt swollen and slightly upset. She had been hopeful, but the feeling had disappeared in the afternoon when Rupert had ridden into the village and told her he wanted to meet. She had then hoped she would not be bleeding, but, now, the passion satiated, she was afraid.

Earlier, he had talked of leaving the island, and her dream world had shattered explosively, but he had wanted her and had pulled at her with a desperation she did not understand but to which she responded easily. With anguish in his voice, he had spoken about his sister, Miss Ruby, and she had sympathized since his opinion was shared by everyone in the village. So when he told her about his fight with his sister over the village, she had been proud of him. She had not known her mother had visited Miss Ruby, but she could imagine how that conversation would have gone. It was not clear why, but her mother found the Barneses objectionable and would often say the meanest things about the family, particularly Ruby. She once asked her mother what the Barneses had done to her, but the woman turned her baleful eyes on her daughter, telling her not to push herself into "big people" business. Audrey recognized the tone, which hinted at violence, and had remained silent, fearful of her mother's anger. Still, she wondered about the venom in the voice whenever her mother spoke of the Barneses. It was the one dark spot on her relationship with Rupert. She did not mind not being able to tell the others in the village; in fact, she had no desire to share her private world in this way, but she wished her mother could bless the relationship.

Audrey sighed softly, moving on Rupert's body. He closed his arms more tightly around her, and she snuggled against him. The air was cold on her legs, but there was something erotic she craved in the nether nakedness, and she did not want to put her dress down, her mind already anticipating the separation from his body. Feeling the wetness, which the air seemed to make electric, she laughed silently when it tickled. Rupert turned his head, careful not to dislodge her, and asked sleepily, "What's so funny?"

"Nothing," Audrey replied, continuing to chuckle more openly now.

He sighed, not pursuing it, but returning to his earlier position. Audrey felt the disappointment that followed his lack of interest, and she said, "Rupert, you serious 'bout leavin' Barbados? Why you want to go to Panama, anyway?"

Rupert had been dreading this conversation, which had to come at some point, and he hesitated before answering. She waited for him, knowing he would be uncomfortable but needing to have her say. She was afraid of what her body may be creating. He did not know, and now that he had mentioned Panama, she feared he would think she was making this up. In any case, she did not really know whether her body had betrayed her or not. The possibility created a tension in her. She hoped desperately she was not pregnant, but there was no way to tell. Even if she were not, he had made the decision to leave without even talking to her about it. He had announced it as what he would do, and it was clear he saw nothing wrong with that. She was hurt because he did not feel her sense of connectedness. When he had spoken, she had stood very still so as not to react, but she could not help but feel the profound sense of betrayal and disappointment the words "I am going away to Panama" had created. She had built a fantasy about her life with him, and he had not done any such thing, so he was willing to leave her and go away. This, she knew, meant the end of the relationship, for few men came back with the same intentions with which they had left. The village was full of women who had children for the men who left for the riches of Panama. Most of the men had either not returned or had found other women before they came back. Some had come back with long-haired Spanish girls who were light-skinned and, therefore, more acceptable. The women talked about this again and again; lying there, Audrey wondered if she, too, would be one of those women sitting under the mango tree discussing the unreliability of men.

"Panama is the only way I'm going to get away from Ruby. She's making things very difficult for me just now. She has no faith in my ability to do anything, and she's always criticizing me. I'm tired of it. You have no idea what it's like to live with someone who thinks she is perfect."

He ended with a sharp sound, almost a squeak, in his voice. She recoiled a little, and immediately feeling guilty, kissed his face, noticing the difference of his smell. At first, she had thought of it as a cleaner smell created by frequent bathing with scents and fancy soaps, but gradually she had come to believe the smell was more fundamental than that, existing deep in the skin that carried its difference so proudly. Sometimes, bathing in the yard with rainwater from the barrel, she would immediately smell herself, but her smell was always different, and she felt a little disappointment at this.

When she responded, it was with this sense of her difference, a difference she could not wash away. The water welled up in her eyes, and she said angrily, "You aint runnin' 'way from Ruby. Um is me you runnin' from."

Something in the night changed when he did not respond immediately. Expecting the denial to come forthwith, his hesitation gave the subsequent denial that peculiar echo of falsehood. The pressure built in her chest as the cry tried to tear itself out of her lungs, but she choked it back, forcing the air down into her stomach and closing off her throat.

"You are not being fair, Audrey. This has nothing to do with you."

His voice petered out, and he held her close, rubbing his face in her long and luxuriantly black hair. Her head moved against his as their bodies separated, and she pulled her dress down as she sat up. The sky wheeled around as she did this, and the deeper darkness of the machineel tree to their left seemed a solid hole in the sky, eliminating the stars. She was so aware of the night, with its secret life and silent noises. It was late. She could tell from the disembodied and brittle sounds coming from far away. Nothing seemed to exist close to them. There was a zone of silence surrounding them; although in the distance, she could hear music, very soft and tinny, coming from a band. The distance was difficult to judge because sound traveled differently at night.

Audrey was trying not to be angry, but the feeling was powerful, and she found it impossible not to think of her possible pregnancy and the fact that he was leaving. That he did not know about her late period did not make his choice any more acceptable. Her mother had been right about him. He was "a serpent, just like all uh dem Barneses," as her mother once said. She had wanted to defend him, but her mother brooked no contradiction. Now, she castigated herself for her stupidity, for believing him. Standing abruptly, she held her arms around her chest, staring out into the darkness, her eyes automatically noting that there were only two lights in the village. One would be the Haynes'. She would have to pass by there when she returned to the village, and she always worried about their dog. The other she was less certain about, but it was probably Miriam staying up, mourning her child. At this thought, her hand dropped unbidden to her stomach, and she leaned into the slight breeze coming from the west, unusual at this time of night. Rupert stood up and put his arms around her.

"I'm sorry, Audrey. I didn't mean that the way it sounded, but I can't stay in Barbados. I feel like I am dying here. All I have to look forward to is becoming just like Ruby. And the thought of inheriting what she has…"

As his voice petered out again, Audrey found herself saying, "Ruby aint goin' dead. People like dat don't dead."

He was silent for a moment, and then started laughing, and, unable to stop herself, she joined him, each caught in the inanity of the relief the laughter provided, sustaining itself through the avoidance of the pain its cessation would entail. It introduced a note of falseness into their innocent lives and, in that moment, destroyed the possibility of understanding and whatever chance had existed that their lust and affection could have developed into love. It was the specter of the skull and the grave, this laughter, and they both continued, recognizing the emptiness it contained but afraid to replace it with a truth that was painful but unavoidable.

When they walked down from the hill that night, the silence closed in, and the stars stared boldly down at their passage, which was so much longer than the walk to her home. This night, the dogs did not bark, as if they too understood the change to which the distant stars bore witness. Long after he had gone and she had sneaked back into her bed, Audrey lay awake, her eyes staring at the ceiling she could not see, her stomach and heart linked in a sympathetic pain she knew bore her ill. She was pregnant and alone. In the next room, the snores of her parents, her mother's particularly, were a counterpoint to the tremulous beating of her heart, and she pressed the pillow to her face in order to stifle her muffled cries. She did not notice that one of the snores had stopped, and so she continued to cry, believing herself unheard.

In the next room, Ruthie uttered a silent prayer to the Christian god but also threw the imaginary dust over her shoulder. She recognized the particular quality of that sound. It was old, too old to be disguised, no matter that the girl was obviously covering her face with the pillow. Ruthie castigated herself, knowing she should have told the girl. Now, from the sound, which came not so much from the girl but from the depths of her history, she too had made the same mistake that had plagued the family. Ruthie breathed out harshly, convinced of her tragedy. She had known from the way the Barnes boy had asked about Audrey that they had a closer relationship than the girl had let on, and if she had lied by omission, then that was serious. Although she had told Audrey to stay away from the Barneses, she should have been specific as to why. Now, from the sounds in the other room, the girl had found trouble, which always stayed by the side of the road, because, as her mother used to say, "If you di'nt trouble trouble, trouble won't trouble you. You haf to get off de road to find trouble 'cause it di'nt come in de road."

Ruthie's body started to shake, and her mind spun, lamenting the secrets that had created this abomination she was sure had occurred.

God have mercy 'pon me. I shoulda know. I shoulda know. And I shoulda say someting. God have mercy 'pon me, she thought.

Turning on her side, she did what her daughter was doing in the room next door, and the silent sniffs drifted up to the ceiling, joining on the roof and spreading through the village, infecting the silences of the night and emphasizing the darkness that moved in mystery and with assurance across the village, causing a universal shudder. Tomorrow, each woman would have a story of a movement in the night, a movement that seemed to crawl under their nightdresses and press into their lives with a cold certainty of their acceptance. And they, too, would remember the silent cries in the night.

CHAPTER EIGHT

BARBADOS 1905

The next morning, Audrey awoke late to a silent house. Her mother would already be in the fields, and her father would be out searching for the work that sustained the family. Although the village did not seem to be benefiting from the Panama money that everyone spoke of, some other places were because he found work from time to time in other parts of the country. In spite of the drought, some people were making enough not only to get by but also to build houses, so her father had work, although he had to walk far away to find it and sometimes returned late at night. Occasionally, when the work was concentrated, he stayed away for several nights, often paying a part of his wages to board with some friend in another village while he worked.

Audrey wondered what he would say when he found out she was pregnant. He had always been more expressive than her mother, having high hopes for her, and his sadness had been evident when she had not been able to get into the school they had just built two miles from the village. The classes at the church never held her attention. A dreamer, she found the spelling and reading and addition and multiplication a thorough mystery. Some other place occupied her mind when she was in class, and, though this place was always vague, it was beautiful, and in it she was rich, and people were graceful and gracious. In her mind, she learned to bow and curtsy and to wear long, flowing gowns that trailed after her when she walked across her marble floors. If she had been asked where these ideas had come from, she probably could not have said, but they had come from the same books she avoided, for in those books there was always beauty and princesses always kissed frogs that turned into handsome princes. Audrey's dreams tended to turn her life into shadow, an ugliness from which she hid, and this did little to fulfill the urges she felt toward escape. The dreams would always end.

When Rupert had expressed interest in her, the land of her books and her dreams opened up before her, and he had become a prince, quite literally on a white horse. Rupert meant an escape that was not simply in her dreams, and the nights with him, standing under the breadfruit tree or lying stretched beneath the impassive sky on the hill that crowned the village, had been the fulfillment of all she had seen in her mind. Her family was supportive, but, since the death of her grandmother, little affection flowed from her parents. This was not an indication of a lack of love but rather a deeply held belief that children should not be spoiled, that too much affection bred familiarity, and that led to insolence. This was to be avoided at all costs.

Audrey laid now, hugging herself, knowing she should get up and head to the fields, but she felt listless, not wanting to move. In a little while, the sun would be high, and the room would become too hot for lying around; but for now, it was still cool and silent, and she wanted the peace.

She thought of her conversation with Rupert the night before. He was going to leave her alone with this baby, and she had no idea what she was going to do. At the thought of her mother's reaction, her heart quailed. Her mother would be furious and would probably beat her. While this frightened Audrey, it was the look of disappointment she anticipated in her father's eyes that worried her even more. Though he generally followed his wife's lead, he was more given to personal comments about his daughter, and she knew he thought her beautiful, commenting occasionally on her good hair, by which he meant straight, and her pretty skin, by which he meant whitish. He also mentioned her thin lips from time to time. He loved her, she knew, and it was his face and the disappointment contained there that would hurt the most. She sighed loudly and rolled her legs off the bed, running her hands along her hair, pulling it into a single strand and twisting it slightly before dropping it on her shoulder, the uncoiling plait falling to her middle. She quickly washed her face, pulled a loose-fitting dress over her head, and soon was flying up the hill on her way to work.

The sun had risen but still lay low in the morning sky. Over a crest in the hill, the land of the Barnes lower plantation lay spread out before her, and in it could be seen the bent backs and bobbing straw hats of the women. Audrey did not want to be here, though, if asked, she would have had no answer as to where she did want to be. She had been carrying a straw hat in her hand and now jammed it on her head, a violent, rebellious motion that captured her irritation. Turning left, she headed across the field toward the grass-piece where the girls of her age learned how to fight the battle against the land. Approaching the field, she saw her mother bent over the long wooden handle of the hoe with which she chopped at the intractable grass. The woman leaned as if she had a pain in her side, and Audrey wondered at the cause. Her mother was slim, unlike most of the women who had widened as they aged into their thirties and forties, and Audrey wondered if this was because her mother had had no other children.

Her light-colored skin stood out in the fields among the deeper blackness of the other women, and Audrey thought about the origin of that skin for the first time. There were many light-skins in the village, though the vast majority of the people were of a deep, purple blackness they called African black, intending no compliment. She thought about her child and pondered the issue of color. The village was ambivalent about color. When friendly arguments arose, contempt was often expressed for the light-skins, indicating they were somehow lesser for not having the same strength and resistance to the sun. Yet, beneath it all, there was the unspoken assumption that they were better off, the lightness of their skin giving them a social advantage the centuries had converted into privilege and, later, inherent superiority. They would not have admitted this in a serious statement, but their profound sense of their disadvantage was often expressed in humor. Where would her child be located on this social spectrum? And how would she be seen after the village found out she had been made pregnant by the white boy from the plantation? These questions should have occurred to her before, but her fear now generated the introspection, the theoretical questions having never before been of any consequence.

Audrey had stopped, and, hearing her name called, she looked around slightly startled, seeing her mother waving to her. She walked over to the woman who stood sweating in the early morning sun.

"You awright, chile? Wha' you standin' 'bout fuh? You aint got wuk to do?"

Audrey hung her head, mumbling that she was all right, but her mother continued to look at her closely, leaning her weight on the handle of the hoe. Ruthie pushed the straw hat back on her head, revealing the unusually light eyes that complemented her light-colored skin.

"You sure? You aint look like you had too much sleep las' night," she added, watching the girl's reaction like a hawk, but Audrey was prepared for the question and simply said she had woken up early and could not get back to sleep.

"You too young to be havin' restless nights. Wha' 'pon you mind? You worrying 'bout som'ting?"

"No, please, Ma. I aint worryin' 'bout nuttin. I just wake up early, tha's all."

"Well, you bettuh go long and do de white people wuk befo'e de black white man 'pon de horse ovuh dere come here an' I hafta gi'e he a piece of me mind. You bring any watuh to drink? It goin' be hot today."

Like ev'ry udder day, Audrey thought insolently, but she answered meekly, "No, Ma. I fuhget."

"Well, if yuh get t'irsty, I got some. Now, guh long an' do de people wuk."

Audrey walked away, heart heavy and mind in a turmoil. She would have to tell her mother some time, but not yet. Her friends were already bowed over the grass, sickles flowing easily in their practiced hands across the tough grass that had to be cut to feed the Barnes stock. This field, which had been lying fallow for some time, was being prepared for cultivation next year, and looking at the expanse of it, she groaned aloud. Angela, who lived a few houses away from her and frequently accompanied her to the beach, giggled, saying, "Dat is how ev'rybody feel, Audrey."

Audrey joined her laughter, already feeling somewhat lighter in spirit now that she was with her friends. Angela had not straightened up, and Audrey was aware of the absurdity of her position. The grass did not grow above two to three feet long, but since it fell down to the ground under its own weight, the girls had to bend over from the waist almost to the ground or kneel to cut it. Angela chose to do the former, so her not inconsiderable behind was pointed arrogantly at the sky, her voice coming from some place lower down and between her legs, giving the impression that her behind was speaking. When Audrey's laughter continued beyond what she considered normal, Angela stood up slowly, gradually uncoiling her knotted spine and supporting her lower back with the palm of her left hand.

Seeing this posture, Audrey abruptly stopped laughing. There were no women in the village who did not complain about their backs, a product of incessant childbearing and this backbreaking work. Audrey thought of the former when she saw Angela rise, and this wiped the smile from her face.

"Wha' wrong wid you? You look like you los' yuh navel string," Angela said suspiciously, and Audrey resumed laughing, answering, "You backside does look like a ship bow when you ben' over like dat."

Angela made a face, looking over her shoulder, trying to see what Audrey had pointed out and, at the same time, saying in an imitation grown-up voice, "Jus' 'cause you got a white people behind, you jus' jealous, tha's all. You want to borrow some uh mine to fill out dat dress?"

Audrey shoved her playfully, and they both bent down to the waiting grass. It was difficult to cut the grass at the pace the overseer required and speak at the same time, but somehow the girls managed.

Before long, Angela said, "Rupert Barnes ride by de fiel' dis mornin' befo'e you get here. He look like he did goin' some place special. He had on good clothes. He wave at me," she finished proudly. Audrey did not answer, and her friend continued.

"You t'ink we wud haffa chance wid he?" she asked, a wicked tone to her voice, and then added sultrily, "Cause I wont mind givin' he piece."

Audrey shook her head, playfully moralizing, and Angela quickly retorted, "If you din't savin' it fuh Jesus, you wud, too. I see how you does look at he. Lemme tell you. If yuh don't use it, it goin' catch cobweb."

Audrey was uncomfortable with the conversation, but Angela's enthusiasm for sex was infectious. She was what was referred to in the village as "easy", not seeming to care whom she went with and, in other girls, her behavior was considered sluttish. Yet, she wore her promiscuity with such naturalness no one condemned her. Her oversized body exuded sexuality in the same way lilies of the night exuded scent, and no one questioned her. She had to leave the church school when she had become pregnant; Angela had joined the grass gang, working right up to the moment she had the child, which had been stillborn. Her mother buried the child, and Angela had returned to the field the next day. She had never spoken to Audrey about the birth and seemed to have no regrets about the child. Once, when Audrey drummed up the courage to ask what it had been like, the girl looked at her for a long time, the habitual smile missing, and replied, "Can't explain it."

Angela had been pregnant twice since then, and both of the children had died, the first in childbirth and the second after five months. Each time, she seemed to shake off the tragedy and simply returned to work. The women did not know what to make of it. In a land where children were prized, Angela's dismissal of her offspring was not only unnerving but also a little frightening. Some of the older women whispered that she seemed to be a "comeback," one who had lived before and could act with impunity in this life. "Comebacks" were not necessarily evil, but it was wise to placate them.

Maybe it because people frighten fuh she dat mek dem accept de way dat Angela behave, Audrey thought.

Audrey did not think Angela was a "comeback" nor was she afraid of her. When Rupert had started touching her, she had been surprised by the feeling, which seemed to start somewhere in her lower stomach and then spread to the space in the middle of her. Afterward, she would feel like she had those times at Christmas after secretly drinking rum, and, her head losing perspective, she felt to be without responsibility and capable of anything. She knew that Angela simply felt this way all the time, and rather than fear, Audrey felt envy, wishing she too could carry that feeling of a seed bursting from its pod always.

"I bet you still uh virgin," the girl now said, smirking, and Audrey, feeling guilty, replied in a false preacher's tone, "We can't all be like you. Some uh we got to save de village fuh de Lord."

Angela burst out laughing again, not missing a stroke with the sickle, and answered,

"Um aint de Lord you savin' it fuh. Soonuh or latuh, it goin' be a natural man dat goin' get it, an' I got uh feelin' I kno' who it goin' be."

Audrey grunted in denial, feeling the truth of her situation strangling her. She had to tell her mother first. As sweet as Angela was, she kept a secret as effectively as a sieve did water. Angela made no pretense about it and frequently told some petulant, betrayed friend that if she really wanted anything kept secret she would not tell her. She never apologized, and everyone forgave her. After telling her mother, she would probably tell Angela. That way, the village would not have to ask her lots of questions. Angela would answer everything.

One thing was certain: She would not name the father of her child. Let them guess. She would be silent. Audrey knew this would bring swift punishment from her mother, but that secret would be hers. Rupert was probably on his way to see about going to Panama, and she had no intention of looking like a fool.

Above, the deep, startling blue turned silvery as the sun reached up into the sky, sending its waves of heat down on the women who bent beneath it. There was no sound in the air, and the heat beat back from the ground, soaking the women in sweat and changing the smells of their bodies. When the twelve o'clock break came, they all headed for the trees that provided temporary and partial relief from the sun. The women ate the cooked breadfruit, yams, and salted fish, and, before long, most were asleep, dreaming of a land that was cool and where grass did not grow so long.

CHAPTER NINE

BARBADOS 1905

Rupert rode easily into Bridgetown, crossing the wooden bridge that forded the pretentiously named Constitution River. It was little more than a trickle at its most aggressive and now, at the height of the drought, was simply a smelly puddle filled with the effluvium of the city. Without the flow of the water to carry it out to sea, the waste had simply accumulated, drawing flies and, from all reports, rats of extraordinary size. Rupert avoided the city when he could, preferring the freshness of the sea at Oistins or the windy spaces of the plantation. He had few occasions to go to Bridgetown, but when he went, he was always surprised at the constant growth. Across the bridge, there was a new store at the head of Broad Street with the Barnes marquee clearly visible, and he shook his head in wonder. Ruby was everywhere. The road was not very crowded, the people having taken refuge from the sun, and he rode, his path unimpeded, toward the squat building that stood off Trafalgar Square, where the men who wanted to go to Panama were examined.

A line stretched for hundreds of yards down Broad Street, where the major stores stood, and since it was early morning, the ride having taken him a couple of hours, he was resigned to wait all day for the line to move. He would have stayed in town the night before had he known it would be like this. The dirt road, pounded level by flat irons and now baked into an iron-like consistency, was dark with able-bodied men. Shy when confronting whites or bureaucracy (which, in this country, was the same thing), the poor had dressed in their best, and many now stood in what were obviously their "Sunday go to meeting" clothes, their felt hats soaked around the foreheads as they stared forlornly at the interminable line stretching ahead of them. Rupert noted the inhuman patience in them, a patience that had come from centuries of waiting, and he curbed his instinct to go to the head of the line, an action to which he knew none would openly object. His generosity was wasted, however, for, riding past the open doorway through which the men were being admitted, he heard his name being called. Rupert, reining in the white horse, looked in the direction of the sound.

A white boy was waving at him. Recognizing Archie Mackintosh, Rupert waved back and pulled the horse around. As he approached, the black men, heads lowered, made way, and he rode through their midst, dismounting and thoughtlessly handing the reins to one of the men who worked at the Karner Recruiting Office. The two young white men walked into the relative coolness of the stone building. Archie had been at Lodge School with Rupert, and though they were not friends, in this circumstance, surrounded by the black men, they felt an unaccustomed closeness. Archie offered Rupert a glass of lemonade from which he constantly brushed the insolent flies that seemed not at all afraid of the perpetually swishing hand. They found a couple of unoccupied chairs and sat for a moment in silence. Then, Archie, his voice heavy with a north England accent, asked, "What brings you into Sodom, old boy?"

Archie had come from England six years before when his father had been posted to Barbados as part of the colonial civil service. His family lived on the south coast and occasionally visited the Barnes' plantation when invited to lunch. He was a source of some amusement, for he had a dry wit the Barbadian boys at the school envied and tried, unsuccessfully, to emulate. He seemed to take few things seriously, and, protected from most punishments by his father's position, he had always gotten other boys into trouble. Archie had a pixie face most of the boys found unattractive—or they would have were it not for his accent, which they wished they had, and the money to which there seemed no end.

Rupert hesitated, watching Archie closely as he said, "I came to sign up for Panama."

To this, the boy burst out laughing, but realizing Rupert had not joined him, he stopped and looked at Rupert closely.

"You can't possibly be serious. Whatever for?"

Rupert shrugged, and the boy continued.

"The place is not exactly safe, you know. The men we send are dying in large numbers, and several are frequently badly injured. Panama is a deathtrap, Barnes."

Rupert looked at the posters on the wall, inviting men to join the adventure in Panama. The pictures showed well-dressed black men with money in their hands. The images were crude but effective, and Rupert could understand why the men outside would welcome the danger rather than stay in the island and gradually waste away. But why was he going? What was pushing him away from Barbados? Still not sure, he blamed Ruby, but that seemed an inadequate reason for his choice. He liked to think it was adventure that called to him, but it was not quite as simple as that, and he had not really invested the time in seeking reasons.

"Anything is better than wasting away here, Mackintosh. This place has no promise for me."

Archie frowned at him.

"And responsibility, old boy? Don't you have a responsibility to the colony? My father says that it needs leaders now more than ever."

Rupert shrugged, replying softly, "Have you met my sister Ruby? That's all the leadership our family needs, and maybe the country, too."

Archie laughed.

"Yes. She's formidable. My father says she's both competent and honest."

"Exactly. That's why she should be the leader," Rupert responded irritably.

"Oh, quite the contrary, dear boy. Either quality would disadvantage her in government, and both would prove positively fatal. Now you, on the other hand..."

Both boys chuckled but stopped abruptly when they heard an explosion of cheering from the far side of the building. They both turned in that direction.

"What's the matter with them?" Rupert asked, watching incredulously as twenty-five or thirty men jumped up and down, slapping each other on the back.

"The successful ones!" Archie replied ironically, the contempt evident in his voice. "They are the ones selected for the 'adventure' in Panama. Negroes are so puerile. Maybe it is good that you accompany them as a spiritual supervisor."

"Spiritual supervisor. I like the sound of it, though it hardly fits me."

Rupert felt a little irritated, though he was not sure why.

"Every priest I know has had an ill-fitting robe."

The boys laughed again. Rupert, his attention drawn by the cheering, was now looking at the far side of the room where almost a hundred men stood, their backs against the wall, waiting for what was evidently a medical examination. He watched as the doctors, all white, asked the men to open their mouths and stared into their throats. With gloved hands, they checked the men's teeth, noting on a white writing tablet those that were missing, broken, or blackened.

The men had to be eighteen years old to qualify, and boys obviously younger than that were turned away. The same was true of old men who were clearly past their prime or who looked ill. The ones who remained, about seventy total, were ordered up to the loft, where they were made to undress. They were asked to cough, and the doctors checked for tuberculosis, listening carefully to their hearts and checking for rupture.

Rupert watched, fascinated, as one man, obviously acknowledging that he was to be denied, grabbed his pants, shoved his hand into the pocket, and offered the doctor, a young white fellow, all the money he had. It was obvious he had expected to be turned down and had brought the money for this purpose. The young white man looked contemptuously at him. Waving his hand dismissively, he turned his back, curtly addressing the next man in line. Rupert felt something in his soul respond to the man who was left holding out his meager bribe, his pants in the other hand and his privates hanging. Rupert turned his eyes away as the man looked down at the floor where the two white boys sat. Archie laughed shortly, saying, "There is your Negro for you. Big man," he added spitefully, looking boldly at the man's middle.

The man, embarrassed, turned away and quickly dressed before hurrying out of the building. Rupert, surprised at his own irritation, replied with an apparent non-sequitor.

"It is unwise to look too deeply into a man's origins in this place."

"What? What origins?"

"Oh, nothing. I'm just rambling. Will I have to go through that?"

"Are you serious? That's just for the Negroes. It is astounding the diseases they carry. Are you quite certain you wish to go to Panama? Most of these people can't do anything else. I don't understand why you wish to go. That is no place for white people."

"Do you think Barbados is? A hundred years ago, the same diseases were present here, and still our ancestors came. Why is this different?"

Archie looked at Rupert more closely, not able think of an answer. Finally, he said, a hint of envy in his voice, "I suppose the comparison is apt. I envy you, Barnes. You have the freedom to be anything you wish. Civilization destroys that possibility."

Archie was obviously quoting his father, and Rupert, who had no patience with speculative thinking, said, "What has civilization to do with it? This is part of the British Empire, isn't it? Why do you think civilization has failed here?"

Archie looked embarrassed and waved dismissively.

"Sorry, Barnes. I did not mean to give offense, but you, in this colony, like much of the world where we—the British, I mean— have gone, exist in a state of possibility. At home, we are rather finished, and that is all our civilization means: the absence of possibility."

Rupert was surprised to hear the boy speak like this. Although everyone knew he repeated things his father said, there was a certainty about his statements and an undertone of despair that made the pronouncements sound authentic. Rupert found himself being drawn, much to his surprise, into the conversation.

"But we are all aspiring to be more British here. What then is the point of the pursuit of that quality which we envy if the end result is the end of possibility, by which I assume you mean hope?"

"No, no, not at all. Not hope. We yet have hope. It is the certainty of the impossibility of our hope that has created our state. Oh, we are still striving, but it is without any sense of the possibility of our own improvement, for deep down we believe we have created the apex of civilization. From there, the only possibility is activity. Much like rats caught suddenly in a bright light at night, we can scramble around, but there is no purpose."

Rupert wanted to ask Archie, whom he was looking at with new respect, where he had encountered these ideas, but was embarrassed to admit his ignorance. In school, Archie had had a reputation for scholarly activity, and, unlike Rupert, he intended to continue his education in England. Rupert had found school a tremendous waste of time, a time to fool around and get the wildness out of his system. He had found the subjects, with the possible exception of history, a total bore, and he had struggled in the classroom. Now, he found himself outclassed and uncomfortable. There was little in the colonial structure to make a plantation owner uncomfortable, his position being so unassailable. Confrontation usually ended with someone deferring, and this had created the habit of intellectual flaccidity, the unused muscle atrophying and the group depending more and more on the strength of their position and the docility of the silent horde surrounding them.

Rupert did not feel that assurance. He knew that somewhere in his past, there was reportedly a slave ancestor of whom no one spoke, and the family had made sure to distance themselves from that long-dead ancestor. Still, he would never have the assurance Mackintosh exhibited, that ability to criticize with apparent impunity the culture that had produced him. When Barbadians spoke disparagingly of the smallness of the island or its lack of culture, there was a painful icicle that lay at the center of the comment, for it also reduced them to that level of insignificance. In their hearts, they wanted the association with the greatness that was Britain. This validated them, placed them in the scale of civilization in a way their own merits could not, and so Rupert clung to the idea of Britain. He did not want to hear Archie's theories because they threatened his own conception of the universe, and, more importantly, they undermined the self that had been constructed so laboriously over the last three hundred years. So when he replied, it was with some acerbity.

"That's nonsense, Archie. You belong to something great. You just don't appreciate it, that's all."

Archie conceded graciously, saying, "You're right, of course. Too much lamenting is not so good, eh? It's just that I think of my father and others like him who are spreading out over the world with their claims of carrying civilization, and I think of how I feel when in England. Why is the excitement always in the colonies? Why are some of the best people England is producing seeking an escape from it to live in the colonies? And when I ask these questions, Barnes, I have no answers that satisfy me. My father is insisting I go to Cambridge, where I'll study history, but I have studied that history. The story is fixed, however artificially, Barnes, and there are no surprises. I would rather go to the colonies, particularly the Americas, which are in a state of becoming. There is mystery there. Possibility, not certainty. I envy you, Barnes, because I will go to Cambridge and study civilization while you, silly though I think your particular choice is, will go to Panama and make civilization."

He stopped, his voice having become forlorn. Rupert did not say anything, taken aback by Archie's passion. Not sure of what to say, he asked, "What do I need to do here to get organized?"

Archie laughed, replying, "Sorry. I almost forgot you had a purpose for being here. Come with me."

The exam was cursory, and soon Rupert was in an office with a single sheet of paper before him. He held the pen for a moment and then signed with a flourish, saying as he handed the pen back, "I am now owned. My first legal job."

The Karner official took the paper and gave Rupert a soggy-looking copy without answering. When he turned around to file the paper, the two boys made a face and laughed silently. Rupert left, his companion walking to the door with him. Outside, the crowd of men had grown, and they were not quite as quiet as when he had entered. Some of the rejected men had not left but had been telling the waiting men they were wasting their time. The crowd had become agitated, and the police were shoving men back into line, and none too gently.

Rupert spurred the horse, galloping quickly away from the square and thinking of what Archie had said. Why was he going to Panama? Why was he so willing to leave Audrey? That relationship had developed with a quiet intensity, giving him no time to assess what had happened. Whenever he wanted to say something, her face, with its open look of admiration and love, had stopped him. Rupert tried to convince himself he had made no commitment, that he had simply done what he had always done. The girls had always been friendly and seemed not to care too much about what he did, so he had been with many of them. Audrey, however, had brought something new to the way he dealt with the girls. In most cases, the girls had approached him, and he had simply responded to them. His interest in Audrey had come, at least in part, from her very lack of interest. He had gone after her because she was remote, but, in doing so, he had removed his usual excuse that the girl wanted him. So, he had been pulled into the relationship, lured by the freshness and innocence of the girl. She had been different, but his actions had made her the same as the others. He did not see this, feeling certain that what he was doing was natural. He had not lost interest but felt something just as deadly, possibly a fear of entrapment, of being lulled into a relationship he was not sure he wanted.

The argument with his sister, knowing she did not intend to help the villagers, had given him the perfect reason to act. He could leave feeling self-righteous, and no one would be the wiser. Audrey would hurt for a while, but she was strong and would soon get over it. As the horse slowed to a walk upon reaching the outskirts of the city, Rupert sensed there was a flaw in his reasoning but also felt excited at what he had done. Ruby would be angry, and that gave him an odd kind of pleasure.

Under him, the white horse moved with a fluid gait, and Rupert straightened his shoulders, glaring arrogantly ahead. In four days, he would be leaving. He would have to say something to Audrey, although he was not sure what. Feeling some discomfort over this, he pulled irritably at the reins, and the horse shied sideways. Regaining control, he resumed the journey, the struggle with the horse having focused his mind in an unexpected way, as he felt his strength confirmed through the control of the sixteen-hand-high horse. He would succeed in Panama, and his sister could go to hell. Audrey he was not sure about.

CHAPTER TEN

BARBADOS 1905

The lights had long been extinguished at the Great House when Rupert went quietly to the barn, saddled his horse, and walked it along the edge of the path, keeping to the dirt to dampen the sound of the hoof beats. Some distance from the house, he mounted and cantered in the direction of the village. There was almost no humidity, and the night, with the broiling sun long gone, was cool. In fact, there was even the smell of rain in the air, and he said a silent prayer, hoping there would be some relief from the drought. He had ridden by the pond at the northern end of the plantation where they had been watering the cattle, but the water had dried up, and the cattle had been shoving each other out of the way to get a drink. For a moment, he felt some sympathy for Ruby. She cared for all this, and her brothers had deserted her.

To his surprise, Ruby had accepted his decision to leave. He had been prepared to fight her, but she had looked at him with surprise, then sadness, then something like respect. It had not lasted, though, and as the idea sunk in, she accused him of deserting her and the estates. They had had words.

Still, she had arranged the party for him tonight and, while making no concession to his decision, had poured her soul into the preparations. Rupert was not sure how he felt about the party since almost no one seemed to think his decision had any merit. They were polite and respectful, of course, but it was clear they thought he was being shipped away because of something he had done. The only person who seemed to understand why he was doing this had been Archie's father, who had been strenuous in Rupert's defense.

Rupert had sat in the middle of the long dining table, his sister across from him and next to her the Paines, who lived on the far side of the island. The Mackintoshes sat next to them, and Governor Anderson, who had come alone, sat next to Mrs. Mackintosh. Rupert, sure his sister was up to something, looked at them all with a slightly jaundiced eye from the beginning. So, while smiling and welcoming the guests, he had been on guard. The expected opposition had not arisen, though the questions had come repeatedly. It had been after one such question that Mr. Mackintosh said, "There is nothing quite so bracing for a young man as leaving home in search of adventure and fortune. It was at one time an expectation. Now, we pamper our young until they are all but useless."

At the far end of the table, Mrs. Seales, a consumptive who seldom attended these affairs, responded, "But Panama, dear? Whatever for? If a young man wants adventure, then Europe is safe enough for that, don't you think? Panama is so…"

She stuttered, at a loss for the right word, and her husband, a bluff man dressed carefully in a long coat and a colorful cravat, his voice heavy with irony, said, "Unsafe, dear?"

"Well, yes. I have heard there is nothing there but jungle and wild animals. Why are they building that infernal canal anyway? It is not natural, you know."

"Well, of course it's not natural, dear. That is why they have to build it. Governor, why do you think the Americans are building the canal?"

They all looked to Governor Anderson, who carefully put down his glass and leaned forward just a little, thinking carefully about the question. When he answered, his voice filled the room with its cultured tones.

"The Americans are engaged in an act of history, sir. They have wealth but no monuments, and this is the monument they have chosen to erect."

Mrs. Seales, looking perplexed, said, "I thought they were building a waterway from the Atlantic to the Pacific."

"And so they are, madam, but no aspiring culture builds simply for reasons of pragmatism. They build for posterity. Most civilizations know intuitively that military victories are transient, that national wealth can be dissipated within generations, and that even populations that sustained the growth of the culture can disappear. When that happens, what have they but the monuments they built in their prime?"

Rupert, remembering the conversation he had with Archie earlier, asked, "Governor, would that also be true of the British Empire?"

There was a short silence before the Governor answered.

"The British Empire is different. Past conquering nations have sought merely to extract wealth from their subject territories, simply creating tributaries of wealth to the metropole. Britain's mission has been different. We have, unlike any earlier civilization, been driven to share our wealth with the unfortunate of the world. Have you read any of John Speke's articles?"

Rupert shook his head, and the man continued.

"He wrote from Africa fewer than twenty years ago, indicating that, because we have a superior civilization, it is for us to provide moral guidance to those peoples of the world who are not quite as endowed by the Creator with the gifts we have so generously been given. 'The white man's burden,' he called it. You must read his memoirs. They are the very essence of humanity and culture, and they constitute the reason the British Empire will not crumble. It is, young man, constructed on the adamantine bedrock of morality."

"But what about the Americans?" an older man who had been sitting quietly now asked with what was clearly an Irish accent.

"The Americans, Mr. McCrory, are the world's first purely materialistic culture, and they will never create a civilization for that reason. After three hundred years in that wilderness, they have no art, no literature, and no music. They are a crude people, McCrory, and that is why they will succeed with the canal. It will take brute force to conquer that sliver of land, and that the Americans have in abundance. Once they have won it, they will not be able to invest it with any symbolism because, sir, for that, one needs a supporting culture and, alas, there the intrepid Americans are most noticeably deficient."

Mr. McCrory was not convinced.

"You know, Gov'nor Anderson, I've lived there, and I think you're selling 'em short. There is bustle about that country. I wouldn't dismiss 'em just yet."

"There is a bustle, sir, in Billingsgate Market. We would not want that to be our precursor to civilization, would we?"

The table erupted at that, but Rupert had been struck by the Irishman's comment, and wanting to try out the idea Archie had espoused a few days before, he asked, "But what if civilizations reach a point of perfection, not for all time or for all of humanity, but within their own selves? What if they stop seeing what is possible and believe only that which is past is possible? Would they not need to be replaced by a more vigorous culture, even one that seemed to have no possibility for civilization?"

Ruby looked at him, surprised and yet proud, and waited for the Governor's answer.

"Has Mackintosh been infecting you?" he asked. "He, too, believes that civilization is determined by our ability to see the possible, and, I daresay, he occasionally suggests that Britain may no longer have that sight. He is wrong, of course, and so are you. Culture is not spontaneous but organic."

Rupert was about to respond when Ruby said, "Are we discussing culture or adventurism?"

For a while, no one responded. Then, Mrs. Seales said, "I am not sure what any of you are talking about, but it has nothing to do with Rupert's leaving. We are going to miss you, son. You must take care of yourself. You know, three of the men from our plantation went, and they died of some awful disease there. There was not enough left of them to ship home for burial as their contract had said. They had to be buried right there."

She shuddered, the rolled flesh jiggling in response, but the conversation had been steered into less contentious channels, and the dinner had continued in this way, tepid and falsely congratulatory.

Rupert reached the hill and, dismounting, tied the horse to a clump of black-sage bush, then walked to the brow of the sharp rise that protected the village from the wind when the hurricanes came but also increased the heat. The people said the hill had been placed there to show God's sense of humor. Nothing came without a price.

He had not seen Audrey since informing her he was leaving. On the day he signed the contract, Audrey had been working in the grass-piece Ruby intended to plant next season, and, while he had joked with the girls, he had had no chance to talk to Audrey. She had not come to the hill that night or the night following, and he had returned to the plantation feeling heavy inside.

It would be better if I just go without this confrontation, he thought, unconvinced.

The young man stared at the sleeping village he would never see again and felt a sadness he could not explain. Here, all was familiar. He had never before thought of the village as home, seeing only the plantation in those terms, but he now sensed the expanse of the lands around him. He realized, with a tightness in his throat, that none of these elements was truly separable. He would not miss simply the plantation but all that it created, supported, and depended on. The village was not separate from the plantation, he realized as the surprising emotion poured through him. It was one and the same thing. In that moment, he knew Ruby was wrong. She was protecting against not some external enemy but only against herself.

Below him was the village, a single light punctuating the darkness, and he wondered if it was, as Audrey had guessed, the light of the woman who had lost her baby to hunger. Ruby was cruel, but there was nothing he could do about it. She controlled everything. He would leave and use whatever he got to help the village. He was not sure how this would be accomplished since he would be paid ten cents an hour, but Rupert dismissed the details, content with the feeling this untested generosity brought.

Above, the late night clouds had come to cover the sky, and, in the darkness, his tall figure stood like a lance linking the sky and ground, a deeper black against the darkness of the night. She was not coming, and something like a sob started from him but was stifled before it could define itself. Rupert turned slowly, shoulders slumped, and walked toward the horse. Within moments, he was gone, heading into a future that would frustrate his hopes and satisfy his ambitions. The *clop-clop* of the horse's hooves pounded like a metronome in the young man's mind as he struggled to control his emotions, and at the center of these feelings, the figure of the young woman figured prominently.

In the village, Audrey laid, eyes open and heart pounding in frustration. Four nights ago, her mother had, without explanation, moved into her room and had slept there ever since. Not able to leave, she now burned with anger. Kirton, the cook, had brought word into the village that Rupert had decided to go to Panama. Audrey had wanted to see him, to tell him she was pregnant, but her mother forestalled that. He would leave tomorrow, not knowing. Would he write? Of this, she was not assured. The men, when they left, changed, returning (when they did return) more sophisticated and less interested in marrying the women they had left behind. Audrey felt the water run from her eyes, drenching the pillow, but she made no sound lest her mother awake and start to question her.

It was close to sunrise when she finally drifted off into something that approached sleep, and she dreamt of a river, the end of which was lost in some interminable distance. It was watered by her tears that ran between her breasts before leaving her crotch in a torrent. In the distance, she could see little figures moving vigorously in the reddish brown water. They were indistinct, and she could not tell whether they were playing or drowning.

CHAPTER ELEVEN

WASHINGTON, D.C. 1976

Jack Haight was tired, the trip to Panama having been some-what more strenuous than he had expected. Still, he was sure this was the place to begin his operations. The conversations were filled with the excitement of the eventual return of the canal to Panama, and there was a new pride in the Panamanians. He liked Panama's excitement because it meant there was confidence, and when people were confi-dent, they spent money. It was money that would overcome the Panamanians' natural suspicion of the United States, he believed.

He was not really worried about the Panamanians, how-ever. They would come around once he began to pave the way with gold. His concern was actually with another American company in Panama City. Centron Corporation seemed to be everywhere, with the center of its Latin American operations based in an innocuous building in the heart of the Canal Zone. He knew Centron Electronics, ap-parently a subsidiary of Centron Corporation, but had been unaware of its Latin American connection. Yet, wherever he turned in Panama, Centron was there.

Having asked to meet with the American consul, he had been met at lunch by both the consul and an official from Centron. The ostensible reason was that, as a businessman with extensive experience in Panama, the Centron man would be able to answer most of Haight's questions with a familiarity the diplomat did not have. Haight had not been fooled. From his years of work as an analyst in the State Department, he knew when he was being sized up. The look in the eyes of an operative when he is asked to analyze and evaluate in order to report back to a control somewhere is unmistakable. Most importantly, he recognized the man whom he had known only as Romulus when he had worked the Vietnam desk.

There is a little gray around the temples, but other than that he has not changed. He's still lean and fit, Haight thought.

Romulus was a wet worker. He was no businessman. Haight was not sure if the man had recognized him, so he had played along with the charade during the luncheon and had been politely warned off, leaving no doubt in his mind that Centron controlled things there. Haight's Plastics and Paints, a major company in its own right, was not welcome. No one had said this, of course, but there was the undeniable warning in the description of Centron's extensive influence in Panama. Haight was not sure why Romulus had been assigned to see him since his interests were strictly business related. While overseas commerce and intrigue often went hand in hand—in fact, he had conducted some of this silent warfare—there was no need, as far as he knew, for a wet operative to be assigned to him. Haight was not worried, simply curious.

Maybe they are short-handed, he thought, smiling.

Still, he was more convinced than ever that Panama was the key to South America. As he saw it, from there, it would be possible to move quickly south into Columbia, then east into the rest of the continent. There was wealth in the continent, but it was not distributed well enough to avoid perpetual unrest, and it retarded business growth since the upper classes could build only so many haciendas. He could not understand why the Latin Americans did not see this.

He had broached this topic with Señor Raul Amador when they had had dinner only two nights ago. Raul Amador had been at Harvard with him, and, while they had not been close friends, their mutual interest in geo-politics had brought them together in many discussion groups. Still, he had been surprised when, on returning to his hotel, there had been a message that the man had called and invited him to dinner.

Amador lived in an old house of delicate design in Panama City. He was fond of pointing out that the fluted pillars were an affectation of his grandfather, who had been a figure of some importance in the Panamanian war of independence against Columbia. He continued to live in it, he explained, to be reminded of the folly of the past and its continuing influence on the future. Raul Amador was the owner of a popular newspaper, *El Liberador*, which he described as his fool's errand. Haight knew Amador was considered something of a dilettante in his own country, but he was insulated by his family's name and the fact that he was one of the wealthiest men in Panama. He was a charming man who seemed not much interested in affecting the politics of his country, though his knowledge was extensive. Haight had asked him about this, and Amador had replied that he was the last of a particular breed, a species with which the United States was no longer familiar.

"I am, Jack, the quintessential amateur politician."

Haight had looked perplexed, and the elegant man, adjusting the silk cravat with the abstract images suggesting snakes crawling, continued, "My family has had too much to say about the fate of this country, and not always for the good. I confine myself to the thoroughly acceptable act of making money and criticizing the government. It does not matter which. *El Liberador es la voz de la gente*. It is probably

the most honorable way I could spend the ill-gotten gains of two centuries."

"But your country is only seventy…what? Four or five years old?"

Raul Amador laughed, a delicate sound with a hint of derision in it.

"Señor Haight, you North Americans insist on thinking of Panama as a real country. Columbia. Panama. What is the difference? Nothing changed when we gained a flag, except perhaps the United States more obviously became a controlling power in Latin America. The caudillos have not changed in two hundred years, and they still make their money in Columbia, whatever the flag."

"And you, Raul? Are you also making money from Columbia?"

Amador continued the innocent smile, slowly sipping the wine, which he sniffed occasionally.

"If you are to do business in Panama, Jack, you must understand one thing above all else. No business is possible in Panama without some agreement with Columbia. Our little misunderstanding seventy-four years ago has not changed that. You are intending to do business in our fair country, are you not?"

Haight nodded, adding, "If I can. The tone seems accommodating at the moment. The Panamanians with whom I have spoken seem more favorably disposed toward the United States since the President spoke of returning the canal to your country."

Raul turned serious at this and nodded slowly, twisting the glass in his hand.

"Yes. There is a lot of hope resting on the return of the canal. I fear it will all lead to disappointment."

"Why disappointment? Don't you think the deal will go through?"

"Oh, I'm sure it will. And you could have avoided the unpleasantries of the last several years if you had acted more honorably–forgive me–toward Panama. You built a residue of anger over the issue of underpayment, which, I fear, you will not soon overcome. No, Jack. The disappointment of which I speak springs from my fear that we will actually get the canal. Everyone now sees this as a solution not simply to our poverty but to our invisibility in the affairs of the world. The Americans have, whatever else they have done, left the idea of distribution of wealth, though they have not themselves implemented this idea, and that will be at odds with what I expect the canal will mean to the Families."

Haight raised his shoulders, cocking his head to one side in a gesture that asked for further explanation. Raul Amador chuckled, ringing a little bell that immediately brought in a black-skinned servant who replenished the glasses with the red liquid.

He raised his glass ironically in a salute.

"To the canal. May it bring us health. Anyway, Jack, to your business. Are things proceeding well?"

Haight thought for a moment before answering.

"I'm not certain. I think there are possibilities here, but, from all reports, the territory seems to have been sown up by Centron Corporation. I had a meeting yesterday during which I got the distinct impression they were some kind of brokers for the country. In any case, they seem to be everywhere."

"Ah, Centron. Yes,they do have extensive influence, not only here but in Columbia as well. You have met with them before?"

"Actually, no. I am aware of them, of course, but we have never had occasion to compete for anything before. I suspect we will soon enough, though. While they have had no interest in paints or plastics, which is our core business, we are in the early stages of moving into electronics. They would, of course, be aware of this. I assumed that explained their interest in us."

Haight was not being forthright. He was concerned about a lot more than Centron being aware of Haight's Plastics and Paints' entry into the electronics business. He was concerned about being unable to get information from what he thought of as routine sources within the State Department, about being met by a man he knew to be an agent who did dirty work for the Agency, and about Centron being so aware of him. Finally, he was concerned because Raul Amador, who had not seen him for twenty years, knew he was in Panama and had tracked him down. He was not fooled by the man's foppishness. Amador was bright, well traveled, and fully aware of the importance of the canal and the retreat of the United States, but he was playing it all down, and that suggested he wanted something. Haight did not know what, but he was sure of one thing. This was somewhat more complicated than he had assumed.

On a whim, he asked casually, "Are you familiar with Culebra?"

For a second, the man's face shifted, and the foppishness disappeared. He recovered quickly, but not before Haight saw something he recognized in the depths of the man's eyes.

"Well, of course I know Culebra. We have a small country here, Jack. Nothing can be hidden. Culebra is in the middle of the country, halfway to the other coast. Why do you ask?"

"No reason really. When I was doing research on Panama the name came up as being quite important in the construction of the canal."

Amador appeared to relax a little, then responded, "Yes. There are many stories of Culebra, often mysterious. There is more legend than fact associated with it, however."

Now, sitting in the limousine, Haight wondered about those legends. Just then, the phone rang, and, surprised, he picked it up. It was Dean. He had just dropped the boy off at the townhouse Haight's Plastics and Paints kept in Washington. Haight had given the boy use of it when he had come to work for him, and Dean would have barely had time to reach his floor.

"What is it, Dean?"

He listened for a short while, then said, "A fire? How'd it happen?"

He listened again, then replied, "No. Don't call the police just yet. I'll be back in five minutes. Are you inside the apartment now? Good. Stay there. Don't touch anything, and don't speak to anyone. You didn't contact the management, did you? Good. I'll be right there."

Haight hung up, a contemplative look in his eye. Someone had broken into the townhouse. This was not an easy task. Not only was the building's security extraordinarily tight, but the company had installed an additional system. He had not been contacted, and that meant both the security system and the fire extinguisher system that should have triggered the alarm had been disconnected. That meant this was no accident. The heavy car spun in the street, causing a stream of abuse to be hurled its way, but soon it was heading north toward the city. He was there in very short order.

Entering the room, Haight quickly assessed the damage. It was a self-contained fire, probably phosphorous. It had burned quickly and thoroughly and seemed to have started near the bedroom, which was a mess. The break-in was intended to look like a burglary, but Haight could see a pattern to the destruction. Someone had gone through the closets and had not found what he was searching for. The intruder had then searched the clothes stacked in the cabinets, and these had been thrown to the ground before they had been burnt. Most of the furniture was slightly out of place as if the attempt at disguising the search as a burglary had been abandoned halfway through. The mattress had been pulled off the bed and then partially burnt. The unknown burglar had cut the mattress and searched it thoroughly. That suggested he was looking for something relatively small. Haight never kept anything of significance here, so it was reasonable to assume they had been looking for something the boy had. Haight walked out of the bedroom and entered the kitchen, where the damage was much less extensive. It was clear the arsonist had not expected to find anything here. Again, the sitting room and the dining room were largely untouched although smoke-blackened. There were few hiding places in these rooms, and they had paid little attention to them. Obviously, the search had been concentrated in the bedroom, and it was also clear they had found nothing because the torching had been intended, he believed, to destroy what they had not found. Haight looked over to where the boy was standing and smiled reassuringly, a gesture the boy clearly appreciated.

Haight said light-heartedly, "As they say in the movies, a fine mess you got us in to. Any idea how it happened?"

The boy shook his head, asking, "Do you think that...?"

He stopped, and Haight finally said, "Dean, if there's something you need to tell me, now would be a good time."

The boy was obviously torn, and Haight turned away, investigating the lock, which showed no evidence of a forced entry. That told him nothing except whoever had broken in was sophisticated, and this he already knew. It took skill to start a controlled phosphorous fire and to destroy as completely as had been done without anyone in the building knowing. These were not skills easily available on the market. Haight was angry, but he did not want Dean, who was barely hanging on, to see it. Still, the boy would have to talk to him. Haight made a call, and the manager soon arrived. If the man was surprised, he did not show it. His opaque eyes took everything in at a glance as he walked, without speaking, through the townhouse. When he returned from the bedroom, Haight said, "Alfred, discretion is of the essence. How long?"

The man looked around, his eyes measuring the damage, and then replied, "A week. Ten days at the most."

Haight nodded his satisfaction, and the manager turned away, heading toward the door. As he reached for the doorknob, Haight's voice stopped him.

"Alfred, your security was breached."

His voice had not changed, but the man froze without turning, and Dean sensed something subtle change in the room. It took a while for him to realize Alfred was afraid. Yet, as far as he could tell, Haight had said nothing threatening. Then, Haight continued, "You will see to it, won't you?"

The man swallowed and, nodding, hurriedly left the room. Haight turned to Dean, saying, "It looks as if everything is ruined, so we will have to get you some clothes. First, though, I think we should talk. Let's go."

Dean picked up the bags he had taken to Panama and followed the long-striding older man down the corridor to the elevators. Soon, he was ensconced in the Watergate and drinking a cup of tea, trying to get over the sense of unreality this whole episode had created. Haight had been on the phone since they entered the room, and Dean went out to the terrace overlooking the city.

Haight joined him, a smile on his face. The smile did not extend to his eyes.

"Sorry about that. Had to make a few calls. I have also taken care of you. You will stay here until further notice. Now, do you want to tell me why someone would break into the apartment? I would guess you have something someone wants. Do you have any idea what that might be?"

Dean frowned. He did not have anything worth stealing. He had no money or jewelry, and his clothes were ordinary. Suddenly, Dean's eyes widened slightly, and he looked at Haight, a question on his face.

"But that doesn't make any sense."

"What doesn't, Dean?"

"My original senior thesis about the Panama Canal. I wanted to do something different with my thesis, so I used information from some letters to build a case. But there was no real proof. Still, that is the only possession I can think of that someone might want. Although I don't know why."

"Were the letters at the apartment?"

Haight was surprised to see alarm grow in the boy's eyes. "No. I left them with a friend of mine. Pam."

Haight felt the worry settle in the back of his neck, and he asked, a little too quickly, "Do you have a number where we can reach her?"

Dean gave it to the man, who dialed quickly. He waited for a while, then said, "There's no answer. Maybe she's out."

Seeing the boy was nervous, Haight asked, "Should we go and see if she's around?"

Dean nodded, his face concerned. Haight said, "Don't worry, Dean. It's possible that someone was trying to find something out about the company. That would explain the break-in. I'm sure your friend's all right."

Haight wished he was as certain as he sounded. It did not take them long to reach the apartment building off Connecticut Avenue. Dean pressed the buzzer several times, but after a while, walked back to the car where Haight waited.

"No answer?"

Dean shook his head. Having found the manager, Haight took him aside and spoke urgently for a short while. The man nodded vigorously and then signaled Dean to follow him. The three men ascended in the small padded elevator to the third floor. The manager selected a key from the ring he carried and opened the door. His gasp told the others something was amiss. Then, the smell hit Haight like something physical, and he stopped, pushing the boy back into the corridor, but it was too late to prevent Dean from seeing the girl lying on the floor, her neck bent at an unnatural angle. The boy's stomach contracted, and he fell to his knees, fighting the vomit that surged up into his throat. Inside, Haight had gone to the phone and was speaking to the police.

CHAPTER TWELVE

WASHINGTON, D.C. 1976

The Washington night had crept up slowly, like suggestive
tendrils of smoke on a windless day. Outside, it was dark, or
at least as dark as the city ever got. In this section of
Washington, Haight felt so far away from the centers of
power, it was as if he had left the planet. Tenement houses
lurked at the edge of the road, seeming to lean predatorily at
the slowly moving black car. Haight had the feeling of eyes
watching, though he had seen no one for the last fifteen
minutes as the car moved deeper into the heart of southeast
Washington. This was an area where even the black residents
were afraid to walk at night, and Haight wondered why the
man he had spoken to had wanted to meet here.

His driver, a solid-looking man well over six feet tall, was
alert to everything, and though from the back seat Haight
could not see his eyes, he knew they were scanning for patterns that did not fit. Antonio Peques had been a linebacker
at Penn State, and his body gave evidence of it. He was dangerous looking. As a player, he had gained such a reputation
for hard hits that running backs were known to fake trips
when they saw him bearing down on them. The body was

intimidating, but it masked an extraordinary mind. Peques had worked in Vietnam as an "advisor" from the late fifties until Hanoi had fallen, and Haight had learned to recognize his signature in the reports he sent back from forays into North Vietnam. When Peques came out of 'Nam, Haight had been in therapy, trying to recover from the trauma of watching America commit suicide in a war it never intended to win. He had sought the man out, recognizing from his last messages that he was angry and brittle–too brittle to survive in an ambiguous world. War, Haight knew, in spite of its brutality, created very narrow paths along which life proceeded, and Haight had sensed in Peques' final reports that he would have trouble re-entering the "real world." It had not been too difficult to find him, and Antonio Peques now headed up the security unit for Haight's Plastics and Paints. Haight had never been sorry he hired him.

After Haight called the police, he made two other calls. One was to Antonio Peques, and the other was to the man he was on his way to meet. Antonio had flown immediately from Charleston on an HPP jet, and Haight felt better immediately upon his arrival. Dean had been taken back to Charleston on the company jet, but not before Haight had ascertained that the letters were nowhere to be found in the girl's apartment. The boy had been useless, the shock having numbed his mind, and Haight had waited with him while he woodenly answered questions about the dead girl. Haight knew he would be better off not having to worry about the boy. He suspected Dean still was not telling him the whole truth, but that would have to wait. Now, he needed information. Something was badly out of focus here. There was no reason he could see for what was going on. All he knew was that the boy had a series of letters that had now disappeared, and a young girl was dead apparently because of them. Dean had seen nothing in the letters except a discrepancy between the official figures given for the depth of the canal and the unofficial statements of some person, probably long dead, whose letter suggested the canal was deeper. Nothing there suggested anything sinister. Interesting maybe, but hardly sinister.

Yet, the girl was dead.

He was angry that his home had been violated, and, if he was going to invest millions in Panama, then he wanted to be certain of what he was investing in. Haight thought of the girl they had left on the floor almost ten hours before. Even in death, she had been pretty, and he felt a fresh surge of anger at the thought of the young life snuffed out for some reason that would not add up to the value of her life. He had lived in that world, had given orders that ended people's lives, but he liked to think those who died had been evil men who sought to destroy the United States. In this sense, he had acted in self-defense on behalf of his nation. Whoever was behind this cared nothing about life. The girl's murder was senseless, but it sent a message, and he had an odd feeling that the message was meant for him. That made it personal, only he had no idea how or why.

The car slowed as they approached a ramshackle bar enclosed by a wire fence that was broken in several places. Only a few vehicles were in the lot, and as his car stopped, Haight noticed they all showed evidence of considerable wear and not too much care. Antonio got out, moved his bulk gracefully around the car to open the door, and soon the two men were inside. As he had expected, all heads turned toward him as he walked in, but the not-so-veiled looks of resentment at the white man's presence were quickly replaced by a hood of disinterest when the onlookers saw the huge, lithe black man with Haight. He quickly walked across the room, which smelled of beer and the pungent, acrid odor of hash, and settled at a table in the corner. The man meeting him would have been watching and would soon come. Haight was not worried. This was the way his informant worked, and he would just have to wait. A tall, full-bodied woman came over with a dirty tray on which used glasses sat precariously, and Haight ordered a beer.

He did not have long to wait. The man who entered was slumped over and weaving just a little. Haight smiled, amused at the transparent disguise. Yet, he knew it would be effective because most people did not see anything except the obvious, and the man's face, crouched over as he was, was hidden. José Nieves sat down, leaning on the table. Haight leaned forward as well and said, "Simple but effective, José. How are you?"

"Hello, Jack. Your call was a surprise. How are you? It has been... what? Eight years?"

Haight nodded, thinking back to the time when this man had come into his life and wondering what risk he was asking Nieves to take now. Yet, Haight had no choice. He had to find out what was causing the shakes in his universe, and Nieves, who had been a field operative in Latin America for two decades, refusing promotions so he would be able to remain south of the Rio Grande, could help. When Haight called the number in Virginia, he had not expected Nieves to get back to him for a while, but the man had been in Washington and was leaving in the morning, so they had had to meet tonight—late, as it turned out. It was now after one in the morning.

"Yes, José. It has been quite a while, and, despite the disguise, you look well."

The man shrugged and waited for Haight to continue. Haight composed his thoughts, not sure where to begin. He did not know the layout of the ground he was treading, and, though he trusted Nieves, Haight was reluctant to show he was fishing, experience having taught him that this always placed the interrogator at a disadvantage. Still, Nieves was too experienced an agent not to recognize that Haight had no information.

After a while, Haight said, "I am rather in the dark, and I need your help. What do you know about what is going on in Panama?"

"Can you be more specific, Jack? Panama is the cross-roads of many worlds. There is always something going on there."

Haight got an answer of sorts. Nieves was hedging, and that meant he knew something.

"José, this is very important. Earlier today, my apartment was broken into and burnt, and a young girl, the friend of a kid I just hired, was killed. There is nothing I am involved in that leads to this. I don't know if the boy is in danger or if I am. I have to know what I am up against, José."

The man across the table remained bent over, and Haight waited, knowing he had no way to force cooperation. He only hoped José Nieves remembered a night on a Cuban beach over ten years ago, when Haight had broken the imposed silence to give him a chance to get off the island before the Cubans attacked. Haight had been reprimanded for this action, and he was hoping Nieves would feel some loyalty to him. Nieves knew Latin America like most people knew the inside of their home, and if anything was going on down there, he would be able to say.

"What do you know about this, Jack? Anything?"

Haight shook his head, and Nieves continued.

"You are aware that conversations involving the return of the canal to Panama are going on right now? There has been very little publicity about this, but there is a struggle within the government over the return."

"But that has always been the case. There's a significant faction in the government— in fact, within the country— that thinks we should not give back what is rightfully ours."

"Yes. But this time, it's different. Latin America has never been a threat before, and administrations could always back down when the nationalists became too rambunctious. This time, Central America is going up, and with us locked in a struggle with the Soviets, there is less room to maneuver. This President also seems to be motivated by altruism—a dangerous principle, to my mind—and so the battle lines have been drawn."

"What do you mean, 'battle lines'?"

Nieves hesitated, and, as the hood slipped a little, Haight saw just how tense the man was.

"Jack, there's a group that has vowed not to return the canal. They see it as American and the return as us giving in to 'Sovietization' of the hemisphere. This is not a fringe group, and it is feared that it exists at all levels of government."

"What has the Agency been able to find out, José?"

"All levels of government, Jack," Nieves replied slowly, looking up into Haight's face.

"Jesus Christ," Haight responded, the stress suddenly visible in his face.

If they could not trust the information gatherers, then things must really be frightening. No wonder Nieves looked spooked. But why would the canal be so important to whatever group was doing this? Granted, it was a symbol of American ingenuity and a source of tremendous revenue, but that seemed an insufficient reason for what Nieves was suggesting. He was hinting at treason, and it sounded as if the Agency was in a state of confusion. That was dangerous.

"José, you don't believe the 'Sovietization' story, do you?"

Again, the agent paused, then said, "No. Something isn't quite right about what is going on. There's a lot of political pressure and business muscle behind this. It's not clear why so many corporations are interested. True, some fear that if the canal is not under American control, then shipping could be disrupted, and that would significantly affect economies and profits, but no one really thinks that is the reason. Something is frightening these companies, and we have no idea what it is."

"Centron!" Haight said suddenly, and the man looked up sharply, the fear evident in his eyes. Haight was surprised. This man lived in the shadows and confronted his fears all the time. If he was running scared, then this thing was somehow outside his experience, and that thought did nothing to reassure Haight.

Nieves stood suddenly, the hood firmly in place around his face. He looked down at Haight and said, "Jack, stay away from Centron. It's bad news. I'm sorry I couldn't help you more."

Before Haight could react, the man disappeared through the room, moving with that swift, unobtrusive glide Haight had seen so often. It was as if the air absorbed these men as they came.

Antonio moved back to the table, waiting for his boss, who quickly left. Outside, Haight watched the shadows that surrounded them. He was worried. Suddenly, the world seemed a much less safe place. Still, he paid no attention to the drunken black man who stumbled out of the bar and noisily relieved himself against the wall. Haight's face wrinkled in disgust, and he quickly got into the car. As soon as the large, black car pulled out of the lot, the man straightened up and was joined by another man. They both got into an old Chevy, the sound of its engine belying the flaky paint and dented fenders. They pulled out and trailed after the black car.

Haight tried to sort out what he knew. *Precious little*, he thought. A man who was trained to survive in the darkness was afraid. A Panamanian newspaperman had shown the same fear when he had mentioned Culebra. A girl was dead, and the boy had lost a packet of letters. Haight leaned back, searching for some pattern in the facts, but he found none. He swore softly, kicking himself for not having asked Nieves about Culebra. Shocked at the man's response to the mention of Centron, he had allowed him to walk away. Yet, Culebra had caused the same look of fear in the eyes of Raul

Amador in Panama that Centron had caused in Nieves' eyes in Washington. Haight could see no connection except for one thing: Romulus. He had claimed to be a senior vice-president at Centron, but Haight knew these men never retired. If he was to find out anything about what was going on, then he would have to start with what he knew, and Centron seemed to be at the center of something important.

He knew the interests of the corporation were diverse, and it controlled a number of subsidiary businesses, not the least significant of which were defense contractors. As far as he knew, the company had no interest in paints or plastics, so it had been a double surprise when Romulus had shown up. The explanation given that the consul had brought an experienced businessman to answer any questions had been plausible, or it would have been had Haight not immediately recognized Romulus. Certain that Romulus did not know he had been recognized, Haight felt this gave him something of an advantage. Still, he did not know what to do next. If his being in Panama was going to be a source of contention, it did raise the question as to whether he wanted a corporate struggle with Centron. As powerful as Haight was with the vast resources of HPP behind him, he would be no match for Centron, with its global interests and a political influence that, given its size, must be worldwide. But putting aside the commercial possibilities, there was the matter of the girl. Thinking of her sickened Haight to the stomach. She had been so young, certainly not more than twenty-five, and she had been murdered simply for being in the wrong place. He had no proof but felt certain Romulus was involved in the girl's death and the break-in at the townhouse.

Romulus was a legend in the intelligence community. He seemed to have been around for all time and had great successes. The man was resourceful and, from what Haight remembered, impervious to fear. Over ten years ago, Haight had been his control on a mission into Cambodia. Officially, the United States was not supposed to be there, but the Vietcong had been using bases in Cambodia to attack American troops. Romulus had taken in a team of five. Even with his battle-weary psyche, Haight had been sickened at the carnage the man caused. When Washington called for them to pull back, Romulus had redefined the mission and, maintaining radio silence for seventeen days, continued the burn-and-destroy pattern of retribution. Haight had thought him dead until, after more than two weeks, the call sign was activated again, and Haight heard two words: "Mission accomplished." The brass had been embarrassed by the action because word leaked out after Cambodia protested, but nothing was done because the attacks on Americans had stopped. Most people walked around this man. Now, he had surfaced as a businessman. Haight wondered what the business was.

As his car pulled up to the Watergate, he glanced at an old Chevrolet that drove past, but it did not stop. Putting it out of his mind, he entered the hotel, looking at his watch. It was after three, and he needed rest. Having left Panama almost twenty-four hours ago, his body was feeling the wear. He would call the house and speak to his wife tomorrow morning. The hard face softened a little at the thought of his wife, the Bostonian who had relocated to the south because of her love for him. She had been a godsend, saving him from the embarrassment of those lonely years at Harvard, where his new wealth had bred insecurity. She had given him a sense of place, and for this, he would always be grateful. His life was invested with a sense of grace and peace that he was not sure would have been possible without her. She would make the boy comfortable, he knew. That was her talent. Dean was afraid and hurt. She would understand this and find a way to soothe him, but the boy would need a distraction, and Haight had just the task for him. He needed more information about Centron, and Dean could put together a profile of the corporation. Haight did not think public information would be helpful, but it was a place to start, and Centron seemed the only lead. One of the things that had been drilled into him in the State Department was never to act without information, and even that which appeared trivial could prove invaluable in putting the pieces of a puzzle together. He would have the boy find out all he could about the corporation and see where that would lead. As he laid down, secure in the knowledge that Antonio was in the adjoining suite and would not sleep while he did, Haight hoped that, with the letters now gone—if that was the cause of all this—there would be no more trouble until he was better prepared. He could not have been more wrong.

CHAPTER THIRTEEN

The tall, muscular man strode into the room where the old man lay. In his hand was a large packet, and this he laid on the table next to the reclining man.

The room always smells like death, he thought.

In the dusk-like conditions that prevailed in the room, it looked like hell. The figure before him had no flesh on its bones, and the eyes stared brightly out from the face, sometimes seeing and, at others, seeming to look away into the distance. Yet, this man controlled an empire, and it was folly not to look behind the eyes and see the bright intelligence still burning there. Five days ago, the man on the bed had invited his old colleagues to meet with him. It had all been a charade. The old man had pretended to be much weaker than he was, and it was all to see their faces when he mentioned the word Culebra. The tall man had heard the word from his place in the next room as he watched the faces and recorded their reactions. What he had seen was fear, not betrayal, and this was what the old man wanted to know. In any case, he had decided to dissolve the partnership with these men. Romulus (as Haight knew him) did not know the significance of Culebra, but the old man attached great importance to it, and that was enough for him. Each of the men who had visited Gordon Heights five days before had died separate deaths, each apparently natural. No alarm had been raised.

One of the men who had been invited had not come and was suspected of the betrayal. Strangely enough, the old man had been amused by the man's absence and ordered Romulus to find him. It was entirely by accident that Romulus found out about Haight's visit to Panama, and he had notified the old man, who surprised him again by knowing exactly who Haight was. Haight had been clumsy, tipping his hand by asking Amador about Culebra. When Amador mentioned this to Romulus, he immediately checked on Haight. The boy with him had been included in the general sweep, and Romulus' agents discovered he had written a troubling thesis. Romulus also found out the boy claimed he had proof, and, as a result, the boy's apartment had been searched. He thought angrily of how clumsily this had been done. It would have been better not to leave any trace of the visit, but the fool he had selected, wanting to make sure he had missed nothing, burned the apartment, thereby alerting Haight. Worse, they found the girl's address in the young man's notebook and a note to himself that he should pick the papers up when he returned from Panama. They had broken into the apartment, but the girl returned unexpectedly, and she had been killed. This had been the height of stupidity and would make his job more difficult. Still, he now had the letters.

The old man had not decided what to do yet, but Romulus felt the slight tension that always preceded action. He had worked for the old man for the last twenty-five years, even when he had officially been with the Agency. Sometimes, there seemed to be no difference between the government and this man who controlled the largest corporation in the world. He may be dying, but his powers of command and discernment had not diminished. Now, he reclined on the stuffed pillows, and Romulus, realizing he was being watched, felt the delicious tendril of fear this man's presence always evoked.

"Mixed results, eh, Thomas?"

The younger man felt his throat constrict, recognizing the condemnation. This was not a man who treasured loyalty, which he had always bought, nor past success, which he dismissed. Yet, there was, as well, an affection Romulus felt at being called Thomas. No one else called him by that name, and those who knew it were buried so deep in the Agency that neither they nor his name ever saw the light of day.

He did not answer, knowing the old man expected no response.

"I assume the packet you have is the proof the boy claimed to have."

He pointed, and Romulus handed him the envelope from which he pulled a bunch of letters. It was too dark to read, but he held them up to the minimal light coming from the table lamp that, turned low and with a thick shade, cast the room in shadow.

He chuckled, a surprisingly gay sound coming from his broken body.

"So it is Rupert's romanticism that threatens to destroy us all. What do you make of the letters, Thomas?"

Romulus recognized the trap and breathed softly, thankful he had not read anything after taking the quick look to ascertain the letters were in fact relevant. Once he had seen the word Culebra, he shut the whole packet up.

He now said, "I can't make any judgment, sir. I did not read them."

Again, the ghostly chuckle came from the skeleton, and Romulus twitched in his chair.

"Very good. Rupert was always the independent one. Not like the rest of the island fellows. He had that streak of romanticism. I should have guessed he would be the one."

Romulus waited for the man to continue, curious about the letters and what Culebra signified but knowing better than to ask. If the old man wanted him to know, then he would be told. Until then, all he could do was wait.

Romulus did not know the strategy in this operation, nor did he know the stakes. This made damage assessment difficult, and that made him nervous. He had to trust the old man, who no longer seemed sure what he wanted. Even as he talked about this Rupert destroying them all, the old man seemed more amused than afraid of the possibility. For a fleeting moment, Romulus found himself wondering whether the old man was all there, but he immediately submerged the thought, almost afraid he would be heard.

"And Haight? You know him, Thomas. What do you think will be his reaction?"

Romulus again recognized the test, so he replied carefully, aware that, while it was a test, the old man used any information and expected an honest assessment.

"Haight is an analyst, sir. I think we have given him a problem he is incapable of not trying to solve. When he was my control officer, I always felt he was motivated by the intellectual challenge of the assignment. He never seemed to realize his analysis meant people would die. I think Haight will investigate this because it is confusing, sir. Unless..."

Romulus stopped.

"Unless we make it less complicated for him?" the old man chuckled. "And how would you propose we do that, Thomas?"

"Well, sir, it appears Haight is legitimately interested in getting a beachhead in Latin America. I don't think that was a cover. I believe he was accidentally caught in this thing with the boy's thesis. Maybe the boy was using him to explore his own thesis."

"If you believe that, then you know him less well than I thought. Did you know that when you disappeared on your little temper tantrum in Cambodia, he stayed with your frequency the whole time even though he must have thought you were dead? What does that tell you, Thomas?"

Romulus understood the point. Anyone who could act decisively while holding two opposing thoughts was too complex to be caught in something not of his own making. Haight may not know what the game was, but he was sure to be playing on his own terms.

Something more ominous was also implied. Haight would be coming after whoever attacked him. Still, Haight was an analyst, hardly a threat in the field. Romulus had never met an analyst who had any competence once his precious data were taken away, and Haight would be no different. Once the old man gave the order, Haight would be eliminated. He was thinking of the most effective way of doing this when the old man's voice broke into his thoughts.

"It wouldn't help, Thomas. Our main problem is containing the possibility of exposure. Haight's death, unlike those of my erstwhile associates you have dispensed with so effectively, would hardly contain the problem, would it? Rather, we must steer him away from what is important and exhaust his energy on the inconsequential. We have to give him a solution to the problem he has yet to define and an answer to the questions he is even now asking. What do you think he will do next, Thomas?"

Romulus thought for a while, then said, "I imagine he will try to find out who killed the girl. That would give him a lead to who is behind this."

The old man snorted, and Romulus felt his stomach constrict.

"Why would he do that? Haight is not without influence himself, remember. Why pursue the killers when he can have the police do that for him? He is an important man, and they will bend over backwards to please. To him, it will not matter who gathers the information. So I ask again, what will he do next?"

Romulus was stumped. Maybe he did not know Haight as well as he thought. The old man continued.

"Watch for anyone who seeks information on Centron in the next few days. Haight will go to the source and derive his strategy from there. Now, leave me. I will expect your report in two days."

Romulus stood and eased quietly toward the door. As his hand turned the knob, the man's voice stopped him. Its timbre had changed, sounding like that of a young man again, deep and resonant.

"Today should not be counted a success, Thomas. You should be more careful, or I may have to re-evaluate our relationship."

Romulus felt the dampness in his palm, which seemed stuck to the door. Turning the knob, knowing no answer was possible or necessary, he pulled a handkerchief from his pocket, briskly and jerkily running it over his neck and hands. Outside, the chill of the night seemed to pull at him, and he almost ran to his car. He had lived in the shadows of the secret world where nations compete in deadly silence and had learned to make the darkness a friend, but tonight, the shadows took shape, and the wind carried the screams he had heard for so long. Romulus knew the agents who protected this man were watching, but he sat in the locked car for a long time before turning the key.

There was still a long drive back to New York, and he found himself wondering about Haight. Whatever game the old man was playing, he would eventually have to kill Haight, and now, away from the old man's influence, Romulus thought playing games with Haight was a waste of time. The way he saw it, without Haight, the boy had no resources to pursue whatever interests he had in Panama. Once he eliminated Haight, the problem became more manageable. The old man would see this soon enough. The small sports car bellowed as he entered the Long Island Expressway, heading for the city. In the distance, the hazy penumbra was clearly visible against the darkness of the night.

CHAPTER FOURTEEN

Rupert Barnes sat on the uncomfortable bed that had been erected for him in the hut next to the river. He was hungry, and the little bell he rang brought a short man of Asian origin. It was not yet dinner time, but they would find him something to eat. He put the newspaper down, thinking of the front-page article about the latest debate on the return of the canal to Panama. The rift between the President and the hawks on the Hill was becoming bitter. Barnes felt a little sorry for the President, who had no idea the can of worms he had opened with the promised return of the canal. In fact, the number of people who knew what the canal disguised was exceedingly small, most of them dead, and, from what he had read in the papers over the last two days, the rest dying more rapidly now. None of them knew the full story of the canal, it was true, but obviously the man in Long Island was making sure no one would be left to testify if anything broke.

Barnes had left Panama City after reading that the five men had died. No one knew of the connection between these men, so the coincidence was not noted. Knowing the deaths were not natural, Barnes had begun to think he should have covered his tracks a little more conscientiously before leaving Philadelphia. He had left the hotel but had kept his reservation for an indefinite stay. It would not fool anyone who was determined to find him, but it was always good to be on the offensive. The man in Long Island liked playing, as long as the stakes were high, and that made him unpredictable and extraordinarily deadly.

They had all been young when they had met so long ago now, but even then there had been a strange sense of humor to the man who did little to mask the sheer enormity of his cruelty. He had always thought big, and the very size of his dreams, combined with his ability to make them wealthy beyond their imaginations, lured people into doing the un-thinkable for him. Barnes shook his head as the images of death came into his mind.

They had all prospered. No question about that. But the price had been high. They had all condemned their souls in the act that defined their relationship, and, in time, they had separated, knowing that something indefinably evil had shaped them and controlled their actions. Many of the men had talked of the man in Long Island having The Power. Barnes had not believed any of this but had watched as the man cultivated this belief in the men from the island with whom he had surrounded himself, exploiting their supersti-tions. In some very strange way, this had separated Barnes from the other Barbados men, for he did not believe in the things they did and had been less susceptible to this influ-ence. He had been, however, very susceptible to the promise of wealth, and this had proved as powerful an influence.

Barnes' body hurt from the long cross-country trip to the place where he had spent so much time in his youth. It was all so different now, having become a low-grade resort that promised the original life of Panama, capitalizing on the rustic beauty of the place to create, for bored tourists, an illusion of the primitive. How different from when he had arrived in 1905.

Barnes had arrived the night before. Only his attendant served him, and contact with the resort's staff was kept to a minimum. Word had it that the man in Long Island was dying, but Barnes had heard that for a long time now.

He must be at least ten years older than I am. No reason to expect him to keel over and die, Barnes thought with an ironic giggle.

He called to the attendant who stood alertly next to the door, and the Asian slowly wheeled Barnes toward the water. The concrete walkway stopped short of the sea, and Barnes sat there, a blanket covering his legs, watching the water, blue and calm except where the waves broke gently over the nearby shoal. *So like Barbados*, he thought and was surprised at the feeling of nostalgia that assailed him.

When he had left Barbados three quarters of a century before, he never intended to live the rest of his life overseas. The whole point of his leaving had been to prove he could make it on his own, and to do this, he would have to confront Ruby, his long-deceased sister, with his success. For a long time, this was his motive. Panama had not been an easy place to live in those days. He glanced around at the resort, thinking of the first time he and the others had come here, north of Colon.

The man in Long Island had pushed them hard on the project they could not talk about. They were housed separately and fed better. Unlike other blacks, these two hundred Barbadians were not paid on the silver standard or even the gold standard that was reserved for the whites from America, but were paid a much higher wage for the same work. These men had been selected as an elite workforce, commissioned to construct a tunnel some distance from the Canal Zone, which was American property, in Panama itself. There was no explanation for the work, and no one inquired too closely when their wages were increased from ten cents a day to twenty-five cents a day and their hours became more regular.

There was, however, one prohibition that was strictly adhered to. There was to be no talk of the work being done, and they were not to go to Panama City. This rule was not left exclusively to the good will of the workers, most of whom were recent recruits from Barbados. For some reason, the man wanted all of the workers on the project to be from the same island, and, without explanation, he had chosen Barbados. The camp, however, had some non-Barbadians. There were fifteen hard-faced men who seemed to be military, although they never wore uniforms. Always armed, they ensured that the workers did not stray.

Barnes and the five men who had just been killed by the man in Long Island had eventually become part of this group of guards. This had given them privileges, one of which was the right to leave the camp.

They had been working for three weeks, including weekends, without a break when, one night, Blackett, who was the most daring of them, suggested they ride to the coast. They boarded the train, and, passing the great hole in the ground, they heard the noise of the place as the train chugged along, for the work of the canal never stopped. They had not been working on the canal for quite some time, having been taken off the year before to work on this project. When their train stopped in Gatun, Blackett, a secret smile on his face, shoved them off the train. Gatun was a wild town, on the railroad line but oddly disconnected from it, and many a West Indian had disappeared there. They nervously descended from the train, aware that they were in a Spanish town, and though the Panamanians did not exhibit the same aversion to black-skinned people as the Americans did, there was a growing resentment as increasing numbers of West Indians arrived to work on the canal. This night, though, there seemed to be not a Panamanian in sight, and they headed away from the town toward the Chagres River.

At the riverbank, a dark-skinned Spaniard with a limp met them, and they all piled into his skiff, not sure where they were headed but intrigued at the possibilities. Blackett was an irritant, but he did know how to find fun, so they sat gingerly in the unstable boat as it headed down the Chagres toward the Atlantic Ocean. It took a long time in the dark to reach the coast, and, upon arriving, Blackett told the man to wait. This created a moment of tension because Blackett refused to pay the Spaniard until they were taken back to Gatun. The man eventually agreed to wait, and the six men went into the jungle. In the distance, the breakers gently rubbed against the shore, and though it was pitch black, Blackett seemed to know where he was headed. They followed, hands resting lightly on each other's shoulders to make sure no one got lost.

After what seemed like an eternity, they glimpsed, in the near distance, flickering lights and quickened their steps, glad to be free of the Panamanian jungle. Though none of the men would admit it, the jungle was too mysterious for their comfort. Born to the open land of their flat island, the jungle seemed too close to their skins, and they recoiled from the chilly touch of the vines and trees as they passed. Unlike Barbados, this place was alive with the unseen, which was real and immediately dangerous. Barnes had seen a jaguar only the week before, near the worksite, and it had arrogantly stared at him, eventually spitting furiously before walking into the darkness of the jungle. He was struck by how quickly it had merged with the colors of the trees, and for several days, he had stayed close to camp. This foray into the jungle was not without some nervousness, and so the lights were welcome.

They emerged in a clearing not far removed from the sea. There were men, whom they recognized as Kuni Indians, around a fire. There were no women to be seen. Blackett knew the leader, and the six Barbadian men were invited to sit with the Kuni. There was little conversation as they joined the Indians in use of the pipe, and the night soon turned silky.

Barnes' breathing slowed, and between each breath there evolved an eternity in which he could see down into the center of the earth. The sea came closer to him, and soon he was engulfed in the waves, his head covered by the crystal blue water. Far above was a light that looked like the moon, although he could remember no moon from earlier. In any case, it was beautiful, and he looked at it reverently, wanting to be closer but reluctant to move. Water was draining into his lungs, but, feeling no fear, he relaxed, accepting the water into his body, which itself then turned to water. The other men disappeared, and he tried to look for them, but his head would not turn, and he stood suspended in the water, feeling the waves trickle into his lungs only to be exhaled through his nose.

Suddenly, the water closed in on him, changing shape as it did. He could feel himself tightening in the middle and wanted to see what caused it, but his eyes were closed. As the tightness increased, the waves of pleasure washed over him, and his eyes opened a crack to see a goddess turning on him. She was from the sea, and her hair fell down in waves, covering her body from his eyes. His heart beat furiously as the goddess held his life between her legs, stretching him out into some place he wished he could identify. The darkness was coming over his eyes again, and his mind seemed concentrated in the one spot of his body the goddess touched. He tried to reach for her, but his arms were too heavy, and he gave in to the thrusting of the woman who sat astride him. He could not keep this up, and soon, he melted into her, becoming one with the hair that covered her face and his body. The cold came when she flew off into the light he thought to be the moon, leaving only the image of her hair in his mind. The world slowly faded to black as he sucked on his thumb.

It was Blackett's voice whispering urgently in his ear that woke him. It was still night, and he was naked. Looking down at himself and seeing the dried dampness that surrounded his middle, he knew his night had been only half a dream. Blackett quickly dressed him, and they headed for the boat, anxious lest the man had left. He had waited, the lure of payment more powerful a motive than his resentment at having to serve the Negroes. Barnes' mind burned with the image of the woman who had come in the night. Before tonight, he had never felt as if everything in the world was concentrated in the single act of sexual completion, but he had been inside himself, feeling something in him wanting to give up all of himself. He was not sure of the cause until Blackett, laughing knowingly, said, "Dat was diffrent, aint it?"

Barnes shook his head, and Blackett laughed even louder, adding, "In all de time we bin comin' here, dat is de first time I see she go wid anybody. Mus' be because of you white skin, boy. Um look like you had a good time. It knock you' ass out."

The other men looked at Barnes, gaffawing, and he asked, "You have all been there before? What did we smoke last night? It certainly took my mind. And who is the woman?"

The laughter continued until Richards answered, "Dem Indians does call it peyote. To tell yuh de trut', I does only tek it fuh me sinuses."

This occasioned another round of laughter and back slapping, vigorous denial and playful recriminations. Barnes watched the camaraderie among the men and was again aware that, though they included him in their games, something indefinable separated them from him. They laughed easily with him, but he could get only so far. Even his act with the woman was playfully assigned to his whiteness, and that stood like a blanket around him always, more often than not a protection but sometimes a hindrance. He wished he had their ease and could talk carelessly about the act and laugh. He felt quite different from that, a little guilty perhaps at having lost control of himself. They, on the other hand, seemed so free, so accepting of the act that he wanted both to eliminate and to duplicate.

"Who is she?" he asked again.

"I don' know, Barnes. She does dance fuh we, dat's all. We t'ought dat you wud like to see she dance. Wat you tink bout de way she dance?"

Barnes tried desperately to remember the dance but could not see a single picture in his mind, which was confused with images of breathing beneath the sea and seeing a moon that had not been in the sky. The men continued to laugh, making jokes at his expense all the way back to the camp.

The train was late, and they arrived in the morning to find the new man who ran the operation standing at the entrance of the camp. The men had become silent as they approached, and he did not move when they reached the gate. They stopped, the man's cold, gray, unblinking eyes on them. He had taken over the project three months earlier, and discipline had been tightened noticeably. Barnes, in Panama for three years, had been working on the project in Culebra for almost a year, and he knew this man was different. Two days after he had arrived, two workers had, against orders, gone into Panama City and flashed their money around. They were later found in an alley, both knifed, their pockets empty. Word had been that one or more of the many thieves in the city had killed them, but another rumor frightened the workers. It was said that the new man had killed them himself to ensure that nobody would be foolish enough to leave the compound. He had done nothing to refute the statements.

Now, he looked through them, staring rigidly ahead, the four military-looking guards standing at attention behind him.

Finally, he said, little inflection in his voice, "Call the workers together. This one will take ten lashes."

He pointed at Richards, who laughed nervously and responded, "You can't do dat. Wha you tink dis is? Slavery days? You try dat shit an' I goin' straight to de British consul and bring you up 'pon charges."

The new man, whom they all called Captain, ignored the response and, with a small movement of his head, signaled the guards, who grabbed Richards and pulled him to a post in the middle of the camp. His shirt was quickly stripped from him, and one of the guards applied the whip, leaving long, blackish-blue welts on Richards' back. The man cried out as the lash was applied, and the others stood silently, staring at the ground, wondering why they had been spared and, more importantly, why they were doing nothing to help their companion. Barnes looked at the mute faces around him and noticed something else: a look of resignation. They flinched in unison with the man being beaten, each lash evoking a silent groan Barnes sensed more than heard.

When the beating was over, they were exhausted, and Barnes, in that moment, realized something about the man they called the Captain. He had known of the collective pain he could evoke with the beating. There was no need to punish them all because each carried the pain and the guilt of the other. Barnes wondered why he had never thought of this before, why he had not seen that they had all inherited the same pain. He had lived with men like these his whole life, and they were still a mystery to him. He had tried to befriend them since he was a child, had even played with the boys in the village, but somehow he had always been on the edge of the village, not really a part of it.

As Richards was cut down, the Captain stared at Barnes, and, before the workers dispersed, he shouted, "Barnes, you should have known better. Come with me."

He turned away, heading for his office. Barnes reluctantly followed, aware of the eyes watching him, conscious more than ever of the uniform blackness behind him.

This had been the start of his relationship with the Captain, and, Barnes now thought, it looked as if it would end where it had begun: Panama. He felt no fear, knowing that death was bound to come and he had lived long and well. What concerned him was how Culebra had become a whisper again and the effect this would have on his family. His wife had died some time ago, and the ache of that loss had dulled, but his sons, both lawyers in Philadelphia, knew nothing of his past nor of the horror of Culebra. He felt sadness at the thought of their lives being ruined by the mistakes of his youth, and gradually that sadness changed to anger. A small sound escaped him, and, instantly, the attendant was next to him, but he irritably waved him away.

Bloody fellow must think I'm going to die any minute, he thought with some annoyance.

Well, he was not going to die just yet, not while he had work to do. His sons were now vulnerable, and they had to be protected.

Barnes sat in the sun a long time, unmoving, appearing to be asleep, but he was thinking. Eventually, his mind came to one focus. There was no point trying to eliminate the man in Long Island. Apart from the fact that it was almost impossible to penetrate the grounds at that fortress he called a home, Barnes knew, in a sense, they were both after the same thing: to prevent knowledge of Culebra from coming out. The man in Long Island was simply taking care of the loose ends. In any case, there was a threat, and if they were protecting against the same thing, then they should do this together. He would have to get a message to the man to let him know he was not a threat. They should combine forces to shut this thing down. When all was said and done, the major problem was still the return of the canal to Panama. That had to be stopped, for if the Panamanians got hold of the canal, there would be hell to pay when they found out what had been built alongside it in the jungle and what had been extracted from their country.

He had seen the man in Long Island the last time the Americans began the conversation about the return of the canal. Demands attached to generous campaign contributions put a stop to that. In this case, the demands were simple to make. He had been surprised at how many of the younger politicians did not even realize the canal belonged to America. Then, the man in Long Island had decided on a strategy of disinformation and cash infiltration. That was over twenty years ago.

This time, it was different, and he had not foreseen the carnage the shift in American sensibilities would cause. The President appeared determined to have his way, and, for the last year, opposition to his position, fueled by Centron's money, had been growing in the Senate. Barnes knew it was better that this President should die than have the secrets of Panama exposed, and he felt certain this was a contingency the man in Long Island had prepared. It would not be the first time they had eliminated a head of state to protect their secrets. The American was no different, simply more difficult. Barnes realized just how dependent he was on the man in Long Island for decisions of this sort, the habit of listening to him having created an expectation of advice that occasionally left Barnes at a loss when that voice was silent. His face suddenly felt older, and the flesh hung down from his throat, giving him the look of a prehistoric lizard lazing in the sun, waiting for some predator to arrive.

He did not have the resources to match the man in Long Island, so it would only be a matter of time before he was found. Barnes was worried about his family because he had seen the man's ruthlessness. He had killed the other five men and would not stop until he was certain all traces of the conspiracy of Culebra were eliminated. Discovery would destroy them all, and this could not be tolerated. Not for the first time, Barnes wondered how he had allowed himself to be attached to this man. There had never been any doubt as to his malevolent will. It had been clear in the way he had driven the workers, developing a schedule that had soon become inhuman. The freedoms the men had come to expect and which made them different from those who worked on the canal had all been eliminated within weeks of the man's taking over.

One thing had improved, though. The pay. He had understood immediately that the workers would exchange their need for social interaction and rest for money, and he had established a bank on the compound in which the men deposited their earnings. A second contract the men signed upon arriving at the camp strengthened the Captain's hold on them by requiring three years of work without leaving the compound. Few men lasted the three years, and Barnes had watched as the Barbadian men labored in the broiling sun and fetid jungle without the amenities of the regular canal workers. In these conditions, they aged quickly and died regularly. Yet, there never seemed to be any end to the number of those who wanted a chance to make the money the man promised. They had come, worked, and died in a variety of ways, not all of them natural, though always explained as such.

Barnes shook his head, trying to rid himself of the memories crowding into his mind. His face, the muscles long atrophied, was hardly capable of carrying emotion anymore. Still, for a moment, he seemed to have grimaced as his eyes looked deep into the past, where his innocence and shame rested. In that time, he had not only been young but alive to the possibilities of the world, believing he had a gift for it. *What a gift that had turned out to be*. Almost everyone from that time was dead, and so many of those deaths were on his hands. He could not really blame the man in Long Island; they had all made choices. His had been wealth and success, and that choice brought his soul to the brink of hell.

Maybe it was this thought that caused the look of shame to enter his eyes. Or it could have been the brightness of the sun that forced him to squint with pain from the glare. He signaled the attendant that he was ready to go in. Barnes knew he had to be careful in approaching the man in Long Island or he would be dead before he had a chance to make his offer. Tomorrow, he would go to Culebra Cut. They had renamed it Guilliard Cut, but for him, it would always be Culebra Cut, the place that had almost broken their spirits.

As the attendant turned the chair, the sun dipped beneath the palm trees and disappeared, leaving a haunting penumbra, like a memory dimly reclaimed. Barnes thought of the nights spent in this wild place and was angry that the young couple who sat nursing their last drink before dinner did not understand they stood on bones that were noble.

The Kuni village was long gone and the woman who had come to him in the peyote dream along with it. Barnes had found passion here, and he wanted to make a sacrifice as the Kuni had done, but the false rusticity of the place was like a fog in which he traveled. The new buildings reshaped the geometry of the beach, and he had no idea where he first made love to the woman who had become his obsession. He signaled the attendant to stop, his watery eyes searching frantically for some sign that would tell him where the old village had stood, but his memory was now too weak. He gave up in frustration, his thoughts becoming less coherent. In this state, the man in Long Island and the woman from the Kuni village merged, seeming to come together in his mind's eye, and he shook his head again, saying, "You are an old fool, Rupert Barnes. It must be time for you to go."

Above the palm trees, the sunlight played with the leaves like a fool who had found paints and an accidental symmetry.

The golden tones shifted, becoming tinged with vermilion and, at the edges, a suggestion of purple. Barnes' mind came to itself, remembering a night long ago that had opened for him a path to the passion contained in his soul but which he could not find in the world he had inherited. He had thought that, in leaving Barbados, those relationships he dimly understood to be perverse would be changed, but Panama had consolidated them, making his role as jailor more concrete, more obvious to the men he had sought to befriend.

CHAPTER FIFTEEN

PANAMA 1907

The day after Richards had been whipped, the Captain called Barnes to his office, and the two stood appraising one another. The Captain was wiry, with that suggestion of strength that comes from fitness and a boundless energy. Ashamed at having done nothing to save Richards from being punished, Barnes now felt an intense dislike for this man who had come into his life with such assurance and strength. Octavius Bryant, the heir to limitless wealth, had no engineering experience, and as far as Barnes could tell, had never built anything. Barnes recognized he did, however, have one superior quality: the total absence of doubt. Bryant understood men, and Barnes, barely twenty, was drawn to this assurance.

Standing before the man, he felt the tendrils of power reaching out from Bryant, catching at the edges of his heart, and though Bryant could not be more than ten years older than he, Barnes felt like a child next to him. After a while, Bryant sat, leaving Barnes standing, appraising him with his gray, speculative eyes. Barnes' anger drained away under that gaze, and, as the silence dragged on, it was replaced by curiosity, followed by a strange feeling of being discarded. Although he knew of the man's power, Bryant had not yet shown just how ruthlessly he was prepared to use it, so Barnes felt no particular fear of him, just this sense of his will being drained away.

"And why, sir, are you here?" Bryant finally asked.

Barnes, perplexed for a moment, wanted to turn and leave but felt compelled to answer.

"You asked me to be?"

"No, Mr. Barnes. I meant why are you in Panama?"

"Much the same as all these men. Panama beckoned. I came."

The man chuckled, shaking his head slightly. Barnes' body had filled out, and, with his height, he was an imposing figure. Body hard from work, he should have felt perfectly capable of crushing the smallish man who sat so complacently before him—except for one thing. There seemed to be something playing at the corners of his mind, sucking his will away. It was not constant, but, whenever he felt a surge of strength, something subtle tickled his mind, curbing the instinct.

"No, Mr. Barnes. You did not come as these men did. You exchanged comfort for this hellhole. Why?"

"I might ask the same of you."

The man raised an eyebrow, the gleam in his eyes more pronounced.

"Hardly, Mr. Barnes. One, you are in no position to ask me anything. Two, you are a worker here. Hardly my situation."

Barnes felt the dominance in the statement and resisted it.

"I came because it gave me a purpose. Much like you, I suspect."

"You suspect wrongly, Mr. Barnes. I am here because I have no choice."

"Then you are a worker, too?" Barnes asked with a smile, and the Captain's eyes shifted slightly, becoming more fixed and glassy.

"Why are you with these men? I am aware of your relationship to them. Why are you searching for some way to redesign nature?"

Barnes pretended not to understand, waiting for the man to continue, and the silence dragged on. Looking out the window that had been pulled back to allow what little breeze there was to enter, Barnes saw a green lizard lying in the sun. The beam caught the occasionally reflective coat of the lizard, flashing a light into Barnes' eyes, and he used the flashes to hold his concentration.

"Tomorrow, I want you to report to me. I want you to assume leadership of the guardhouse. It is more becoming than what you do," Bryant abruptly said.

Barnes was ambivalent. Though recognizing the monetary value of the promotion, he did not want to be indebted.

"No words of gratitude, Mr. Barnes?"

"Probably useful to wait until I find out what I'm agreeing to, don't you think?"

"Well said. You're dismissed."

Barnes had just turned away when the voice came again.

"And you may have the night off. The Kunis will be waiting."

Barnes turned slowly, looking into the smiling face with the iron gray eyes, seeing nothing that made him comfortable.

Later that night, he headed for the railway alone, having made no arrangements for the visit to the village. This time, Gatun looked more ominous than ever, the smell of fish strong, the moving shadows suggesting a presence just outside the consciousness. He stood on the bank where the rickety boards that passed for a dock pointed down the river, uncertain what to do next. Then, a figure, walking with a slight limp, approached, and Barnes' heart jumped in anticipation. The smell of fish was strong on the Spaniard's body as he walked by, beckoning Barnes to follow, and soon, he was in the small boat, heading down the river.

Only when he was on the water did he think of the stupidity of his actions. This was dangerous jungle, and men disappeared all the time. What relationship Blackett had with the Kunis, he did not know. He was not even sure what had happened to him the night before, but the woman was like a fire lit in a very dark night. She had become a beacon to his senses. All day long, he had been consumed with the desire to see her, to touch her again. In his three years in Panama, there had been many faceless women who came in the night with their practiced expressions of love. He continued to write to Audrey, but gradually, the early passion for her faded, and increasingly the letters had become a response to what he believed to be her need. Still, in the frontier society of Panama, few women had caught his eye. Men watched their women with a closeness that threatened violence always, and he stayed away, taking his pleasure in La Boca or Colon in the darkness that carried sounds not his own. He had no clear image of the woman who had been with him the night before, but he felt certain he would recognize her. After that, he was not sure what his actions would be.

As the skiff slid silently down the river, Barnes saw the lights flickering in the trees, and he wondered what lay back there. This land was still largely a mystery to them, and most of the West Indians confined themselves to Colon and Panama City, particularly La Boca. In the jungle, there was mystery and the unknown. Even the Panamanians from the city were not familiar with the secrets of the jungle, the Spanish, after four hundred years, having carved only a foothold along the coast. In the night, the sounds of the jungle were magnified, and he could hear the scream of a jaguar. Barnes wondered if it was the one he had seen only days before. It had looked at him disinterestedly, but he had not moved, fearing movement would precipitate an attack. The eyes had seemed to be of two colors—yellow flecked with black—and the two colors had crossed into each other, giving the impression of being crosshairs. The impartial malevolence of the creature's eyes reminded him of the Indians' eyes, that flat glance that seemed to accept the universe as a plaything for their gods, and their fates merely a history written by those beings whose statues stood with such gruesome authority in the most improbable places.

What would he say to the woman once he found her? Would he find her? What if Blackett had fooled him, and the drug had created the hallucination?

As the boat drew closer to the sea, the smell changed, and his heart pounded. The Spaniard sat, all but invisible in the stern of the skiff, sculling skillfully, seemingly without disturbing the water.

"Do you know how to get to the village?"

But the man did not speak English, and Barnes tried in his pigeon Spanish to ask the same question.

"Donde el camino al pueblo? Anoche pasado?"

The man laughed sharply at the abominable Spanish, but he understood and nodded vigorously, pointing into the forest in the direction Barnes assumed they had gone the night before. Soon, he tacked the boat toward land, leaving the current that ran swiftly toward the sea. Barnes could hear the breakers and was once again aware of the pounding of his heart, although it now seemed to be pounding in a kind of delayed rhythm. Soon, they were walking swiftly through the forest, and, in no time, they arrived at the village.

He must know a shorter way, Barnes thought as they strode into the center of the clearing.

The scene was as the night before, the men sitting in a circle, smoking. Two men moved aside to make a space for him, immediately handing him the pipe. Barnes did not want to lose consciousness as he had the night before. He wanted to see the woman, and asked, *"La mujer? De anoche pasado?"*

The Indians looked blankly at him, their eyes turned inward, seeing some world he could not. They understood no Spanish. This was in itself strange, since, as residents of a coastal village, they would have come into contact with the Spanish. The Spaniard solved his problem by saying something rapidly to the Indians, who looked at him more closely and pointed to a hut situated away from the compound. He stood, heading for the hut, but a firm, though not threatening, hand placed against his chest quickly blocked his path. Clearly, he was not to go there. For a while, he considered resisting but, recognizing the futility of this, sat down, accepting the pipe and, in frustration, inhaling deeply.

Soon, the world changed, and the jungle moved apart. In the distance, next to a hill, was the jaguar, sleek, long canines exposed. Barnes felt the chill of a breeze but could not tell where it came from. The jaguar moved and, in an instant, was next to him. The fear started deep inside, and he struggled not to scream, knowing the scream signaled his surrender, and that meant his death. He was trying to squeeze his body into a smaller space that had opened up behind him, but the jaguar was smaller and could follow. Still, he instinctively burrowed in, feeling the space encase him.

Then, the jaguar disappeared, and, in its place, there was the woman, dressed in a cloak of molas. It was brightly colored and fell below her knees. Her golden earrings glistened in the uncertain light, and in her nose was a ring, also of gold. Her legs were covered by anklets and calf stockings, and her clothing was designed with a series of fishes and monkeys, along with small statuettes of what looked like a stone jaguar. These were woven into the fabric in an alternating pattern of bright reds, blues, and golds. Streaming through the fabric was a strand of green that looked like the color behind the jaguar's eyes, and, sometimes, when the woman moved into the light, the monkeys changed into panthers and snarled at him.

It took him a while to realize she was dancing, and he watched, transfixed by the movement of the colors and her body. His mind was moving around the room, viewing her from different angles and finding her pleasing from each. Looking down on his body, he saw that it had become inert, curled into a ball on the dark ground, and the woman was taking the giant mola off, placing it, now unwrapped and wide enough to cover the floor, on their bodies. She was kissing him along the edges of his soul, and he heard her voice inside him, asking him to free himself and to lay within her, and this he did, feeling her close softly around him. As he sank into the maelstrom of her passion, the sky lightened and moved away from him at a frightening speed. He held on lest he fly away with the sky. A long time later, the sky fell, with equal rapidity, back into place, the darkness descending, and in the darkness, he sensed her absence.

When Barnes awoke, the darkness was solid, and the men were stretched out on the ground, asleep. Shaking the Spaniard awake, he left, snaking through the darkness toward the river.

For weeks, this went on. The days were full of his new duties, and the nights laden with the incense of this woman who was half dream, half wife. Then, one Friday, he slept through the night. In the dawn light he awoke, and the mist laid heavy on the water and the land. Waking alone in a hut that was set some way back from the sea, he stepped outside to relieve himself and saw the woman squatting in the trees, an assertive stream coming from her. She looked across the clearing and stared full into his eyes, giving evidence of no shame or any particular awareness of him. When she came back to the hut, he saw her for the first time without the haze induced by drugs, and he gasped. Her face was burnt on one side so that it looked like a crisp, the disfigured flesh composed of ridges and flats that seemed like an alien landscape. Barnes could not look away, and she did not turn away, allowing him to see the full horror of the burnt flesh. Her eyes stared out of the flat face with a half-amused look as she waited for his reaction. He was both moved and revolted, and she stood, allowing him to grapple with his choice. Finally, he went over to her, gently touching the destroyed flesh, and she placed her hand over his.

Now, Barnes sat in the darkness, the attendant just outside the door, wondering how his life would have been different had he not met Leila and fallen in love with her. The Panamanian night had descended, and the attendant gave him his pills. Barnes wondered if tomorrow, at Culebra, he would again hear the screams that had haunted his nights for so long. The word had been spoken again, the American President's zeal for fairness to Panama having frightened someone. That someone had reacted to the word Culebra. The man in Long Island was closing up this episode, and Barnes was the last loophole. With Barnes dead, there would be no direct evidence of the horror that had taken place at Culebra sixty-three years before. Barnes had left that behind, had constructed a life in Philadelphia that was the essence of respectability. Wanting no contact with the old days, he had never returned to Barbados, thus ending his relationship with Audrey. He wondered now if she was alive. He doubted it.

As his memories became muddled, and the two women played in his mind, his head fell forward, and, soon, Barnes slept.

CHAPTER SIXTEEN

Charles Lemieux stood on the hill across from Cucuracha slope, watching the rain pelt down. The grass under his feet had been pounded with the downpours that had come in waves for several days now. He had engineered projects all over the United States, in land that was inhospitable to human life, but he had never seen anything like this. Even now, the weight of the rain slammed into his shoulders in its inexorable thrust to the ground, the drops puncturing the earth, leaving almost perfectly round holes. When he had left Ancon Hill, where his headquarters were located, it had been overcast, but by the time he had reached this hill, he had been drenched. It never ceased to amaze him how the rain came. High up in the hills had appeared what looked like mist, and this had been quickly followed by the long, drawn-out shush of the water slapping against the broad leaves of the rubber and medlar trees. Then, within seconds, the sound changed, reminding him of the time he visited Niagara Falls. The water became a roar, and the tension involuntarily increased in his body as it sought to duck the onslaught. It hit him with the force of some malevolent spirit seeking to obliterate all evidence of his presence, and Lemieux hunched his shoulders against the weight of the rain, thankful he had not been foolish enough to come out without his slicker. There was no wind to speak of, but the rain itself created a vacuum that tugged at the slicker, whipping the bottom around.

Lemieux was not thinking of the discomfort of the rain, however. He was looking anxiously at the towering height of Culebra Cut. Though anxious, he could not help but feel pride in what had been accomplished here in the last three years. From where he stood, the belly of the earth laid exposed, evidence of the tremendous effort that had gone into making the cut. Culebra had been an impossibility for the French, and it had broken their spirit, but arriving in Panama, he had been impressed with what the French had accomplished. In Washington, it was believed the French had failed, but that first morning, when he walked out to Culebra, he had known that, if this was failure, then it was a magnificent failure indeed. The Cut was impressive, descending foot after perilous foot into the bowels of the earth. This would be the heart of the canal, if the sea-level waterway was to work. They would, in effect, be attempting to move ships through a mountain range; to make that possible, the mountain would have to be cut down. It was at Culebra that the lowering of the mountain was taking place.

Looking down, he thought of what the engineering professor at West Point had said: "Engineering, gentlemen, is merely dependent on mathematics. It is not mathematics. It is the organization of the human will in the pursuit of a common purpose." At West Point, he had discovered his love of engineering, and there, too, his admiration of Ferdinand De Lesseps had grown into idolatry. He had studied the Suez Canal's engineering and understood what the professor meant. De Lesseps was not an engineer, but he had organized the effort so productively at Suez that he emerged as a legendary builder. Lemieux understood that organization, more than engineering, was keeping him ahead of the disaster that always lurked in the heart of success. Like most engineers, he felt the pull of superstition, that "something" that did not explain why a bridge fell when every precaution was taken or why a rail flies apart when it is designed identically to every other. Now, he was definitely feeling the tug of that superstition.

Across from him, Cucuracha Hill was soggy after days of incessant rain, and the men's nervousness was evident. Lemieux recognized the danger of a slide, but the work could not stop. Below him, the huge, ninety-five-ton Bacyrus shovels dug into the side of the mountain, chewing obscenely huge chunks out of the earth, then wheeling to deposit the tonnage into the continuously moving trains that carried the waste away from the site. This was the secret of his success at Culebra. He had immediately revised his opinion of the engineering needed to complete the work started by the French, as, under pressure from Washington, he had been forced to begin the digging before he was ready.

The politicians wanted proof for the American people that they were winning the battle. The outpouring of nationalism over the canal had surprised him, as he had been sent off from New York with a military band and 21- gun salute. The Vice President had been there, and several senators had come to make speeches. Embarrassed for the most part by the fuss being made over him, Lemieux was even more aware of the level of expectation everyone had. This would be the most expensive project in the history of mankind, and the politicians would need to justify the cost.

The meddling had begun almost at once. His intention had been to spend some time analyzing the engineering problems, but with the first appropriation coming before the Senate, the (not at all subtle) message was to get a move on. It angered him that these people, who did not understand the problems he faced, were giving him orders. He had written to the Vice President, explaining that it was folly to proceed without a thorough analysis of the geology of the cut at Culebra, where he would begin the assault on the canal. Taft had written a short note back, saying, "Good engineering, poor politics," and suggested he proceed.

Lemieux had no choice after that and had begun digging, using the old French excavators upon which De Lesseps had depended. The same problem that had plagued the French also plagued him: disposal. The trucks could not get rid of the dirt quickly enough, and so the efficiency of the scoops was destroyed. It was not simply a question of more trucks, although he had tried that as well. This had only added to the confusion as the trucks got in each other's way. Still, the illusion of progress had to be maintained, and he sent reports indicating the tonnage moved, not mentioning that most of it sat in the cut itself. A desperate note to Edward Bryant explaining that the interference from Washington was making things impossible had been rewarded by a lessening of pressure within days. Bryant also sent him new shovels. Lemieux could not thank the man enough.

Now, walking along the brow of the hill, he had an uncomfortable feeling in his stomach. Below, he could barely see the Bacyruses. Looking like otherworldly beetles of gargantuan size, snarling and smoking, they attacked the earth, dumping dirt into the trucks that sped over to the continuously moving trains carrying the detritus away from the cut. The rain was now pouring down with such power that he could not see much beyond the edge of the hill.

The road had turned to mud and slid around under the weight of the truck. Descending the hill slowly and with a great scraping of gears, Lemieux saw the drop that fell to the bottom of the cut. The people in the United States did not understand the size and scale of what they were doing here. He had just seen a report, published by the Department of the Army, indicating that, this year, thirty-seven thousand cubic yards of dirt had been removed from the cut. What did that really mean? How could that be made real to people whose digging experience was limited to turning their flowerbeds? For most of the people making the decisions, even this was not true. Most of them had their sod turned for them.

Lemieux tightened his jaw in anger, thinking of the cable that had come today. President Roosevelt was coming to the canal, and Lemieux thought of all that could go wrong. If the President felt the project was not going quickly enough, there would be additional pressure. Senator Nolte from Louisiana was still a problem. He opposed the Panama route, favoring a canal through Nicaragua, but having lost that debate, Nolte had not given up his opposition to the project. He was critical of the Canal Commission and had made thinly veiled criticisms of Lemieux himself. The President was supportive, but even he had shown some hesitation as the funding estimates had been revised upwards time after time. Senator Nolte was asking about costs, and the President was showing some sensitivity to the criticism.

The truck reached the bottom of the mountain, and it bumped along the floor of the cut, occasionally getting stuck in the clinging mud. Glancing at the great gouges in the earth, Lemieux felt some ambivalence. Like all engineers, he felt a unity with the structures he built, much as a sculptor would. Sometimes, he could not help but feel that the earth was crying out at the cuts that laid her body open, exposing the insides for all to see. Looking at the great striations packed one on top of the other, he felt he was engaged in a violation of something sacred, that he was destroying something beautiful. What would he create in its place? In his mind's eye, he already saw the water flowing along the great cut. He purposely avoided images of ships on that water because his soul rebelled at the thought. Recognizing his sentimentality, Lemieux sighed loudly, causing the driver to look at him.

"Are you okay, sir? Pretty hairy driving around today."

Lemieux nodded, staring at the black workers who were furiously moving around, digging and loading.

The Negroes used to be a real problem, he thought.

They had been so ignorant of modern machinery. He had watched one of them, having just arrived, look curiously at a wheelbarrow, walking around it, not sure what to do with it and, thinking the fellow a dunce, had lamented again the decision to use the West Indians. He had worked with the Chinese in the western territories, and if he could not get white men, then they were best for this kind of work. That had been his recommendation, but, having been overruled, he had gotten the West Indians instead, and they had proven to be a major problem. Their productivity had been a third of what a white man from Ohio just off the farm would be. They were now still less productive than whites he had brought in from the United States, but the difference had practically been eliminated.

Lemieux watched as a group of them, carefully carrying the thirty-pound boxes of dynamite on their heads and shoulders, walked swiftly along the ledge where they were blasting. The incidences of death by explosion had dropped precipitously once the West Indian Negroes learned to allow for a safety margin. In the first year, he had lost more than eighty of the fellows, until someone realized they had stuck rigidly to the timings they had been given, allowing for no flaws in the fuses. Once this had been corrected, the number killed or maimed in these explosions dropped to a more acceptable rate and now hovered around thirty a year.

Very respectable in the circumstances, he thought as the men put the boxes down, swiftly stuffing the brown sticks into the holes. He ordered the driver to stop and immediately felt the truck sink a little into the mud.

On the slope, the men had lost the joviality that seemed so much a part of their character. Lemieux smiled, thinking, *it's like a symphony*.

They were dressed in the khaki burlap pants and the white cotton shirts of the blasting company, although they all worked directly for him. The shirts were stuck to their backs, exposing their tensile strength. Few were heavily muscled, but they were lean and stringy. One man, the blasting leader, gave an order Lemieux could not hear. They had developed a rhythm. The leader brought his hand down sharply, and the men, each grabbing a stick of dynamite, shoved it into the already dug holes. At another sign from the standing man, they drew their hands back to the box, and the process started again. Now, as Lemieux watched, the man made a motion, and all the men looked up at the same time. Then, they nodded in unison before hurrying back the way they had come. The man who had been giving the signals now came down the ledge, spooling after him a long, black wire. Lemieux thought with satisfaction about how he had solved the problem of the wet fuses, which had haunted the project in the early days, by using an old railroad trick to avoid the delays that were costing a fortune. He had welded together a series of railway ties, one on top of the other, from the blast site to the detonation site. This gave a dry housing for the wire and had improved his efficiency immeasurably.

As the men returned to the floor of the cut, a siren gave three loud shrieks. Most people knew where the blast area was and did not stop work. In minutes, Lemieux actually saw the hail of flying dirt before he heard the blast, but when he did, it was as if some hell had opened in front of him. Instinctively, he closed his eyes, the assault on his eardrums forcing the reaction. Something trembled in the very sinews of his body, much like a tuning fork in response to being struck, and thinking about what the men went through all day, every day, Lemieux shook his head in wonder. Before the wet mud had settled, the trucks, looking like inquisitive beetles, were on their way up the slope, and, as the all-clear siren sounded, the trains were being maneuvered into place to receive the detritus. The group of West Indian Negroes, he noticed, had all lit cigarettes and were smoking while the trucks cleared the place they had just blasted.

Lemieux noted that the white-skinned fellow, Barnes, was no longer with them. He had always been a bit of an oddity, speaking in that surprising accent and living with the Negroes. Lemieux wondered how a white man could fall to this level and made a mental note to do something about placing him in a more responsible position. He hoped the fellow had not run off. Men were disappearing at a rate he found unacceptable, and, worse, he had no idea where they were disappearing to. Worried about it, he had mentioned it in a report, but this prompted a cable from Edward Bryant, who warned Lemieux not to emphasize his failures, implying that it was hard enough for the President to keep the support of the Senate. Bryant had also inquired whether he had a shortage of laborers, and when he replied that he did not, Bryant told him to stop worrying about the little things.

The message had been clear. The government wanted progress reports, not explanations or complaints, and since there was no shortage of laborers and everything he asked for was being provided, he had put it from his mind. Still, the absence of the white Barbadian was a reminder of how easily, on a project this large, one could ignore a detail.

Lemieux motioned the driver to take him back to Ancon Hill, and soon the truck was wheezing up the steep incline. Reaching the top, he looked back, the worry lines clear as he stared at Cucuracha Hill. The truck jumped as another blast sounded, and he wondered about the wet mud sitting atop the granite that was the bedrock of the canal. Unconsciously, he tapped his hand against the metal dashboard of the truck, a gesture the driver wondered about.

CHAPTER SEVENTEEN

PANAMA 1907

Claudette Binai-Lemieux was happy. She watched closely as the West Indian maid set the last piece of cutlery on the table and turned to see if her mistress approved. Claudette nodded her satisfaction, and the brown-skinned woman left the room. She walked to the rain-drenched windows, looking to see when the truck would appear. Outside, the gloom of the Panamanian rainstorm sat heavily on the atmosphere. They had not seen the sun in days, but she did not mind. The darkness created an intimacy she enjoyed when Charles was at home, although he was often gone for long hours. She had taken to Panama. Never had she felt more useful and more at ease. There had been so much to do when they arrived, what with the campaign against the yellow fever and malaria and all. She had volunteered as a nurse in Ancon hospital, and those days, working with John McCormick day and night, had been hectic.

McCormick believed that if they could eliminate the mosquitoes, they would be able to eliminate the disease. This was not universally accepted in the medical profession, and he had had to fight to implement his plan. Charles had supported him, had even threatened to resign if McCormick was not given full medical authority, including the ability to request budgets. Still, in the first year, the black workers had succumbed in droves. Claudette had not actually worked in the ward with the Negroes but had heard the news from the others. Charles was afraid for her safety, but he knew she was comfortable in the hospital.

McCormick had managed to clean up the areas around Ancon Hill where the whites lived, but he was having more of a challenge with the Negro areas. Claudette did not know why it was so hard for them to understand simple directions like "don't leave water lying around." They had all but ignored the instructions, and so they were still dying.

In this assumption, Claudette was incorrect. She did not know that little attention had been paid to the workers' quarters until the disease had been practically eradicated on Ancon Hill. The West Indians had continued to die until it was understood that, if the disease existed in one area, then nowhere was safe.

She still volunteered at the hospital, but the sense of urgency was gone now. *No white person has died in over a year*, she thought with some satisfaction, recognizing she was partially responsible for that.

Claudette sauntered back into the room and looked around at the quarters they had appropriated. The French had built well and had been criticized for it. Charles, sensitive to this, had not wanted to repeat that mistake, but Claudette had no interest in being cooped up with other officers and their wives, so she asked Charles to fix up the chateau that had been abandoned by the French Directeur General. They had never had their own home, always living at the Army's expense in houses that functioned in the way they were supposed to, i.e., they kept the cold and the rain out. The nicest place they ever had was the apartment in Washington that had been provided for them during the debate over the location of the canal. When she had seen the chateau and fallen in love with it, Charles refused to repair it. For the first time, she had not accepted his judgment and had written to Margaret Atherton, the young woman she had met at Edward Bryant's home. Soon after, Charles received a cable indicating that Bryant thought he should have a home in Panama, the work being hard enough even in the most comfortable circumstances. Bryant had provided a line of credit from which the Colonel could draw to build his home and had put no limit in the cable. Charles had looked at her speculatively but had said nothing, and so the matter ended.

She looked around the room, which stretched away from her into the verandah surrounding the house. In profile, it looked like a castle, with the grounds enclosed by a low wall ending in postern gates at each corner. Built on a hill that sloped gently down to a level section, it contained a small garden, the flowers within which were now cowering under the onslaught of the rain. They had replaced the flooring of the house with stained pine, and even in the dull light, it shone. Claudette was very proud of what she had done with the house. It had lost the officious mood the French Directeur General had created, this replaced by a warmth she found comforting.

From outside came the awful scraping of the truck's gears as it made its way up the hill, and she went to the door.

As Lemieux entered, she shouted playfully, "Wait! Wait!"

Lemieux stopped, a look of alarm on his face. She hurried up, quickly removed his dripping slicker, and pushed him back outside, pointing sternly at his mud-caked boots. He did not resist and allowed himself to be seated on the verandah, where he pulled off the boots and sat them down on the floor before standing in his socks and walking into the house. She kissed him as soon as he was inside, and he kissed back, always glad to touch her. Then, tucking her arm into his, she said, "You must hurry. John will be here for dinner any second now."

Lemieux slapped his hand to his forehead, softly swearing.

"I had forgotten. How much time do I have?"

"Just enough to change, dear, but you must hurry."

Claudette came into the bedroom as he was putting the finishing touches to his cravat and looked at him speculatively, noting the square cut of him and laughing at that improbable jaw.

He has lost weight since he came to Panama and is more tanned. The tan looks good on him, but I have the devil of a time keeping out of the sun, she thought, looking past him into the large, egg-shaped mirror and admiring the whiteness of her skin.

I have been very careful with my parasol, she thought with a smile.

Lemieux noticed the smile and said, "Admiring ourselves again, are we?"

Claudette made a face, and they both laughed, heading, arm in arm, to the stairs. As they were descending, John McCormick's vehicle could be heard climbing the hill. A year ago, Lemieux had promoted McCormick to major and had provided him with separate quarters, a reward for the conquest of the diseases. There were still cases of yellow fever reported, but it was not the fearful killer it had been. The workers knew this, and morale had improved. Productivity had also increased, and Lemieux looked like a genius, but he knew McCormick had been the hero and had said so to Washington. McCormick had never married, had never had the time, so intent had he been on his pursuit of the diseases that challenged his life.

As he sat, he said, "I just heard the President is coming to Panama. Is that true, sir?"

Lemieux nodded resignedly, and McCormick, a little surprised at his boss' lack of excitement, continued, "But that's quite an honor, sir. This must mean he continues to be supportive of the project."

"I would be somewhat more comfortable if we did not have continued instances of yellow fever in La Boca."

McCormick colored, although he knew Lemieux intended no criticism. He had done wonders in three years, and they both believed that his failure to clean out La Boca, where the Negroes lived, was largely due to their not heeding his instructions. Still, he felt uncomfortable with the Colonel's observation.

Lemieux had noticed the slight hesitation, and added, "Of course, you cannot be blamed for the irresponsibility of the Negroes, but we must find a way to solve that problem. I cannot afford to have the President come down with even a cold when he is here."

Claudette had been listening to the conversation and said, "But the President is a practical man, isn't he, Charles? He understands the difficulties you face here, no? He has, after all, led troops into battle. Don't you think he knows the extent of what you have accomplished? Both you and John?"

Lemieux smiled at his wife and replied softly, "The President is, above all, a politician. If I succeed in making him look good, he will support me. If not...."

His voice trickled off, but they all understood what he meant. John McCormick looked at his boss, admiring the strength he saw there. The project was actually going well, and they were ahead of schedule. Bringing in the giant Bacyrus shovels had been an act of genius, and the speed of the work had increased immeasurably. The organization was awesome, and McCormick knew that fewer than ten men in the world could have done what this man had done. He had already excavated more dirt from the canal in three years than the French had done in seventeen.

"You know, sir, I am beginning to believe this is possible. What has been accomplished so far is awe-inspiring."

Lemieux laughed and, turning to his wife, said jovially, "I want you to note, dear, that the Major had no confidence in the project. He came only to advance his career."

McCormick colored more deeply, making his naturally ruddy features positively crimson.

"No. No, sir. I did not mean to suggest—I had every confidence—I was certain...."

He stopped, watching Claudette and Charles Lemieux laugh at his confusion, and soon, he laughed too. Lemieux continued to chuckle, raising his hand to indicate he was joking.

The butler, a young fellow from Jamaica, placed the soup before them, and they ate quietly for a moment, enjoying food as only men who work from sun up to sundown can. Claudette watched them as they ate, noting how Charles had changed in the three years in Panama.

He is less fastidious about his table manners for one thing, she thought with a smile, noting how he shoveled the soup into his mouth as if it were his last meal.

John McCormick had not lost his care, and he delicately scooped up the thick soup the West Indian cook had concocted. Lemieux had lost all semblance of youthfulness in the last three years. The worry lines, now a permanent feature of his face, seemed to drain down into that pugnacious jaw, giving the face a fiercely simian look. She laughed to herself as she thought of him roaring at some unfortunate officer who had fouled up.

The men, having finished the soup, picked up their conversation again, but Claudette was not listening, instead thinking of Panama three years before. She had not been prepared for the land, which betrayed the paucity of her imagination. In her mind's eye had been a picture gleaned from her reading, a picture of beautiful landscapes and impressive but welcoming mountains. She had read of the hardships of frontier life, but it was impossible to imagine Panama. Stepping from the ship, she had been assailed by the primordial nature of the place. Panama was a dark land. In spite of the sun that burned with such ferocity, she was always aware of the dark jungle. Even today, now that they had carved so much out of the middle of the land, it lay unknowable and phlegmatic around them. Men were dying here. John had done an admirable job of conquering the diseases that had haunted the French, but this land was not beaten. Outside, the rain poured down as if some malevolent god had opened the bottom of heaven and was intent on drowning them all. She understood the lines in Charles' face because, although she did not show it, the land frightened her. There was something old and evil about it, something that betrayed its inhumanity. These fears were kept from Charles, and she knew he was grateful for this, not wanting to be responsible for her discomfort.

She had never been close to blacks before and was still adjusting to that. She now knew her maid well enough to see a basic humanity there and was still surprised at the commonality of their concerns. Sheila's husband worked on the dynamite gang, and Claudette would watch the woman tense up each time the siren sounded. Whatever she was doing would be put on hold for those long moments until the all-clear siren was heard. Then, she would relax again, becoming the self-effacing person she had learned to be. Claudette wondered what her life was like, this living between heaven and hell, this constant worry about the destruction of someone she loved. Charles had the responsibility of managing the greatest construction project in the history of man, but he was never in physical danger, and she wondered who had the greater weight, she or her maid.

Suddenly, she asked, "Charles, how many men do we lose in a year?"

Both men, their conversation interrupted, looked surprised at the question, and Charles asked gently, but with a hint of caution in his voice, "Whatever do you mean, dear?"

Claudette was not sure what she meant but plunged on. "Well, I know you're concerned about the number of men who die each year. I simply wondered how many they were."

Claudette was surprised at the look of relief that passed over the men's faces before Charles answered.

"Something on the order of twenty to twenty-five deaths now that the yellow fever and malaria are nearly under control. We do have hundreds of injuries, though, and, in many cases, that is as devastating as losing a life. Many of them are never productive again."

Claudette was surprised at feeling disappointed in Charles' answer.

"Is that considered acceptable? Is that a high number?"

"Yes, I would say that these are acceptable. It's impossible to build on this scale without some losses, but since we have all but eliminated the disease, we have brought our losses well within the bounds of acceptability."

John McCormick added, "Actually, for the scale of the project and the difficulty of the terrain, the losses are extraordinarily low. The mortality rate, if you exclude the early days when the yellow plague was about, is actually lower than what it was at Suez."

They both looked satisfied at this, but she was leading up to something and thought she had better get it out.

"How many of the deaths have been white men?"

They both looked at her strangely, wondering what she was up to. Finally, McCormick answered, "We have had no deaths of whites since last year—at least, not by disease or injury. We did have a couple of deaths by natural causes, but that is understandable. There are almost no white laborers on the canal now. Most of those who were here returned to the United States after the malaria outbreaks. The labor force is almost entirely Negro. They were brought in because of their natural resistance to tropical disease."

"But, John, they are the only ones dying from the disease now."

McCormick shrugged, indicating he was perplexed by it too, but Charles was watching her closely, a questioning look on his face.

"We know why that is happening, Claudette dear. The Negroes have not been following the rules John laid down. They need to be watched all the time, much like children. John, do you remember when they were first brought here? They had never seen most of the equipment we were using. These are a very backward people, dear. We do our best with them, but if they ignore the warnings, what can we do?"

"But, Charles, when John first came and told our people they had to clean up the area and get rid of the water, he was practically laughed at. No one believed the diseases could be carried by mosquitoes or that they had to clean up the stagnant water to get rid of the disease. In fact, you had to dismiss the resident doctor at Ancon Hospital because his opposition was so distracting. We sent out the brigades of fumigators to rid ourselves of the stagnant water, and you imposed fines to make sure that our people listened. There has been no such effort in La Boca, has there?"

It was not often that Charles lost patience with her, but he was looking at her closely now, and the jaw was stretching forward. Not certain why she had brought this up, Claudette was a little perplexed herself. She had thought of the maid, and, suddenly, the questions were there. Now, seeing opposition in her husband's eyes, Claudette subsided, and the men went back to their conversation. Still, she wondered why fumigation had not been insisted upon in the Negro districts.

Some time later, the two men went out on the porch to smoke, and the smell of tobacco filtered into the room, leaving her with the feeling of being in the arms of a man she could not see. In the years they had been together, her love for Charles had not diminished. She still felt like a school girl around him and knew him to be gentle and kind with a streak of what she thought of as nobility in him. He had attacked the challenge of the canal as if it were something he had been born to do; the arrangements, the organization, the terror of this ungodly climate and this heathen land he had grappled with as if they were physical beings he could see and struggle against. She had watched the chaos of the early days give way to order as he arranged the men into useful gangs that functioned like a living, breathing machine. He saw this as a struggle to convert men with wills, however perverted, into a single will-less machine that obeyed a single brain: his. He had said more than once that if the Negroes could be directed like the Bacyrus shovels, he could complete the canal in half the time. This always elicited a laugh, but tonight, she felt something was wrong with that statement.

Claudette walked up to the second floor of the house. The wraparound porch gave a view of both the canal area and the broad Pacific, which rose and fell every six hours with frightening regularity. Upon first seeing the severe drop the tides caused, she had been awed. Charles had taken her and several other officers' wives to the old city, and they had seen the marvel of the ocean. As the water retreated, its level dropped thirteen feet in two hours, leaving boats that only an hour before had been floating gaily, stranded and leaning on their sides like giant fish that had been caught and thrown on some muddy beach. This had early on convinced her of the incomprehensibility of this land. There was something they did not understand about this place, and she shivered involuntarily.

Outside, the rain continued, obliterating the sky, forming a solid, metallic, leaden sheet that shut the world down around her. Claudette placed her hands over her ears as she had seen the Negro children do, and the rain seemed to be speaking to her, its sibilance encouraging her to give way, to come out. In her mind, the lancets of water became metal, capable of piercing her body. Claudette yanked her hands from her ears, but the threat of the rain continued, promising no end.

Still, until a moment ago, she had been happy, glad to be sharing in the glory of this enterprise with her husband. What had changed? It seemed illogical that the thought of her maid could so radically alter her mood, and yet she could think of nothing else. Or maybe it was her recognition that Charles was changing, becoming older with the weight of the canal on his shoulders. Yet, this was a glorious enterprise, and she felt even now a thrill at the thought of its grandeur. Still, there was this feeling of foreboding, of something impending.

"I know it's just the rain. Why am I being so foolish?" she asked herself quietly, hearing the reassuring laughter of the men downstairs.

John is a good friend to Charles, she thought, overwhelmed with gratitude for this quiet man who had made her husband's triumph possible.

Something was worrying Charles, and she wondered what. He was concerned that the President was coming, as anyone would be. There would be preparations to make, and he hated taking time away from the real work of the canal. Yet, construction was as much an act of politics as it was one of engineering and commerce, so the visit had to be a success.

Still, when she had asked about the number of workers lost each year, they had looked slightly guilty and had obviously been relieved after her next question. This feeling of being left out fueled her upset. It was not like Charles to leave her out of things, although this canal had started them on that track. Like his relationship with Edward Bryant. That was still a mystery to her. It seemed he was always there when Charles needed help with equipment, politicians, or funding. Charles seemed comfortable with the explanation that the man was simply a patriot who wanted to make sure the canal was built, but she just did not like being left out, and now it seemed that Charles was keeping secrets from her.

Claudette knew she was not making sense, but her thoughts kept spinning around in this dark, formless world, and she wished Charles would come upstairs. Her mind needed something solid to hold on to in this inchoate world that had come right up to her door and crossed through the portals. Suddenly, she felt weak, a band of dull pain stretching across her forehead as the spray from the rain bounced up from the patio floor into her face. She pulled back sharply, and the pain increased. Standing slowly, Claudette walked into the sitting room that occupied one side of the second floor and, blowing out the lamp, closed her eyes, trying to will the pain away. Outside, the sharp, tearing sound of the torrential rain beat into the ground, and beneath it all was the periodic boom of the powder gangs continuing their work. Nothing stopped the work on the canal, and this was a source of pride for Charles.

She had seen these men during the day, packing and tamping the dynamite charges, and she now wondered if Sheila's husband was out there in the torrent, trying to keep the fuses and the wires dry. This was dangerous work, and she felt certain the maid was downstairs in her little room, worrying. Claudette walked down to the basement. She had fixed it up for the maid. Charles had been outraged at first, but she had wheedled the concession out of him. Sheila now stayed in the house four nights during the week and was allowed to go home to La Boca on Thursdays, Fridays, and Saturdays unless there was some affair at the house. It was not safe moving about La Boca at night. A woman walking alone in that neighborhood was easy prey, so she would have Sheila stay sometimes five or six nights a week. Sheila never complained, so Claudette assumed she had done the woman a favor. After all, who could prefer to live in La Boca?

The maid sat facing the small window that looked out on the western side of Ancon Hill.

She has not heard me, Claudette thought, more convinced than ever she was right to come and see the woman.

The maid, in the dim light of the kerosene lamp, looked spectral, insubstantial, her thin shoulders, hunched forward, fading into the dimness of the wooden wall against which she leaned. Claudette felt she was intruding and experienced an unaccustomed shyness. She hesitated, uncertain whether to go forward or not.Before she could make up her mind, the woman turned and stood suddenly, smoothing her flowered dress as she rose. Her eyes, unprotected for a moment, showed surprise and what seemed to Claudette to be anger.

Before Claudette could be sure, Sheila dropped her eyes to the floor, mumbling, "Sorry, mam. I din't see you dere."

Claudette made a dismissive noise, encouraging the woman to sit and seeking out some place to seat herself. There was only one chair in the room, and this the woman shoved carefully over to her, seating herself on the edge of the bed, while saying, "You did want me to do somet'ing, mam?"

"No. Actually, I came down to see how you were doing in all this rain. It seems like it will never end, doesn't it?"

The woman chuckled shyly, her face lighting up as the muscles relaxed, and Claudette thought with some surprise, *My goodness, she is pretty. How come I never noticed that before?*

"Dat is how it does be down here in dis part uh de worl'. You should see how it does fall in Barbados durin' de rainy season. Just like here."

Claudette nodded, watching the animation in the woman who had only a moment before seemed so depressed.

They really are like children, just as Charles says, she thought.

"How long have you been in Panama, Sheila?"

"Let me see now. I come ovuh in 1900. Lauriston come ovuh some time befo'e dat to wuk wid de French. W'en dem left, he stay on to wuk in Panama, an' den, in 1900, he sen' fuh me. I bin here ever since."

"Don't you miss your home? I mean, did you not leave your friends there? That must have been hard."

The woman paused, considering her answer, and Claudette thought she had gone too far, but Sheila soon continued.

"I mos'ly miss my mudduh and my chirren."

"You have children? You never said anything about children."

The woman hung her head again, staring at feet that were wide and splayed from incessant walking.

There is strength there, too, Claudette thought, noticing the thin, cord-like muscles of the woman's foot. *She's as skinny as a rake, but she looks like she will endure forever.*

Claudette glanced at her own feet, which were covered with leather slippers Charles had brought back for her on one of his trips into the country. She could not help but notice the difference, even as she continued to evaluate the other woman.

They are so secretive, like children with little nuggets they keep to themselves. Looking at her body, who would have thought she had a child, never mind children.

"How many children do you have, Sheila?"

"T'ree. Two boys an' a girl. My mudduh does take care uh dem fuh me."

Claudette did not know what to say. How could anyone just leave her children and go off to a foreign place to live like that, she wondered. She had seen the black women with the children of the officers' wives, and they were always so attentive. How could they just leave their own to take care of someone else's? It was perplexing, and Claudette glanced at the woman who had raised her eyes in the presence of the ensuing silence. The whiteness of her eyes shone in the flickering light, giving the woman a slightly alien appearance, almost as if she had fire inside her.

The woman had been formulating a question that, when it came, surprised Claudette.

"How come you an' de Colonel don' have no chirren, mam?"

Claudette felt the blood rush to her face and was on the verge of blurting out that it was none of the woman's business when she forced herself to stop, remembering it was she who had broached the subject. In any case, anger would make her look silly. She thought about it for a while, knowing she was going to lie.

"Do you think Panama is a fit place to raise a child? It is so deadly. I would be afraid. Many of the children born here die early. I see them at the hospital all the time."

The woman was watching her closely as she spoke, both understanding the lie. Claudette suddenly felt uncomfortable and looked around for something to occupy her eyes. Finding nothing, she sat, the comforting silence of a moment ago gone. Still, something remained of the ease, and she wrapped herself in this, struggling with the truth of her body. She could not have children. None of the doctors had been able to find out why. Charles was kind about this, explaining that his work did not allow time for child-rearing anyway, but the very fact of his denial always stood like a rebuke in her mind. She looked around sharply, realizing the woman was speaking again.

"What did you say?"

"I jus' say dat ev'ry woman should have a chile. No mattuh w'at try to get in she way."

Claudette felt that something in their roles had changed. The woman now sounded more assertive, confident in her female strength, and Claudette felt her anger rise. Again, she pushed it down, recognizing the woman meant no harm. She was no longer sure why she had come. As the woman stood up with her, the roles were re-established. The maid hung her head, and Claudette said goodnight.

Reaching the stairs, she turned, remembering her purpose.

"Sheila, is your husband working tonight?"

The woman looked up quickly, surprised at the question, and when she answered, there was a pronounced hesitancy in her voice.

"Yes, mam. He wid de dynamite gang tonight."

Claudette nodded and walked upstairs. The two men were still on the porch, and she could hear their whispered conversation. John McCormick would soon be leaving, and she stepped out, feeling the spray from the rain insinuate itself into her skin.

"Well, John, you'll have a nasty drive back down the hill tonight."

He agreed and wished her goodnight. Claudette walked upstairs to her bedroom and undressed slowly, conscious of the sound of the pounding rain. In her ears, it was like a baby's cry, petulant and insistent.

CHAPTER EIGHTEEN

PANAMA 1907

Downstairs, Charles Lemieux was thinking that the rain was going to present a problem. He could not see the hills through the sheets of water cascading down from the heavens, and he was worried about the impact on the digging. They had had more than twenty inches of rain so far this week, and this was only the beginning of the rainy season. Work was slowed by the rain. For one thing, the West Indians, much to his surprise, were uncomfortable working in the rain, and, although they had adjusted, their output dropped dramatically. He was also concerned about the possibility of slides from Cucuracha Hill, though he had said nothing to McCormick.

What really worried him, though, were the continuing disappearances of men from the work gangs. He was not accustomed to sloppiness and wanted to get to the bottom of it. A rumor had started among the West Indians that someone was carrying people off, and, while dismissing it publicly, he wondered whether there was any truth to it. The jungle was untamed, and he was not certain that some of the Indian groups were not still wild in there. He had heard one of the dynamite men say there were "suckuyas" in the woods, and he had laughed at the superstition of these simple people. When he had asked the maid what a "suckuya" was, she had laughed shyly, asking him what he knew about "suckuyas" but had explained that they lived out in the woods, waiting to suck the blood of the unwary. He had shaken his head, laughing at her, and, immediately, the hood had come down over her eyes. He was not ready to buy the "suckuya" theory, but something had to be done if morale was not to suffer. It was this that he and McCormick were now discussing.

"We have to find out what is going on with these men, John. The rumors are growing, and some of them are quite odd. We can't afford to allow a problem to develop. There's already some anxiety among the Negroes over the return of the yellow fever. It would be disastrous to have them become skittish over these disappearances."

"Actually, it has already become more noticeable since that big, white fellow disappeared. Barnes. Wasn't that his name?"

Lemieux did not know, but McCormick had hit on the thing worrying him most. The man's whiteness and accent made him highly visible, and Lemieux worried that his disappearance would prompt a reaction the black workers' had not.

"John, I need to get to the bottom of this thing before it gets out of hand. You know how rumors can destroy a project. I remember when I was working on the rail in Montana territory in '94, somehow word got around that someone had discovered a gold mine fifty miles away from where we were. I knew it was false. Had been cabled the news from headquarters and told the contract workers so. I lost seventy percent of my civilian workforce in eight days. Completely killed the project. I can't go out there myself, but I need someone I can trust to ferret out what's going on. I've heard these men are being dragged off by everything from jaguars to something the West Indian Negroes are calling 'suckuyas', whatever they are. I can't have this. Particularly not now the President's coming."

"You're right, sir. If this isn't solved, it could raise questions about leadership. And..."

McCormick saw Lemieux wince, recognized the unintended cruelty of his remark, and stopped, an apology on his lips. He had no idea how much that thought weighed on Lemieux's mind. In the last six months, nearly sixty men had run off. The purchaser and a few others who were missing men from their individual gangs knew of this, but he had kept the problem close. With the President's impending visit, however, scrutiny was bound to increase. He had secretly been investigating the hovels in Colon, Panama City, and particularly in La Boca, as these were the areas where the West Indian Negroes were clustered, but the disappeared men were not showing up there.

In fact, a second story was beginning to emerge, one that did not make any sense but had to be investigated anyway. In addition to the "suckuya" story, the West Indians were saying a spirit jaguar was dragging the men off. They said it had the power to change its shape to that of a woman. In some stories, she was Indian; in others, she was white, but whatever she was, she could lure men from their women and children. That is what Lemieux found strange. The men were leaving their families, disappearing into the depths of the Panamanian jungle without a trace. He had his men looking for a jaguar because it was possible that men were being dragged off, but they had found nothing. He had no jurisdiction outside the American ten-mile-wide sphere of influence and was reluctant to go to the still new Panamanian government with his problem.

In any case, he was not certain what the new government in Panama could do. Since their country had been carved out of Columbia three years before, the Panamanians had lived in a state of fear only partially relieved by the American presence. Columbia, along with the rest of Latin America, had seen the outstretched hand of the United States folded into a fist, and they had trembled, wondering when it would strike again. Still, the government would have to be contacted if the men continued to disappear. Remarkably, there had been no questions about the requests for more and more men. Whenever he faced a difficulty with the Commission in Washington, Edward Bryant appeared like an angel, smoothing the way, clearing obstacles, persuading men, and through that support, the canal was moving forward.

McCormick, afraid he had given offense with his last statement, had been waiting for the Colonel to continue, and now Lemieux said, "We have to investigate the stories about a jaguar dragging men off. I want to do this quietly. So far, there's been no real fuss, only the whisperings. If, however, I send in a party to look for it, I give the story credence; and if we fail to find it, then we have a real problem on our hands."

Lemieux paused, then added carefully, "There are also the political considerations."

There was no need to explain. He had just authorized McCormick to go into Panamanian territory to pursue whatever was taking the men.

"I'd like to go, sir," McCormick replied, excitement in his voice.

"You realize if you do, I can't accept responsibility for you in Panama's territory. If for some reason you were caught, I would have to deny any knowledge of your being there."

"I understand fully, sir."

This was the reason he had invited McCormick to dinner, and, now, with the doctor's agreement, Lemieux again became aware of the sense of foreboding that had been present all day.

Maybe, he thought with a wry smile, *I've been talking to those West Indian Negroes for too long. Next thing you know, I'll be looking over my shoulders for a "suckuya." Whatever that is.*

He stood, and McCormick did likewise. For a long time, the two men looked at the pouring rain in silence, each wrapped in his own thoughts. McCormick agreed to take three men and leave before daybreak, heading into the deep jungle north of the canal where the men seemed to have disappeared. In the distance, Lemieux heard the rain-muffled sound of the exploding dynamite and shivered.

This is a strange land, he thought.

The two men shook hands, each wishing the other well. Neither man guessed this would be the last time they would see each other.

CHAPTER NINETEEN

PANAMA 1907

Lemieux awoke quickly, his senses alert. Something had awakened him, but, not sure what it was, he laid, allowing his mind to collate the night sounds. Everything was quiet. Suddenly, he sat bolt upright. That was the problem. Everything was quiet. He rose swiftly, trying not to awaken Claudette whose naked body lay face down next to him. Lemieux quietly dressed, the sense of foreboding coming back with the force of a hypnotic suggestion. He pulled on his tunic, counting the minutes since he had awoken and not heard a single explosion. That could only mean one thing. Work had stopped for some reason, and there were no good reasons for work stopping. He could now hear the sound of a truck's engine straining as it climbed the hill, and that was enough to confirm his fear. He walked swiftly down the stairs, buttoning his collar as he went. As he pulled open the door, the driver, soaked and with a mad look on his face, shouted, "The Cut, sir. Culebra. It fell."

Lemieux felt the coldness come over him, but he straightened his shoulders and said calmly, "Slowly, Corporal. What happened?"

The young soldier gulped and started again. This time, he was much more controlled.

"The south face of the Culebra Cut has fallen in, sir."

"Thank you, Corporal. Casualties?"

"It looked like a lot, sir, but I didn't go down in the hole. Captain Boyle sent me here as soon as it happened."

By this time, they had reached the truck, and the corporal took off down the slippery hill. Driving in the approaching dawn light, Lemieux wondered if his luck was finally turning. He knew, as most engineers did, that the completion of large projects was part genius and mostly luck. He had been very lucky so far, and, if the early fatalities due to yellow fever were excluded, this project had so far proceeded with a minimum loss of life. People died all the time in the Cut, but the numbers had been well within the projected range. Now, this slide threatened to change that. He urged the driver to hurry. Taking one of the trains at Miraflores, they flew down the tracks, but soon had to stop because the railway had been twisted. Lemieux walked to the front of the train but could see nothing in the dark. He swore sharply and ordered the train back to Miraflores. Here, he got into the truck again and headed east. When the truck stopped by the jungle at Pedro Miguel, Lemieux jumped out and scrambled down the incline into the heart of the cut. By the time he reached the bottom, his hands were raw, and his tunic bore the marks of the red clay that formed the topsoil of the land. He jogged across the bottom, using the smoke from the waiting train on the other side as his guide. Men were standing about, and, quickly calculating the cost of this, Lemieux swore again. Soon, he was steaming down the north tracks toward the cut at Culebra.

As the train pulled up, he could make out not so much the slide itself but the changed shape of the hill against the lightening sky. Captain Boyle met him as he stepped down before the train had fully come to a stop.

"Well, Boyle, what happened here?"

"The south face just fell in, sir."

"Damn it, man. I can see that. What the hell caused it?" The captain collected his thoughts, then replied stiffly, "The rain, sir."

Lemieux was about to respond when the man added, "And the fact that we have been cutting too vertical a path through the rock, sir."

Lemieux looked at the young captain, aware of the implied rebuke. Boyle was a geologist by training and had earlier warned Lemieux that the structure of the rock did not allow for the kind of cut being made. Now, however, was not the time for the debate. Lemieux asked if there were any casualties.

"I'm not yet sure of the number, but I do know it is considerable, sir. This slide came all the way across the bottom, and the cut is completely blocked. I am sure we've lost the dynamite gang. That's ten for sure. One of the Bacyrus shovels is buried, and that's another eight men. We are attempting to dig some people out of the locomotive, but there is not much hope they'll be alive. I have the gang bosses trying to get a count right now."

As they talked, the sky lightened, and now Lemieux saw the sharp incline that had been created by the fallen mud and rock. He shuddered at the thought of those hundreds of thousands of tons raining down on the artificial valley below.

"Two things, Captain. One, when I crossed over at Pedro Miguel, I saw your men standing around. We already have one tragedy. Let's not create another by wasting time. I want them back to work immediately. Standing around will do them no good. Two, get me up on a hill so I can see the damage that's been done."

The Captain turned away, giving orders quietly to his second in command. Within minutes, Lemieux heard the mournful sound of the siren coming from the direction of Pedro Miguel and smiled thinly in satisfaction. He and the

Captain reboarded the train, which took off down the track deeper into the Cut at Culebra.

Twenty minutes later, having climbed to the top of Contractors' Hill, Lemieux stared speechless at a scene from hell. He struggled to keep his face expressionless but was not successful, and an awed "My God" escaped. For half the distance between Gold Hill and Coal Hoist Bend, a distance of close to a mile, the cut had been filled in with the fallen soil. His first thought was that nothing could have survived under so much dirt and clay. The whole face of the cliff had disappeared into the cut, and frantic, small figures in the bottom were trying to scrape away the dirt that had buried the men there. How many men? Fifty? A hundred? He had no way of knowing until a count was done, but what consumed his mind was the size of the slide. The fallen clay had pushed across the fifty-foot floor and maybe about fifteen to twenty feet up the side of the opposing face. Looking black in the morning light, the clay lay in what, from this height, seemed an even, soft spread across the canal, joining the two halves of the country that his skill had sundered.

Trapped under the tons of rock was the twisted form of a locomotive. The engine and the first three cars were undamaged, and these lay in ironic splendor in front of the horror behind them. From where he stood, the train seemed like a giant worm struggling to pull itself from beneath some ponderous load. Lemieux continued to stand, staring at the holocaust below. Everything was out of place, and at the far end of the slide, a truck was perched in preposterous balance on top of the mud. It seemed unscathed, perfectly capable of driving off, except there was no road, only a precipitous drop of fifteen feet to the floor of the cut. Lemieux stood, not sure what order to give, his mind stunned into uselessness by the sheer scale of the disaster. The young Captain also stood waiting for the order that would activate the energy still waiting below, but Lemieux continued only to stare, something inside him uncomprehending, grappling with what the human response would be to this malevolent act of nature.

As the sun rose higher in the sky, Lemieux turned to look at the half of the cut that had escaped the slide, and this brought something approaching sanity back. Yet, he recognized that the normality of the section of the cut leading southward toward Pedro Miguel was just as absurd, just as frighteningly unreal.

In the new light, the cut lay exposed to the sky, and Lemieux stared at the red clays that had become the bane of his existence. He was standing on a terrace above the Panama Railway tracks that ran along the rim of the cut. In the bottom, work had restarted, two trains of two cars each, U.S. 213 and 209, moving with a swift yet ponderous dignity toward the trucks waiting in the shadow of Gold Hill, the cliff he had created. A banana tree had managed to survive this destruction, and it waved in splendid isolation on the man-made hill, surrounded by the ascending lines of smoke from the trains. To the right of the tree, a larger column of smoke was billowing upward, and Lemieux realized he was seeing the result of the gigantic explosion he had heard only moments before.

The West Indian dynamite blasters really have mastered the art, he thought.

They had become more proficient, and the pace of the excavation had increased. Now, a group of them, tiny figures from this height, were lifting the wooden ties to create new rail lines as the huge shovel was moved to where the blast had left its deposit. Lemieux knew he should do something, say something, but he did not want to look back to the left. Where he now looked was the Panama he was building. It was orderly and manageable. To the right was chaos, and he wanted to see only what he was creating, not its antithesis. Finally, heaving a great sigh, he turned to the captain.

"Well, Captain, you have been patient. Out with it."

The young man straightened his spine but said nothing. Lemieux continued, his voice less threatening.

"Come on, Captain. Let's hear what you are thinking. And that is an order, soldier."

"Sir, I have indicated before that the geology of this section of the cut would not allow us to cut these narrow walls. If we persist, sir, the slides will continue."

"What do you suggest, Captain Boyle?"

The captain hesitated, and Lemieux made a sucking noise with his teeth, showing his impatience.

"It would be easier to demonstrate with a drawing, sir."

"Describe it, soldier. If I don't understand it, we can go to the drawing."

After a moment's hesitation, the captain bent down and drew what looked to be a series of ice cream cones in the mud. The rain had eased somewhat, but it still came down fairly hard, and the shapes were difficult to maintain, but the design was clear.

"The geology of the cut is structured like this drawing, sir. You will note that most of the weight is distributed at the top. As we have cut away at the bottom, the top has become too heavy, and it will slide. That is what happened this morning."

Lemieux nodded, then moved briskly down the slippery slope. The captain hurried to catch up.

"Let's get down there and see how much damage has been done."

When Lemieux reached the site of the fall, the smoothness he had seen from the top of the hill was nowhere apparent. The huge mudslide had picked up the giant machines and tossed them all over the bottom of the cut. Injured men lay everywhere, and in a tent where a makeshift hospital had been set up, a black-skinned man was bellowing in pain. Lemieux forced himself to look where the man's knee had been wrenched away from the socket and now lay at right angles to the thigh. That leg would have to come off, and he reached over and held the man's shoulder, looking him in the eye all the while. Lemieux was not sure the man knew he was there. All around him the carnage was evident, and the place had taken on its own smell, that of blood freely flowing and laying exposed in the heat. It was a smell like no other, and it assailed the nostrils. Lemieux had not smelled anything like this since Cuba in '98, when the bodies would pile up too quickly for the medics, and the smell would fester in the air. He had hoped never to smell that particular odor again.

"Captain, I want every available train turned into a transport to get these men to the hospital. Those with the best chance of survival go out first. Find out as quickly as possible our death count and report to me. And I want you and the director of construction to report to my office at five this afternoon. I expect a plan to stop these damned landslides by then. Ask the trainman how far down the Cut he can get. I want to see the rest of this."

The captain saluted crisply and said, "Yes, sir."

As Lemieux was about to board the train, the Captain, looking at the devastation surrounding them, asked, "What will we do now, sir?"

Lemieux studied the Captain's face for a moment and then replied, "We keep digging, son."

CHAPTER TWENTY

Haight put the phone down slowly, his face masked in thought. He was a tall man, well over six feet, and his body, though it had lost some of the suppleness that had made him a ferocious tennis player in his youth, still carried the marks of the athlete. He was not thinking of tennis now, however. The police had called. They were treating the young girl's murder as a priority but had found out nothing. Not that Haight was surprised. If Romulus was involved, the police would be out of their league.

Dean Greaves had written a report for him. It was intriguing, but Haight wondered what it all added up to. Still, something was there. His anger had grown in the week since the girl's death. He understood death, but it had never been this close, and the look of shock on the boy's face had aroused something cold in him. Dean was still in a daze, blaming himself for his friend's death.

Haight had asked him to find out as much about Centron Corporation as he could, largely to take Dean's mind off the girl. Not expecting much, he had been surprised at what the boy had turned up. Centron was powerful, controlling shipping, rails, and air freight in a world-wide network that had no national boundaries, no discernible attachment to philosophical or religious groups, and no government. It was everywhere. Gold and diamonds in South Africa, oil in the Middle East, sugar throughout the Pacific. The report revealed not so much a corporation as a universal business state that functioned like a government–with one notable exception. No citizenry restrained its actions. Haight knew the power of corporations, but even he was surprised at the size and scope of Centron.

Two things worried him. First, Centron was a major supplier of advanced arms to the United States' military. That would explain the difficulty he had getting information from his colleagues in the State Department. No one really wanted to fool with the defense contractors, never being sure who was protecting them.

Second, Centron was an unusual corporation. While Dean had been able to identify the board members of the subsidiary companies controlled by Centron, he had not been able to find a single director of the umbrella corporation. Haight could deduce from this that either the corporation did not exist–and it obviously did–or it was not a corporation in any conventional sense. The only way to ensure that kind of secrecy would be to have a wholly owned company, but that did not make sense. The combined assets from Dean's preliminary analysis suggested that Centron subsidiaries were worth several trillion dollars. No one could generate that kind of wealth without selling stock. Something must be off with the report. Yet, he had the same feeling about this as he had about the boy's senior thesis. It seemed incorrect, yet someone had been willing to kill for it. Now something was again telling him to trust the boy's research.

Height walked to the table where he had placed the thin envelope and sat, deep in thought. There was a link between the boy's thesis and the corporation, but what was it? Dean had tried to trace the development of Centron, but the corporation was actually not that old. It appeared in 1963, registered in New York. Yet, Haight knew that even if the name was new, the wealth that created it had to be much older, and now Dean was trying to track down the genesis of the individual companies within the giant corporation. The defense companies were the ones of immediate interest since Haight knew from experience they always played fast and loose with the rules. The boy was slowly tracking down the financial sources that created each of these companies, but so far he had had little noticeable success. Dean was now following an interesting strand of financing for Dayton Electronics, one of the Centron companies that made guidance systems for fighter planes. Haight was not sure the boy would find anything useful, but he was getting a bad feeling about where things were headed.

He also did not like being one step behind whoever was controlling these events. Somehow, they had known he would be in Panama and had met him with someone he knew. That seemed careless, but he had never actually met Romulus before. If he had not broken the rules and sought out Romulus' identity when the man had been loose in Vietnam, Haight would not have recognized him. Yet, it showed an incredible confidence to send the man to meet him. Also, although Dean was blaming himself for the girl's death, Haight was not certain that his own questions had not been the spur to action from the other side, so the feeling that he might be responsible also nagged him. This was an unreasonable response and not one that was particularly helpful, but he could not shake the feeling.

Something else bothered him. José Nieves had disappeared. Haight had been trying to find the agent for three days and so far had not even been able to get a hint of where the man had gone. Frustrated, he had called the State Department and asked for Jeremiah Hanscom, who had been stationed at the embassy in Chile. Hanscom had retired twelve months before, but Haight had been given his home number by State. Once Haight mentioned Panama, Hanscom had been cautious but agreed to meet. They had been at Harvard together, part of that idealistic group of graduates who entered the State Department in 1956. Also, he owed Haight a favor. When, in 1970, Haight had operational control for Southeast Asia, Hanscom, caught in his own war in Chile, had secretly asked Haight for help. Haight had diverted operatives from Vietnam to help with the problem, and Hanscom had been able to prosecute his little war without appealing to Congress. This had all been done on the quiet, and Hanscom knew Haight had taken a terrible risk for him.

The first sentence of Dean's report was graphic. "Centron is like an octopus," it read. Haight turned the pages slowly, trying to make connections where possible. It was amazing how pervasive the influence of the corporation was. It had subsidiaries in the United States, England, France, Germany, Australia, and Canada. From what he could tell, it controlled most of South Africa, and its holdings in Asia were mind-boggling, with plants in North and South Korea, Vietnam, and Japan. Even China had succumbed to the influence of Centron. There were rubber plantations in the Pacific and cocoa in the Far East. It surprised him to find that, with this worldwide reach, the company had its headquarters in Panama City. From what the report indicated, only a tiny fraction of the corporation's interests was located in Latin America. Haight sat back, thinking. Why would a corporation of this size be headquartered in a place as remote as Panama? There did not seem to be any compelling reason for that. Centron controlled a huge shipping fleet, and Panamanian registry was not unusual, many companies doing this for a variety of reasons, not all of them illegal. Many banking houses had found Panama amenable to their interests and were beginning to locate branches there, but there seemed no reason for Centron to do so.

Yet, there they were, sitting in the middle of the banking district, right off the Via Espana. Why? Why had they needed to check him out? What was Romulus' connection to all this? Haight had not been able to find out if Romulus still worked for the Agency, and, in fact, no one seemed to know who Romulus was. Above all, Haight wondered what Nieves meant when he said no one could trust anyone else. That sounded as if something was going on in the government itself. Why would Panama and the canal raise such emotions? It is true the United States had invested hugely in the construction of the canal and had basically kept it going for the last sixty-plus years. Capital and imagination had built the canal, not labor and geography. Ownership properly belonged to the one with the imagination to conceive the project and the will to command the labor that built it.

That is the way of the world, he thought.

He could understand the opposition to the return of the canal. However, the conflict did not appear to be a sufficient reason for the U.S. government to be threatened by internal struggle. Haight had little respect for politicians, but one thing they knew how to do was compromise, and this was precisely the kind of situation where they would. So what was creating the problem? Why were some of the politicians so stuck on hanging on to the canal? And what had this to do with the boy's senior thesis? Or the death of the girl?

Haight stood, realizing he was getting nowhere. He needed more information before he could answer any of these questions. This pure analysis was frustrating, and he knew a frustrated analyst was a danger to himself and those around him.

His thoughts turned to his wife and her safety. He called security at Haight's Plastics and Paints. The retired FBI agent who served as deputy director of security for the company came on the phone with a seriousness Haight always found reassuring.

"Hello, Andy. I have a favor to ask."

"Course, Mr. Haight."

"This may be nothing, but after the break-in up here, I was thinking maybe we should have someone at the house for a while. Just as a precaution, you understand."

"Yes, sir. Better safe than sorry. I'll put someone on it right away, sir."

Haight hung up, feeling uneasy that he was being out-thought. He was not sure what–or whom, for that matter–he was protecting against, but as more information came in about Panama, he was becoming nervous. In the near distance, the imposing cupola of the Capitol glinted in the dying sunlight. At the other end of Pennsylvania Avenue lay the White House.

The brackets of world power, he thought, wondering what role these two buildings played in the mystery in which he now found himself enmeshed.

Haight had been with the State Department a long time and was only now healing from the agony of Vietnam. The insanity of the war had forced him deeper and deeper into a neurosis in which the truth had become irrelevant, and reality had been a phantasmagoric spectacle. Death had become a number and life expendable in that war that could not have been won. He had slowly deteriorated into drink, analyzing the data that came into the dark rooms below the huge complex in Virginia. As the lies of victory had become public truth, his mind had given way, and finally he had had to take a leave of absence. That leave might have saved his life. It had certainly saved his mind. Through it all, his wife had been a steady, calming influence in the brittle energy his mind had created, an energy that constantly threatened to spin out of control. She had been his salvation and his solace, the one hold on a reality that had crumbled each night as his overactive mind saw the horror of a battlefield he had never experienced. Reality had to be reconstructed every morning, and Madeline's face had been the point of reference when he had tried to shed the torture of the night, seeking the safe haven that lay in the daylight.

Haight felt a certain nostalgia for those more innocent times when he had, full of idealism and fire, gone into the government. America had then fired the imagination of the world. It stood for good in a world where too much evil had been seen. There had been, among the group who entered the State Department that year, a sense of history, of destiny, of certitude that they would make a difference. They had come through Harvard with a daily diet of the evils of the Soviets, and the repression of the Hungarian Revolution had simply crystallized the burning sense of righteousness they brought to the job. Haight had worked long, awful hours in the pursuit of the glory he thought the United States' due. For a decade, the burning zeal had endured and, indeed, increased as the country confronted the evil of communism and began to win a tenuous victory over the hearts and minds of the more enlightened people in the emerging world.

Vietnam changed all that. Haight sighed, feeling the heaviness come between his shoulders, as was always the case when he thought of the loss of innocence that Vietnam represented. Vietnam had ripped away the veil for him, had exposed the platitudes for the lies they were, and as he had watched this, lost in a world that seemed to have no stability, anything and its opposite had become true. The moral certainty of a decade earlier had disappeared, and he had, for a long time, lived in a fog induced by alcohol, self-deception, and the interminable statistics out of Southeast Asia that, after a while, he no longer believed but faithfully reported as truth. The mental breakdown had been almost a relief. The doctors said he was simply protecting himself from the stress, the tiredness that comes from constant pressure, but he had known better. Haight knew that, in losing his innocence, his belief in something that was good and pure, he had lost his self. Were it not for the face of his wife, he would still be searching in the hazy land between reality and unreality, calling out in fear at the ghosts that lurked there. He looked over his shoulder where the picture of the elegant woman sat on the mantel of the fireplace. Not conventionally beautiful, Madeline Haight had a dignity that made beauty irrelevant. The picture had been taken on the front lawn of the family mansion just outside Charleston, South Carolina. In it, she wore a white dress with a high collar and ruffles.

She looks almost Elizabethan, he thought with a wry smile, walking into the room and running his fingers gently over the face of the picture.

There was an unaccustomed gentleness in his eyes and a softness to his face as he gazed at the photograph. He would return to Charleston tomorrow after speaking to Jerry Hanscom. He was driving himself since Hanscom had insisted he come alone. As he pulled out of the underground garage and headed toward Route 50 East, Haight never noticed the black Cadillac that jerked away from the curb, melting easily into the traffic.

When he pulled into the parking lot of the Nag's Head Inn, Haight was wondering why Hanscom had chosen a place so out of the way.

Who would guess that this place is less than three hours from Washington? he thought. *It looks like Mississippi.*

The inn was picturesque though and situated close to the sea. Haight could smell the acrid seawater in the air and, if he held his breath, could almost hear the sound of the sea moving against the shore. The parking lot contained several cars that, from the license plates, must have belonged to tourists because the states represented were from all over the East Coast. Jerry Hanscom was being smart. Not only was the place remote, reducing the possibility of an accidental sighting, but since most of the people were tourists, Haight's presence was easily explained to any locals. Haight smiled, comforted by the professionalism.

Once inside, he quickly located Hanscom, and the two men were led to a second-floor, minimally illuminated dining area overlooking the inlet from the sea on which the inn was built. Hanscom, Haight noticed, looked carefully around the parking lot before he sat. There was, however, nothing out of the ordinary, and he leaned back in his chair, saying in a hoarse voice, "You have certainly stirred up a hornet's nest, Haight."

Haight was surprised at the abruptness of the address, and he replied, "Believe it or not, Jerry, I have no idea what I've stirred up. Maybe you can fill me in. Everybody seems skittish about Panama."

"And you don't know why?" Hanscom asked suspiciously.

Haight shook his head.

"Then you must be the only one. Everyone's trying to distance themselves from Panama until the crisis is resolved."

Haight frowned, but in the darkness the other man could not see his face, and so he asked quietly, "What crisis, Jerry?"

The man hesitated, then said, "The government is locked over this issue. The President wants it, but some very powerful men are against it, and it's not all political. There is talk of a group of major corporations that have been blocking this."

"Centron?" Haight asked innocently and noted with satisfaction the intake of breath.

"What do you know of Centron, Haight?" came the breathless query, and Haight, a little impatiently, responded, "Practically nothing except that it seems to control every industry that is worth controlling, and that everybody seems to be in a panic when I mention it. What is the story with Centron, anyway?"

Again, the man was silent for a while, and Haight waited.

"When I was in Columbia, the word was like a ghost. Everyone knew of it and, yet, no one knew it. People spoke of Centron in hushed tones. I'm not sure most people fully believed in its existence, but it was always there."

"Jerry," Haight interrupted impatiently, "it is a corporation, registered in New York and Panama City, for God's sake. I don't understand what you're talking about."

"Haight, describing Centron as a corporation is like saying a gale-force hurricane is a windy day. It is much, much more, and no one seems to understand its purpose. We think it's American because so many of its interests, when we have seen expressions of them, seem to coincide with our own. You will note I said 'coincide' because we have no idea whether it supports us or not. We have no idea who runs it or what its purpose is. It has, on more than one occasion, bailed out the U.S. government in Latin America, though. Many of our actions down there seem to attract Centron's attention, and, very often, Centron provides political and financial aid."

"You mean that we–and by 'we' I assume you mean the Agency–are accepting help from an entity we don't know?"

It was now Hanscom's turn to be impatient, and he said shortly, "Don't be naïve, Haight. You have lived with the politicians. We have an impossible situation in Latin America. Do you think we are going to look a gift horse in the mouth?"

He paused, then added carefully, "Actually, word is that you had their help as well."

Haight looked sharply at the man sitting in the dark and, a nagging doubt in his mind, he asked quietly, "What do you mean? What help?"

"Well, I only heard this fourth hand, and then only sketchily, but as I understand it, your big victory, the secret one in Cambodia, was organized by Centron."

Before the man was done, Haight blurted, "Romulus!"

Hanscom asked quizzically, "What? Who is Romulus?"

Haight, realizing his error, responded, "Oh, just the name of that operation in Cambodia. It was a perfectly straightforward mission. At least, as straightforward as anything in that war was. What had Centron to do with it?"

"Like I said, it was just a fourth-hand rumor, but word was Centron had co-opted the mission and was pursuing its own agenda. For us in Latin America, it was not too hard to believe. We had seen it too often in our neck of the woods. We assumed you guys in Southeast Asia were aware of Centron, too."

Haight sat silent for a long time, thinking of the disappearance of Romulus for that two-week period, his sudden re-emergence, and the bloody massacre that constituted the "victory" for which they had both been saluted. He could never explain why he had reported the mission a failure and Romulus dead but then continued to repeat the call signal on schedule for two long weeks, refusing to accept in his heart what his mind had already determined. Nothing had ever been said about Centron being involved in the operation. Maybe that was significant, but right now, it was more important to find out what Hanscom knew.

"What does all this have to do with what is going on in Panama right now?"

"Most of this is speculation, Haight, so you will have to evaluate it on your own. The word is that there is some relationship between Panama and Centron. No one seems sure what it is. What we have been able to determine with some certainty is that Centron's origins are roughly contemporaneous with the building of the Panama Canal."

"You keep saying 'we.' Who is the 'we'?"

In the darkness, the man stirred uneasily, and Haight could sense the discomfort in the atmosphere. He decided to spur things along.

"Look, Jerry, I have no idea what I'm in. I've asked what I thought were innocent questions, and already a girl is dead, and my place in Washington has been broken into and burnt.

I have a very frightened kid living in my house right now whose life may be in danger. If you know anything, Jerry, I need to know what it is. I have no cover here at all and no backup."

The man continued to be silent for a while, and when he spoke, the hoarseness was more pronounced, like someone had grated his throat.

"Haight, you are worried about a couple of lives? You have no idea what these people are capable of. When Chile started to go up, a group of us wanted to encourage them, and Washington was going along. All the intelligence suggested that Chile would have arrived in the same place without our intervention. Then, through the secret corridors came word that Centron wanted the timetable accelerated. It could not wait for the natural change of government we knew was bound to come. And like that, Washington changed its orders, and we were told to make the revolution happen. We protested, of course, and in three days–three fucking days, Haight–seven of the most senior agents in the northwestern sector of South America were dead, and the names of four others were given to the Chilean government as a warning. And Washington did nothing, Haight. Not a goddamned thing. Eleven men were eliminated in three days because they had a different interpretation of the situation."

Haight was shocked at what he was hearing but felt compelled to ask, "Do you know what the relationship is between Washington and Centron?"

The man answered quickly.

"No. I didn't know why I had been spared. I had been very vocal in opposition to the plan, but once that had happened, I requested a transfer that was granted in no time flat. I spent the rest of my time in Washington, and I retired as soon as my time was up. I had no faith in State or the Agency after that. It was always spooky working with the Agency boys, but they had been eliminated as easily as the

State Department's men were. I just wanted to get out, and I did as soon as I could."

Haight could understand the man's fear, though he did not feel much better informed than when he had arrived. Still, he had to analyze the data, and the first rule of data analysis was not to collect and analyze at the same time. It was too easy to miss data elements when you stopped listening. It was getting late, and he had to drive back to Washington. It did not look as if Hanscom knew much more, and if he did, he clearly was not telling. Haight realized they had not eaten and, feeling guilty, asked the man if he wanted to order anything but was told no. Haight pulled out a fifty-dollar bill and laid it on the table for the waiter, standing as he did so. Hanscom continued to sit, clearly concerned about something. Haight, not wanting to seem insensitive, stood leaning against the rough, wooden rail that enclosed the balcony.

After a while, Hanscom said, "Jack, don't trust anyone where Centron is concerned. And if you intend to do any financial traces of the company, don't do it by computer. It's too clumsy, and they will track it back to you. I can't define the relationship between the government and Centron, but I can tell you that relationship exists. And one last thing: After I got back to the United States, I was practically going insane trying to figure out why some of us had been spared, and I received a message."

"A message?"

Hanscom moved, and, in the darkness, Haight could not see what he was doing. Then, the man handed Haight a sheet of paper. Haight walked over to the doorway and held the paper close to his eyes. On the sheet was a single sentence that read: "It is never necessary to punish all of the guilty. Punishment of one atones for their sins."

"What the hell does it mean?"

"I've never been sure, but I have always been struck by the tone. Sounds like a person who believes he is a just god or something. I can only tell you it scared the hell out of me when I got it, and I am still scared today. Which leads me to my next point, Haight. I owed you. I consider my debt fully repaid. Don't call again."

With that, the man took the piece of paper and disappeared down the stairway.

Haight, disgust in his voice, said, "Goodbye."

Outside, a summer chill had come, and, hunching his shoulders, Haight walked briskly to his car. Because he had not seen the black Cadillac that had followed him from Washington, he never noticed that it was no longer in the parking lot, nor did he think much of the man who had just left him and who would lose his life this night for having talked to him.

Three hours later, he reached his townhouse in Washington and immediately called Dean.

"What else did you find out, Dean?"

"Well, sir, after we spoke, it occurred to me that one way to trace Centron was not just through the individual companies but the oldest companies. I started with those that were older than fifty years, but too many showed up, so I went to those more than seventy-five years old, and there were only two. One is Craven Shipping, and the other is Southern Railroad. I'm still working on Craven Shipping, but it's clear, even with the limited amount of work I've done, that it is huge. It is also structured in the same way Centron itself seems to be structured; that is, it's an umbrella group that controls several other shipping lines. The same thing is true of Southern Railroad. That, too, controls a whole complex of rails across the southern United States. I haven't tried to work out their total freight, but it must be incredibly large."

The boy stopped, and Haight heard the shuffling of papers. Then, he said, "It seems that an Edward Bryant started both these companies. The rail company is first registered in 1886, and the shipping company seems to have started around 1901."

"Keep digging around and see what you find. Anything else? If not, may I speak with Mrs. Haight, please?"

When Madeline Haight came to the phone, he immediately felt his mood lighten as the strong New England voice with its faint hint of Englishness seeped into his ear.

"Well, Jack, are you coming home any time soon, or shall I file for divorce?"

Haight laughed, responding, "If those are my choices then I'll be home immediately. Has Dean spoken to you about what's going on?"

"Not much. He has been very busy with the work you have given him, and he's struggling with the girl's death. Yesterday, I found him staring at a photograph of her. He didn't want me to know it, but I believe he was crying."

"He seems very focused on the research when he speaks to me. He's never mentioned her."

"He's a man, Jack. He's trying to fight this through on his own. Can you imagine what it must be like to have walked out of Lehigh one day and be caught up in something like this the next? I've tried to leave him alone. By the way, I was pleasantly surprised at your sensitivity in giving him the work to take his mind off the girl's death. You do surprise me from time to time."

Haight laughed again, pleased at the compliment. She was, however, continuing, her voice more guarded this time.

"What are you mixed up in this time, Jack?"

Haight felt the pleasure drain rapidly from him. When he answered, his voice was distant and uncertain.

"I'm not sure I know. It's all a mystery to me, but it's a dangerous mystery, and people seem to be afraid of it."

"What about your friends at State?"

"That's the strange thing, Madeline. The fear seems to be concentrated there. I can't get a straight answer out of anyone."

"That ought to be answer enough then, don't you think? By the way, are you worried about the boy's safety?"

"Not really. I haven't seen any evidence that anyone is after the boy. They wanted his papers, and they have those. Why bother with him?"

"Then, may I ask why you are sending a guard over to the residence?"

Damn, Haight thought. He had forgotten to tell the deputy director not to mention the added security at the house, and the man must have called her immediately. Still, Haight did not want to frighten her, so he lied.

"That's just to make the boy feel comfortable, Madeline."

"Well, I fail to see how an armed guard around the residence can make anyone more comfortable."

Haight knew he had been chastised, but the guard would stay. They soon hung up, with Haight promising to take the company's jet down the next day.

Pouring himself seltzer water over ice, Haight returned to the balcony. He had not been entirely honest about one thing. He did know who Edward Bryant was. The man was a legend, one of the giants who had seen in the American century and had provided it with the means to travel by ship and rail. Haight remembered that the man had died tragically when, well over sixty at the time, he had tried to build a new city somewhere in the South American jungle. Now, if the boy's research was accurate, here he was, right in the middle of the problem Haight was trying to solve.

Haight sat very still. There was no noise this high up, and the lights of the city made a hypnotic backdrop to the workings of his mind.

What did he know for a fact? A girl was dead because she had been in possession of letters written seventy years ago. A boy had guessed at something involving the Panama Canal, and this had apparently started a chain of events that led to the girl's death. An agent he knew from the past had shown up to meet him, obviously thinking Haight would not recognize him. Two agents from the Latin American theater, Nieves and Hanscom, had both indicated that something was afoot within the government, and the agencies were stymied because it was impossible to know whom to trust. Both had suggested that the troubles had something to do with the return of the canal to Panama. A shadowy but powerful corporation, Centron, had emerged as somehow being linked, maybe even a spur, to these events. No one seemed certain of, or willing to explain, what its role might be. One thing was certain though. Everyone so far had been afraid of something, and these were not men who were easily frightened.

Haight knew that half the battle of analysis was identifying the beginning point, but what was the beginning point? Was it the letters? The boy was uncomfortable talking about them. He could not accept the boy's silence anymore, because if the letters had come from Dean's aunt, then she, too, was an exposed asset. Romulus would not hesitate to eliminate all possibility of exposure of whatever information they were trying to hide. If that were true, then the boy was in danger as well. Haight was glad he had sent the guard to the residence but now felt as if he was being watched from afar, not aware of who, or where, the watchers were. He sat up, looking at his watch, surprised to find that it was after one in the morning.

He picked the phone up, and when Dean answered on the first ring, Haight said, "You should get some sleep, Dean. If you don't, you'll be no use to me or yourself."

The boy mumbled something, aware of the irony of the statement. Haight quickly got to the point.

"Look, Dean, I've tried to respect your privacy, but we are beyond that point. I assume you made copies of the letters. Does your aunt still have the originals?"

There was a long pause, and Haight said impatiently, "Dean, are you still there? If you have copies anywhere, I need to see them. Immediately, if possible."

The boy cleared his throat before answering.

"Mr. Haight, I took the originals from my aunt. She didn't give them to me. I can't explain what came over me, but when I saw them, I knew they would be helpful to my research. She would not have allowed me to read them, so I took them."

The last words were said defiantly, as if he expected criticism, but Haight had no interest in how he had gotten the information.

"Do you have copies?"

"Yes. I left another set with my mother in Brooklyn. She has no idea what's in the packet, though."

Haight thought for a moment, then said, "Could you let her know I will be coming to pick up the packet?"

"Okay, sir. I'll call her right now."

"No need, really. Why don't you wait until tomorrow morning rather than waking her up? I probably won't leave here until around eight."

Dean having agreed, they hung up.

Outside, forty stories below and opposite the high rise where Haight sat thinking, two men also sat. The big man with the slight accent had called and told them where to go. They had parked the car at an angle so they could look up the front of the building, and, though Haight would have sworn he was unobserved, the night glasses they kept trained on the fortieth floor had identified him on the balcony. They relaxed now that they knew where he was, and one of them called a number to convey this information.

Upstairs, Haight fell asleep on the couch, his long legs stretched out across the burgundy-colored Persian carpet. His last thought before falling into a deep sleep was that he was overlooking something.

CHAPTER TWENTY-ONE

WASHINGTON, D.C. 1976

Romulus put the phone down, aware that knowing where Haight was had made him no less tense and impatient. He still had no idea what the old man in Long Island was up to, but something was different this time. Romulus thought it was stupid, if the information was so valuable and dangerous, to allow anyone who had access to it to live. He had cautiously mentioned this to the old man, who had laughed weakly and said, "All in good time, Thomas." It was almost as if the old man was luring Haight on. Just as he had predicted, Romulus had recieved reports of multiple inquiries for information about Centron, and it had become very clear that someone was putting together a profile of the corporation.

Romulus did not know all of the inner workings of the corporation, but he had been around the old man long enough to understand that much about it was secret. The old man had not been this involved for many years, and though Romulus would occasionally be summoned to the mansion, this had become more rare as the man had weakened with age. Sometimes, he could see the frustration as the man struggled with a body that was closer to the grave than to life. The incredible mind that lay encased in the dying body remained sharp, and the old man seemed to know everything that went on in the vast empire that was Centron.

The old man had no heirs, Romulus being the closest thing to a relative. They had been together a long time. Forty years to be exact. Even then, the man must have been in his fifties. In the dark room, Romulus picked up a drink, allowing his mind to drift back to when he had first met the man. It had been 1936, in Friebourg, where his father, Thomas Werner, had been secretly organizing the town in opposition to the French "occupation," as he had called it. In Berlin, a man had started to talk of the Fatherland, and he, thirteen at the time, had felt pride in this new word. His father had been a butcher, but when people found out about his association with Berlin, they had shown a new respect for the meat-cutter, and Romulus (Thomas at the time) had learned his first lesson in power. He had become a terror in the town as the inchoate violence crystallized into a policy of insiders versus outsiders. Understanding well his father's concern with the deterioration of the Fatherland through the encouragement of the weak, he had begun to practice the skills that would later make him feared. Watching the pain on the faces of the victims (mostly small children at the time) had given him an exquisite pleasure. He had learned to hate, with a purity that was almost pristine, any semblance of weakness and had taken a particular pleasure in hurting those who showed fear and cried.

It all ended rather abruptly. His father had been found dead in an alley not far from the butcher shop, both of his hands cut off. Young Thomas had been awakened by a tall man in a dark coat and had known even then that his life was about to change. When the man took him from the house to the alley where his father laid, Thomas had felt nothing except, briefly, anger. The man explained that he could identify the killers but indicated that, if Thomas took his revenge, he would have to leave Germany for good. He had nodded, and the man took him from that horrible alley into a new world. First, though, he was driven to a house just outside of town, and there committed his first killing. The man had placed a gun in his hand and pointed it while the boy pulled the trigger several times, emptying the gun into the two men who had been asleep in the room. It was his first experience of the dizzying feeling that came with killing, the sense of power and pleasure, until later he learned how to control it.

Now, sitting in the dark, Romulus felt the memory of that night exciting him. He had never touched a woman, and though he commanded men, never associated with them either. He was loyal to one person: the old man in Long Island, the only one who could incite fear in him. In America, young Thomas had watched as Germany was overrun by the weaker races who surrounded her like a pack of hyenas. Careful not to investigate too closely what role his benefactor had played in the dissection of Germany, he did know that the old man had supported the Marshall Plan, which poured money back into the country after the war. He had financed Thomas' education, and Thomas always had the sense that the man was there, watching over him.

It had been easy, with the man's enormous wealth and influence, to have Thomas placed in government, and, as if he knew exactly what Thomas craved, the old man had arranged for him to become part of the secret world of the CIA. There, Thomas Werner became Romulus. He thrived on the work, and when the United States became involved in Vietnam, and that war was conducted without any recognizable rules, he found his home. Throughout it all, he served his benefactor's interests. Every one of his assignments had a commercial tinge, and he would get a call from the man or some representative soon after he had been assigned a mission, indicating that this or that needed to be done, all in the context of the official mission.

Romulus learned to fear the man when, in 1948, he had been summoned to a farmhouse in western Maryland. Three men escorted Romulus to a basement where, much to his surprise, there was what looked like a chair used for electrical executions. The men had grabbed him, strapped him into the chair, and placed the conducting band around his head. He sat under a single spotlight, listening to the urbane voice of the man explaining why he had to die and the nature of the pain he would feel. Romulus had fought the urge to beg for his life, certain he would die. He heard the quiet hum of the electricity when the generator had been activated and stiffened in anticipation of the jolt. For a long time, he heard nothing except the generator, for the voice had stopped, and as his fear grew, his body became drenched in sweat, every muscle stretched taut. His mind had felt brittle, and just when he had been losing consciousness, the lights had come on. The man, immaculately dressed as usual, had strolled into the room, a smile on his face.

At first, Romulus felt a wave of hatred, but the man slowly released him, unconcerned with his anger. When Romulus tried to stand, his legs had not worked, and the man lifted him. They had stood like this for some time, body to body, eyeball to eyeball. Something indefinable passed between them, something that made Romulus a slave to the man. The chair had not been purely for Romulus' benefit, for soon after, three men were brought in. The first was placed in the chair and questioned. When he provided unsatisfactory answers, the man quietly turned away with an air of resignation and turned the generator on. Only one of the strangers had been left alive when the man had gotten the answers he wanted. Romulus had never forgotten that night. Moved to the inner circle after that, he served the man faithfully, part son, part slave, but loyal in every way.

That is why he was so confused about what was going on with Haight. It made no sense to hesitate now. Yet, the old man had been right in anticipating the inquiries about Centron. They now knew it was the boy who was doing the research, and, though public information about the corporation would not ordinarily amount to much, Haight's particular talent was interpreting data and seeing patterns. Romulus was becoming impatient, but the old man had warned against precipitous action. He regretted now not having read the letters. Though aware of the dangerous direction of his thoughts, he was beginning to feel vulnerable simply following orders. Clearly, he would have to get his own information.

He picked up the phone and dialed. It was answered on the second ring, and Romulus, without introduction, said, "Pick him up and take him to the house in Pinewood. I'll be there soon."

Romulus felt the little prickles of fear playing around his heart. Having taken an action without the old man's consent, he had to succeed. His relationship with the old man had always contained the kind of affection a master has for a slave. Unlike the slave, Romulus was very well compensated, but the attachment was functional. If he caused the old man's plans to go astray, he would be killed without a moment's thought. In spite of this, he needed to be better informed because, sooner or later, the conflict would break out into the open. Haight was still gathering information and, until he was certain of the stakes, would not act. That was the difference between him and basement dwellers like Haight; they lacked the capacity to act without their precious information.

Haight would not have lasted five minutes in Vietnam, Romulus thought.

If there was one area of comfort, it was that Haight seemed to have as little information as he did. Romulus knew that a pattern of questions, if followed long enough, could become a road map, and sometimes it was possible to get ahead of a man in this way. He would do this and hope the old man did not find out. In the darkness, Romulus rubbed himself and soon unzipped his pants. It was only minutes later, when his breath was returning to normal, that the drowsiness came, and he fell into an uneasy sleep.

A hundred miles east of where Romulus slept, two men moved out of a darkened car and swiftly crossed the small lawn that fronted a house. An hour earlier, the woman had set the alarm, and they would have thirty seconds to disarm it once inside the house. The window in the den proved no problem, and each man kept a silent count in his head, ticking off the seconds. The alarm box was conveniently illuminated, and the numbers were quickly entered. Their tennis shoes made no noise as they slowly ascended the stairs, and, upon reaching the door of the bedroom where the man and his wife slept, one of the men handed the other a handkerchief. They silently entered the room, going to opposite sides of the bed. Swiftly, they clamped the handkerchiefs over the noses of the sleeping couple. There was only the briefest struggle, and then both bodies went limp. Within minutes, the male was trussed up in the back of the car, which headed west on Route 50. The driver was very careful. The man they knew as Romulus was coming, and they had seen him work. There would be no screw-ups.

CHAPTER TWENTY-TWO

BARBADOS 1976

The old woman drank the bush tea slowly, straining the white, watery, heavily sugared beverage through her gums. A breeze had sprung up, and, given the slight chill, it would soon rain. A certain heaviness had pervaded her spirit for the last few days. She had come to the conclusion that the boy had taken the letters, and the loss left a vacuum. She sighed, turning sideways on the long wooden bench and, in doing so, faced away from the land where she still grew "ground provisions." At least, she had until very recently. Now, she rented the ground to a St. Lucian woman.

She had not been able to adjust, the way so many in the village had, to the new supermarket in Holetown. That thing had upset the way the village worked. Now, the markets were dying, and everybody seemed to prefer the food they stocked on the long shelves. And it was putting everybody out of business, too. She sucked her lips, making a rude sound.

It really is a shame how dese worthless people just left Carter like dat, she thought. *And some uh dem still owe he money.*

At that moment, she heard the accented voice of the St. Lucian woman, who must have returned from the field, saying, "Miss Audrey, you talkin' to you'self again?"

The old woman had not heard Antoinette approach, and, surprised, she responded, "You shud stop creepin' up 'pon decent people, Antoinette. Dat is wat you people does do in St. Lucia?"

Antoinette did not reply, and the old woman said, "Wat you do in de ground today?"

The old woman could almost hear the pout she knew was on the younger woman's face.

"I did weedin' down by the grasspiece. Yuh know, if we cud find a man to get dem rocks out uh de grasspiece, we cud expan' de groun'. Right now, we aint doin' nutting but wastin' dat land."

"Wunna St. Lucians gettin' worse dan Bajans. All wunna t'inking 'bout is lan'. Wunna aint had no lan' in St. Lucia?"

Again, Antoinette did not reply. This baiting was not unusual, and she would just have to wait it out. The old woman was continuing, but now her voice had lost its stridency, becoming almost nostalgic.

"In fac', wunna aint like de young Bajans, at all. Dey don't want to work. Dat is why all uh wunna tekking over de jobs. I couldn't fin' uh single Bajan who wud come an' work de lan' fuh me. In fac', if you hadn't to come along, I don' know wha' I would do."

"You sayin' t'anks, then?" the younger woman asked mischievously.

Immediately, the voice was strident again.

"Don' mek me vex. Wha' I got to t'ank you fuh? You livin' better here dan in dat little islan' you come from."

"St. Lucia bigger dan Barbados, Miss Audrey, so you can't call it a little island."

"Dat just go to show how ig'rant wunna people is. St. Lucia bigger dan Barbados!" she ended indignantly.

The younger woman sat on the step, protecting herself from the sun. There was nothing new about the conversation, and there was no way to win, so she changed the subject, moving it into safer territory.

"W'at you t'ink 'bout de Americans givin' de canal back to Panama?" she asked.

The old woman sucked her gums again but did not answer. When the younger woman looked around, the old woman's eyes were closed. She called Miss Audrey's name softly, but there was no answer.

Antoinette, seeing the steady rise and fall of the woman's flat chest, said, "She somet'ing else. One minute she arguin' wid yuh, an' de nex', she gone. Ole an' foolish," she ended affectionately.

When she had come from St. Lucia, the old woman had taken her in until she could find a place to live. That was almost ten years ago. Antoinette decided to let her sleep and soon walked away.

She was wrong, however. The old woman was not sleeping. The question about Panama had simply reminded her of the letters, and her mind had drifted back to Rupert. She wondered what had become of him. In the last few days, she had found herself thinking about how her life would have been if Rupert had not gone to Panama. She heaved a sigh that seemed to come from some deep and inaccessible part of her. Until the morning the ship left, she had not realized how much she had built her expectations around Rupert. In her heart, she understood that life with one of the Barneses had always been a dream, but the memories still remained.

She had not gone to meet him the night before he left, but the next morning, rising early, she had rushed off to Bridgetown, hoping to see him before the ship sailed. Having no idea where to go, she had asked and been directed to the Careenage, but the boat taking the men out to the ship had already made its last trip. The Panama-bound ship, sitting in the inaccessible distance at the mooring, had been pointed out to her, and, dejected, she had walked back to the village.

As the days passed, the reality of her pregnancy pressed in upon her, and she fought the despair. Her mother watched her closely, though now that Rupert was gone, she had moved back to her own bedroom. One morning, her mother stared as Audrey brought up her breakfast in the corner of the small yard. She could no longer protect her secret, and, straightening up, her sides aching from the violence of the retching, she looked directly into her mother's eyes.

"You got anyt'ing to tell me, Audrey?" the woman asked.

She stood foolishly staring at her mother, whose face showed only calm. It was a calm Audrey feared because it suggested her mother was controlling herself, and Audrey knew from experience her mother was no good at it. Her father joined them, and they stood in this uncomfortable triangle, waiting. Fearing her voice would break her mother's control of her emotions, she kept quiet. Across the yard, the woman's posture gradually changed, becoming more erect, as if someone was shoving some hard, straight object through her. Audrey was in a quandary. She did not wish to speak, not wanting her voice to change the link that had grown between the three of them. On the other hand, her mother might see her silence as rudeness. In desperation, she nodded, and her mother immediately went into the house, soon returning, body rigid, with a hard, black leather belt.

Unlike previous beatings, her mother said nothing, her lips pulled together in a tight line. Audrey felt no fear. She, in fact, began the walk across the yard to meet her mother, whose rigidity faltered for a moment as she stared uncomprehendingly at this sacrifice. Her hesitation did not last long, and Audrey felt the weight of the woman and the belt on her shoulders, her back, her legs, everywhere. She did not cry out to reduce the punishment but stood silent, flinching with each lash. It was a strange beating, these two women, connected by blood and the lash, standing across from each other, both aware of the finality of this action.

In the corner of the yard, her father watched, saying nothing, but yet a part of this strange goodbye, this ritual of leaving. Only when the belt connected with her eye, and the blood spurted out, did her father intervene. There was no resistance as he gently held her mother's arm when it reached the top of its swing. They stood like this, her father looking forlornly at her mother and her mother looking with the weight of disappointment at her. The anger dissipated quickly, for her mother seemed older and tired. Shoulders curved, in her eyes, Audrey saw, to her surprise, what looked like fear. The woman's lips moved repeatedly, and after a while, Audrey made out the words, "Nothing good aint goin' come uh dis." Her mother did not explain what those words meant, and Audrey, consumed by fear, did not ask.

Three days later, her mother sent her to the far north of the island to live with an aunt, her father's sister. Her aunt was strange and lived alone, close to the sea in Cove Bay. It was a lonely existence, out there where the sea constantly pounded the land, the sea spray flying high in the air and hanging for long moments, but she was glad to get out of the village. And since her aunt never questioned her about the child, she lived in relative peace.

There was one prohibition. Her mother had instructed her not to contact anyone in the village until the baby was born or tell anyone she was pregnant. The village had been told she was getting out of hand and had been sent away.

Audrey did not mind. The peace of the backwoods suited her, and her aunt was attentive, though often forgetful. She was patient and caring, and Audrey grew to feel a great attachment to, and dependency on, her. The long days in the far north were different from anything she had ever experienced. Almost self-sufficient, growing all she needed, her aunt only occasionally went into the village to buy a few groceries from the small shop there. Unlike so many women her age, she did not attend church. Once, when Audrey asked her why she did not go, the woman took the big-bellied girl by the hand, leading her over the rocky track to the cliffs. She stood there, feeling the wispy spray from the waves that pounded into the cliffs and was blown by the wind onto the land. Her aunt held her head back, her eyes closed.

Finally, when Audrey asked her what she was doing, she replied, "You don't feel it?"

"Feel what?"

"God."

Audrey muttered a prayer under her breath, but her aunt laughed harshly, saying, "Dere got mo'e God out dere in dat wave dan in dem people church. Most uh dem worshippin' de devil an' don't even know it. Look at de rainbow ovuh dere in de middle uh dat spray. Tell me dat aint God."

Audrey was worried, but looking at the rainbow, felt the power of the colors. Her aunt suddenly reached out and, resting her hand on Audrey's swelling stomach, said something Audrey did not understand, at the same time waving her other arm at the sea and the rainbow in the spray. When Audrey asked what she had said, her aunt looked at her slyly and responded that she was praying, adding after a while, "Somebody got to pray fuh dat chile. It aint natural."

"Wha you mean?"

But the woman continued to rest her hand on Audrey's stomach, and to say something under her breath. Audrey was uncomfortable but did not want to offend, so she allowed her to carry on.

Still, she wondered why her mother had said nothing good could come of her pregnancy, and her aunt was saying that her child was not natural. Her mother had been hurt and disappointed, but her aunt never worried about the pregnancy, never said anything to suggest she disapproved. In fact, it seemed quite the contrary. She enjoyed any life coming into the world.

However, when Audrey asked her what she meant, the woman replied, "Don't min' ole people. Mos' uh de time dey does be right only by accident. Never min' wha I say. You goin' have a beautiful chile."

Audrey was not satisfied. Later that night, she lay on her pallet, trying not to notice the smoke that lingered from the fire hearth on which her aunt cooked. She wondered if both her mother and aunt knew or suspected she had been impregnated by a white man, and it was this they considered unnatural.

Why her mother should feel this way was unclear, since she was so light-skinned herself. Many of the children in the village were brown-skinned, so somebody was having babies with white men. Still, it was like some dark secret everybody knew, but nobody wanted to face. Some of the women got money haphazardly from the men, but more often than not, they had received all they would by the time the child was born. It had become worse when all the men from the village headed off to Panama. It was unnatural the way the women had to work the land and support everybody, and Audrey wondered if she would be any different. Rupert was now gone a few months, and she had heard nothing from him.

Her mother came to St. Lucy periodically to see her, and Audrey waited anxiously for any news of Rupert, but she was always disappointed because the woman never mentioned the "Barnes boy." Her mother was herself pregnant, and Audrey felt both embarrassment and a kind of comradeship with her. They spoke more easily now, and her mother appeared to accept Audrey's pregnancy. One day, she questioned Audrey closely about whether she was going any place where she might be seen. Audrey answered that she was not, but her mother continued to question. After a while, her aunt yelled to her mother to stop bothering "the girl." That started a passionless argument, but eventually her mother ordered her again not to go out, adding, almost to herself, "Dat would spoil ev'ryt'ing."

Audrey looked at her quizzically but said nothing. Every time her mother came, she would mention Steven Thornhill, whom everyone called Hurricane. He had always tried to talk to Audrey, but she had ignored him. She was not sure what her mother was up to, but she had no interest in Hurricane or anybody else except Rupert. Yet, what had he promised her? She would awake at night sweating because she dreamt he had been hurt and could not write.

Thus, her fantasy was created, but it was preferable to the alternative, and in any case, it was possible he was hurt. A small number of the men had returned to the village, but not one came back as he had left. Something was always wrong with them. Most had missing limbs and stayed in their houses. These were often nicer than others in the village, because built, as it was said, with "Panama money." They were an odd bunch, staring out their windows, not saying much to anyone, shouting at the children to stay off their property. This, in particular, was strange in the village because, although people were property conscious, this exclusion was never extended to children. Audrey had not talked to any of these men until Angela's father had come home. He lived with Angela's mother but was married to a woman in the next village. When he came home from Panama, his body crushed, his wife had not taken him back, and Angela's mother, in spite of the criticism and the unsolicited advice of the women, had allowed him to move in with her.

It was while visiting Angela that she saw the crushed man. He was covered by a blanket, though the day was hot. Audrey had tried not to look at the broken body, but her eyes flitted to him time and again. He had become angry and, finally, called Angela over to him, ordering her to take off the blanket. Angela had asked why, and he had responded, looking accusingly at Audrey, that he wanted to satisfy "Miss Eyes" over there. Angela had hesitated, but he insisted, and she pulled the blanket off the man. Underneath, he had been wearing a vest, and this Angela pulled up. Audrey had involuntarily screamed, for the flesh had been torn away, and a thin layer of leather stretched from the hip to just under the man's arm, covering half his chest. The ribs were gone, and all that was left was this leather band-aid that held his insides in. Before Audrey could think, she darted from the house, her flying body followed by the sour laughter of the man and Angela's sobbing.

Alone at night, fearfully wishing nothing like this had happened to Rupert, she would get up from the pallet, quietly open the door (easy with the constant noise of the pounding sea), and walk out into the night. It was strange that, in the village, she had always been afraid of the night, but out there where there was nothing but the ocean, the short shrub that clung gallantly to the thin soil of the sea-spattered cliffs, and the coconut trees waving like giant sentinels in the distance, she felt no fear of the night. Her aunt changed something in her. The woman would often head into the depths of the woods, searching for herbs, and Audrey would accompany her, gradually becoming comfortable among the trees and the darkness.

So, Audrey would walk toward the sea, feeling the shaking of the land as the giant breakers flung themselves into the north coast. The Caribbean Sea and the Atlantic Ocean met there, and the meeting was not gentle. The north coast was a constant swirl, the two waters pressing against each other for dominance. The north coast bore none of the characteristics of the western Caribbean, but was constant white water that boiled and frothed and threatened. Standing on the edge of the cliff with the sound of the waves in her ears and spray on her face, Audrey would reach out her hands to something in the night, feeling alone between heaven and earth.

In de dark, I musta look like a mad woman, she now thought, laughing quietly. *It is a wonduh I di'nt fall in de sea. An' as dey say, de sea aint got no back door.*

It was now hot, but, unwilling to move, Miss Audrey swung her feet under the long bench, continuing to dream. In her mind's eye, Rupert was still young, still the tall, white boy with his skin turned a light brown by the sun. She still saw him on the horse, and, even today, when everything inside had dried up, the nights they had spent lying in the dark on the ground after a drizzle still fired her imagination. He was the first person she was sure had loved her, her mother having always been distant, and her father, though occasionally affectionate, moody. The other girls in the village had been friendly, but she had never thought of that as love. When Rupert approached her, something opened to him, and she lived in a land of fairy tales and sweet touches. She had been surprised at the feelings her body could generate, never having, until then, understood what Angela meant when she talked about "feeling sweet." After Rupert left, she tried to reproduce the feelings, and sometimes she could lie very still and let her mind drift back to some moment they had spent together. The night she frequently allowed to fill her mind was when she was certain she had become pregnant. They had been making love for several weeks, and though she enjoyed the feelings that coursed through her body, it had been nothing like what Angela described.

And then, just like that, on that night, she had felt her mind spinning, and somewhere in the distance she heard her own voice crying out something inarticulate. Deep inside her mind, she had known this was a mistake, that she should make him stop, but her will betrayed her, and she clutched at him, feeling the lines of pleasure run along the divisions of the nerves and muscles on the inside of her thighs until her spirit seemed to be trying to escape her body through her flexed and straining toes. Her eyes had been closed, and when she opened them, the sky had been blocked out by the man. His body was a hole in the night sky, and she had fallen in.

The old woman stirred on the bench and sighed deeply. She heard, along the road next to the house, someone going by in a horse and cart.

Must be Pa Pa, she thought. *Not too many people usin' donkey-cart nowadays. Even poor people drivin' car now.*

As if to confirm her thought, a voice hailed her from the road, asking if she wanted anything from the shop, and she answered quickly, indicating that the St. Lucian girl had brought all she needed, but thanks anyway. Pa Pa hailed her again, and she listened to the gradually disappearing sounds of the wheels as the cart moved past her home.

"Rupert cause me too much trouble," she said aloud. "But I shoulda know he would."

All the signals had been there, and her mother had recognized them. Audrey knew that she, too, had been warned. The dream had started almost at the same moment she began to lie down with Rupert.

In the dream, she always comes to an abrupt wakefulness, and immediately, the relaxed look of sleepiness leaves her face, replaced by a number of minute lines.

A low sob escapes her, and it must have been heard outside because her mother knocks on the door. Audrey wipes her eyes in the cloth of the flattened pillow, and says, "Yes, please?"

"W'at wrong wid you, Audrey?"

There is guarded concern in her mother's voice.

"Not'ing. I doan feel good. My belly hurtin' me."

"Well, if it doan stop soon, I goin' gi'e you somet'ing fuh it."

Audrey makes a face, and her mother walks away, satisfied that it is not very serious. As soon as her mother leaves, Audrey jumps up and, shrugging off the loose, cotton nightgown, hurries to the broken piece of reflective glass that serves as a mirror, looking at her reflection. She runs her hand over her stomach. It is flat, giving no indication of the life that lies hidden inside. Her hair, black and long, is her pride, and she flings it over her shoulder in that uniquely feminine motion. She fancies that her breasts are getting larger. Suddenly, the face in the mirror changes, crumpling a little, and she runs back to the bed, again seeking the darkness of the pillow. The heaviness is in her body, and though she knows her mother will soon be calling to her, she is unable to move herself to get dressed.

The dream slowly dissolves, and she is remembering her fight with Rupert last night. They had met on the hill to the east of the village. She does not mind sneaking out of the house to meet him because this secrecy, this privacy, makes him more hers. As they sit close to each other on the fallen leaves and talk, she wonders if it is a good time to tell him and how she will tell him, what words she will use. Rupert had talked about getting away from the island and his sister, and she is frightened, a new experience for her. Audrey looks at the trickle of spring water that passes by their feet and watches as a small flower (a hibiscus, she thought) drifts slowly by, occasionally catching some unseen snag, but inexorably dragged downstream.

"Audrey," Rupert says, "suppose I went to England. We still have family there. Wouldn't that be great?"

"I suppose so," she answers, her voice low.

"You suppose!" His voice holds a fake outrage. He does not understand her. "What do you mean 'you suppose'?"

Audrey continues to stare at the stream. The flower has now disappeared. Suddenly, Rupert falls back on the ground, reaching out and pulling her on top of him, saying as he does, "You could come with me, Audrey."

His voice, lazy as always, holds the note of exaggerated sincerity that accompanies the lie they both accept. Audrey lays half on top of him, conscious of his body. Something inside her turns over, and she thinks of her own body. The morning has confirmed her fear. She is pregnant. She had waited for five weeks, hoping against hope her period would come, but nothing had happened. Strangely enough, there is no fear. She has an undefined faith in… something.

"Hey, what are you crying for?"

Rupert's voice breaks into her thoughts, and she presses her head closer to his chest as he automatically strokes her hair.

"Don't cry, please. I'm never going to leave this place anyway," he finishes with a bitter laugh.

He does not understand, and she cannot stop crying. She feels something crystallizing inside him, something hard and ugly, and knows he is fighting the feeling her crying has evoked. He sits up, in the process pushing her away.

"Audrey, you don't have to act like that. I was only dreaming about leaving. You know I wouldn't leave you."

She wipes her eyes with the back of her hand and, looking at the young man, asks earnestly, "You sure 'bout dat, Rupert? No mattuh wha' happen?" and Rupert, seeing that she is more controlled, nods. She continues, "Suppose somet'ing happen dat you di'nt expect at all?"

"Like what? Give me a 'for instance.'"

"Well…I don' know. Okay, suppose my foot get cut off?"

The crisis is over, or seems to be, so Rupert laughs and says, "No. That's out of the question. No one-foot woman for me. Suppose you had a child, and it had one foot, too?"

He laughs hard, again falling to the ground. The mention of a child has started Audrey's mind on the thought she had been on the verge of forgetting, and she does not join his laughter. Rupert does not notice, however.

"Rupert, wha' you would do if I did pregnant?"

He thinks for a long time, then says, "I suppose we would get married."

He sounds unsure, and she asks, "You don' know wha' you would do, right?"

He does not answer, and she adds, "Well, Rupert, I pregnant."

He looks up sharply, eyes narrowed and nostrils flared, and Audrey feels the newly discovered strength drain from her with every labored breath he takes.

"You are not serious."

There is no question in his voice as he gets to his feet and looks down at her, his face tense.

"You are not serious, Audrey, are you?"

She nods, crying. He is silent for a long time; then, he pulls her to her feet. His face has closed, and his eyes shine in the darkness.

"How could you?"

He shakes her, then thrusts her away from him. Audrey feels a part of her dying. She has lost feeling in her left side and thinks her heart has stopped as she struggles for speech but nothing comes out, and her mind wrestles with the emotions she feels. He holds her arms tightly, and she welcomes the pain.

Finally, she gasps, "It aint my fault, Rupert. Not my fault."

"Then whose fault is it? Mine?"

He is out of breath and is pacing back and forth between two mango trees, almost as if they are boundaries he cannot cross. She watches as he withdraws into himself, feeling a curious pity for him. He really is not so big after all.

Rupert, she thinks, *you don' got to worry.*

She hopes to transmit this to him but says nothing. Even in her rejection, she cannot shame him. When he speaks, however, she, for the first time, feels something akin to hatred for him.

"Audrey, you have to get rid of it."

"No."

There is a note of finality in the word, but Rupert, his sensitivity dulled by fear, does not notice.

"You have got to. You can't have a child. It's not...not...fair," he collapses weakly. There is nothing left of his defiance now, and that alone has given grandeur to his insensitivity. She wants to console him, but the distance is too great.

"Don' worry, Rupert. I goin' be alright."

She is not bitter, not even angry, only empty, and this surprises her, even as she stares at Rupert, who is crumpled against a tree, staring at the stream. She walks over to him, ignoring the slight stiffening when he feels her hand on his arm.

"Don' worry, Rupert. You goin' be alright. Nuttin goin' happen. I got to go home now."

He turns, silently following her lead. As they walk out of the darkness created by the trees and into the pale ghostly night light, Audrey feels split into two beings. Her fear and anger, for the moment quiescent, are buried. She thinks of her life and the life inside her. The thoughts are not unpleasant, so she smiles, and looking at Rupert's serious profile, she whispers, "It alright."

"You goin' mad, yuh kno'."

The old woman started, not recognizing the voice at first, still lost in the remembrance of the old dream. It was the St. Lucian woman, Antoinette.

"Wha you dreaming 'bout, Miss Audrey? I bin here fuh ten minutes watchin' you sleep. I bring yuh food, but I di'nt want to wake you. Wha you did dreamin' 'bout? You did movin' 'bout a lot. I did watchin' to mek sure you di'nt fall off de bench."

"Wha' I dreamin' 'bout is my bidness. I don' know where wunna St. Lucian people learn manners. Lis'nin' to people when dey talkin' to demself. I aint know where wunna people come from at all, at all."

Angry, torn between the world left in the dream and the woman before her and wanting to be alone, she told Antoinette to leave the food and go. The younger woman, accustomed to her rudeness, sucked her teeth. Taking the lunch inside the house, she placed it on the wooden table, covering it with a soiled cloth. Upset with the old woman, she did not stop on her way out but shouted over her shoulder that, "somebody should know bettuh dan to sleep out in de hot sun 'cause somebody else goin' have to tek care uh dem wen dey sick." The old woman snorted, continuing to sit arrogantly on her perch. She would eat soon enough. In fact, she had been eating less and less these last few days. Hunger had become distant, and, now that the letters were gone, she seemed to be living in the past more and more. In fact, she was not always sure what was the past, easily slipping in and out of her memories, her dreams, and her life. This did not disturb her. What did worry her was the boy who had taken the letters, and the relationship between them he did not know about. He believed her to be his aunt, not suspecting that the relationship was much closer than that.

This led her to think of her mother and the deception they had engaged in so long ago. The old woman could see her mother's face clearly. Light-skinned, or what the villagers called "yellow," the woman had exuded confidence, and some of this rubbed off on her daughter. Everyone said they looked more like sisters than mother and daughter, with their identical light-brown skin and their long, black hair. The hair, which Ruthie hated and would from time to time cut off, was very unusual in the village, where most of the women had thicker, more densely packed coils. The long, black hair was a source of envy, and Audrey never did understand her mother's objection to it, although her claim that it kept her neck hot was believable. Audrey had never felt the need to cut hers, and all her life it had been a source of pride. Even now that it was gray and her scalp could be seen through the thinness at the top, she still brushed it every morning and plaited it into a single, long strand that lay even now behind her back.

But her mother...her mother... The woman sighed softly, thinking of the strong woman who had saved her so long ago.

CHAPTER TWENTY-THREE

Barbados 1906

Ida-May Haynes hurried past Ruthie's house, down the dirt road bordered on both sides by the wooden houses of the villagers. The air seemed to crackle around her as she tried to get more speed out of her pudgy legs. The hen pecking hopefully into the dry dirt was too slow in moving, and Ida-May's foot, a considerable weapon at any time, shoved it roughly out of the way. It ran away, clucking indignantly. Ida-May was unconcerned; in fact, it is doubtful she was even aware of the hen since the collision must have been comparable to a battleship plowing into a piece of flotsam. Pendulous breasts leading the way, Ida-May swung into the side alley that led to the meeting place: the mango tree. The tree was deserted, but this did not deter her.

Giving herself two seconds to catch her breath, she lifted her voice and yelled, "Elsie. Vida. Sylvie. Lottie. Gloria. Ruthie. Wunna come out here now."

So saying, she squatted and wriggled around, trying to find a portion of the tree that would comfortably fit the contours of her not-inconsiderable bottom. Failing to find comfort, she sighed, settling for the least discomfort. The effect of her shout was only slightly less than magical, as from every gate emerged a woman, so that by the time Ida-May had contoured her body to the tree, she had an audience of nine. When Ida-May yelled like that, it meant only one thing: she had news. The women waited expectantly, no one daring to hurry Ida-May. They knew that sooner or later—most likely sooner—she would tell. Old Pa John once said that if Ida-May ever tried to keep a secret, it would literally choke her; indeed, one could tell from her rising bosom the effort this attempt at suspense was causing her.

She took a deep breath, surveyed her audience, and noting that Ruthie was not there, said, "I jus' come back from de tenantry, and you kno' wha' happen?"

She paused dramatically, practically daring anyone to guess. Finally, Lottie, who was less afraid of Ida-May than most and a little upset, said, "No, woman. We doan know wha' happen. Why you don' stop dis foolishness and say wha' yuh got to say."

Ida-May stared at her indignantly, then looked away to the other women, pointedly excluding her.

"Go to hell, Lottie. You always inna hurry. I suppose you dat way wen de lights go out, too. I don' kno' how you man does put up wid you. Tek yuh time, lady. Tek yuh time is wha' I say. If yuh rush de brush, yuh spoil de paint. No need to hurry. Wha'ever goin' get do, goin' get do, is wha' I say. But not you. You always inna hurry. And you aint goin' nowhe'."

The women groaned collectively, knowing Lottie was not one to take this upbraiding from anyone, least of all from Ida-May. They feared that now they would have to wait until the two women settled this before they heard the story. Lottie resented Ida-May, and, now, she stepped closer to the big woman, her voice dangerously low.

"And wha' de hell you mean by dat? Wha' you mean I aint goin' nowhe'? You talkin' like you goin' somewhe'. If I aint goin' nowhe', you kin tell me whe' you goin, Ida-May Haynes."

Ida-May was the very picture of forbearance. Composing her face into something resembling a smile, she attempted to avoid the impending quarrel.

"Look, girl, I aint lookin' fuh nuh fight wid you. I say wha' I say, an' I forget it. Why you want to mek uh big t'ing outa wha' I say?"

"You kin forget it, but I won't. You always tryin' to walk over people, an' you expec' dem to siddown an' let you do it, too. Well, maybe dese rest will let you walk over dem, but not me. So you doan forget dat. Doan forget dat I kno' t'ings 'bout you, too. So don't start me up."

The challenge had been thrown at Ida-May, and the pointed innuendo was not lost on the other women who now backed off to the two sides of the combatants. Ida-May raised her head to the sky in silent communion. When she brought her head—and presumably, her spirit—back to earth, she was ready. Her mammoth breasts heaved with the intake of breath.

"An' jus' wha' you kno' 'bout me, young woman? Jus' tell me dat. Wha' de hell you kno' 'bout Ida-May Haynes, yuh little harlot?"

"Goddam you! Who you callin' uh harlot? It aint me who got a man in Panama an' does lef' de house ev'ry night God sen', when my man bustin' he ass in some faraway country dat nobody aint even hear 'bout befo'e, and go down to de tenantry. It aint me dat does do dat, Ida-May."

Ida-May's face, large at all times, had become bulbous with rage, but she was still trying to control herself. Unfortunately, this was an unaccustomed role, and the effort was costing her. Voice carrying tremulously in the stillness of the women's attention, she said slowly, "But looka muh crosses. Don' t'ink dat I don' kno' wha' you tryin' to say. I kno' wha' sluts like you does say behin' my back. But ev'rybody know dat me an' de gentleman in de tenantry is jus' friends, and I faithful to my husban'. So I don' care wha' you say, Lottie Green."

Lottie laughed, a harsh, cruel sound, and Ida-May winced.

"You husban'!" Lottie guffawed, bending forward and resting her hands on her knees. "You husban'? Wha' husban'? Ever since, you walk 'bout tellin' people dat you marri'd to Joe, but you is such a foolish bitch dat you doan kno' ev'rybody kno' you is a liah. People does only preten' to believe you to save you face, but ev'rybody kno' dat you aint marri'd."

Ida-May was on her feet by this time, her arms, which hung shaft-like down by her sides, ending in hands that constantly opened and closed. Breathing hard, prominent ligaments in her thick neck corded, she tried to keep her hands at her sides.

One of the women, Vida, now worried, implored, "Lottie, Ida-May. Why wunna doan stop dis foolishness befo'e it go too far. Wunna goin' be sorry after, yuh kno'. Wunna better stop now or wunna goin' be sorry. Mark my words."

"Shut yuh tail, Vida," Lottie, sensing victory, shouted out of the corner of her mouth, not taking her eyes off Ida-May. "If Ida-May want uh fight, I willin'. Somebody got to show she dat she can't be sayin' wha'ever she like 'bout people."

"Wha I say 'bout you, Lottie? You tell me wha' I say dat aint true. You shou'nt talk 'bout people 'cause ev'rybody know 'bout you. Nobody aint goin' marri'd you 'cause you aint no good. Dat is why you can't keep uh man. You always got to be runnin' from man to man 'cause you aint no good. An' now dat ev'rybody man gone 'way to Panama, people aint goin' put up wid you runnin' down de few men dat lef' in de place. You ain't nuh blasted good at all, at all."

The voices had been rising, and the villagers, mostly women, gathered to see the outcome. It looked like a real bacchanal was going to develop, and no one wanted to be absent since this would be news for a long time to come.

Mimsie was shouting, "Ai, ai, ai. Tell it to she, Ida-May. Doan let she talk to you like dat. Tell she 'bout de underwears dat she carry 'way from Jordan store."

The crowd broke up with laughter. They all knew Mimsie, and it was the general opinion that the only thing she loved more than a fight was more fight. Even Vida, who had only recently attempted to stop the developing conflict, was suffused with laughter, and the two fighters, aware of their central importance, psychologically girded on their armor and prepared for battle. The crowd, aware of the subtle change in the women, fell silent, expectant. The difficulty was how to get the two women to start fighting. They were only inches apart, each with her face leaning toward the other, but those few inches were a no-woman's land, and anyone crossing it would be deemed the aggressor. Each woman stared at the other, eager to fight but unwilling to give up that slim claim to being right.

Then, Mimsie, laughter in her voice, shouted, "Looka dem two cocksparrow. Uh lotta hollerin' but no action. And I kno' dat Ida-May frighten as hell fuh she skin. She can't fight. She only big, but she aint nothin'."

Ida-May turned to shout some obscenity at Mimsie, and, in doing so, must have invaded the no-woman's land, for Lottie reached out, and, hands cupped and fingers flared into talons, scratched at Ida-May's face. Ida-May screamed, pain and hatred in the sound, and swung a clenched fist at Lottie's head. The blow was ill-timed. Since Lottie had been advancing, the fist missed, but the forearm collided with her head, and she reeled off to the right. Ida-May walked deliberately over to her and again punched her in the head. There was something masculine about the way she fought, and the outcome seemed determined.

Mimsie dug her elbow into her neighbor's ribs, hissing, "I bet yuh uh pint uh peas Lottie don't las' two mo'e cuffs."

The woman, holding the tender spot on her body where Mimsie's elbow had connected, shouted back, "You t'ink dat somebody is uh ass to bet w'en Lottie look like she 'bout to fall down. Look. She can't even stan' up."

It is uncertain whether Lottie heard the little interplay and responded or whether someone actually shoved her into Ida-May, but suddenly she was moving rapidly forward. Ida-May had no time to avoid the collision, and Lottie's head practically disappeared into her stomach. There was a great gush as the wind flew out of Ida-May's lungs, and Lottie, sensing the momentary weakening, fastened her teeth onto the nearest thing that presented itself. This, unfortunately, happened to be Ida-May's bulbous left breast. The shriek that knifed through the air silenced the crowd, for there was genuine horror in the sound. No longer were the onlookers laughing. They looked around guiltily at each other. Each knew what needed to be done, but no one wanted to be the first.

Then, Vida, a little frightened, said, "We bettuh stop dis befo'e dey get in real trouble. Somebody go an' get Ruthie."

That was all that was needed. The women surged forward as one and, after a struggle, succeeded in detaching Lottie from Ida-May's breast. Ida-May's dress was torn, and the nipple of the breast, like some dull eye, peeked out for a second before she closed her hand over it. The teeth marks were clearly visible, and Ida-May lay curled up, moaning, all the fight gone out of her as Lottie looked down on her mountainous victim, breathing hard. She tugged half-heartedly away from her captors. Not that she wanted to fight anymore, but honor demanded an effort be made to finish off the loser.

When it became clear they were not going to release her arms, she settled down, saying at the same time, "Dat should teach you not to bad-talk people, Miss Ida-May Haynes, married woman. You should t'ank de Almighty God dat dese people pull me off yuh, yuh don't know? If not, I wudda did really maul-sprig yuh ass. So you can t'ank God fuh dese people."

Ida-May, who had been moaning and holding her breast gingerly while being helped to her feet by two of the women, was on the verge of replying when a strong voice sounded.

"Hol' up, all uh wunna," Ruthie shouted, and the women stopped. Stepping slowly into their circle, dominating them even while holding both of her hands under her huge belly, she asked, "Wha' start dis?"

Vida opened her mouth and then closed it, looking questioningly at the other women around her. One by one, they lowered their heads, no one volunteering an answer.

"Yes. Dat is wha' I t'ought. Fightin' ovuh nuttin again."

She turned her eyes on the two combatants, and they both looked away. The tension was gone from the group, but no one could figure out what to do next. Slowly, willless, the crowd began to disperse, going in various directions.

Ruthie heard Ida-May say as she moved, bent from the waist, "She lucky dat I trip 'pon dat tree stump. Dat is all I have to say."

After a while, only Lottie, Sylvie, Gloria, Vida, and Ruthie remained, and Sylvie snorted, saying, "Yuh kno', we never did fin' out wha' it is dat Ida-May come to tell we."

There was a moment's silence as the other women looked at her. Then, they all burst out laughing. The laughter rang loud and strong as the women leaned forward, holding their bellies—all except Ruthie, who was staring down the road at a tiny figure weaving back and forth in the haze of the brutal sun.

Her eyes became watery as Miriam stumbled and fell, then got to her hands and knees and slowly pushed herself upright. The figure meandered back and forth across the road, oblivious to time but still aware of place. The laughter stopped.

Miriam had not lasted long after her child died but, for a few weeks, had kept up the appearance of normality, going to work on the Barnes' plantation and coming home to "cook, wash, starch, and iron," the litany used in the village to describe and circumscribe the women's work. Then, one day, Miriam had not come to the field, and, at lunch, Ruthie had gone to her house to find it empty. Miriam disappeared for almost a month. When she returned, it had been almost impossible to recognize her. The flesh had fallen from her body, and her eyes had sunk back into her head, giving her a skeletal look. Deep in her eyes, a fire burned, and when the fire became too hot, they would commit her to the mental hospital in Black Rock. When the fire cooled, Miriam watered it with rum the Barnes' plantation produced. It looked like the fires were cool now.

The women had become silent and fidgety, not wanting to confront this "firehag," as they had begun to call her. Most of them believed the child would not let Miriam go, that it wanted blood for its death. It had come back in the mother and now stalked the night, searching for blood to suck. When this had first been said to Ruthie, she had angrily cursed everyone in sight; since then, the women had avoided mentioning Miriam when Ruthie was around. Now, they were uncomfortable and wanted to leave. Ruthie could not believe that some of these same women had lost children of their own.

Dey gettin' on like Miriam is de only one wid troubles, she thought, moving out of the shade to go to the woman who was struggling to stay the course.

She walked carefully, her hand on her big belly, and when she reached the woman, took her in tow, bringing her back to the mango tree. The smell of rum came off Miriam, but it could not disguise the less subtle smells of her body. She was a walking miasma, some strange combination of urine and feces, sweat and vomit, and that fetid confusion of menstrual blood that had not been washed away. On top of this

Ronald A. Williams

was the sour-sweet smell of the rum. Ruthie, from the corner of her eye, could see the women tossing imaginary dust over their shoulders to ward off the evil, and her heart began to hurt. Holding her stomach more securely, she closed her eyes for a second, and when the pain subsided, she smiled at her friend and said, "We aint see you fuh uh w'ile, Miriam."

The drunk turned her rheumy eyes on the woman who had spoken and, squinting, said in a hoarse, harsh voice, "You too ole to be breedin', Ruthie. You's as big as uh house. You gotta mek Deighton keep he pants on 'pon uh night."

Ruthie laughed, replying in kind, "You evuh kno' uh man dat cud keep he pants on?"

The mad drunk chuckled and sat down on the tree stump, looking at the other women who seemed huddled together for mutual protection against this apparition. And, indeed, she looked like something from hell. Her dress, now of indeterminate color, was torn in several places, and the women looked away in embarrassment because she was not wearing underwear, and all her self was exposed. They would have left, but Ruthie held them with her eyes, so they stood watching, fear on their faces. From time to time, they turned away, averting their eyes from the horror of this destroyed woman—but then, they could have been just avoiding the smell. The woman continued speaking to Ruthie, practically ignoring the others, and though they did not want her to speak to them, they still felt ignored. This irritated them.

"Well, how t'ings in de village, Ruthie?"

Ruthie thought about what had changed.

"Carlyle an' Burton left fuh Panama two weeks ago. Angela pregnant again. An' we lost t'ree children to some kinda fever last week. Other dan dat, not'ing aint happen. De sun still hot; wuk still hard; an' de rain still doan fall. Nuttin aint change."

"An' Ruby Barnes still uh bitch," the drunk added, cackling, and the other women joined her. She looked at them,

234

squinting, and said to Ruthie, "Oh shite. I t'ought dem was duppies. Dem look jest like duppies, but dem laughing now, so dey can't be. Right, Ruthie?"

Ruthie said nothing, and the other women's laughter disappeared. They were offended now, and Ruthie made a slight motion with her head, ordering them not to respond.

"Whe' you been, Miriam? Nuhbody aint see you fuh weeks," she asked the mad woman.

The answer was quick and unequivocal.

"I did down in St. Peter. Somebody tell me dat de chile was down dere, so I went to look fuh she."

It was almost nine months since the death of her child, but she was still looking for it. There was no use telling the woman her child was dead. Ruthie knew Miriam's lucidity, if such it could be called, would end soon. Miriam always searched for her child just before her mind completely gave way and she was committed to the hospital again. Ruthie felt her heart swelling, filling up with something—blood maybe—that caught the breath in her throat, and, for a moment, it seemed as if her breathing would stop. The women had stepped back when they heard mention of the child, quickly throwing dust over their shoulders. Ruthie felt the urge to do the same, but the woman's eyes held her. Still, something pulled at her mind.

The woman continued, "I di'nt find she, though. She mus' be someplace else."

The last words were said almost in a whisper, and Ruthie, ignoring the smell, reached down and hugged Miriam. Both started to cry. Ruthie lifted her from the stump and walked toward her house. She had been on her way to see Ruby Barnes, but that could wait now. She would wash the woman and give her something to eat. Then, she would ask Deighton to take her to the mental hospital. The group under the tree watched the two women move slowly down the road, their differences so obvious—one skinny as a rail, the other big with child, one well-dressed and the other decayed. Yet, as the haze created by the sun absorbed them and they trudged down the white limestone road that was baked to a resistant hardness, it was impossible to tell, when they disappeared in their mutual embrace, who was supporting whom.

CHAPTER TWENTY-FOUR

BARBADOS 1906

Miriam became incoherent as Ruthie washed the stink off her but was as relaxed as a child in her hands. Ruthie used two buckets of water—precious now that wells were beginning to dry up—to clean the dirt off her. The grime laid on Miriam in layers, and rubbing her wet skin only caused it to come off in rolls that turned the water brown in moments. Ruthie struggled with her emotions, determined not to cry, but she could not stop herself when the woman started to sing "Rock of Ages," her voice clear and strong for a moment. Ruthie stopped, but Miriam reached out for her soapy hand and put it back on her body, looking her directly in the face and smiling vacuously. When Ruthie allowed her hand to sit there, the woman gently began to rub Ruthie's hand over her body, singing all the while. Then, for a moment, awareness gleamed in her eyes, and she reached out and wiped Ruthie's face free of the tears that were streaming down her face. She ran her hands over Ruthie's big belly, and, slowly, a perplexed look came over Miriam's face as her hand continued to rub the woman. Suddenly, her hand stopped, understanding gleaming in the depths of her eyes. Ruthie nodded, and the other woman smiled. Then, gradually, the dullness came back into her face, and she began to mumble incoherently.

Later, Ruthie watched helplessly as Deighton loaded Miriam into the cart, in which she sat docilely, accepting her fate.

Now, as Ruthie walked into the Barnes' drive that divided the front lawn on which several guinea birds strutted, she wondered if the village would ever be free of the Barneses. The land stretched away in the distance until it disappeared into the sky and the heat waves, and she was overwhelmed by the thought that everything she could see, including practically herself, the Barneses owned. Her mother had been born one year after slavery ended and had tried to explain that things were so much better now, but Ruthie had never been able to see how. They all still worked on the Barnes' plantations, they owned no land, and they lived at the mercy of whichever Barnes happened to be in charge. Even the overseer could still whip them from time to time. True, they were no longer owned, but she was not sure what that all added up to.

She stopped in the hot sun, staring at the house that dominated her life and shaped the village. Miss Kirton, the cook, called softly to Ruthie, who walked over to the kind-faced old woman.

"You come to see Miss Ruby agin? Dis is uh bad time. She got important comp'ny. De gov'nor an' som uh dem big-shots from town in dere eatin' lunch. You goin' haf to wait 'til dey gone."

"How long dat goin' be, Miss Kirton?"

The old woman shrugged, a singularly eloquent movement, and turned away to check something on the wood stove. Ruthie sat, not comfortable but certain she was going to talk to Ruby Barnes. She strained her ears to hear what might be going on in the house but heard nothing except what sounded like male laughter. The kitchen was hot, but

Miss Kirton seemed unaffected by the heat, moving slowly about the kitchen, removing lids, tasting, shaking her head in dissatisfaction, adding some mysterious substance, tasting again, nodding, and replacing the lid. Ruthie was hungry. She had fed Miriam but had forgotten to eat, and, now, the tantalizing smells of Miss Kirton's cooking caused her stomach to growl. Miss Kirton said nothing but brought the woman a calabash of yam soup. The white meat of the boiled chicken floated around the bowl, and Ruthie was on the verge of digging her spoon in when Ruby walked into the kitchen.

Surprised, Ruby stopped, then asked, "What are you doing here?"

The spoon stopped halfway to the bowl; then, Ruthie allowed it to drop all the way in. Ruby continued to glare at her, expecting an answer. Ruthie did not stand, and this was not lost on the white woman.

"I come to talk to you, Miss Barnes."

"What about this time? No, don't tell me. I'm busy. Why don't you come back tomorrow?"

Ruthie looked directly at the woman and replied, "I rather wait 'til you done doin' wha' you doin. Dis important."

For a moment, it seemed as if Ruby was going to order her out, but something in Ruthie's face issued a warning, and Ruby paused, then said, "All right. You may wait. I cannot promise I will be with you in any hurry, though."

Ruthie continued to sit, staring at the woman, who, having made up her mind, turned away, speaking to the cook. After she left, Ruthie continued to eat, commenting to the cook that Ruby was a real dragon. The older woman did not answer.

Ruthie occasionally rubbed her big stomach, and, after a while, the old woman asked, "W'en it due, Ruthie?"

"In a couple uh weeks, Miss Kirton."

"Boy, Deighton musta bin su'prise wen you get in de family way. He musta did t'ink dat he was past dat by now. It funny how God does work. In mysterious ways, girl. In mysterious ways."

Ruthie did not reply, finishing off the soup with a flourish. Now in her forties, her pregnancy had taken everyone by surprise. She touched her stomach gently, unsmiling. The day dragged on. Miss Kirton hummed as she prepared things, and from time to time, the butler came in hurriedly, grabbed some delicacy and rushed out again. He never said anything to Ruthie, never even looked at her. The shadows slowly shifted from under the buildings and started to stretch to the east, thin black stalks on the dusty ground. Ruthie tried to be patient, but she was angry, sure that Ruby was taking her time because she knew Ruthie was waiting.

Finally, she asked irritably, "How long it does tek fuh dem people to eat?"

The old woman chuckled softly and shook her head.

"Yuh nevuh can tell wid dese rich people, gal. Dem doan eat; dem does 'dine'. "

She said this last word with a fake upperclass accent, and Ruthie, surprised at the irreverence, laughed suddenly. The old woman looked at her and said, "Good. You too purty wen you laugh." Then turning serious, she added, "Doan le' life get yuh down, dearie. De ole people used to say 'dey aint nuttin to life but deadin'. You 'member dat, Ruthie. You got to live fuh youself, too."

The woman stopped as if thinking she had gone too far, but Ruthie had never heard her speak this way before, and she wanted the woman to continue. So, she asked, "Miss Kirton, beggin' you pardon, but kin I ax you uh question?"

The old woman nodded, and Ruthie, asked, "Las' time I did up here, you say dat Miss Ruby Barnes aint as bad as she like to mek out. Wha' you did mean by dat?"

The old woman smiled and replied quietly, "Only dat nobody aint as bad as people believe dem to be, nor as good as dey believe demselves to be. De mistress is a strange one, Ruthie. She got troubles, too."

Ruthie sucked her teeth loudly and apologized quickly as the old woman's eyes narrowed.

"Sorry, Miss Kirton, but wha' trouble Ruby Barnes could got? She got mo'e money dan God."

"Doan blaspheme, chile. Money aint ev'ryt'ing, yuh know. Look how dem wuthless brothers uh hers all run off an' lef' she wid all de plantations to worry 'bout. You tink dat easy, Ruthie?"

Ruthie, however, was in no mood to be generous.

"As long as she got slaves like we to wuk de lan', Miss Kirton, it aint dat hard. She doan do nuttun but stand 'bout an' watch we wuk."

The old woman's face changed, and she said, "Slavery."

There was resignation in her face, and Ruthie waited for her to continue, but she went back to her work. Ruthie was, however, building her courage up to ask the question that everyone shied away from.

"Miss Kirton, you was born in slavery days?"

The old woman did not turn around nor did she answer for a long time, and Ruthie thought she had angered her, but when the woman did answer, her voice was mild.

"Now, I kno' dat you mudduh tell you dat is one question you doan ax people. But, yes, I born in slavery days, sorta. I born in 1836, durin' wha dey call de apprenticeship period. Dat is wen de British people decide dat we should be slave fuh four years mo'e aftuh dey set we free."

Ruthie did not understand, and she asked the woman to explain.

"Well, it so happen dat wen de law pass to set we free in 1834, de plantation owners claim dat dey need some time to ad'jus' an' dat we di'nt kno' how to tek care uh weself, anyway. So de English people keep we slave fuh four mo'e years, so dat we could learn responsibility. I born ha'fway through dat period dey call 'apprenticeship'. "

Ruthie was surprised nobody had told her about this, and she was curious.

"So wha' wunna do durin' dis apprenticeship time?"

"Wuk like slaves," the old woman laughed loudly. "De white people aint foolish, gal. Dey free we from dem tekking care uh we, but not from de wuk. Not from de wuk."

The old woman turned back to the stove, and Ruthie wondered if the people in the house were still eating. She did not ask, however. Outside, the shadows had lengthened, looking like cornstalks that the buildings were pulling behind them. It was getting late, and she wondered when Ruby would be done. In the meantime, she just sat.

On the other side of the house, Ruby was thinking about her. The luncheon had not been expected to last this long. She had invited the governor; his wife; Mr. Waldron, a planter who had plantations near hers on the eastern side of the island; a couple of British civil servants; and the commander of the local garrison. They were relaxing after lunch on the eastern porch, which showed off the gardens to good effect. It had been too hot to venture out into the sun, but the beauty of the Barnes' gardens was legendary, and with the breeze coming off the ocean, the afternoon had been very pleasant. To the east and north, the gardens stretched away, layer upon layer of color confounding the eye and dazzling the senses. The gardens had been around since 1776. At least, that was the first reference to them she had seen in an early memoir she kept locked away in a vault in the cellar. They were her pride and joy, and throughout the drought, they had been tended, no matter the cost in water. Now, Ruby wondered how long she would be able to keep this up. The wells were drying up, and, as she looked to the east, the sky remained that startling blue so many artists of Caribbean seascapes had captured. Right now, the azure sky looked like hell itself to her. If it did not rain soon, many would be ruined, and even the Barnes empire could not continue to produce at a loss. The plantations were draining profits like a run-off after a rainstorm.

I hope there's a rainstorm somewhere in my future. Maybe there's a way to make the gardens pay for themselves. People are always talking about them. Maybe they would pay to see them, she thought.

She was just getting excited about the idea when she heard her name called. Ruby looked at her guests, who were waiting expectantly for an answer to something that had obviously been asked.

"Forgive me. I was thinking about the rain—the lack of it, rather. Now, what is required of me?" she asked playfully.

"Waldron here was wondering whether you knew how the Americans' canal is progressing. Your brother being there and all that."

Ruby smiled thinly and answered, "I fear that Rupert is not one for writing, Mr. Waldron. I received one letter from him when he first arrived, and that has been the extent of our communication. He seemed to be adjusting then to the place. I must say, it sounded rather awful to me."

"Frontier life, Miss Barnes. Never pleasant, but exhilarating."

This came from Waldron, a small, wizened man with an enormous wife who asked sharply, "And what would you know about frontier life, Morris? The most adventurous thing you have done is bathe on the east coast of the island."

"But that, Mrs. Waldron, takes considerable bravery. The breakers there are ungovernable, I have heard."

This came from the Governor. It was not clear whether he was being ironic. Ruby, hoping to avoid an argument, replied, "And so they are. In any case, the newspaper said just the other day that the Americans have been removing dirt at an incredible rate."

"The bloody thing is draining all the workers from the plantations. We are having trouble sustaining the work with all the men heading off to that bloody canal. Only last week, four of my best workers left, saying they were going to work for more money in a day in Panama than they would get for a month on the plantation."

This had come from Waldron. When the others nodded sympathetically, he continued, "The worst part of all this is their damned insolence now they have an alternative to the plantation. Just the other day, one fellow whose grandfather and father have worked on my plantation came to me and said he thought I was exploiting the workers. Me! Exploiting the workers! I gave him one slap across his face, and he scampered out of my way. But can you imagine the insolence of the fellow?"

"It's the price of lifting up the world, Waldron," the Governor said playfully. "Sacrifices must be made. When I was at Cambridge, old McMorris Laughton, history lecturer, used to say that civilization is a constant. To provide some to others is to lose it yourself. He lived in Africa, and from some of his antics, I would have to say he was correct."

They all laughed, raising their glasses and saluting each other. Ruby wondered what they were talking about. Waldron was right about one thing though. The workers were becoming irritatingly insolent. This brought her mind to Ruthie again, and she was glad the woman had been made to wait.

Serves her right, she thought. *Coming to the house without so much as a by-your-leave and expecting me to stop everything to pay attention to her. She needed to be put in her place.*

She said aloud, "I have the same problem as you, Mr. Waldron. We are losing more and more workers every day. In fact, most of the work on the land is now done by the women."

They all looked at her, surprised, and Waldron replied, "I didn't realize it was that bad over here, Miss Barnes. Your productivity must be down quite severely."

"I'm quite pleased to say that is not the case. Actually, in at least one respect, there's been some improvement. I have many fewer injuries on the job. For some reason, the women seem to be much more careful than the men. They don't work as quickly, but they compensate by working more steadily. It's quite extraordinary, really."

The men were silent, but Mrs. Waldron, with some pleasure evident in her voice, said, "Yes, that is quite extraordinary. And only women, you say. Quite extraordinary."

"But when the crop comes, do you think they will be able to do all the work necessary to get your fields cut and in the factory in a reasonable time? Patience may not be a virtue then. You will need to get the canes cut quickly. Do you think they will stand up to that?" Waldron asked.

Ruby surprised herself, defending the women's skills with more certainty than she felt.

"Actually, yes. They have given me no reason to believe otherwise."

Mrs. Waldron was still thinking, though, and said, "There is something unnatural about a village without men. Don't you think so, Morris?"

Her husband adjusted his small frame in the large chair and sniffed the air like a muskrat coming into daylight.

"Odd. Very odd," he declared, looking at the Governor, who seemed amused by the whole thing. "What do you think, Governor Harris?"

The Englishman smiled comfortably before replying, "With all due respect to Miss Barnes, whose competence we have all come to admire, I am exceedingly fearful of a world composed of Amazons. That, sir, is man's greatest threat."

He bowed to Ruby and Mrs. Waldron and, picking up his pipe, continued to smoke.

Waldron, after a while, said, "Hear, hear, Governor Harris. The bloody world is perplexing enough without us allowing nature to be upset."

"You know, in England, the suffragettes are making a case for women's equality and are insisting on the right to vote. They are not voting here, Miss Barnes, but you seem to have found that equality."

Ruby realized she was being discussed along with the other women whom she employed and, for a moment, was not sure how to answer. The conversation continued, but Ruby was caught in her own world, paying scant attention and wishing the luncheon would end. Her mind kept going back to Ruthie waiting in the kitchen, and, for the first time in years, she felt uncertain. One thing was certain though. If that woman had come to bother her about helping those women in the village, she would throw her out forthwith. The shameless thing was pregnant again and was not even embarrassed. Ruthie and she were the same age, and it was disgusting to see that big belly protruding in front of her.

Ruby became aware of movement and came out of her daydream. The Governor had stood, his head surrounded by blue, aromatic smoke. The others were pushing chairs back and standing, and Ruby joined them, smiling her "so soon?" Soon, the carriages were disappearing down the long, white limestone driveway, and, breathing a sigh of relief, she sat for a moment before ringing a small, silver bell. When the butler came, she ordered him to clear the tables and to bring a jug of lemonade. This done, she asked that Ruthie be brought to her.

Ruthie came through the door, huge stomach swinging before her, and Ruby felt disgust rise in her at the sight. Pointedly looking away toward the east where the sea beat against the shore, she said haughtily, "Maybe we can save ourselves the trouble of a long conversation. If you are here to ask for some kind of break for those women in the village, don't waste your time. Until the crop season ends, I cannot spare a single worker."

The expected outburst did not come, and she reluctantly turned her head to see Ruthie looking at her. There was no anger in Ruthie's face but a speculative look that hinted at sorrow. Something about that look forced Ruby to turn all the way around, and, for a while, the two women stared at each other, waiting.

Finally, Ruthie said, "This aint 'bout de women, Ruby. Dis 'bout you an' me."

Again, though she chafed under the insolence of the address, something about the woman forced Ruby to hold her tongue. She waited. Ruthie seemed reluctant to speak now, and something told Ruby she did not want to hear what the woman had come to tell her.

"You know why I here, don't you?"

Ruby shook her head, uncertain of herself.

"De boy mek Audrey pregnant, Ruby."

Ruby made a small noise, sounding as if she was in pain, and turned away again, staring into the distance. Her arm had involuntarily been raised as if to ward off some attacker, and Ruthie, in her own hell, stood waiting for the woman to absorb the enormity of the statement. Ruby turned again, face bloodless, eyes pleading, and mouth trembling.

When Ruthie spoke, anger was in her voice.

"It is wha' we' get fuh all de secrecy an' de lies. Somebody shoulda tell dem, but de secrecy did too important. Now, look wha' happen."

Ruby looked disdainfully at her accuser, but, before she could speak, Ruthie continued, "You di'nt want nuhbody to know wha' you father do, so de whole ting had to be secret. Not dat I did want it spread 'bout either, but look wher' we is now."

Ruby pointed at Ruthie's big belly and said, apparently inconsequentially, "And you?"

Ruthie hesitated, and then, in front of Ruby's horrified eyes, she raised her dress to expose two pillows tied around her waist. Ruby gave that small cry again and fell back in her chair, uncomprehending.

Ruthie rearranged her clothes as Ruby muttered, "You are not pregnant. Why?"

"Because de girl goin' have a chance fuh some kinda life. Wha' kinda life you feel she goin' have if she have a chile now?"

Ruby shook her head, replying, "But you just said she was pregnant. What are you saying?"

Ruthie sat down uninvited, and Ruby was too shocked to react. Seated together, it was easy to see a resemblance between the two women. They had the same long, black hair and, though Ruthie was darker, the same bone structure and facial features.

Ruby sat silently as the other woman explained, but she was not listening. Her mind had gone back to a day long ago when her father had taken her to the village. The girls were playing jacks in the road, but Ruthie had left, going to the same house her father had entered. Uncomfortable, after a while, Ruby followed them. As she entered the yard, her father had been hugging Ruthie and, before he saw Ruby, had given the girl money. Something in the way he looked at Ruthie had told Ruby all she needed to know. The girl's mother had seen Ruby but said nothing, standing in the door with a look of satisfaction on her face. In that moment, Ruby had known that Ruthie was her sister. Something indefinable changed in her feeling about the village that day, and, when her father saw her, she had stared at him, a look of pure hatred on her face. She had turned and walked away from the village, not stopping when her father caught up with her in the open carriage. It had been her last walk to the village to play with the girls, for the village became a threat from that moment. Any thought of speaking to her mother about what she had found out also died, as one look at the frail woman made it clear her father's infidelity was no secret in that house. Something inside her had hardened against her mother as well.

Now, the village was threatening again, and the same woman was the cause. Ruby stood, leaning on the balustrade that ran around the house.

After a while, she asked, "And what do you want from the Barneses this time, Ruthie?"

Ruthie's eyes narrowed dangerously.

"De same ting dat I always did want from wunna. Nuttin. Nuttin atall. I don' want a ting from de Barneses."

"Then why are you here? You must think I can do something for you."

Ruthie hesitated. Then, she responded in a surprisingly small voice, "Not fuh me, Ruby. De Barnes do enuff fuh me a'ready. I wud be jus' as glad if I nevuh see one uh wunna again. But yuh kin help de girl."

Ruby waited, and Ruthie, much less comfortable now that she was going to be a supplicant, sat staring at the green stalks of the sugar canes waving in the distance. The silence dragged on as the two women sat in the approaching dusk.

Then, Ruthie said, "We goin' have to leave de village."

Ruby spun around as if this was the one thought that had not occurred to her.

"Why?"

Slowly, but with growing emotion and anger, Ruthie poured out her venom in her explanation. When she stopped speaking, Ruby sat, her body twisted away from her sister, her thoughts all scrambled, and the horror of what they were going to keep a secret sitting heavily on her mind.

Before Ruthie left, it was agreed that Ruby would have her attorneys convey to Ruthie possession of a property on the west coast of the island where she, her husband, and the girl would live. There, away from the village, they would protect the secret to which they were now sworn.

As Ruthie was walking down the steps, Ruby asked softly, almost shyly, "Why did you take so long to tell me?"

The other woman stopped but did not turn as she answered.

"I dint want to say nuttin, but only yestiddy, I feel dat de secrets between de two uh we never lead to anyt'ing good."

There were no goodbyes as she walked out into the dusk, and the other woman sat, watching her disappear, uncertain of her feelings, but somehow relieved.

CHAPTER TWENTY-FIVE

Panama 1908

Barnes waited impatiently at the mouth of Balboa Bay, across which he had taken a skiff to the edge of the city. He now sat near the silent shore, waiting for the man. It was dangerous for him to be in this portion of the canal since he had disappeared two years ago to live in the forest at the compound. Compound! How innocent that sounded. The place had been converted into an armed camp. During the first year of the Captain's control, the project had changed from what appeared to be a secret part of the canal construction into a mine. Over time, the personnel had changed, and men whose hard eyes suggested they lived in a place far removed from the land they guarded had come. The camp had grown, and security increased. Richards' flogging had changed the tone of the camp, which, until that time, was not excessively controlled. The Captain, Octavius Bryant, changed all that, and the men now endured a routine of labor that paralleled the canal's miles to the south.

Still, no one left. They were very well paid, and though there was nothing to spend the money on, the men dreamt of a time when they would leave this fetid jungle and be back in Barbados, where they would be "somebody," with lots of money to spend. They dreamt of buying land and living like the rich, which, in their imaginations, meant like the whites. Like him.

He had an odd relationship with the men. They accorded him the respect that went with his color, but there remained a distance he could not traverse, try as he might. His relationship to the Captain did nothing to reduce the distance, for Barnes had prospered since the Captain arrived, and the men instinctively understood that his color was not an inconsiderable weight in his position of authority. Barnes knew they were right. The Captain had been very clear with him on that score and had promoted him. Now, Barnes managed the labor of the enterprise. He was responsible for feeding the engine of the mine, which consumed men quickly and created labor shortages with frustrating regularity. At first, the men were secretly recruited with the promise of significant increases in wages, but as men had disappeared, the task of recruitment became more difficult. Someone in the United States was siphoning off men from the canal to provide manpower for the secret project in the jungle, but they could not keep up with the demand, and so the kidnappings had begun. Barnes was not sure why he had allowed himself to become part of this, but something about the man they called the Captain seemed to make sense of it all.

The men who had come to the camp with him two years ago were nearly all dead, through natural exhaustion and sickness. Out in the jungle, malaria was still a threat, and men died quickly, in brutal pain. Richards had not died. He had settled into a pattern of obedience after the beating, and the man, once a natural joker, had ceased to laugh, becoming the most productive worker in the gang. He did not speak to Barnes, but as the others had died, he redoubled his efforts. Richards was first into the mine each day and last out, clearing more ore than any other man. At first, Barnes had been pleased with the production, but, slowly, it dawned on him that the man was engaged in a form of suicide. Somehow, Richard's spirit had left him, and he was forcing his body to find it. Barnes' mood changed from satisfaction to despair. One day when Richards had been working so furiously that the other men complained, Barnes asked him why he was going so fast. He had intended the question as a joke, but the man turned the most deadened eyes on him and had not answered. Then, Barnes saw something that explained the distance he always felt when with the men from his country. For the briefest moment, the deadness had disappeared, and something frightening showed behind the eyes, a strangeness that was less comforting than hate. Anger he had been prepared for, hate even, but the sense of being alien, of not being recognized, chilled him. That was the last time he had spoken to Richards; though he saw him every day, Barnes knew the man was oblivious to him. He had been nullified.

In two years, much had changed. The Captain was extracting gold from the Panamanian soil and was moving it across the isthmus to the east. Every four weeks, the hard-faced men came and packed the bags on to mules. They came in the early evening and left in the early morning. Before they entered the village, the way was cleared, and men were sent to their quarters. They did not fraternize and were given quarters separate from the men who worked in the mines. After almost a year of these periodic visits, it was impossible to identify any of them. The rules of the camp had also changed, and now, no one left except the Captain, Barnes, and one or two senior men whom the Captain trusted. The men objected strenuously to this, but the Captain had done two things. First he increased the per-day wage. The second thing, however, had been more effective.

One of the men had tried to leave the camp. It was never known whether he intended to escape or simply to take off for the night. The next morning, they found him outside the gate to the village, his body already turning black from the poison shot into him. The Captain was standing over the body, looking at it with a smile. He had said nothing, but the body was left for two days and then had disappeared. Barnes was both disgusted and fascinated by the man's actions, for many hinted that the Captain had committed this act. Also, at that time, men began to catch glimpses of dark bodies flitting through the jungle, always just beyond the realm of certainty. Somehow, the jungle had come alive.

Barnes was tempted to follow the men who came to take the tons of gold out of Panama, and he wondered what the government in Panama City would do if they knew they were being cheated in two ways. The Captain had laughingly told him of the deal the government of the United States had made with the Panamanians. They were to be paid a quarter of a million dollars for possession of the land that, in perpetuity, would constitute the sphere of influence of the Canal Authority. A quarter of a million dollars! Barnes was certain many times that amount was being extracted from the land now.

When he said this to the Captain, the man laughed, replying, "It's a good business arrangement, Rupert."

Barnes could not see how this was good for the Panamanians and said, if caught, he would probably rot in some Panamanian jail. The man shook his head, still chuckling.

"You really have no idea what you are part of, do you?"

Barnes waited, sensing this was something of which the man was proud. The Captain settled into his chair, staring off into the darkness of the forest. It was close to midday and sweltering, but the man seemed not to notice the heat as they sat on a small promontory created by the excavation of the mine. Few men were about, most being in the mine. The work was brutal, and the men were almost always too tired to eat.

Barnes was still not used to the soul-draining nature of the work, and he sometimes still entertained notions that the labor was freely given. This was no longer true, and something he dared not voice nagged at him, something he thought he had escaped when his father died. He had been so certain his father was wrong, that something was fundamentally corrupt about the society they had created in Barbados. Seeing himself as part of whatever changed when slavery ended, he avoided the word that played at the edges of his brain and made his success in Panama a hollow thing.

The Captain does not know the import of his question, Barnes thought.

The man, however, continued.

"Everyone is getting a good deal here. The Panamanians have a country we have helped them to obtain and the prestige of being the location of the latest wonder of the world. The United States government will soon have a major engineering triumph to point to on the world stage, and we will have wealth, Rupert. My father is fond of saying there is no disadvantage until someone feels cheated. No one feels cheated here. So there is no disadvantage."

Barnes was uncomfortable with the argument, but his mind turned toward the personal nature of the reference to "my father." It was the first time the man had given a hint of a life beyond the clearing. He wondered about the Captain, who was obviously wealthy and well financed. Barnes felt certain it was the father he had mentioned who was the power behind him, but the man remained silent.

The Captain and Barnes had an odd relationship. It bordered on friendship, but there was never any question that the man was in charge. He kept Barnes off-balance because the relationship drifted between these intimations of friendship and the brutal display of power. As a result, Barnes could not get to the heart of the man but found himself strangely drawn to him. He could not comprehend that the man who was capable of killing so casually could sip a cold drink and talk of politics and human nature.

They sat in silence for some time after the man's comment about his father. Then, he turned to Barnes and said, "Have you ever wondered why I singled you out, Barnes?"

Barnes thought for a while, then said, "I assumed that, as you have intimated, you did not want a white man to be laboring."

The man chuckled softly, his face crinkling like a squeezed doll's.

"Is that what you think? That I didn't want a white man to be a laborer? I suppose that's partially true, but it is not the most important reason."

"Then what is?" Barnes asked, a little impatience showing.

The Captain sipped slowly, Barnes doing likewise. Around them, the midday sun beat down, casting startling shadows in odd shapes as it sought to penetrate the density of the rain forest. Barnes was struck by the stillness of the day. It was almost as if the forest was waiting on the man to speak. The shadow and light formed a jigsaw puzzle, and his mind drifted toward the ground as he tried to fit similarly shaped pieces together in his imagination. It was a frustrating exercise, for as the trees' branches shifted slightly in the light breeze, the configurations on the ground constantly changed, and Barnes found his mind becoming exhausted by the exercise.

"We are not so different, you and I."

Barnes realized he had drifted off.

"What did you say?"

"We are not very different. We are both products of exhausted blood. We have ancestors who have done too much, and it has left us tired, desperately trying to prove we are worthy, in one way or another, of being who we are."

Barnes looked at him curiously, not fully understanding what he meant.

When he did not respond, the man continued wistfully, "That may be the epitaph of the twentieth century. 'We sought to achieve'."

Barnes had never seen him like this. The Captain was not ordinarily a contemplative man, driven more by action than thought, but something about his voice sucked Barnes in, forcing him to engage the thought, so he asked, "And how do you see us to be the same?"

"Oh, not the same. Merely similar. The difference is you still have illusions about proving your worth. I once asked you why you were here. I was certain you did not know the reason. We are all refugees from the nightmare of our past, Barnes. You just have not determined what your nightmare is."

"And have you figured out what yours is, Captain?"

"Captain. An idiotic title, but I suppose it will do. You may, however, call me Bryant. That is, after all, my name. And, yes, I have figured out my nightmare. It is the same as yours. It is the fear of not being good enough, of being less than our pasts. That is why we are both here, Barnes, seeking to show we are worthy of our heritage."

Perplexed, Barnes still found the man's voice hypnotic. The black men in the camp had begun to say the man had "the power." Somewhere in their ancestral memory was a belief that some men were born closer to the ancestors than others, and though they did not inhabit the world of the dead, they brushed so closely against that world, they inherited some of its power. This was manifested in a man's ability to command other men who could not understand the source of the power that sapped their will. In some men, it manifested itself in the use of the voice as an instrument of control. Men would act in response to the voice before they realized what they had done. Barnes had dismissed this as African superstition, but now he wondered. There was something calmly persuasive about the man's voice, and Barnes replied lamely, "I am here to make money."

Bryant chuckled silently again, sipping his drink.

"And so you shall, Barnes. So you shall. But it will not satisfy you. It is only a facsimile of your need, isn't it? You need to have someone acknowledge your success, right? Your sister, perhaps?"

Barnes looked around sharply, staring in surprise at the chuckling man.

"What do know about my family?"

"Oh, come now. No histrionics. You don't believe I would not have checked, do you? In any case, I think your sister has a connection to the past you do not. We are fighting, Barnes—you more than I, it is true—to sustain our instinct for command. Your sister has that. She understands how civilizations are built—with truth, vision, and strength of purpose. They cannot be constructed on morality, for that inevitably weakens the instinct to command. That is what I fear we are losing in the twentieth century, and that is why you are here, Barnes. To regain something of what the Barnes men must have been like a century ago. It would be a shame if it had passed to your women."

The man laughed, and anger rose in Barnes' throat. He sensed something vile and decayed in Bryant, but it had the sour-sweet smell of power too, and Barnes knew he would follow this man because of that scent.

Shamed by Bryant's words, his anger at Ruby returned. He had written to her only once in the three years since leaving the island, and she had answered with a brief, factual letter that told of the difficulties of the drought and the impossibility of finding labor. Her well wishes had sounded like a dismissal. He continued to write to Audrey, at first because he missed her and then out of a sense of duty and perhaps habit. She never answered, and it dawned on him she might not be able to read or write. He did not know and was ashamed at his lack of knowledge about her. Still, he wrote regularly and always included money for her. In some ways, not receiving an answer allowed him to believe he was making a sacrifice, thus justifying his betrayal. Also, her not coming that last night allowed him to muster up a false anger that insulated him against his guilt.

He had no contact with the canal workers anymore, but word would filter back about the continuing influx of men from the Caribbean, and once in a while, someone who knew him would arrive in the secret compound. No longer did he try to befriend these men. Richards' flogging had separated him from the other Barbados men, and, as he had been promoted, that distance had grown. In some ways, he was moving backward in time, away from the world he had believed he could create. There was something elemental about the work in the jungle, and he knew the Captain was right. Morality was not the bedrock of this world.

The madman still had not come. As Barnes looked around in the darkness, the small skiff rocked dangerously. Why did he come to see this man? Why had he saved his life? A year ago, he found the man wandering near the secret compound in the jungle. On his way back from the Indian village, an apparition had risen from the ground, startling him out of his wits. Reaching instinctively for the gun he now carried at all times, Barnes had been about to pounce when the figure groaned and leaned against a tree. The man had looked like something from a nightmare, groaning loudly when Barnes held him. When his arm disappeared inside the man's body, it had taken Barnes a while to realize that the side was torn away. He was the most grotesque thing Barnes had ever seen, his body cantilevered to the left at an impossible angle. Barnes shuddered to think of the strain on his spine. How he had managed to come so far into the jungle without being killed, Barnes did not know, but he was faced with a dilemma. What should he do with the man? To take him to the camp would be to condemn him to death; but if he left him to wander about the jungle, it would only be a matter of time before the man was found and killed. Knowing what he was doing was stupid and cursing himself for it, Barnes quietly turned the man around, heading toward the river. There, he found the Spaniard, who took the man to the town of Gatun. That had started these periodic journeys to see the madman. Barnes could not understand why he did it.

Now, Barnes was waiting again for the man's arrival. In the distance, he heard a shuffle and peered into the darkness. As the bent shape came into view, Barnes eased the skiff to the shore and stepped out. When he said, "Goodnight," there was no immediate reply, but he handed over a packet of food, and the man sat.

After a while, the madman said, "Water almost gone," and Barnes breathed a sigh of relief.

The man was lucid tonight. Sometimes, he made no sense at all, carrying on about landslides and leopards in the jungle. Barnes hated this. He had never forgotten the look the jaguar had given him, and the thought of the beast haunted him. Tonight, though, the man seemed coherent.

Barnes said in reply, "Yes. The tide has been going out for some time now. How come you are late?"

The man turned his body carefully in the night and replied with a high-pitched cackle, "Uh get los' in de past. Dat ever happen to you, Barnes?"

Barnes shook his head. Then, remembering the man could not see him in the darkness, answered, "No. What do you mean, Anderson?"

"Oh, jus' sometimes yuh mind does go aroun' in a circle like yuh get catch in a w'irlpool, an' yuh can't get out no matter how yuh try."

"You having nightmares again?"

"Well, not nightmares exactly. I just does remember de t'ings dat happen before."

It made Barnes nervous when Anderson talked like this because it was possible he had seen the compound in the jungle, and Barnes knew what would happen if the man ever said anything. Though he might not ordinarily be believed, the men's disappearances would give credence to his story. Barnes was not too worried about anyone entering the deep jungle in search of some shapeless vision a madman created, but the danger could not be entirely overlooked. If rumors got back to the Captain, Barnes was sure the man would be silenced. So he asked cautiously, "What things, Anderson?"

"You ever t'ink 'bout Barbados, Barnes? I remember you w'en you was a boy, yuh kno'. You fadder uses to bring you down to de Anglican church fuh Sunday school, an' all de boys used to want to be you. You remember dem days?"

Barnes said yes, wondering where the man was going. He soon continued.

"Barbados create one odd relationship between us and wunna, yuh kno'. One odd relationship. It always had we wantin' to be like wunna. Yuh kno', dat is why a lot of de fellas lef' de islan'. Somehow, dem t'ink dat by comin' here, dey would get rid of dat urge. Dat Panama would give dem self-respec'. But yuh kno' wha' happen? Lots of dem now t'ink dat dey might have jump outta de frying pan into de fire."

He stopped, and Barnes, surprised, found himself waiting for the man to continue. When he did not, Barnes asked quietly, "What do you mean by that, Anderson?"

"Well, most uh dem come here to get 'way from de wuk on de plantations. Ev'ry day wukking fuh white people an' getting' next kin to nothin' fuh deir wuk. Deadin' 'pon de plantation an' never ownin' nuttin. How anybody could become like white people dat way? All yuh ever do is give up yuh youth an' yuh body to de ground, an' in de end, wha yuh got to show for it? Bad back an' artaritis in yuh hands."

Barnes felt something inside him quail at this reference. Somehow, he knew what was coming.

"My fadder wuk 'pon de Barnes plantation 'til he dead. He body jus' give out one morning. We went in to see why he di'nt come outta he bed, an' he was dere layin' down as peaceful as ever, like he did goin' soon get up, except de top part of he body was white. All de blood went down to he back, and he face did white, white."

The man paused, then added with a giggle, "I guess he get to be a white man, after all. W'en he dead."

Barnes kept quiet. He had certainly not expected this. More often than not, the man was maudlin, creating the fantasies that seemed to sustain his imagination. Barnes would listen to him half attentively, responding to the sound of the friendly, familiar accent. Tonight was different, and Barnes was intrigued and uncomfortable.

"But why is it so important for you to be white?"

The man did not answer directly.

"Why you lef' Barbados an' come to Panama, Mr. Barnes?"

It was Barnes' turn to laugh as he replied, "It seems as if everyone is curious about that, Anderson. I was asked that question very recently and was told my answer was wrong. Once, just before I left, an English friend told me I was on my way to build a civilization."

"Den, dat is de answer to your question. Only white men would lef' home to build civilization. Most people content to do dat where dey live already."

This time, Barnes joined in the laughter. It was, however, a bitter laughter as he thought of what he was constructing in the Central American jungle. It was a far cry from any civilization he understood. He had joined the Captain in the forced labor of several thousand men, many of whom he knew would not survive. In the last two years, he had become very well off and had accounts in banks in New York. He was succeeding. But at what?

When he responded, however, his voice was light.

"Touché, Anderson. But why did you leave?"

The answer was quick.

"Woman troubles. Dat is de reason half uh dese fellas here. Most uh dem runnin' from some woman or other."

"But I thought you said they escaped the island to find whiteness? Do they have two reasons then?"

"It is one an' de same t'ing. Most uh dese fellas feel dat dey can't married to dese women 'cause they aint got nuttin to give dem. It easier to lef' dem an' live bachelor where dey can eat, drink an' wear de same t'ing as de white people wid-dout worryin' 'bout supportin' nobody."

"I suppose that makes some kind of sense. I—"

Before he could finish, the man cackled again and continued.

"But Panama trick dem, yuh kno'."

Barnes waited.

"Yes, boy. Panama done trick dem bad fuh so. Dem come to find whiteness, but dey now butt up 'pon a new fangled kinda slavery here. 'Though most uh dem don' kno' it."

Barnes was silent. Around them, the night had its own sounds, the boat occasionally bumping against the rock, causing, from time to time, a little splash. The silhouette of the broken madman stood out against the dim backlight of the town, and Barnes felt something tug at him. He had saved this man. Barnes clung to that thought with a ferocity that made his teeth grind, and, closing his eyes, he listened to the ponderous silence of the mighty Pacific that stretched in inky blackness behind him.

Why had he saved this man? Why did he continue to see him, each time exposing himself to danger? The compound could only be reached by a walk that took him through the depths of his fears in the absolute darkness of the jungle. It was stupid to do this, but something pulled him out of the jungle and away from the wet warmth of Leila once every month to see this man. He had watched the other Barbadian men die, and each death had deadened a part of him until he had become objective about pain and the men's dying. One he had killed himself, but by then, he had felt no attachment to them. Duty had driven his action and controlled his arm. Until he had found this broken man wandering in the forest, he had learned to stay within himself, to let the world treat others as it will, and to protect himself always. This man, however, had stirred something in him, and he could not explain why.

The thought of the new enslavement bothered him, but he quickly shoved that thought down into some inaccessible recess of his brain.

Inexplicably, his mind jumped to Audrey, and he thought of her smell, her thin nose, and, above all, her hair, which he thought impossibly long for a black woman. Yet, he had loved its texture, the feeling of slight resistance that accompanied the pulling of his fingers through it. He had written to her only yesterday, feeling the falsehood, the encrusted emotion, and the hollow half-truths of the letter to be a burden. Still, sitting in the salt-filled air, he thought of the warmth of this girl who must be a woman now, and the reality of her was like an ax in his brain. As the silence lengthened, Barnes imagined the girl he had held. Did he love her? If he did, what did it mean now? How could he have loved her and left so easily? If he did not, what was it that kept him writing to her? If he loved Audrey, what was his relationship to Leila?

The two of them are so different, he thought.

The two women coalesced in his mind, and he struggled to separate them, closing his eyes and concentrating hard, forcing Leila out of his imagination and allowing Audrey to come into full focus.

She stood next to the breadfruit tree where they had met, her eyes, brown and luminous even in the dim light of the tropic night, full of innocence. It was the look of trust, unspoiled by betrayal or deceit, that he had treasured in her. When she looked like this, there was a pain in his heart, and he wanted to fold her into himself, if that had been possible without soiling her by the touch. That look had allowed him to go for a long time without touching her, awed by something in her that was unspoiled. He would look at her skinny body hidden by her drape-like dresses and think her the most beautiful, purest thing in the universe.

Sitting in this unformed land, Barnes felt again the tension that would arise in him, the unaccustomed dryness in his throat when he spoke to her of innocent things while feeling his raging passion. In the darkness, every act was private, and simple speech carried an intimacy he treasured. Whatever he had known about girls deserted him with her, and he felt fear at the innocence of her. She was not resistant, neither in words nor will, but in spite of herself, unknown to herself, some purity in her stood in unconscious rebuke of his instinct. Their relationship had been constructed on this repressed tension, and he had believed her to be unaware of it and immune to it until the day she challenged him with the words that changed their relationship. Her half-playful comment that she would remain a virgin unless he did something had forced a hardness in him because he had felt not simply challenged but shamed by this young girl.

She had intended no insult by the comment, but his maleness shoved this from his mind. From that fateful statement—said in innocence, most likely—their sexuality proceeded with a fearful inevitability, and as she had given way to herself and him, she had changed. The innocence was lost in the sounds of her quiet screams, and he had been frightened by the quality of those screams, most of all because he could not match them. Somewhere inside him, his pleasure was aborted; though he felt his nerves tingle, felt the muscle in the middle of him become bloated with blood and the thrilling power of his seed seeking a complement, there was always an unfulfilled need that sat at the back of his pelvis, as if there was more to come that could not be drained out of him. So her satisfaction, her languor, built resentment in him, and where once he saw innocence, he had come to feel frustration and anger. As she laid on the hard, uneven earth, slipping into sleepiness, he would stare into the star-filled night, wondering why he felt such hunger still.

Barnes looked at the sky and, not for the first time, thought how much the night in this country reminded him of Barbados. Staring skyward, he saw the oddly shaped configuration of stars resembling a boxcart, the same he could see from the hill above the village. Maybe that was why he thought of Audrey, but he knew that something far more intimate spoke to his relation to the people and the land that had nurtured him.

The madman next to him had been quiet for some time, and, unexpectedly, Barnes reached out and touched him lightly on his shoulder, their first contact since Barnes had brought him out of the forest. In the darkness, as the broken man's warm, bony body turned soft and welcoming under the unaccustomed caress, Barnes felt momentarily peaceful.

Finally, he stood and, looking down at the man, said, "I have to head back into the other world. Or maybe the netherworld would be better."

To which the man replied, laughing, "Go, young Orpheus."

"What?" Barnes asked with his own uncomfortable snicker.

"Go. Pursue your Eurydice."

Barnes, with great perplexity in his voice, said, "You are a surprising one, Anderson. What other tricks do you have?"

The man, however, had relapsed into his more usual vacuity and did not reply.

As Barnes was turning to leave, Anderson said, "Beware de leopard, Mr. Barnes."

Barnes thought how strange it was that the man always changed accents but supposed it was the madness. As Barnes stepped into the small boat, the misshapen man had begun his own trek back to the light of the city. Barnes felt the warmth receding from him as he pushed off from the shore. Over his shoulder, the darkness of the jungle stood like an alien universe, threatening and beckoning at the same time.

CHAPTER TWENTY-SIX

PANAMA 1908

Barnes awoke with a start from the unsettling dream, immediately wanting to get out of the workman's hut where he had spent the night. It was still dark outside, and he quickly stretched and left, heading into the deep jungle. There were no roads beyond where the Europeans had attempted to slice a path through the land that joined the great oceans. Balboa had failed, and, later, so had the French. Still, each attempt had carved a little of the wildness from the jungle, and around the area of the Canal Zone, there was at least the illusion of civilization. Half a mile into the dark land, that illusion disappeared, and Barnes labored along, swinging his machete at the vines that always crept back across the Indian paths.

The land was not silent. He had assumed this upon arriving in Panama and seeing in the distance the dark, mysterious heights surrounding Colon. That first year, with its pounding rain and sludgy streets, had been hard for him. Bred to comfort and the support of a servant population, he had done little hard work. The pick he plunged into the ground with great enthusiasm, desperate to prove to the black men around him he could keep up, became leaden before the sun reached the mid-morning sky. He had swung lower and lower until he could not straighten up far enough to generate the power necessary to break the earth. Aware of the stares and the whispers, he tried to keep going but eventually stopped, bent from the waist and leaning on his pick handle. He had stood like that, eyes closed and arms hanging loosely, until the foreman took him to the shade. There he had sat, numb with exhaustion and embarrassment, as the work went on around him.

No one had urged him back to work, and he knew the black men recorded this. He watched as the men were driven in this fight against nature itself, reflecting on the magnitude of what was being attempted. The granite walls of the great cut towered over him, proof of the tremendous effort that had been exerted over the last thirty-five years as two world powers tried to join the great oceans. The stone had gleamed in the early morning light as the sun's rays bounced off it. The walls were seventy feet above his head, and, from what he had heard, they had to dig down to a depth of one hundred and sixty-eight feet. He had shuddered at the thought of the work that simple number implied.

Six months later, there had been no appreciable change in the depth.

I became stronger, he thought, passing with some difficulty through the densely packed trees.

He had been gradually climbing for hours, but a clearing ahead marked the end of the climb. A river ran across the clearing, and he normally walked along the edge until it was possible to cross where the rocks formed a natural bridge. It was also the point where he could cross unobserved, a precaution that was always taken, although anyone in this place probably knew more about staying unobserved than he did.

Barnes soon became aware of a soft, padding sound in the jungle. Then, the silence returned. His eyes searched the dense undergrowth, but he saw nothing. Reaching the clearing, he breathed a sigh of relief and was just about to sit when he looked to his right. His breath left him. Standing on the edge of the river was a jaguar. In the brilliant sunlight, Barnes could see few details, but he intuitively knew it was the same one he had seen outside the camp. From his oversized pocket, Barnes pulled out the gun he now habitually carried. It was not much but provided some solace.

In the sun, the color of the creature seemed to change, and some of the legends he had heard in Panama came to mind. Animal and man simply stood, staring at each other. Barnes was not inclined to challenge the animal, knowing jaguars were unpredictable creatures. Still, he was not going to stand all day waiting for the animal to make up its mind, so he picked up a stone. As he moved, the animal turned squarely toward him. Barnes froze. The low-slung shoulders, built for speed and climbing, were pointed toward him. Still, it did not look aggressive, merely curious. Barnes decided to wait, and, after a while, the creature turned and began lapping the water. It drank for a long time, but immediately afterwards, slouched away into the darkness of the jungle. Barnes walked carefully toward the point where the animal had disappeared, but it was nowhere to be seen, and he hurried on, anxious to be gone. Quickly crossing the river and feeling somewhat more comfortable with the water between him and the giant cat, he settled into a steady, ground-eating stride that carried him quickly toward the compound.

It was late afternoon when Barnes walked past the hidden guards. Immediately, he knew something was wrong. There was a quietude that was not peace, and the air itself carried a tension. Few men were around, and these appeared to be waiting for something. Barnes strode to the headquarters hut, grateful to be out of the sun. Inside, the Captain sat facing the door, the gloom obscuring his face.

Barnes stood at attention as the Captain said, "It seems you have exhausted our guarantee, Barnes."

Barnes did not have to be told what the Captain meant. Immediately after Richards had been flogged, the Captain placed him on twenty-four-hour underground duty. After a couple of months, Barnes had asked that the man be allowed to come back above ground. The Captain had not argued the point but had asked for a guarantee that Richards would not try to escape. He never trusted the good instincts of a humiliated man, he had said. Barnes had given his guarantee, and the Captain, smiling, had accepted it. Since then, Richards had been a model worker, and Barnes' faith seemed to be justified. Now, something had changed. He waited, and, amused, the Captain said, "As you have probably guessed, Richards has disappeared. He was your responsibility, Barnes. You find him and bring him to me before my men do, and you live. If they find him, he won't survive."

Barnes stood stunned for a moment, not believing the man would kill him. Then, thinking of Bryant's past actions, he quickly re-evaluated his conclusion. Octavius Bryant would kill him without a thought. Nothing was going to stop him from completing what he had come here to do. If Barnes was a hindrance, however incidental, then he would be removed. Barnes turned slowly away from the man whose face he could not see and walked into the brilliant sunlight. Minutes later, armed with a rifle, a machete, a rations bag, and a water bottle, he set out from the camp. The unreality of the day was emphasized by the gentle movements of a black man who was sweeping the yard. Barnes headed south toward the canal, moving along the track they had carved out over the last two years.

He had to find Richards before those bloodhounds who worked for Bryant got to him. Now having worked with those men for two years, he still did not understand them. They lived apart from the other workers and were hired personally by Bryant. He had no doubt they would kill

Richards if they found him first. Around him, the dimness of the jungle amplified his fear, and he pushed on, following the faint track that disappeared from time to time. Knowing where Richards would go added wings to his tired legs, and in spite of a nagging stitch in his side, he closed his mind to the pain and moved more quickly.

He frequently had to swing the machete to clear vines that invaded the path. Why had Richards run now? Barnes had been certain, as had everyone else, that Richards had settled down. True, he was always alone, but, in this, he was not singular. The work was wearing, and the only incentive was the high wages. The men were willing to accept the brutal conditions because they saw wealth, or at least comfort, at the end of the work here. Men, therefore, sometimes worked themselves to a zombie-like state until all they could do was sleep, write letters, and rest before returning to the back-breaking, bone-crushing work they performed underground. Richards was an extreme case, and so they left him alone, allowing him to outperform everyone, taking this as a sign that he had accepted his fate. Apparently, he had fooled them all.

Barnes felt a wave of anger and, for a moment, was giddy. Richards had fooled him, too; and now, with his escape, he had placed both their lives in danger. Richards'— and his— only chance was for him to find the escaped man first. Out in the jungle, the trackers would be expecting Richards to head for the canal since it offered safety of a sort. The Captain would be sealing off, as best he could, any means of reaching there. The Captain had influence in the Canal Zone, and Barnes was certain that, even if Richards reached there, he would die before he could talk to anyone. Richards knew this, and so Barnes was betting that the man would not go there. He hurried on, following his instinct.

Three hours later, he got off the train. Having never before approached the river during the day, he was concerned the Spaniard for whom he was now frantically searching would not be around. At night, although Barnes had no consistent schedule to go to the village, the man always appeared when he needed him. In the daylight, everything was different. Barnes stood peering down the steep bank at the water where many canoes were tied up, but the man was not in sight. He walked along the wharf to the scattered huts that stood in splendid isolation and, since no one was about, poked his head inside one of them. It was empty, and, striding quickly, he investigated five huts before, coming around a corner, he saw an old man sitting on the ground, a corn pipe in his mouth.

Barnes asked about the Spaniard, and the old man chuckled, saying in English, his voice hoarse, "So you are the one. We have all wondered who you were."

"What do you mean?"

"Hey, hey. We don't get too many visitors here at the end of the world, particularly not regular ones. You are a celebrity of sorts."

Barnes was curious but impatient and asked, "Do you know where I can find the Spaniard?"

"Hey, hey. Always in a hurry, too."

The man reached behind him and brought out a conch shell. This he placed carefully against his lips and, adjusting it minutely, blew. There emerged a mournful sound that seemed to be calling beyond the edges of the village. The sound hung in the air for a long time, and Barnes stood in the hot sun, waiting.

Then, the old man said, "Hey, hey. Here comes Charon now."

It was the first time Barnes had heard the Spaniard's name. He quickly thanked the old man, dropped a coin for him, and walked over to the Spaniard.

"Charon, I have to get to the village as quickly as possible."

The man looked at him perplexed, and Barnes realized he had spoken in English. From behind him, the old man spoke in Spanish too quickly for him to understand, but something changed in the Spaniard's eyes, and he turned away, heading to the river.

As they entered the small, unstable boat, Barnes said, "Charon, I—"

Before he could finish, the Spaniard looked at him dully and said, "My name not Charon. Village make joke."

Barnes apologized and asked, "What is your name?"

But the man was busy extricating himself from the tangle of boats that clogged the bank of the river and either did not hear or simply did not answer. As the boat headed east, Barnes was struck by the difference in the river's character during the day. The silence that had been his constant companion for the last two years was gone, replaced by a bustle that he sensed more than saw. Sometimes, through the infrequent breaks in the trees, he glimpsed sparsely occupied villages, and occasionally, something dark and long moved in the water. There were alligators about. Suddenly, the boat seemed very fragile. Water lilies covered the river, adding to its mystery and its slight and sudden movements. In the back of the boat, the Spaniard whose name was not Charon steered casually, almost, it seemed, without thought, and the land slipped by, sometimes hazy in the distance, sometimes startlingly clear.

Barnes thought of Richards and again wondered why the man had run off. Richards was making lots of money, winning with monotonous regularity the monthly bonuses Barnes had instituted close to a year ago. In the years since the flogging, as the humor drained out of him and he seemed to confront the rock of Panama as a personal enemy, his body had hardened and thickened, and even the strongest men in the camp gave Richards a wide berth. Barnes had not thought of how to bring this man back but realized that, if Richards did not want to return, there was precious little he could do without killing him. This worried him. He had no intention of hurting Richards, but his life hung in the balance, too. He suspected Richards felt betrayed by him. The other men had also done nothing, but he knew they had expected him to intervene in the flogging. Instead, he had done nothing, accepting the Captain's judgment. Richards would understand this and would have no assurances of Barnes' good intent. Persuading the man he meant him no harm would not be easy, but he would save him from the Captain. And he would save himself.

Barnes asked the Spaniard to hurry, but the man ignored him, pointing the skimpy boat into the middle of the passage that ran swiftly toward the Caribbean shore. The river changed, becoming less dark, and the water lilies disappeared, replaced by a white foam that covered everything. A mist had also arisen, and this cut them off from the shore. The white froth stretched before them, and unable to turn in the unstable boat, he guessed it was the same behind him. The mist and froth joined in the distance, creating in Barnes a feeling of deep loneliness and isolation. The Spaniard was humming a song Barnes thought he knew but could not quite place, and he concentrated on the sound that was frequently just below his hearing. The melody tantalized him, and he felt suddenly that the sound was coming not from the Spaniard but from the mist itself. He shook his head violently, causing the boat to rock from side to side, and the Spaniard stopped humming, looking at Barnes with baleful eyes. Barnes sat very still.

The mist cleared gradually, leaving the earth glittering in the sunlight. Before the boat pulled onto the bank of the river, Barnes jumped out, hurrying toward the village. It was empty. Leila's hut, too, was empty. He turned just as a woman came from one of the huts. She raised her small, pear-shaped face up to him, and in her eyes he saw the knowledge.

Richards lay on the floor, his arm flung across his eyes, his bulk filling up the hut. Barnes stood at the door, waiting. Slowly, the man removed his arm and looked squarely at him.

"De devil sen' you to get me, Barnes?"

Barnes nodded, and the man glanced at the rifle Barnes carried.

"You goin' need dat. I aint goin' back dere."

Barnes nodded again, and Richards sat up.

"I have to take you back, Richards. You won't escape, and if the others catch you, they will kill you. The Captain said he would spare your life if I brought you back."

Surprisingly, the man laughed easily.

"Mr. Barnes, I aint got no life to lose. You kno' dat as well as me. You de straw-boss now at dat place, so you kno' how we all livin' dere. And dat sure aint no life, I kin tell you."

Richards cocked his head to one side, a sly look on his face. Then, with a slight note of wonderment in his voice, he asked, "It aint my life you worried 'bout, right?"

Barnes looked away, aware of the smokiness of the hut. The clay pots were all over the floor, and on the walls were a multitude of molas, several of which depicted a jaguar in various postures. One, its face lowered to the ground, slim shoulders hunched, staring at something unseen in the distance, caught his attention. Half of the face was human and looked as if it had been scarred.

"Look like a haunt, don' it, Barnes?"

There was something mesmeric about the molas, and Barnes tugged his eyes away, gazing uneasily at Richards again.

"We should be heading back, Richards. If possible, I'd like to be at the camp before nightfall."

Richards pushed himself up from the ground, his eyes riveted on the rifle in Barnes' hand. As he stood, the hut seemed to shrink, and Barnes involuntarily raised the gun, backing out the doorway. The village had filled up, the women standing silently in a wide circle. As Barnes turned, Richards leaned against the hut. The man was exhausted. Barnes lowered the gun and, taking Richard's weight on his shoulders, helped him back into the hut. He could smell the heavy sweat of the man's body, was aware of the strong beat of the heart that pounded under the dirty shirt. Barnes was irritated. He wanted to get back to the camp quickly, but his captive had already fallen asleep and was breathing heavily. Barnes laid across the doorway and was soon asleep himself.

When he awoke, the night had closed in. Richards still slept, and Barnes went to the village center where the men had returned. He was never sure what they did. They sat in a circle, short bodies hunched over the meals. Barnes walked into the circle and sat, accepting a clay plate and eating ravenously. The men continued to speak in a language he still could not understand, and he listened now to the musical sibilance of the speech. Having lived on the edge of the village for two years, he still did not know these people. He came in the night, drank, smoked, and lost himself in Leila's world. They sat, night after night, apparently doing nothing, and around them, their world seemed not to change. In the last two years, there had not been the slightest modification in any of the huts. Each dwelling sat in a moment of time, a place where things existed eternally, it seemed. Leila never changed the position of anything in her hut, and on those occasions when he had shifted something, she always moved it back. Barnes thought how comfortable he was in this world of unchanging routine and wished he could stay here, away from the threat that lay behind him in the jungle.

Sipping the bitter brew the Kuni drank, Barnes thought of leaving with Richards. They could head down the coast toward Colon. He had no idea how far the town was, but this was the Caribbean. How difficult could it be? He could take a ship from Colon to Barbados and end this nightmare.

At the thought of Barbados, a tightness entered his chest. How could he fit back into that society? He had written to Ruby only once in three years and could not subordinate himself to her again. In Barbados, he would have nothing but the plantations. Here, he was free to direct his own life. Barbados would be right one day, but it was not yet time.

He would take Richards back. All he had to do was to get to the camp without being seen by the men who were out searching. Barnes inhaled deeply and soon felt his mind changing shape. Somewhere in the dimness, the woman with the burnt face walked into his mind, and he stood, heading for the hut. He would leave in the morning and take Richards with him. The man's strength would not be a problem now. Richards was weak, and with the gun he would be able to get him back to the camp. His only worry was whether the man was strong enough to make the return trip on foot. Barnes meandered across the sandy loam of the village center, his eyes already beaded and centered on the open doorway that beckoned.

CHAPTER TWENTY-SEVEN

WASHINGTON 1908

Charles Lemieux placed the long-stemmed crystal wineglass carefully down on the blue-gray, marble table and slowly wiped his lips. Aware of the beauty of his surroundings, he did not hide his admiration. The chair in which he sat had been brought from Africa on one of Edward Bryant's trips, and it was solid, made of ivory, and covered with zebra hair. Lemieux had sat gingerly at first, almost afraid to relax on this exquisite piece of artwork. The whole room appeared to be a museum, filled with collected artifacts from the man's constant travels. They had been drinking for some time, and Bryant had become more languid in his movements. Lemieux sat back, thinking of what the man had said. He was in Washington on a short leave, ostensibly to shore up political opinion in Washington but really to get away from the tropics for a while. He had begun to worry about Claudette, who had developed a terrible fever six months before; although she had shaken it, she had never fully recovered, seeming to lack her usual vivaciousness. Bryant had found out about it and arranged passage home for both of them on one of his luxury ships.

Lemieux's presentation before the Senate two days ago had received a standing ovation, although two southern Senators had probed him about the delays. Panama was not giving up without a fight; as they dug, the land resisted with landslides, floods, fever, and heat. Men continued to come from all over the Caribbean, but something was different. They were as strong, as hungry for the gains they believed they would make in Panama, and they worked as hard, but something was different. They seemed to have become fatalistic, digging into the land with a quiet determination to survive.

Above all, fear had come to the canal. Lemieux picked his glass up and drained it, knowing Edward Bryant was watching him closely. He had aged since Bryant had last seen him, and the difference was startling. His hair, now cut very short, was completely white, and the short beard was of the same color. In order to stop the landslides, the tops of the artificial cliffs had been widened. At first, he had been conservative, but as the slides continued, the tops of the cliffs consumed more and more of the labor. The top of the canal was now close to three times the width at the bottom, and still, from time to time, there were slides. He was losing men constantly, and it was wearing him down.

Deep down, he knew it was not the canal that had shaken his faith. Two years ago, he had sent his friend to find out what was taking off his workers, and John McCormick had never returned. He sent two expeditions in after them but found nothing. The canal had become a burden after that, and what had been an adventure had become a task. He still occasionally thrilled at the challenge of some particularly difficult piece of engineering, but now those moments were farther apart, and he had noticed the worry in Claudette's eyes.

His mind was just drifting back to the image of his wife when Bryant asked, "How serious are you about changing the design of the canal? I don't believe your proposal was well received."

Lemieux did not immediately answer, the phrasing of Bryant's question worrying him.

"Quite serious, but I understand I will need backing on this."

"But why is it now necessary, after three years, to change the design? From all reports, you are proceeding well. Is it worth the political struggle?"

"I think so, sir. We've done very well. If this were a conventional construction project, I'd be thrilled. But it's only possible to understand the magnitude of what has to be accomplished in Panama if you're there. The sheer scope of the project can't be conveyed by maps, scaled drawings, or reports. We are, quite literally, cutting a country in half, sir, and the depth of that country is only now becoming evident."

"We had the statistics before you left, Charles. We knew exactly how far down we had to dig in order to make a sea-level canal. Now, you are springing on the Senate, without any notice, a major change in the plan. That has made things immeasurably more difficult."

"I understand, and I apologize, but I did not want the Senate to be prepared by someone else. I think that, with all due respect, I am the only one in the world who is fully qualified to discuss the canal in detail. The statistics were all useless. I didn't realize until I arrived in Panama that they had all been bought from the French. We had done no independent surveys, and the French sold us the surveys from the earliest expeditions. The primary map I had to use when I arrived had been drawn by a French surveyor who had never left the comfort of Panama City. It dated back to 1885."

Bryant waved dismissively.

"Be that as it may, Charles, it does not explain why it took you three years and millions of dollars to find that out. There are questions being asked."

This was the first Lemieux had heard about questions being asked, and he looked at Bryant for an explanation.

"Well, you have to admit that it is quite unusual for a project director to send reports of consistent progress, never indicating there are conceptual problems with the design, and then, three years into the project, suddenly to discover that the project is ill-conceived."

"I never said anything about the project being ill-conceived, sir. I said if the Senate intends the canal to be completed in the timeframe for which the nation is prepared then they had better be willing to change the design of the project. As things stand now, we cannot complete a sea-level canal in the eight years they expect."

Bryant looked pensive for moment, then asked, "What is the truth, Charles?"

Lemieux hesitated, then, heaving a sigh, replied, "Mr. Bryant, if we continue at this pace, the canal, according to my best estimates, will be complete in 1935."

"1935! What the hell are you talking about, Lemieux? No one has speculated that it could take until even 1920. All the estimates have been somewhere between eight and twelve years. You'll never be able to sell that the canal will be built in close to thirty years."

"My point exactly, sir. That is why we can no longer proceed with a design intended to cut the mountains down to sea level. We must change the design."

Bryant thought for a moment, and then said slowly, "What do you have in mind, Charles?"

"Well, sir, it's back to the old idea of a step system that would take ships over the mountains. I—"

Before he could finish, Bryant snorted.

"You mean a lock system. I thought that idea was properly exploded. Wouldn't that involve some fancy damming of the rivers?"

"It does. Would you happen to have a map of Panama here, sir?"

"Actually, yes. I do."

Bryant walked from the room, returning shortly with a large, very detailed map of the country of the isthmus. He spread the wax paper map over a large table. It was a beautiful map, and Lemieux wondered who had done it. After three years in Panama, they still had not created a map with this kind of detail. It even had buildings set in relief against the greenery of the terrain. Impressed, he whistled softly.

Bryant laughed, saying, "It is a beauty, isn't it?"

It was more than that. The map was constructed with an artist's eye and showed the country to good effect. The deep greens of the rain forests were faithfully reproduced, and the representative buildings in the two cities of Colon and Panama City were almost real. Someone had spent a lot of time on this map.

He did not have time for admiration, however, and pointed to a snaky blue line on the eastern edge of the isthmus, saying, "That, sir, is the key to the lock system."

Bryant bent closer to the map and read, "The Chagres River?"

"Yes, sir. If we are to build a step canal, our major problem will be to control the Chagres."

Moving his hand slowly, lovingly, over the map and tracing his way down to the Atlantic coast, Lemieux continued.

"If we could harness the river, sir, and redirect it along the channel that has already been dug, that would give us a fair portion of the canal."

"You make it sound simple, Charles, but I see two major problems immediately, apart from the obvious one of how you can control the river. First, if these topographical shadings are accurate, the river is some height above sea level, and, here, it looks as if it drops off fairly quickly. So you will have the problem of raising the ships up to the height of the river. Second — and here I am guessing—what about the natives who live along the river? They will have to be relocated, right? There could be some bloodshed. Are you prepared for that? Is the Senate?"

Lemieux was impressed. Bryant had immediately hit on two of the main issues. There were others, but these had consumed much of Lemieux's thinking in the last several months. Also, though Bryant had dismissed the control of the river as the "obvious" problem, Lemieux had been surveying the river for a while now and knew its redirection would not be easy. In fact, that was the major problem.

"You're absolutely correct, sir. I'm not certain how troublesome the native population will be, but I'm certain it's nothing we can't handle."

Bryant did not look pleased, and finally he said, "Is that a military assessment or a political one, Colonel?"

Lemieux got it immediately, and said with great certainty, "Both, sir."

"The control of the river and the construction of the locks: Is that what you have determined to be the major challenges, Colonel?"

"Yes, sir."

"Then, I think you are mistaken, Charles. I'm willing to entertain the possibility, in engineering terms, that your lock canal could be built. God knows I've built railroads where everyone thought it was impossible, so I won't gainsay that. The locks will be a challenge, but they could be built. The river I'm less certain of, but I've dammed rivers before as well, so I think that this, too, could be done. What I fear you are underestimating is the political challenge, my boy. Stick to your sea-level canal. Add a few years to the construction timetable and sell this to the Senate. You will get no support on the other."

Lemieux's heart dropped. He was being told that Bryant's help would not be forthcoming if he changed the design of the canal. Lemieux felt an urgency to persuade the older man who stood looking down at the map, and he was on the verge of speaking when Bryant said, "Have you really thought of what we are attempting here, Charles?"

The man was still looking at the map, but something in his face had changed. His body, though relaxed, seemed alive with energy, and Lemieux could see the light in his eye.

"I remember when I was laying tracks in the Northwest. It was impossible, they said. No one would be able to track the Rockies. It was too wild. Too inaccessible. Too cold. Too everything. But I always knew that at the center of every great design is not simply imagination, not simply money, but determination. I didn't out-engineer the mountains, Charles. I simply outlasted them and gave my body as a sacrifice for the victory."

He stopped, his face alight, the memories flooding into his mind. Lemieux saw and wondered.

When Bryant continued, his voice was low, reflective, as if he were talking to himself.

"Panama is not an engineering project. It is a signal for the century. A statement of American power, it is true. But ultimately, it is a statement of man's triumph over nature. We have never built on this scale before. What it took nature millennia to create we are attempting to undo, and we are much more controlled than nature ever will be. Panama is the signal of human purpose, not simply human ingenuity. It is as much a philosophical statement as it is an engineering one."

He stopped, and Lemieux, curious, said quietly, "But you have always insisted it was practical not idealistic."

"And so it is, Colonel. Practical, yes. Idealistic, no. The canal will make money for me, and I would like to see you become part of what I have created. If you succeed at this project, you will have deserved it, but you should not think that philosophy is separate from pragmatism. All the great constructive works of mankind are both practical and philosophical, so it is possible to deduce from the works of any culture what its beliefs were. The Pyramids of Egypt were both practical and religious. They formed a gateway to another world. They were also storage bins for the journey as well as astronomical measuring devices. The Aztecs created great monuments that were both to appease their gods and to ensure their crops grew. Man's instinct has always been to construct that which is greater than himself, and that is, ultimately, a religious instinct, but he has had to be concerned with the mundanities of construction, and this has always tempered his idealism. When people die in the act of sacrifice, it always makes that act more practical."

Lemieux did not say anything, and Bryant continued to stare at the map, running his hand over its uneven surface.

After a while, the man smiled and said, "I have seen in you, Colonel, great determination and surpassing skill. You are truly an extraordinary builder. The organization of the zone, from all reports, is excellent, and you have practically beaten the disease problem. All of this is excellent. What I have never seen in you is the spark of madness that all builders of civilization have."

He stopped, looking, his head cocked, at Lemieux.

"I have found that, on the whole, insanity is a highly undesirable trait in an engineer," Lemieux replied with a laugh.

"In an engineer, yes. But I said in a 'builder,' not an engineer. The two may be the same, but they do not have to be, and frequently, it is best that they are not. We are constructing civilization here, Charles, not canals. Do you see that?"

Lemieux, a little worried about the direction in which the conversation was going, replied, "I understand the civilizing instinct, sir, but isn't the British experience in Africa pretty much exploding the myth of the possibility of bringing civilization to backward races?"

Bryant laughed and, wagging his finger, said, "Indeed, it is, but the British, like every superior culture before them, made a fundamental error. Do you know what it is?"

Lemieux shook his head.

"Every conquering culture, with the accidental exception of the Romans, has tried to take civilization to men, and, by and large, they have failed. They have failed because they have assumed it is necessary to conquer men in order to transmit culture. We are the first culture, Charles, to understand there is another way. It is through the conquest of nature itself that we will transmit our culture. We understand that man is simply a proxy for nature, and in the conquest of nature lies the conquest of man. Primitive man has always worshipped nature. Substitute yourself for that natural wonder he seeks, and he will enslave himself. The Romans came close to understanding this but lost their sense of purpose."

Lemieux nodded, replying, "Very interesting, sir, but what has that to do with building the canal?"

Bryant sighed softly before answering,

"It is everything, Charles. It is why you are ordering men to their deaths every day. It is why you live in such primitive conditions. It is why you endure the misery of the tropics. It is, ultimately, why your concerns with time and cost are irrelevant. You must build the great canal, Charles. Don't be misled by the possibility of shortcuts and economies. They are distractions. Build the monument, not the canal, and you will find that you will have built a fine canal as well."

Lemieux did not know what to say, and he looked carefully at the map, nagged by the thought that something on it was out of place.

"A sea-level canal, Colonel Lemieux," Bryant continued. "That is truly grand. A monument. Your lock canal is simply engineering. It is not worthy of you."

"A sea-level canal, sir, will be expensive in materials, time, and, most of all, men."

"And what, Colonel, should the price of civilization be? How do you determine what is an appropriate cost? We have the means and the money. All we need is the will."

"And the men, sir?"

"Ah, yes. The men. You will find them in abundance. The supply is practically endless. And what's more, you will have ennobled their miserable lives. If they die, they die with purpose, knowing they have been part of a greater enterprise than themselves. In those islands, they have been purposeless for close to three quarters of a century. They are flocking to you because you have given them purpose again."

Lemieux was not certain of this. The West Indians had come with enthusiasm and a quiet determination to succeed. Never having worked with blacks before, he had not wanted these men, preferring the Chinese, with whom he was more familiar, but he had come to see that these men from the islands had an equal capacity for settling into a task. The whites who had come from the United States had quit and headed back to the home country, unable to stand the heat, the hurricanes, the pounding rain, and the death. Those who now remained were less productive than the West Indians, but they were paid on the "gold" standard: a higher wage for the same work. Lemieux did not find this unacceptable, but he did find it inefficient since he lacked the most powerful means of encouraging white laborers to produce more.

What had kept the system intact for the last three years was the absolute poverty of the black men. Happy to receive the comparatively high salaries, they did not complain; in any case, he always had the power to deport them. This condition was changing, and, as he had been leaving for New York, some of the men were trying to organize a group to discuss the wage disparity. So he was somewhat less certain than Edward Bryant that these men were purposeless.

Lemieux turned away from the map as Bryant rang a small bell, and a manservant went to fetch the Colonel's coat. Lemieux felt certain Bryant's mind was elsewhere, but as he walked out, his boots ringing on the marble steps, Bryant said, "Think well, Colonel. Remember that it is civilization itself you serve."

Lemieux nodded goodnight and walked briskly in the chilly air toward the carriage that awaited him.

CHAPTER TWENTY-EIGHT

WASHINGTON, D.C. 1908

Less than an hour later, Lemieux walked into the Southern Arms, where Bryant had reserved rooms. He was a little uncomfortable in the luxury of the place, but Claudette was loving it. She was not as active as she had been before the fever and spent much of her time inside the room. For this reason, he was happy with the arrangements. Lemieux poured himself a large glass of whisky, took a sip, and leaned his head over the back of the chair. Where did he stand with Bryant? The conversation had been cordial, but something subtle had changed in their relationship. For the first time, they were in opposition.

In his mind were two designs. He agreed with Bryant that the sea-level canal would be more majestic. The term "sea to shining sea" would have an even greater significance if that canal were built. The waters would rush headlong toward each other, and finally—in his mind, this always happened at Culebra Cut—the two oceans would meet, slapping each other in their final violence. The energy would drive them high into the air before they would fall back to the depth that would allow the first ship to pass through.

He, however, would be old. The French had first promised a sea-level canal in eight years, and then, when confronted with the difficulty, the estimate had been revised to ten. Lemieux now knew a sea-level canal would take much longer, and he would not survive the building of it. The cost of the canal was already staggering, and if he tried to explain that he intended to triple the cost, he would be laughed out of Washington. Lemieux drank deeply from the glass. He was at a crossroads. If he ignored Bryant, his sponsorship would disappear; if he did not, he was certain to lose the support of Congress and the President. He was about to get another drink when Claudette came into the room. Lemieux smiled and raised the glass in an ironic salute.

"I see Mr. Edward Bryant did not have enough liquor."

Lemieux laughed, accepting the rebuke, and, placing the glass on an ornamental table, put his arm around his wife's shoulders. She leaned into his body.

"How was your visit to the great man?"

"Enlightening. He is beginning to sound like the President. He surprised me tonight, though. Talked about us constructing civilization in that damned place."

"Aren't you?"

Lemieux groaned histrionically.

"Not you, too. I couldn't stand it."

"Seriously, Charles. Aren't you constructing a civilization in that jungle? It seems that way to me."

Lemieux shrugged, not answering the question, but continuing, "Well, Bryant's idea of civilization is to have me complete the sea-level canal. I told him it cannot be done— at least, not in the time the Senate has declared and not with the budget that has been allocated. I don't think there is sufficient political will to sustain this project for the next twenty, thirty years. I've never worked like this. Budgets are guesswork, timelines are speculative, and the engineering demands are unheard of. Yet, the country is holding its breath for the completion of this project. Bryant thinks we should build the sea-level canal because, as he says, we are building for the ages."

Claudette was quiet. Her husband continued.

"He sees the canal as America's great statement about its civilization, the act before which the 'lesser races'—his words, not mine—will bow down. As proof, he cites the thousands of West Indian Negroes who are flocking to the canal."

"Why do you think they come, Charles?"

"They come, Claudette, because, like the Chinese in the West, they are poor, hungry, and looking for a means of bettering themselves. They come because Panama offers a way out of the misery those islands represent. They come probably because we lure them with advertisements that misrepresent life in Panama. I don't know why they come, but I do know they need us."

"But isn't that exactly Mr. Bryant's point? They cannot fend for themselves; they have been able to build nothing in those islands."

Lemieux hugged her closer, soothed by the evenness of her voice, and responded slowly, "For me, the issue is the canal. History will not judge me on the basis of my civilizing instincts but on how quickly and how well I build this canal. After all, when all is said and done, it is just a huge ditch. I am the one who has to build it. I can't lose this commission."

Claudette ran her hand over her husband's thinning hair. She had never heard that particular tone in his voice. Still, she understood. In the last six years, the canal had become his life, and it had been exciting. Until two years ago when he lost McCormick.

Something changed after that, and the canal, which he had fought for four years to build, had become a burden. The grief had not affected his work, and he continued to be the terror of the great cut, forcing the soul-destroying work with what seemed to be his will alone.

She touched his hair, aware of the whiteness that had re-placed the deep black of only twenty months earlier.

I am no better, she thought. *The sickness has changed me, too.*

She had lost weight, and none of her clothes fit anymore. Fear rose in her chest, the same she had felt when the fever was at its worst. They had placed her in the isolation chamber. She had not anticipated what that experience would do to her. She had shut men away in the isolation wards when the fever came and their insides became mush. Placed in the tank that shut her off from all human contact, she now understood the inhumanity of isolation. Too weak and dehydrated to cry, the tears welled up inside her, and something dark had come into her mind. It might have been fear, but it was something outside of her, something from far away and very alien.

One night, she awakened, her body dripping, to find Charles looking down on her. Watching him, she experienced the most painful moment of her life, for he had been crying, the water flowing down his face. There was no shaking of the shoulders, no sobs, just this deep sense of for-lornness coming from this large man with the pugnacious jaw. It was as if the water flowing from him purified something in her soul, and she determined she would survive. The darkness gradually receded, and she had come out of the isolation chamber, somehow renewed, though without much strength.

Claudette remained in bed for a long time after returning to the house on Ancon Hill, and Charles nursed her when he was at home. The West Indian woman moved into the house on a permanent basis, and, over Charles' objections, Claudette allowed the woman's husband to visit from time to time. The sickness changed much in their relationship, and, though still close, their intimacy had decreased. They still regarded each other with fondness, but it seemed as if the triple tragedy of the landslide, McCormick's death, and her illness and near-death had destroyed some part of what they understood as their selves. In some indefinable way, he stepped down into the canal, and his feelings went with him. Now, he was obsessed with the idea of finishing the canal and could not bear the thought that someone else would re-place him. He had persuaded himself that the trip to Washington was to give her a reprieve, but the reason, she understood, lay in what was consuming him now: getting those in Washington to change their minds about the con-struction design.

The Senate had been polite but had not been open to the changes he suggested. He had expected Bryant to see the logic and provide support, but this was not the case. Feeling sorry for him, she asked, "If Mr. Bryant doesn't support you, what will you do?"

Lemieux shook his head.

"I have no idea."

They both fell silent. Lemieux refilled his glass and drank deeply. Claudette watched, a deep sadness in her soul.

Suddenly, she said, "What about the President?"

Lemieux looked at her, surprised.

"What about the President?"

"Well, he has been supportive. Why not go directly to him?"

Lemieux thought for a moment, the possibility floating around his head. Finally, he sighed, saying, "I don't have that kind of access. I wouldn't know how to approach the President."

"What about contacting the Vice President, Charles? He invited you to do so when he visited us in Panama. I don't think he was simply being polite. Why don't you write to him?"

Lemieux looked uncertain, then said, "You may be on to something, Claudette. I think I will write to him. With any luck, he will invite us next weekend. He could be the conduit to the President."

He reached over and kissed her playfully, hurrying to the writing table.

Later, as Lemieux sat sipping from the almost-empty glass, he finally figured out what had been wrong with the map at Bryant's home. The name Culebra appeared twice. One was in the giant ditch he was digging. The other had been deep in the jungle. He had never heard of another Culebra, but then, that may not mean anything. It would be easy to overlook a remote village. He would ask about it though. It was curious.

CHAPTER TWENTY-NINE

PANAMA 1908

Barnes was angry. In the center of the compound, the men had been gathered, and Richards strained against the ropes that bound him. Barnes, held by two of the cold-eyed guards, was struggling to escape as he shouted at the man who sat in the covered chair, quietly sipping from a glass. Octavius Bryant was unconcerned. Without raising his voice, he spoke to the men (now close to a thousand in the camp). The contrast could not have been more marked. With the exception of the guards who ringed the compound, their rifles ready, the faces surrounding him were black.

Barnes was red with anger, the cords in his neck showing clearly from the strain as he shouted, "You said you would spare his life."

The short man chuckled and shrugged.

"No, Mr. Barnes. I believe I said I would spare yours, and I have."

The Captain had a long spear in his hand. The tip was slightly blackened, and Barnes knew it had been cured in poison. Barnes felt his breath come quickly as the Captain held the spear to his eye, pretending to scrutinize the point.

"You said he would be spared if I brought him back. You are a bloody liar," Barnes angrily responded.

A look of irritation passed over the Captain's face, but it was quickly gone, and the easy smile returned. Richards stopped struggling as the Captain stared at him.

"Looks like it's second time unlucky for you, eh, Richards?"

He placed the tip of the spear against the man's leg, close to his groin, and Richards flinched. Barnes felt the tightness in his own groin. He had seen what the poison did to animals.

Then, Richards stared at him, and he saw deep in the man's eyes the recognition of a betrayal that was older than they were. There was acceptance and something that seemed to speak of a broken trust, not of a promise made but of something deeper, more ancient. The eyes were red-flecked, but in the center, Barnes saw something of himself, something dark and unforgiving. The whole jungle, the whole world appeared to be reflected in the dark brown pupils of the giant's eyes. Barnes found himself giving way to Richards' universal accusation, and the Captain, sensing this, turned toward Barnes, the complacent smile gone.

"An even trade, Bryant. Him for me."

The Captain's eyes narrowed. Then, he said, "A trade maybe, Barnes, but hardly even."

The day had become oppressive, and the sun, which never quite penetrated the deep darkness of the jungle, created a heat that seemed to be coming from the ground itself.

Unlike everyone else, the Captain was not sweating.

The man, thought Barnes, *is immune to everything.*

"What exactly will you trade me, Barnes?" he asked with a slight laugh.

The two men released Barnes. He looked around the clearing. They had been there for two years, but, unlike the earlier days, he did not know these men. They were hard and uncultured, and he kept away from them. The faces stared at him, a mass of darkness in the lighter dusk of the forest. In the trees, the sound of the wind moved along the leaves high above, and he wondered who bore witness to this barbarity. In front of him, the smiling face with the dead eyes waited.

Barnes said, "I'll pay you for his life."

The Captain waved a dismissive hand.

"Tell me, Barnes, that you do not mean money. Tell me you intend to offer something valuable."

Deep in the Captain's eyes, Barnes saw not simply deadness but hunger, for behind the smile was an unbearable loneliness, something ancient and painful. It was primordial and so beyond his understanding that Barnes was not sure what he saw. Money would not be the price.

Barnes did not answer, and the man did not press him. The heat grew as the two stood face to face.

The men watched, feeling something invade the clearing and hang from the trees like a vine, yet alive and real. They started to look around, sensing in the wind the presence of something they knew but of which they did not dare to speak. Still, as they looked up, seeking some spirit, they saw only the waving leaves and the suggestion of a sun that stood hidden behind the thick branches. They stopped wiping their faces, and the sweat ran freely down, disappearing into their necks and giving the khaki shirts a dark, stained look. From the corner of his eye, Barnes saw them bend slightly and throw imaginary dust over their shoulders. He could not see their faces, but in that act there was a communion of which he felt strangely a part. They were from his homeland, if such it could be called, and he had to make an effort, no matter how small, to help them. Barnes did not want this, could feel his mind rebelling against this unnecessary restriction of his will, but the undifferentiated faces held him, and the possibility of a bond teased him.

Barnes sensed that the Captain saw this conflict plainly enough. The choice was not of great importance to the Captain, but he wanted the conflict.

"Mr. Bryant, there is little I have beyond money," Barnes finally said.

The Captain chuckled, replying, "Quite the contrary, Barnes. Everything important is beyond money. I suspect you know what I mean."

"Loyalty?"

The man chuckled again, shrugging his shoulders.

"Devotion is more what I had in mind, but loyalty will do. Are you pledging that, Barnes?"

The man was staring intently at him now, the smile gone. Barnes hesitated and then nodded.

"And what is contained in that pledge, Barnes? More importantly, what is excluded?"

He glanced at Richards, who stood with a curious look on his face, then added, "What is the purchase price for his life? How do you value it, Barnes? And what are you giving me?"

The smile had returned to the man's face, and Barnes, aware he was saying something momentous but not sure what it was, replied, "Everything you want."

Then, surprisingly, the Captain asked, "Are you a gentleman, Barnes?"

Barnes shrugged, replying with a short laugh, "What an odd question. You should know the colonies do not produce gentlemen. We're all rogues of one sort or another."

The Captain laughed loudly, nodding his head vigorously.

"Do I have your pledge then as an honorable rogue?"

The tone was playful, but Barnes knew the question was asked in deadly earnest, and he replied seriously, "Yes. I pledge everything."

The short man beamed, and he slapped Barnes on the back, shoving him toward Richards and saying, "He's yours then. I hope you've made a good bargain."

Barnes was not sure he liked the sound of that, but he walked over to Richards and cut the man's bonds. The big man collapsed on him, and Barnes, calling to some of the men for help, carried the giant over to his hut. Inside, they laid him down on the simple wooden bed and gave him water to drink. The other men left, but Barnes waited for Richards to gather himself.

It was a long time before Richards spoke. The giant's voice was weak.

"You is a strange one, Barnes."

"How so, Richards?"

"You mek some kinda bargain fuh me, right? Som'times, we does say dat you don' kno' who you is. An' a man dat don' kno' who he is kin be dang'rous to heself. And to udder people too."

Barnes was not sure he wanted to be lectured by this man, so he replied, "That's a strange form of gratitude, Richards. I'll accept your thanks, anyway."

The man on the bed, whose long legs overhung the edge, did not smile as he responded, "T'anks? I aint sure dat you deserve t'anks fuh wha you do. I kno' you inten' to do de right t'ing, but I aint sure dat yuh did dat."

"What the hell do you mean, Richards? This sounds like more of your nonsense. Soon, you'll be throwing dust over your shoulders, too."

The big man chuckled at the anger in Barnes' voice.

"Mebbe I shou'd, Mr. Barnes. Excep' I don' t'ink it wou'd mek no diff'rance. We all in dis now, so it is only a matter of seeing how it all come out. Jest remembuh. Nuhbody don' give nuttin widout getting' somet'ing back. So de question is, wha' you want from me? An' you shou'd be axin' yuhself wha' dat devil out dere want from you."

Barnes looked down at the huge man, now reduced to this state of weakness by his refusal to accept what had been his fate, and felt contempt for him. His huge muscles were useless against the fate he had inherited, and all he could do was rail against a world that had cheated him in some way. He could not even accept the gift of life. In the end, the huge body was nothing. It could be harnessed, much like a jackass, and made to do the bidding of one whose will was superior. Barnes was not sorry he saved Richards. In fact, he felt good about it, but it rankled that the man seemed so unmoved by what had been done for him.

Barnes looked away, and Richards, seeing the look, said, "I suppose you t'ink dat I ungrateful 'cause you mek some kinda deal wid de Captain to save me, an' I don't say t'anks. Right?"

"It had occurred to me."

Richards looked into the corner of the hut. When he spoke, his voice had lost its stridency. It was nostalgic almost.

"Yuh kno', Barnes, de fellows always had a hard time wid you. We all kno' wha' family you come from, an' dere aint no real love los' between you family an' de men what lef' dat village. You was always tryin' to mek out dat you was one uh we. Dat you was just like we. From 'pon de boat w'en we come over from Bimshire, you did trying to be one uh de boys. Ev'rybody kno' dat. But de mem'ries too long, and de hurt too deep, so nuhbody di'nt want to get too close to you. De fellows kno' dat sooner or later you goin' go back to you kind. An' dey right, too. You an' me is de only ones dat left from de fellows dat come out togedder. Where all uh dem is, Barnes? Under de ground. Under de water. Bury in de trees. But all uh dem dead. Dead. Except fuh me an' you. You carryin' somet'ing so heavy, Barnes, dat you don' kno wha' to do wid it. Yuh can' bear it, an' yuh can' put it down. Ev'rybody kno' dat. So w'en you mek yuh deal wid dat man out dere, doan lie to yuhself dat it is me dat you savin'. You shou'd t'ink 'bout yuhself."

The man stopped, out of breath, and Barnes looked at him, seeing the strong pulse pounding in his neck. Mesmerized by the power of that pulse, he wondered whether his beat as strongly. The reference to the one buried in the trees had been directed at him. Until Richards said that, Barnes had thought his actions of a year ago unknown, but the man was clear. Barnes watched the pulse, wondering what he had done in saving this life. As the silence stretched on, he thought of the man buried in the jungle who had run away with a small bag of gold dust stolen from Barnes. Barnes had sent three guards after him but after two days had himself stalked off into the jungle. Early the next morning, they caught the thief, and Barnes, finding the gold gone, felt a rush of madness. Something with flashing colors seared his eyes, and when the colors had cleared, the man lay in his own blood at Barnes' feet. They had buried him in the jungle.

Now, Richards knew. Barnes waited for the man to continue, but the silence simply dragged on until a man rushed to the door of the hut and shouted, "De Captain give we de rest uh de day off. He goin' have a celebration, he say."

Before Barnes could ask what the celebration was for, the man was gone. Barnes followed him into the muted sunlight. There was indeed some kind of celebration going on. Benches had been arranged in a general square, and food was being placed on them. Two giant pits were being dug for the barbecue. Barnes sauntered across the clearing, relieved at the happiness in the air but with a nagging fear of the Captain's generosity. It concerned Barnes that everyone accepted the absence of the normal rules of law in this place, accepting that the Captain had the right to decide on issues of life and death. There were few instances of fighting or killing in the camp. This was a right the Captain reserved to himself, and the swiftness with which he had used the whip in the early days had dampened the men's inclination toward confrontation with each other.

The Captain was sitting on the slight mound, and it occurred to Barnes that there was something very old about the man, something that spoke of an experience beyond what Barnes was likely to know. The Captain motioned him to sit on an empty chair, and Barnes gazed down on the men below as they scurried from fire to table to hut preparing the feast.

"Why the feast? What exactly are we celebrating?" Barnes asked.

"I thought you would understand. It is not every day I have someone swear loyalty to me, Barnes. The celebration is for you. Look at them running from place to place, happy they have a little time for themselves. I mean the white men. At least, we understand the blacks. They are no better than they should be. But look at the whites, Barnes. What do you see?"

Barnes looked and saw men scurrying about preparing food. He said so.

The Captain shook his head.

"Much more than that, Barnes. What you see are men with the ability to shape their own destiny. With all the advantages in the world—their skin, an open land, and the absence of a restraining law—they have only been able to 'find work.' Not to create wealth, or build civilization, but to 'find work.'"

His voice changed, and a kind of bitterness crept in.

"It is these men I despise, Barnes. The Negro I can forgive for his indolence and his lack of imagination, but I cannot forgive these men. They are worse than the Negroes because they were not born to, or for, servitude. That lot was given to the unfortunate Negro. These men, however, have usurped the Negro's position, have carved from their innate superiority the marks of inferiority. They behave much as the Negro does. In fact, one could even say they have copied him, what with their enjoyment of his music and all."

As if to prove the point, a white man at that moment picked up a large tub and began to beat an uneven rhythm on the bottom. Two black men soon began to ridicule him, suggesting he had never seen a drum before. Within minutes, several of the men had acquired makeshift instruments, and the jungle began to reverberate with the sound of the music. At first, there was a competitive strain in the middle of the percussion as each man strove to outdo the other. There was a good deal of laughing as someone would mishit, and the beat would break down. After a few minutes, however, the beat steadied, and the large wash-pans carried an undertone on top of which the smaller pans began to rattle. The flute had a difficult time keeping up, for the player, a thin Irishman, had never played to music with this strain of violence before, and he constantly lost his place, much to the amusement of the black men who had begun to clap their hands and stomp their feet. More men were congregating in the clearing, adding their voices to the percussive sounds of the crude drums.

Suddenly, something seemed to force the music into a rhythmic shape that suggested curves and bent lines. The men started to dance, a wild, senseless movement that quickly coalesced into a circle, with the large men moving with hypnotic grace in a circular line that snaked first in one direction and then in the other. The food was abandoned, and everyone was in the clearing performing some kind of ritual. The voices stopped when the dance began, and the circling men became silent. The diameter of the circle shortened with each reversal of the movement, and the musicians lay hidden in the center as the huge flood of bodies circled and closed on them.

Still, the music did not stop, and the Captain no longer smiled. As the circle was on the verge of crushing the invisible musicians, the Captain raised a whistle and blew three sharp blasts. Immediately, the music faltered, and the dancing stopped. Without being told, without a glance in the direction of the hill, the men drifted back to the pots and pans they had left or returned to huts from which they had emerged. The musicians were the last to leave, returning their "drums" to the tasks from which they had so recently been borrowed.

Barnes felt the loss. During the bacchanal, unseen under his chair, he had been tapping his feet. Something in him had stirred to the music. This thought brought his mind to Audrey. He stood and, ignoring the call from behind him, headed for his hut.

On a night when the sky had disappeared behind the dark clouds that covered the moon, Audrey had taught him how to dance to this music. The crop had recently been concluded, and the bands were practicing for the festival. From the center of the village, they heard the drums beating with a powerful, thrusting rhythm that caused Audrey to move sinuously around him, occasionally touching him with her hips, hands, back, and breasts. In the night, as the drums pounded, she danced, seeming in the dark night to be a jack-o-lantern, arousing in him something hard and fierce, something that tore at him for release and begged that his insides be emptied.

They had fallen to the parched ground, feeling, for the first time, the madness of their passion and clawing at each other as they surrendered themselves. In the night, the thrusts of the drums were counterpoint to their love; and as he looked up to the sky, the strain showing in the thin ligaments of his neck, he cried out for her, and she answered, wrapping her thin, strong legs around him so he would not escape. He burst, leaving only a sobbing emptiness and the hidden cry-water on the side of his face. The breath left him, and he laid inside the warmth of her, enclosed by the love she exuded. She had cried, aware for the first time of the fruits of passion, and would not let him go, closing around him with a tightness he found reassuring.

They laid for a long time, still in the satisfaction of their passion, and the drums had beat strong and steady into the reaches of the sky, the notes seeming to drop like a blanket upon them. She started to move again, and he strengthened before her urging, rising up to a mountain from which he looked down on her body. He tried but could not sustain his height, and he fell back to her, sinking into her body, feeling the depths of her so that she cried out. The blood pounded in his ears, urging him into some place he did not recognize. Then, he saw the water coming toward him and was aware of the sweat on his body and hers. Somehow, he found the water, and took her with him, heaving himself toward the wetness that soaked his parched soul. Her voice became a beat that matched the drums, and she called something inarticulate, yet familiar. When she screamed, he felt something come apart, breaking into several pieces and gushing out of him into a place he could not follow but tried his best to. The gasping brought him back, and Audrey kissed him again and again, which was unusual for her. He felt the power of his maleness for the first time. Meanwhile, out in the night, the drums continued to beat their urgent message.

A long time later, as they silently dressed, she started to dance again, wordlessly following the dictates of the music. The village had gone to sleep, and it was as if the band was with them, the music played only for them. The tempo changed, slowing to evoke some sadness the men must feel, and the bass drum carried a heavy, ponderous note that seemed to come just a moment too late, causing his mind to stop each time when the note fell a fraction behind his expectation. It was disconcerting to feel this break in time, and he struggled to keep the beat in his head. They stood, half dressed, waiting on the music. When he said that the beat was off, Audrey took his hand and, in the darkness, showed him how to move to that unsyncopated rhythm, seeking out the deeper tonal unity beneath. It took some time, but he got it, and he never again felt quite so free as when his body had identified the spaces in the music and fitted itself within them. They had danced as one that night, feeling a mystic bond, and he had floated on a sea of notes.

Now, feeling guilty about Audrey, he turned restlessly on the bed. Outside, there was the laughter of the men, but he had no desire to join them, having begun to feel he was the sacrifice at this feast. The emotion choked him, and, still trapped in that night of the dance, it was some time before he reached for his writing implements.

Later, having written the letter, Barnes returned to the mound. The day had settled into its own silence, so the hum of the men's voices came from a distance, the occasional laughter cracking surprisingly in the stillness. A sense of unreality pervaded the place. Only hours ago, these men had almost been witness to what amounted to an execution, and now they were enjoying themselves as if their memories had been amputated.

"Why did you come to Panama, Barnes? Your family has means; you have property and social station. So why?"

Barnes said nothing, and the Captain continued.

"Are you so uncertain of your place in the social order? Are there moral doubts, I wonder? If my choices are to become your choices, then you'll have to leave those doubts behind. I'll need that loyalty you've promised. We've been here for three years. I expect, at our current pace, this project will take another ten years to complete. That means, at some point probably not too distant, we'll have a labor crisis. These men will not want to remain here under these conditions, and as they become restless, there'll be a need for harsher discipline. That will be your responsibility."

Barnes was struck by the timeline and asked, "Do we have ten more years of gold in this mine?"

The Captain smiled, then said, "It's not yet time, Barnes. Let's just say the project is bigger than the mine."

Barnes raised his eyebrows, but the Captain waved dismissively, saying, "You'll find out when you need to know."

Just then, one of the white men, the telegraph operator, came jogging up the hill. The Captain motioned him forward, and the man, bending from the waist, handed the Captain a piece of paper. Instantly, the man's face changed, and, after a moment, he said, "Maybe the time has come, Barnes. Our lives are about to change."

He stood, and it was as if something had changed in the atmosphere. Barnes felt the tension return to the air. Slowly, the men became aware of the brooding presence standing above them, and the noise died. One by one, they stepped away from the tables and returned to the depths from which they had come. The clearing was soon deserted, and the Captain walked down the hill and into the office. He soon came out, dressed in a wide-brimmed hat that covered his neck and face.

Looking at Barnes intently, he said, "I'll be back in two days. You have control of the camp. The guards will follow your orders."

With that, strapping the rifle over his shoulder, the Captain headed into the dense jungle. Barnes watched as he disappeared from view, thinking how quickly the jungle swallowed a person up.

Entering the office, he saw the telegram on the desk and picked it up.

MET WITH PARIS STOP DID NOT PERSUADE STOP SHORTENED LINE NOW STOP WILL ENTER IN ONE MONTH STOP.

It was signed "ODIN."

Barnes almost laughed. ODIN seemed a little strong for a code name.

As Barnes stepped into the sun-mottled clearing, Richards, leaning weakly against the door of the hut, waved, a smile on his face, but the man's eyes were hard with hatred.

CHAPTER THIRTY

WASHINGTON, D.C. 1908

Charles Lemieux felt good, and he lifted the bottle of champagne to his lips, doing a pirouette and grabbing Claudette by the waist. She laughed gaily, twirling with him, feeling strong for the first time in a while. He had been magnificent before the Senate and had gotten his wish. He would have his lock canal. They were leaving for Panama in two days, and he was looking forward to that. One thing nagged him, though. Once it had been clear that Lemieux intended to pursue the new course, Bryant had called to say he had urgent business out of town and would be in touch. Lemieux had tried to contact him before the Senate hearings, but Bryant had disappeared.

The meeting with the Vice President had gone better than Lemieux could have hoped, since, as it turned out, Taft had wanted to move in the direction of a lock canal anyway. A meeting with the President had been arranged within days.

He was shocked to see, in a large sand pit, a perfect replica of the canal, and Lemieux smiled at the intended compliment.

"Thank you very much, sir," he said.

"Nothing at all, Colonel. Fantastic work you are doing. It deserves all the accolades we can give, doesn't it, Howard?"

The Vice President nodded slowly, showing his acceptance of the judgment, then adding, "However, Mr. President, Colonel Lemieux intends to modify his approach. He wants to explain his new idea."

"Yes, Yes. I know. The locks. Come. Show me."

Pointing to the model, Lemieux said, "Mr. President, this model presupposes that we will be able to join the two oceans, and we could do that over time. The problem is, we will need more time than we projected."

The President looked at him closely, asking, "How much more time?"

"Probably twenty-five years."

"Twenty-five years?" the President shouted, his hands working furiously. "This nation cannot wait twenty-five years, Colonel Lemieux. Why will it take so long?"

"The estimates were pure guesswork. The French, sir, underestimated the difficulty of reducing the Continental Divide to sea level."

" Twenty-five years! Even you will be gone, Howard."

After a while, the Vice President said, "Mr. President, Colonel Lemieux believes we can make our original schedule, but only if we move immediately to a lock system."

"The original schedule? We finish in ten years?"

"Sir, I believe that with a lock canal we can be finished in fewer than ten years. More on the order of eight years."

Lemieux was not as confident as he pretended, but he needed the President's help.

"Eight years, you say. What is the basis of this new calculation, Colonel?"

"Well, sir, we have solved almost all of the technical problems. The one imponderable is digging down the mountain at Culebra to sea level. If we could get around that problem, we could complete the work in one-third the time."

The President walked across the lawn, his head bent, clearly thinking of the politics of the change. Four years ago, he had held out until the last minute before committing to the sea-level canal. Now, he would have to do a public about-face and, in so doing, risk criticism. He would have to be particularly concerned about those senators who, from the beginning, had favored Nicaragua for the canal.

Lemieux glanced at the Vice President, a question on his face, but Taft shook his head and said quietly, "Let him think it out. It is a good sign that he is taking time with this."

Finally, the President walked briskly back, asking as he came up, "Will it cost more or less, Colonel?"

"What I am proposing, sir, will cost one hundred million dollars less than the current plan and save us a great deal of time."

"You are saying that this project will cost one hundred and forty-seven million dollars, Colonel?"

"Yes, sir. The majority of the cost is contained in cutting down the mountain to sea level. If we eliminate that, we save time and money."

"What aren't you telling me, Colonel? I have the utmost respect for you, but if it were this simple, someone would have proposed it before."

Lemieux smiled, attracted to the man's intuition and good sense.

"As you have correctly guessed, sir, there is a problem we will have to solve. The Chagres River will have to be dammed and controlled. May I use your model, sir?"

"Since you are changing the whole thing, this may not be worth anything now. Sure you can use it."

Pointing to the wiggly blue line that ran along the eastern end of the land, Lemieux said, "That, sir, is the crux of our problem and the solution to our questions. The river is slow moving. Damming it will be challenging but not impossible.

In fact, sir, damming the river solves a series of problems. We will have a functional disposal point for the dirt that is coming from the ditch. We will also be able to redirect the river so that it flows where we want it, and, most importantly, we will create the means by which the canal will actually be completed."

The President looked at Lemieux quizzically, and the Vice President, to whom the engineer had already explained the plan, said, "Mr. President, he intends to use the dam to create a lake here."

Taft pointed to a small blue mark in the middle of the model and, slowly, understanding dawned in the President's eyes.

He nodded, saying, almost to himself, "Yes. Yes. I see what you mean. If you dam here," he said, pointing to where the Vice President had just done the same thing, "this will force the water into this small lake. You will, in fact, be enlarging the lake to a capacity far beyond what is now there. If that works, you will have made...what? Half the canal through the creation of this lake?"

The excitement in his voice was palpable, and Lemieux felt the satisfaction that comes from having someone else see into your mind and give their approval of what is there.

Suddenly, the President asked, "Is there enough water to satisfy what you are asking of the river?"

Lemieux felt relaxed enough to quip, "Not having enough water will be the least of our problems, sir."

"And what will be the greatest, Colonel?" the President asked quietly, looking up from the model. "Forgive me, son, but I have learned through hard experience always to look a gift horse in the mouth."

"Well, Mr. President, the asset is also the liability."

The man nodded, accepting the paradox as only the military mind can. Lemieux continued.

"The real challenge here will be damming the Chagres, sir. The river is much larger than is suggested by the model, and what we do not know is the flow rate of the water during the rainy season. That will determine, to a large extent, how much effort we will need to put into the damming. Although the flow rate will be somewhat faster in the rainy season, every model we have made suggests it is within manageable limits."

"'Manageable limits.' I think I've heard that before. Would you care to be more specific?"

"Well, sir, the flow rate of the Chagres in the dry season is about a thousand cubic feet per second. Let's say in the rainy season that rate quadruples. At four thousand cubic feet per second, the engineering difficulties are not severe."

"Didn't the French try to dam that river?"

Lemieux, surprised at the depth of the man's knowledge, replied carefully.

"The French miscalculated where the dam was necessary. By choosing here," he pointed to the model at a place named Gamboa, "they increased the stress factor by five. It would be our intention to construct the dam at Boohoo. That reduces our problems considerably."

He really had no idea why the French dam had failed, but what he speculated seemed plausible enough. He also knew they were now coming to the part of the problem that engineering could create but could not solve.

"Colonel, how far north does our zone extend?"

Lemieux pointed to a spot just beyond the northern edge of the lake.

"And when we redirect the river, where will the northern boundary be then?"

"Somewhat further north, sir."

"Inside Panamanian national territory," the President said resignedly.

"Yes, sir."

The President looked away contemplatively, his large hands clasped behind his back.

Finally, he said, "Colonel, four years ago, I said to you that the canal was the United States' statement to the world that the twentieth century was going to be our century. This I firmly believe. I also believe the Panama Canal is the single most important act to which this country has so far committed itself. We cannot allow so great an enterprise to suffer any taint of illegality."

Lemieux knew the President was thinking of the way in which Panama had been created a few years before. He had just lost his libel lawsuit against Joseph Pulitzer since the court found there were many peculiar circumstances surrounding Panamanian independence. The President had been accused by Pulitzer of protecting the French investment in the canal since his own relatives were secret stockholders. The threat of American naval power, which had been used to confront Colombian claims to Panama, was, therefore, seen as the President's way of protecting his own interests. He was very sensitive on this score, Lemieux knew; and though he blustered a lot about having taken Panama, he was thin-skinned on the issue of how history would view him and his accomplishments. Having just lost the lawsuit, however, Lemieux knew the President would be disinclined to expose himself unnecessarily. There was no evidence he had orchestrated the rebellion of the Panamanians, but it was certain he had ordered the Nashville to sail for Panama, to be followed closely by the Atlanta, the Maine, the Mayflower, the Prairie, the Boston, the Wyoming, the Marblehead, and the Concord. This, more than any resistance from the Panamanians, had sealed the fate of the Colombian soldiers who had been sitting in the holds of their ships. It was the war that never was, but when it was over, Columbia had been humiliated and Panama was a country. The circumstances surrounding this act and, more importantly, the mauling he had recently taken in the press for his attack on Pulitzer now gave the President pause.

"Well, what do you think, Howard? Are we sufficiently over those attacks in the press to attempt this? I don't think Panama will be a problem, but Columbia may take the opportunity to show this as another example of my 'gunboat diplomacy,'" the president sneered.

"We certainly wouldn't want to be accused of that, Mr. President."

Both men laughed before the President replied, "Well, I did defend myself well against the charges, didn't I?"

"You most certainly did, Mr. President. With respect to Panama, I believe you were accused of seduction and proved conclusively that you were guilty of rape."

Both men laughed uproariously, and Lemieux recognized the words of Elihu Root, Secretary of War.

"But seriously, Howard, how will this play on the Hill?"

"Mr. President, the problem will be in changing the plan. However, if the Colonel can be persuasive about the reduction in cost and the shortening of the timeline, it should be possible to get the Senate to go along with him."

"Well, Colonel, do you think you can handle the Senate?"

"With your help, Mr. President, all things are possible," Lemieux responded.

"He'll make a politician yet, God protect him. I believe it is with the help of your benefactor Bryant that you have been able to move mountains. Where is he on this?"

"Actually, I did meet with Mr. Bryant. He is not inclined to support this change."

The President looked up sharply, first at Lemieux and then at the Vice President.

"Why?" he asked.

"It is not entirely clear, sir. As near as I can tell, he wants to make the building of the canal the most difficult challenge this country has faced. It seems, to his mind, this is the way for the United States to put its stamp on the twentieth century."

"Edward Bryant the romantic. Who would have thought it?" the President said, almost to himself, and the Vice President replied with a chuckle, "A romantic who owns half the country. I'm not sure it is romanticism that drives Bryant."

"What do you think does? He certainly has enough money. Maybe he's motivated by patriotism."

"As you wish, Mr. President, but I would bet anything he sees money in this. He's not the kind who contributes his time and money for nothing."

"Howard," the President continued, "find out if Bryant will oppose this politically or whether he will just stay on the sidelines. If the latter, I want to proceed with all due speed to bring the Senate in line. Any problems you foresee with that?"

"No, Mr. President. There will be some squawking about dictatorial manipulation of the Senate calendar, but we have the votes."

That was two weeks ago, Lemieux thought with a smile. The Vice President had been true to his word, and the Senate had behaved. His face clouded as he thought of what faced him when he got back. The West Indians were becoming more certain of their indispensability to the project and had fomented a movement against the two standards of pay that existed. A petition, surprisingly well written, pointing out the injustice of the system, had been sent to him.

He had wanted the Chinese, a proven commodity. They were distant from their homeland and unable to find the wherewithal to return if they were dissatisfied. The West Indians' overblown conception of themselves as British citizens made them more difficult to handle because they were not averse to haranguing the British Consul to intercede for them. While this was not as effective as they seemed to think it would be, it did create the sense of a negotiation between two nations and had bred dangerous attitudes of equality in the Negroes. This, probably more than the complaints themselves, he found irritating.

"Penny for your thoughts."

Claudette's voice caused him to sit up.

"Sorry. Must have drifted off. I was thinking about what to do with the petition from the West Indian workers when I return."

"One challenge at a time. You did marvelously well today. Even Walters from Louisiana, in spite of his protestations, was impressed. You should be very proud."

"I think we did well, but it simply leads to the next problem, and I'm concerned with Edward Bryant's objection. I can only hope he does not oppose us. I got the impression this was important to the President."

"Well, if Bryant were going to, don't you think he would have done so through the Senate?"

"I hope you're right."

He could not, however, get rid of the nagging feeling that things were not all right.

CHAPTER THIRTY-ONE

BARBADOS 1908

Ruthie sat in the doorway of the small bungalow watching the boy as he walked tentatively across the yard toward the mesh fence that kept the fowls inside. At the far end of the yard, Audrey was hanging clothes on a wire. It had been two years since the girl had given birth, but her body was unchanged.

Still skinny as a rake, Ruthie thought, watching her daughter stretch to reach the line.

The girl had become surly after the birth of the child, as if she resented her mother having taken the child from her by the subterfuge, and Ruthie's eyes moistened a little. She muttered something about being "a foolish woman" to herself and quickly rubbed her eyes. Audrey heard her voice and looked around, a question on her face.

"You saying somet'ing, Ma?"

Ruthie shook her head, not trusting her voice. She sometimes felt lost now that Deighton had left the island for Panama. He, too, had changed after the birth of the child. Immediately, he had complained that the carpentry business was not paying much because nobody had any money. The drought was beginning to affect everyone, and even the so-called well-off black people could no longer afford to fix things. With less work available, he had become alienated from the family. Deighton had always been a quiet man, not imposing himself on the house, but now, he became demanding. She had been disappointed but not surprised at his decision to leave the island. The breaking point was the house Ruby Barnes had given them. He understood Ruthie needed to leave the village because the subterfuge would not have worked otherwise, but he resented her having arranged it without his knowledge. Ruthie was lonely but not angry. She despised Deighton's weakness but understood his pride.

Looking around the place Ruby had given them, Ruthie felt gratitude to the woman. The bungalow was larger than the other village houses and was situated close to the sea, which pounded every night with a forlorn hollowness she found strangely haunting. It had taken a while to get used to the newness of the place because she had lived on the south coast all her life. For the first time, she had felt out of place, away from where her "navel string was buried." She sat now, watching the boy waddle over to the fence, trying to creep up on a cock that watched him carefully. He pretended to be leaning on the fence but would move ever so slowly, from time to time, in the direction of the cock. The cock, in turn, would high step away, never going very far, but far enough to be out of the boy's range.

Suddenly, the boy jumped at the cock, and Ruthie was just about to laugh when she noticed that the cock, instead of running away, had turned, its crown raised. Before her alarm could register, it sprang at the boy. Ruthie saw the red welts before she heard the boy's scream and was coming to her feet when she saw Audrey flying across the yard. As the cock turned for another pass at the screaming child, Audrey descended on it, her hands like talons, reaching for its neck. Realizing that it was under attack and trapped against the mesh, it sprang at the charging girl, its feet, the claws of which were razor sharp, outstretched. The body of the cock slammed into the girl's face, and she stepped back. This was all the cock needed to beat a retreat, and Audrey rushed to the boy, who stood, arms held rigidly at his sides, mouth open, the screams coming without pause. As she reached for him, he shoved her hands away and ran clumsily across the yard to Ruthie, who swept him up, hugging him to her breast and soothing him with soft, cooing sounds. Gradually, the sobbing subsided until the boy was making only a whimpering sound.

Ruthie continued to pat his back for a while, but becoming aware of the silence, she looked to where Audrey stood. Blood dripped from her face. Her lip was split. The girl stood, not responding to the pain or the blood, and Ruthie, taking Audrey's hand, led her to the small gallery. She pressed a cloth hard on to the cut to staunch the flow and held it there. All the time, Audrey continued to look toward the hills in the east, silent witnesses to the drama.

High above, the pitiless sun beat down, and Ruthie groaned at the thought of having to return to the fields. She was already late, and the overseer would have something to say. She kept the cloth on the girl's lip, thinking of what had happened to them. In this village, there were even fewer men, and the women had not been eager to have her. That had not been the only problem. She had moved into the Barnes' house, and the women did not understand how she fit, living in the house of the rich people but working in the fields. They did not know if she was a spy for the Barneses, so they kept their distance. It had been hard, this feeling of exclusion, but she learned to take her lunch alone under whatever shade was present or she went home under the accepted excuse that she wanted to see how the child was doing. Two years later, she still did this, though it meant a trek through the broiling sun.

Ruthie took the cloth cautiously from the girl's face and stared at the ugly gash. Placing Audrey's hand over the cloth, she went into the house, made a poultice, and returned to the gallery. Audrey had dropped the cloth on the floor, and her mother picked it up, a little worried.

Then, she said, "It not too bad, Audrey. Just got to make sure it don' get infect. It goin' be alright."

Audrey looked toward the fields, where the long stems of the sugar canes waved in the breeze.

The ole people uses to say dat God move and talk in de wind, Ruthie thought.

She had no idea if this was true, but, on a day like today, she accepted it because, without the breeze, it would have been impossible to breathe. This was the hottest weather she had ever experienced, and it would be worse back in the fields with no protection from the sun. Reaching for the wide-brimmed cane hat, she stuck it on her head. The hat reduced her, immediately making her anonymous. She said goodbye quietly. Audrey did not respond until her mother was on the last step. Then, she asked petulantly, "Why he always go to you?"

Ruthie heard the resentment in the girl's voice, and her heart quailed. She did not want to have this discussion but knew it was unavoidable. The two women stared at each other, recognizing something inevitable and terrible in their stance. Ruthie was torn. She had no way to express the sympathy she felt, yet she understood the girl's anger. Everything that had been beaten into her, however, forced her to see this as confrontation, and when finally she spoke, her voice was harsh and low.

"You should be grateful. He come to me 'cause dat is what we, all two uh we, decide w'en he born."

The child stood on the gallery, watching, not understanding, but sensing something was wrong. He had stopped crying and stood with his shirt raised to his nose, which he probed with a finger. Alert to the tension the women exuded, he called out in an insistent voice, "Ma!"

Both women looked toward the boy, but he was staring at the older woman who stood, her shoulders now slumped, at the bottom of the steps. Something in her face crumpled, and she turned away, walking slowly, with labored steps, toward the cane fields that beckoned. She could not cry. Somehow, somewhere, some time long ago, the water inside her had dried up, a victim to the cruel sun that shone brilliantly down upon this dry and dusty world. Inside her, however, something poured within her soul, soul-water that gushed and washed away nothing except her remaining restraints. She stumbled slowly, blindly along the cart path that divided the cane fields, aware of the short cous-cous grass that reached over to caress her as she passed.

The snort of a horse caused her to look up. The light-skinned overseer was staring silently down at her, and something rose in her spirit.

"Don' say nuttin. I aint in de mood," she said.

With this, she walked past him, heading to the huge tree stump where the other women in her gang stood waiting. The overseer was angry because not only had she been late, but she had kept the other women from working as well. They were clearing a field, cutting down trees and pulling the stumps. Sawing the trees down had not been too difficult, although the women had never done this before, and the long, two-handled saw had been tricky to manipulate at first. Still, they had gotten the hang of it, and it had become a source of pride when their newly acquired rhythm had accelerated the work. They had started on the field two weeks ago, and after two years in the village, she was finally beginning to be seen as one of them. They depended on her strength and her skill. Now, without a word, she picked up the traces of the two bullocks. Next, she fixed the leather straps around the base of the tree, and, as the women joined her, grabbing hold of the straps, she raised her hand with the short whip in it. For a moment, everything was still as woman and animal waited for the signal that would throw their combined strength against the resistance of the giant stump. The overseer sat astride the horse, watching. Ruthie knew this was the reason she could get away with much that the others could not. She was valuable because, however grudgingly, the women accepted her leadership.

Ruthie dropped the whip onto the backs of the bullocks, and the women began to pull. The tree stump moved fractionally, then stopped. She could see the strain on the women's faces, and inside her stomach, something tightened and stretched. The stump was on the verge of moving, but they did not have enough strength. She raised the whip again, and they all stopped pulling, the women spinning away from the traces, breathing hard, and the animals standing around stupidly. This had been going on all morning, but no one wanted to ask the overseer for more bullocks. Ruthie stood for a moment, waiting for the women to regain their breath and staring at the overseer who sat calmly astride his horse, smiling. He was waiting for her to ask for help. She was a bit of a mystery to him. She lived in a better house than he did, but he had no instructions to treat her differently. Careful with her at first, he had gradually tested whether she had any ties to the Barnes family. As he had given her more onerous tasks, there had been no recriminations, and, gradually, his caution had been replaced by something approaching contempt and, later, indifference. He found her arrogant and sought opportunities to humiliate her. Still, they had found their spaces in the social landscape. He was even lighter skinned than she, and Ruthie wondered whether he had gotten the skin the same way she had.

Turning back to the women who were breathing less hard now, she raised the whip again. They attached themselves to the traces and again the strain showed in their necks, the tendons standing out clearly. Eyes closed, their heads were pointed to the sky as if in some silent prayer to a god that demanded not only their supplication but their pain. Ruthie watched the tableau, her heart on fire. There was something reductive about the look of their haunches as they pulled, the same tension showing in them and the bullocks. A low hum came from the women as their teeth showed from the strain. They were at the end of their strength.

Before she could stop them, however, the overseer yelled, "Pull, damn it."

The women redoubled their efforts but to no avail, and Ruthie shouted, "Stop."

The women dropped the traces, spinning away and leaving the bullocks heaving. The overseer nudged his horse forward until the shoulder brushed against Ruthie's back. She spun around sharply, throwing her hat off with the motion. The overseer stared down at her, looking into eyes that were light like his. Seeing something boiling up in him, she waited, staring directly into his eyes. He leaned down from the horse.

"Don't contradict me again. All of you too blasted lazy. That is why that tree aint moving. Now put your back into it. Come along now."

The women moved back to the traces, pained looks on their faces. She raised the whip. The women were frozen, caught between the two wills. The overseer nudged the horse forward again, and Ruthie stumbled backward. She caught herself and stood still, the whip raised.

Looking directly at him, she said slowly, "I can get dis tree out de ground in a minute. It near comin' out now. All we want is a little mo'e power. Why you don' help?"

The women gasped as one, and the man, too surprised to answer, just stared at her. Ruthie continued to look at him, no pleading or arrogance in her face, just reasonableness he found hard to understand or resist.

Finally, dismounting, he said, "You can use de horse."

Within minutes, the horse was attached to the traces, and Ruthie raised the whip again. This time, the stump came halfway out of the ground. Ruthie whipped the bullocks and the horse, watching the hooves skid on the dusty ground. On the third try, the stump, with a terrible screeching, came out, leaving a huge hole. The women pranced away from the traces, clapping their hands and laughing. Ruthie watched them, a smile on her face and a feeling of triumph in her heart. They unstrapped the overseer's horse, and he mounted, riding away without comment, but they could see in the way he held his back straight and rigid that they had won something. No one had given them permission to stop work, and there were other stumps to dig up, but Ruthie ordered a break.

As they sat down in the shade of the trees, she surveyed the women, all of whom were sweating profusely.

Dey aint no different from de friends I lef' in de other village, she thought. *Even de clothes is de same. And particularly de eyes.*

There was that same deadness that came from being left alone with children and work that broke their backs and their spirits. Most of the women had lost their men to Panama, and few heard from them, so they learned to live in empty houses and emptier beds. Their bodies hardened and became muscular. Ruthie looked at her own hands, calloused and broken in places, showing the scars of her life, and she knew that each one of them looked into the secret places of her soul and saw the same scars. Listening to them now, not understanding their chatter but enjoying the hum of their voices, she felt tired but protected, sharing, in some way she could not explain, the lives of each of these women. She still did not know them well, but, in an odd way, they were the same as Vida, Lottie, Mimsie, and Miriam. She had heard the same screams in this village as she had heard in the other, the same secret shufflings in the night as they satisfied their bodies with the few men left in the village, ignoring the conventions of husbands and boyfriends. They carried these men to their beds because they needed them, if only to feel alive and part of a universe that demanded connections.

They shared these men, expecting nothing of them and giving nothing except their bodies and, from time to time, a meal. Panama had reconstructed their world, and now their conventions were approximate, never precise. They lived contingent lives, made more difficult by their poverty and their dependence. So the little triumph of the stump was important. It certified them to themselves and made a period in their lives. It reduced their contingency and made them purposeful. Ruthie looked at the women, all of them tall, and she felt sorry for the men who dared lay between those legs.

This brought her mind around to Deighton. When he left, she had held herself in, pouring her energy into the two children. She had married Audrey off to Hurricane, and the boy was growing up normal, which was the most that could be asked from these times. Deighton wrote frequently, and, unlike most of the women, she had a good idea of what was going on in Panama. His letters conveyed the terrible loneliness that most of them felt, but there was something else. He was proud. It was all over the letters. He was associated with something great, something he thought would change the world. Ruthie did not understand this. It seemed so stupid to leave your family to dig a ditch so that ships could cross over a country.

And dere is somet'ing unnatural about dat, too. If God intended dat people should sail ships across dat part of de world, he would have put water dere. But dat is just like man. Always flyin' in God face. Never payin' attention to de fact dat God does work in mysterious ways his wonders to perform. Man always havin' to try and perform his miracles, too. Tryin' to improve 'pon wha' God do. It did all foolishness in de long run, she thought, *cause man's work can never stan' up, anyway. Dey always changin' t'ings, tryin' to mek dem better, but deir t'ings always come to nuttin.*

The time drifted on as Ruthie sat thinking, and the women, glad of the break, talked quietly among themselves, not wanting to disturb this strong, hard, yellow-skinned woman who lived in the big house but worked in the fields and who could talk back to the overseer without getting slapped down. She seemed to be at rest for once, and they were quiet lest they rouse her and she put them back to work. This was an unexpected holiday, and they did not want to do anything to change that.

Ruthie, meanwhile, drifted away, thinking of the man who had left but who still loved her. He had been angry when she accepted the house from Ruby Barnes, but she could not tell him Ruby was her sister. She had never been proud of that. Now, that foolish girl had gone and had a child by her uncle. Deighton could never know that. The child gave no sign of being deformed or mentally warped (the result, she believed, of family getting on top of family), but everybody knew that something bad was bound to happen when that sort of carrying on took place. It did not matter that Audrey did not know. Ruby would not tell anyone, and neither would she.

If dat mean dat Deighton have to run off to dat place where God aint come yet, I will accept dat as my punishment, 'cause, as sure as God mek mornin', nobody goin kno' wha happen to Audrey, she thought fiercely.

She had the girl married now, and that was that. Hurricane was one of the few men left in the village, and he had moved to the west coast about a year ago, after he and Audrey were married.

De boy got to put up wid a lot, though, Ruthie thought, sighing.

Audrey had gone through with the marriage because Ruthie threatened her with constant beatings if she did not, and after silently resisting for a while, Audrey gave in. Ruthie was sure she had done the right thing, although she could not shut her ears every night to Hurricane's puffing and Audrey's silence. Something had gone asleep inside the girl, and Ruthie knew the Barnes boy was the cause.

Now, she worried about the letters the Barnes boy was sending to Audrey. Ruthie had to walk to the post office in Holetown to get the mail. She had been picking up a letter from the Barnes boy every few months and, after reading them, hid them under the cellar. He sometimes sent Audrey money, and this Ruthie saved. She had not thought of what she would tell the girl when the Barnes boy came back and asked about the letters, but she knew Audrey needed to stay away from him, and the letters did not help.

This relationship between her family and the Barneses always turned out badly. She still remembered when the white man would come to their house bearing gifts. At first, she had not understood since he gave nothing to any other child in the village. Her father always left as soon as the white man came into the yard, and this, too, confused her until, one night, her mother and father had fought quietly over the man's visit. She had tried to shut her ears, just as she tried to shut them now to Hurricane and Audrey, but it became clear who she was. It had explained a lot to her ten-year-old mind. Her color, for one. Although there were many light-skinned children in the village, she was lighter than most, and her color was always a source of concern and pride. She had often asked her mother why she was so light, but the woman had said it was because she had been born in the daylight.

Ruthie had believed this until the night she heard her parents fighting, and her mother had asked plaintively, "But wha' I could do? Wha' I could do to stop he?"

Ruthie had been perplexed by the question, but when her father called her mother "no good," something else fell into place, and she realized her father was not her father, but the white man was. Long after they had fallen asleep in the room next to hers, she had laid awake, staring into the darkness, trying to rearrange her thoughts about the white man. She had intuitively known to say nothing about her new knowledge, so she continued as before, accepting gifts from the man when he came and silently wondering why she was not like Ruby Barnes, who rode with him on the horses and, more often, in his carriage. The difference between her station and Ruby's had become a festering wound that was constantly irritated by the sight of the white girl in her clean, new clothes and the ease she exhibited. The white girl would come into the village from time to time to play with the girls, for there were only boys on the plantation, and Ruthie would watch her, envious and resentful of the mantle of privilege the girl wore so unconsciously.

Unlike the other girls, Ruthie did not defer to her and, in fact, constantly challenged her, until Ruby had become convinced Ruthie hated her. This was not quite the truth, but what Ruthie felt was hardly any better. Ruby could not understand why the light-skinned girl objected to everything she said, but she feared, just a little, something in Ruthie's attitude that she secretly thought of as insolent. So, control of the girls had become the battleground of their wills. The girls knew this and tried to avoid showing favoritism. Yet, they were proud that Ruthie fought back in a way they could not, and they had urged her on, if not in words then in some secret spirit communication they all shared.

Ruby understood this, too, though she was willing to brave the possibility of losing the battle for control of the group in order to escape the horrid loneliness created by her brothers' unconscious bullying. Ruthie did not know this, so she fought the white girl always, sensing in her the same will and knowing that the same blood flowed in their veins. Her resentment had grown until the day in the yard when she saw the look on Ruby's face as their father hugged Ruthie. Ruthie never forgot that look of horror. The girl had become like the chalk they used on the boards at school, and something strained came into her eyes as they slowly shifted from confusion to some kind of understanding. The look had stayed firmly fixed in Ruthie's mind, and it was the mark and the extent of her triumph. She did not have the horses or the carriage, but she had that look. The white girl disappeared from the girls' lives after that, and Ruthie, to this day, felt this to be her victory. Somehow, the girls understood this, and, though not knowing the cause, accepted her leadership from that day.

That was what made the move to this new village so difficult. She missed her place in the other village. The dozing women around her all looked unfamiliar. After two years, she was still new, still not fully accepted as part of the group. A wave of emotion rose in her chest, forcing the air out of her lungs. Ruthie felt like crying. For what, she did not know, but something painful was inside her. Not a sharp pain that was recognizable and could be assuaged, but one so diffuse, so indeterminate in its location inside her body, that she was not sure it was there. Yet, its presence was evident in her shortness of breath, and, to end it, she called to the women, "Wunna goin' sleep all day? Get up and do de people wuk. Come now."

She stood up briskly, showing an enthusiasm she did not feel, and the women, groaning at the end of the impromptu break, reluctantly stood up with her. Ruthie watched the sky, squinting in the glare, aware she was seeing something odd but not sure what it was. Only after one of the women said, "It look like de rain might come," did she realize that, to the east, at the fringe of the hills that obscured the horizon, there had appeared a strand of dark clouds. It was a long time since they had seen clouds to the east, and, for a moment, she had not been able to identify them.

Rain! God, let it come down.

Intent on watching the cloud, she did not see the overseer ride up. It was only when the harsh voice interrupted her thoughts that she turned to him.

"You people inten' to stan 'round all aftuhnoon? Dere is mo'e trees to get down today, yuh kno."

Ruthie was not sure why, but the man's voice did not bother her as it normally would, and she called the women, gathering them like personal followers and leading them to the next tree to be cut down. As they took up the long, two-handled saw, Ruthie noticed two figures in the distance walking with what appeared to be some haste across the field. Ruthie turned away, not recognizing them but thinking they would get there sooner or later. She signaled Dorothy, a large woman with enormous thighs, that she was ready to begin, and the woman placed the saw against the bark of the mahogany tree and pulled deliberately, a motion Ruthie returned. Soon, the rhythm was struck, and the saw flew steadily back and forth, each pull eating into the hard, resistant wood of the tree. As she sawed, Ruthie remembered the awkwardness of the early days when they did not understand the use of the tools, and the women had screamed at each other in frustration while the overseer laughed or yelled offensive names at them. It had been difficult to get them to act in concert, uncertainty leading them to make mistakes. Ruthie was proud that she was responsible for the elimination of that insecurity. There was no evidence of it now as the saw flew back and forth, slicing into the very marrow of the tree. Still, this was hard work, and the women spelled each other frequently, trying to conserve their strength.

As Ruthie sat, awaiting her turn at the saw, she glanced at the approaching figures, a suspicion dawning in her mind. Standing, staring at the two shimmers in the heat waves that were now getting closer, she took a step in their direction, a sudden fear rising in her chest. It was Audrey and the boy. A worried frown appeared on her face as she strode out of the shade into the sharp burn of the sun. Her anxiety changed to anger at the thought of the boy out in the heat. The sawing stopped. Ruthie heard the boy crying and was about to shout at the girl to lift him up when she saw Audrey's face. It was stricken. Ruthie felt the fear that always sat at the back of her mind come in a wave. Audrey arrived out of breath, and Ruthie picked the crying boy up, resting his head against her shoulder.

Finally, the girl said, "A man jus' come by de house and say dat Miriam dead."

CHAPTER THIRTY-TWO

BARBADOS 1908

Ruthie walked from the west coast to the south, where she went into the undertaker's parlor to look at Miriam's body. It was not yet prepared, and Ruthie struggled not to gag at the sight and smell of the woman. The stench of decomposition hung in the air, and Ruthie's first thought was not to show her disgust lest she insult the woman. She was surprised to see the whiteness of Miriam's skin and, underneath, the dull darkness that seemed to be reaching up to the surface. Ruthie was not afraid of the dead woman, but there was something eerie about the stillness and the strange coloration.

She stood, mesmerized, staring at the decomposing body and thinking, with some guilt, she was somehow responsible. Maybe if she had not left the village, Miriam would have been all right. This was not true. The woman had died a long time ago, when her child had expired, its empty stomach distended and its silent cries reaching deep into the secret recesses of the women's hearts. Ruthie, from time to time, could still hear this silent, noiseless cry that signaled the child's presence. The women would look away when this happened, and Ruthie had scolded them for it. It was not their fault, she knew. They just did not want to see the suffering, but, in some way, they had all left Miriam to her own fate.

She aint change at all, Ruthie thought, looking at the decomposing face that still bore some resemblance to the woman who had been her friend.

She did not touch the body, her beliefs preventing this, but she did not run away from the unwholesome smell of the dead woman, seeking, it seemed, in the union of smell to find some solace, some forgiveness. The silent body conceded nothing. Ruthie left the undertaker's home, desolation in her soul.

Coming into the village, Ruthie was surprised at the deterioration. The houses were dilapidated, and the gardens showed signs of neglect. Walking in the fierce drizzle, she noticed that Lottie's gate had half fallen off, giving a forlorn quality to the village that went beyond the broken windows and rotting wood. Ruthie stopped, an odd action in the rain. As she stood in the middle of the road, no one came out, and a feeling of desolation fell on her. The low sky possessed a feral brightness that lay just behind the dark, glowering clouds, and she felt trapped between the sky and the earth. There was a weight on her shoulders, crushing her. A whimper escaped her, and, confused, she moved on to the old house in which she had lived. It was now rented to a family who paid her when they could.

As she stepped on to the rectangular, limestone blocks that served as steps, the door opened suddenly, and a sharp-faced man practically pulled her inside. Ruthie, not accustomed to being touched so roughly, quickly extricated her arm. The man stood uneasily, chastened and uncertain what to do. Ruthie sat down without being invited, and the man's wife and three children stood over her, their discomfort evident. It took her a while to realize they were awaiting her command. Somehow, she had become an owner without knowing it, and the thought unsettled her.

"I come fuh de funeral tomorrow. Wunna got any space w'ere I could spen' de night?"

The new occupants, aware of their vulnerability since she never insisted on the rent, instantly agreed. The three children, all seeming about the same age, about four or five, stared at her as she sat on the rickety pine chair, waiting for the cup of hot tea she had been promised.

When it came, the wife, a small, mousy woman who seemed not much older than the children, asked, "Mrs. Greaves, you did know de woman who dead well?"

Ruthie looked up, all her disdain draining away. The dirt on the woman's face gave her the same look of brittle vulnerability Miriam had had. Her eyes were those of a hunted rabbit, the brightness suggestive of an insanity that was not far away. Ruthie could tell the children were a burden, probably her husband's idea, and feeling a sudden comradeship with the woman, she said, "Come, chile. Siddown here."

The woman cautiously sat, and Ruthie reached out, patting her hand. They sat in silence for a while, listening to the rain, unsure of its meaning. Then, Ruthie said, "Yes. Me an' Miriam did friends since we did little girls. She did a funny one, though."

"Wha' you mean?"

"Well, Miriam nevuh seem to unnerstan' dat life did somet'ing serious. W'en we was girls–back w'en God was a chile–she was always in trouble fuh one t'ing or another. I remember one time she mudder sen' she to buy flour from Miss Drayton. You won't know she; she dead a long time ago, but she uses to sell t'ings in de village. People uses to say dat she was a slave w'en she was young. Anyway, Miriam mudder sen' she to buy flour from Miss Drayton, an' de girl di'nt come back home 'til de sun getting ready to go down. An' worse dan dat, she aint got nuh flour. W'en de ole lady ask Miriam wher' she went all day, Miriam, quick so, tell she dat she did in church all day, prayin'. Well, de ole lady know Miriam, so she grab she by she han' and march down to de Church uh God wher' dey all went to church. Well, de church close up tight tight 'cause nuhbody aint dere. Miriam mudder asked she how she could get in de church if de church shut up, and Miriam, quick so, answer back, 'De Lord turn me into a spirit, Ma.' She mudder was so surprise dat she bu'st out laughing."

Ruthie started to chuckle; then, sensing the water coming into her eyes, added, "Course, dat di'nt stop she from cuttin' Miriam ass right dere in de road. Wid everybody watching, she raise up de girl dress and maulsprig she backside. All de time, wid ev'ry lash, de ole woman was saying, 'Hard ears, yuh won't hear; own way, yuh goin feel,' and everybody laughing and pointing at de holes in Miriam bloomers."

Ruthie's voice drifted off, lost as she was in the memory of that faraway day. Outside, the drizzle continued, giving the ground a new scent, one that smelled of an exhalation from the dry earth. There was something old and decayed about the smell, something that spoke of sweat and blood, bladder-water and cry-water. Ruthie had not been aware of it before, but, somehow, the memory of days past brought it to the edges of her senses.

She watched, from the corner of her eye, the young woman who clearly wanted to ask her something.

"Well, wha' yuh t'inkin'?"

The young woman hesitated, then asked, "You kno' anyt'ing' 'bout slavery?"

Ruthie understood the question well enough. The girl wanted to know if she had been a slave. It was considered impolite to ask that question, everyone being so anxious to forget that time.

"Only wha I hear 'bout. Miss Drayton dat I just mention wud only talk 'bout it to de ole people, but sometimes, we wud hear some uh wat dey talk 'bout. I don't kno' too much, but from wha' I unnerstan', it sound like it did pure hell fuh dem people. I hear Miss Drayton say one time dat she husband, who did dead befo'e I born, get beat wid a whip by one uh de Barnes 'til he skin practic'ly tear off."

Both women shuddered at this, and Ruthie continued, "An' ev'rybody had to work mornin', noon and night. Yuh kno' what dem say. 'Dere aint no rest fuh de wicked.' Well, lemme tell yuh. All uh dem slaves musta been plenty wicked."

They both laughed, and Ruthie touched the woman's hand again. Then, the younger woman asked, "You kno' dey find you frien' in de grasspiece widdout any clothes? Flat 'pon she back, wid she legs open like she did waitin' fuh somet'ing. She clothes did fold up neat neat, an' she use dem as a pillow."

Ruthie turned to the woman. She had not heard this, only that Miriam had been found in one of the Barnes' fields not far from the Great House. Of course, Miriam was mad, so there was no telling what she had done. Still, what the woman described sounded odd, even for Miriam.

The next day, standing by the graveside, Ruthie thought again of the conversation with the young woman and wondered what would have induced Miriam to take off her clothes. The women were shuffling around, and she realized the preacher was done with his sermon, or, at least, he had stopped. All eyes had swiveled to the left, staring at something. Ruthie turned. Ruby Barnes was making her way cautiously through the mud of the cemetery. She wore a long, black dress, foolish in the rain since it dragged on the ground, and a black veil covered her face. Her gait, though careful, was unmistakable, for even making her way between the mounds of the graves, Ruby Barnes stepped on the ground as if she owned it—which, in fact, she did.

Ruthie was uncertain how she felt about this woman coming to Miriam's funeral until Lottie sidled up to her and whispered, "It is she dat kill Miriam, yuh kno'."

Ruthie did not know how this was intended but felt certain it was true.

CHAPTER THIRTY-THREE

Haight hurried up the steps of the building, which stood over a mile and a half from the main road. Maple trees shaded the long drive that curved back and forth through well-cut lawns. Anglesey House, the home of Colin Anglesey, represented old money—very old money. Although Anglesey never claimed his ancestors came over on the Mayflower, everyone assumed they had, and he did not disabuse them of that thought. He knew ancestry had its advantages.

Haight wondered what the man would be able to tell him about Panama. They were not friends, but Anglesey, like Haight, had been a cog in the vast machinery of the State Department, and though his role had never been clear, Haight knew he was a field man. Like Haight, he had gone to Harvard, and like Haight, with no real need to work, he had gravitated toward the government. They had met a few times at affairs in Washington and had occasionally exchanged information. Haight had been able to help him from time to time but had never asked for repayment. The man's sense of honor made him feel indebted, and this had passed for friendship over the years. Haight had not seen Anglesey since taking leave from the service following his breakdown, so Anglesey's call earlier that morning had been a total surprise.

He and Dean had been trying to make sense of the letters. The later letters, those written around 1912, were tortured and difficult to understand, except for the fact that something monstrous had happened. The writer had clearly been looking for a way of talking about the event without disclosing what it was or his role in it. Haight found the mystery a little irritating after a while, and, were it not for Nieves and Hanscom, the two agents who had dropped out of sight after talking to him, he might have dropped the whole thing. There was a mystery here that his every instinct told him was dangerous. Nieves could have just gone to ground to wait this thing out, but Haight was no longer sure. Two days ago, he had called Hanscom, whose wife was frightened and terribly worried. Her husband had disappeared, and no one seemed to know what had happened to him. Nieves' disappearance might have been overlooked, but to assume that both agents had taken off immediately after talking to him was pushing coincidence too far. Haight was beginning to see the pattern. Someone with lots of resources and power was cutting him off from the trail he was following. That someone also seemed to know every move he was making. This, more than anything, worried him.

He was getting in pretty deep but could not stop. Dean was bravely carrying out the tasks assigned to him, but Haight could see the fear in the young eyes. This angered him. No one should have his innocence stripped away so early.

Now, as Haight parked the car in front of the magnificent mansion, he wondered what had prompted Colin Anglesey to call him. The man had been cryptic on the phone, and Haight had known immediately the call concerned Panama.

The oak door with the shining brass knobs opened as he walked up the long marble steps. The house was relatively new but had been built in an archaistic style suggesting something from the nineteenth century. Haight had been there once before, at an affair held in honor of some agreement between the Soviets and the United States. He was not sure of the details but, given who had been at the dinner that night, he knew Anglesey traveled in pretty rarified air.

Haight handed his coat to the black butler and was led through the house to the rear. Colin Anglesey was sitting on a marble patio overlooking a pair of tennis courts. In the distance, the bucolic landscape of northern Virginia spread like a painter's idea of paradise. The view was magnificent, with the greenery of late spring reaching up toward heaven like a suppliant's hand. The black man had announced him, and Haight stood gazing at the distant landscape as Colin Anglesey came up, his hand outstretched.

"Hi, Jack. How have you been? I haven't seen you since…when was it? Four years ago at the signing?"

Haight stuck his hand out, nodding as he did. Close up, Anglesey looked even more the patrician, dressed in a long, white pair of tennis slacks and a matching sweater. Haight was led to a cushioned wrought-iron chair that sat on the side of a table with a basket of fruit on it. "What do you think of the view?"

"Absolutely incredible, Colin. How did you find it?"

"Actually, one of my companies has owned the land for quite some time. We were thinking of turning it into a winery, but the soil wasn't right. In any case, someone asked me to take a look at it when we were making the decision, and I fell in love with it. It's wonderful to wake up to, I assure you."

Haight could not agree more. He was, however, impatient to get to the purpose for his visit, and as if Anglesey had read his mind, he said, "I suppose you're curious about the call. Well, that's only natural." He paused, then added,

"A number of people have been made nervous by your inquiries, Jack."

"Which inquiries, Colin?"

"Come now, Jack. You've been asking around about Panama, and that has made very important people uncomfortable. There's much that's going on there you don't understand. I've been asked to suggest caution to you."

"In other words, I'm being warned off. What's so important about Panama, Colin? Why has it been necessary to kill to protect whatever it is these 'important people' want to hide?"

Anglesey's face turned sour.

"You aren't becoming maudlin, are you? You know better than most that death is the ultimate form of diplomacy. There're always deaths to account for in any operation. You know that."

Haight felt his stomach turn. Colin Anglesey had the reputation of being a cold fish, but Haight was surprised and disgusted by the callousness of the man's comment.

"Not civilians, Colin. We've always made the distinction. The girl's death was totally unnecessary."

"A mistake. Insufficient control over the operative. That will be dealt with, Jack. What is important is your next move. They know you've been tracking information about Centron. That was not wise. You have no idea what you're digging into."

"You're right. I have no idea, and that's why I have been digging. Maybe if I knew what was going on, I wouldn't have to dig anymore."

The offer laid between the two men, both of whom had seen so much deception in their lives, and finally Anglesey said, "It's big, Jack. There are people who will stop the canal from being handed back to the Panamanians. I don't have to explain this to you, but the canal controls shipping around the world. They cannot afford to have this disrupted. Central America is very dicey, and we need this foothold."

Haight listened in the way an analyst listens, for the changes in pitch that would signal the lie, the half-truth, or the truth that was intended to deceive. Colin Anglesey was good, as good as Haight, and his voice betrayed nothing.

Haight asked, "What's the relationship between all this and the girl's death? She was not involved."

Anger had crept into Haight's voice, and, seeing the smile on Anglesey's face, he stopped.

"Life is never simple, Jack," Anglesey replied, a great tiredness in his voice. "The boy's speculations about Panama raised questions best left unasked."

"What questions?"

"His speculations about the depth of the canal. There are issues here neither he nor you understand. The answers to his questions frightened a lot of people. Which brings me to the question of the letters. They know you have them. You were seen leaving the boy's mother's home in Brooklyn with a package. I assume it contained the letters."

There was no point denying this, so Haight nodded, and Anglesey sighed, asking, "What do you make of them?"

Haight shrugged, knowing he had the upper hand at the moment because, though they had stolen the set from the young girl's apartment, they could not be sure they had all of them. Something in the letters had frightened someone. Haight was certain Anglesey was not speaking for himself, but he did not know the level of Anglesey's involvement or whether he was frightened. Anglesey seemed composed, but he was a professional.

Anglesey removed a thin cigarette from a packet on the table and, placing it in an ivory holder, lit it and inhaled deeply before blowing a stream of blue-gray smoke high above his head. He cleared his throat and said, "There was an accident a long time ago."

"What kind of accident?"

Anglesey hesitated, then added, "It was a difficult time, Jack. Our national pride was on the line. The French had failed miserably in Panama, and we had capitalized on this. The canal became our statement about the shift of the balance of power and world leadership from Europe to the Western hemisphere. We could not afford to fail. The very honor of the United States depended on our success."

Anglesey paused, then continued.

"I don't know how much you know about the building of the canal, but we had originally decided to build a sea-level canal just as the French had. By 1908, it was clear to everyone that this would take too long and cost too much money. It was at this point the strategy shifted, and the decision was made to build a lock canal, the kind of canal that exists today. It was still a glorious achievement but considerably less than was intended when we started. The dream had been the joining of the Atlantic and the Pacific in one continuous flow of water. This had been the dream since Columbus, and Europe had failed repeatedly, the French failure being simply the latest. Now, America was compromising, too. There had been a group of very powerful opponents to the Panama Canal from the beginning. Many of the senators from the Southern states objected to the Panama route, arguing instead for a route through Nicaragua. The reasons for this may not today be immediately obvious, but—"

"The Civil War had ruined their economies, and a Nicaraguan route, with its proximity to the Southern ports of Louisiana, Mississippi and Alabama, offered the possibility of restoring their prosperity through trade," Haight said, impatiently.

"Yes. That was exactly it. When the Senate voted over the objections of these senators to change the mode of construction, what had been an argument made on the basis of economic progress became allied to the one around national pride. It made for unlikely allies, but you know how that is. 'The politics of convenience,' I think you once called it. After 1908, politics and power became allies, and suddenly the

South had a champion who had been an opponent. He had vast resources—"

Again, Haight interrupted, a dawning comprehension evident in his eyes.

"Edward Bryant."

This time, Anglesey was surprised, and it showed.

"My compliments, Jack. However, that is a dangerous name to know."

"Why?"

"Do you know who he was?"

"Yes. He was an industrialist. From what I understand, probably more successful than the other big names from the nineteenth century like Carnegie and Rockefeller, but much less well known. I believe he disappeared somewhere in South America."

Anglesey nodded, clearly impressed, then added, "He was much more than that, Jack. In many ways, he was the money and the muscle behind the canal. He made a fortune from the railroads and another in shipping. The canal was to be his grand gesture. He, as much as the government, supported the building of the canal financially. Between 1903 and 1908, he made sure the project stayed on course, supplying it with shipping at reduced rates, funding in times of difficulty, influencing the Colombian government from time to time, and generally providing the support in Washington to ensure the project kept on track. Then, in 1908, all that support disappeared, as did he, although his influence continued to be felt for some time after that."

"Where did he go?"

Anglesey shrugged, indicating ignorance, and Haight recognized in the gesture the lie. He was being told some kind of truth, but not the whole truth. Anglesey was misdirecting him. This was not all bad because it meant he was on to something. It also meant they did not know what he knew and where his influence lay. The latter explained why they had watched but had not tried to get rid of him.

Not wanting Anglesey to know he had seen the lie, Haight repeated the question.

"Somewhere in South America. What's important is he continued to finance another project in Panama."

"Another project?" Haight asked.

"Yes. He was disappointed that America was giving up the dream to join the two oceans. He withdrew his support from the official canal and began secretly to build a competing project in the jungle. It was foolhardy but just the kind of thing he was famous for doing. As you know, he made his original fortune building railroads where it was said they could not be built. This latest action, however, placed him in jeopardy in two ways. One, he was now operating outside the constraints constructed by the government of the United States, and this placed him in conflict with the President—first Roosevelt and then Taft. Secondly, he was illegally building his city on Panamanian territory. While this did not constitute a major problem, the new Panamanian government being weak and dependent on the United States, it created an area of vulnerability. The other project was secret, but it was difficult to disguise so large an operation. Bryant had been a friend and supporter of Roosevelt, who, when he found out about the alternative project, chose to ignore it, seeing it as the folly of a very wealthy man. However, the rumors started to escape from Panama that men were disappearing from the canal into the jungle. Roosevelt did nothing about these rumors because the pressure from the Southern senators had suddenly disappeared. The canal was proceeding smoothly, and the public was enthusiastic, so the President saw no reason to raise questions about what he privately called 'Bryant's Folly.' By the time Taft became President, the secret project, with all its anomalies, was so established that he could do very little even if he wanted to."

Haight was intrigued.

"You mentioned 'anomalies.' What were the anomalies?"

Anglesey hesitated, and, again, Haight got the feeling he was being told half the truth. Certain Anglesey was acting, Haight stared at him, the picture of interest.

"Well, you've read the letters. You know some things were going on that were not entirely kosher."

It was a good answer, yet no answer at all. The perfect feeling-out response. It did tell Haight that Anglesey had read the letters though.

He did not bite, and Anglesey continued after a while.

"The secret project had the same problems as the official one. Labor. The canal's leaders had raided the Caribbean islands for men, and this was also where the secret project went. For example, between 1908 and 1915, the two projects extracted close to thirty percent of the men from Barbados. That, as I understand it, was what your new employee was studying when he ran into the letters on which he based his hypothesis."

Anglesey paused, taking a sip from a glass that had appeared on the table.

"There was one problem that had been solved in the official project that was not in the secret one," Anglesey continued. "That was the problem of malaria and yellow fever. From all reports, the mortality rates were so high that eventually the group in the jungle resorted to kidnapping from the official project. Men started to disappear into the jungle, and the commander of the project, a Colonel Lemieux, sent an unofficial expedition to see what was going on. The crew never returned, and Lemieux could never get anyone to pay attention. Not surprising, considering his benefactor, Edward Bryant, was also in charge of the secret project. In any case, the death count was astronomical, and the project was failing when someone got the bright idea to use the Indians in the area as a labor force. Well, that pretty much destroyed the project because the Indians reacted badly, and, in addition to the high mortality rate from malaria and yellow fever, now was added the attacks, which took place more and more frequently. Eventually, they had to abandon the project because they could not replace the labor force."

Haight sat silent, unaware of the watery spring sun that had emerged from the hills to the northeast. He tried to picture the place that must have been killing these men so long ago, but he could not. In Panama, he had stayed in the city, protected by the illusion of civilization, with full markets and modern cars that ran along highways suggesting connectedness to a modern world. The cuisine he had eaten was international, the garment stores and the banks recognizable, all identifiable as links to a world that he knew and understood. This world that Anglesey described was unfamiliar. It was as if he had not really seen the country, as if it had covered itself with a cape that blocked out the malevolence in its eyes. Much of what Anglesey had said made sense, but something nagged Haight, who watched the slender, aristocratic windpipe bobbing up and down as Anglesey drank.

"Why is this a threat today, Colin? Why are people dying today to protect what seems an embarrassing, but hardly fatal secret?" Haight asked.

Anglesey hesitated, then replied cautiously, "'Fatal' is a matter of perspective, isn't it? Much like in 1908, economic and political interests have coincided. You have been investigating Centron, so you know its interests are vast. Even a cursory look—and we know your look has been anything but cursory—will suggest its base wealth is generated through shipping. Centron will not allow the canal to go from its control. It's as simple as that."

"Not so simple. I thought the government controlled access to the canal."

Anglesey shrugged again, and Haight understood the gesture. Still, he asked incredulously, "That whole military structure, the whole Southern Command, is there to protect Centron's interests?"

"It's not that sinister, Jack. Let's say the interests of the government and those of Centron intersect at a variety of points."

Haight felt his tension rise. He was close to something, but Anglesey was telling him just enough to get him to stop his investigation. Still, he had to press ahead, not giving away the fact that he knew less than they assumed he did.

"You mentioned political interests. What are they?"

"Well, it's rather confounding, really. Fifteen thousand people died in that jungle. No one would believe the United States' government had nothing to do with the project or, at least, did not condone it. "

"Why would anyone care what Barbados or Panama thinks?"

Anglesey sighed, saying, "You ought to pay more attention to what is going on around you, Jack. Some jackass blew up a Cuban airliner just off the coast of Barbados a little while ago, and the finger has been pointed—wrongly as it turns out this time—at the Agency. The last thing this President wants is a weakening of the relationship with the third world. More importantly, the Agency agrees with him on this, although on very little else, but for very different reasons. There can be no movement of the English Caribbean toward Cuba, and this airliner episode has created a good deal of sympathy for Castro. If, in this atmosphere, a report comes out saying that thousands of West Indians were allowed to die in the Panamanian jungle, what do you think the effect would be?"

The question hung in the air, and Haight understood. He knew the Agency worried about the Caribbean because all the conditions for revolution were there. Haight had not been too involved with the area, having been a Southeast Asia expert, but he had heard the reports. The ex-British colonies were poor, uneducated, and without prospects. Cuba was aggressively promoting revolution in Latin America, and the Agency had its hands full containing the communist country's influence there. The last thing they would want is for the English Caribbean to start looking at Cuba as a model. So far, that had not happened.

Still, two people were missing, and one was dead. He could not accept what he was hearing as the reason. Betraying his ignorance was dangerous, but he could not resist the question he next asked.

"What of the rumor that there's a split in the government over this Panama issue? My intelligence suggests the Agency can't be trusted on this, that the President may be out there on his own, and, at best, his policy will be undermined."

Anglesey looked uncomfortable for the first time. He lit another cigarette but was no longer as assured as he had been. Haight knew this was the real reason he had been invited to Anglesey House. They had not known whether he was aware of the plots being hatched, but they knew Haight had his own contacts and his own protections, and this meeting was designed to find out where he really stood.

The pattern was clear. First, he had been vaguely warned by Anglesey, then gradually he had been brought into the circle of information. Now his patriotism had been subtly appealed to. Haight had no doubt he was being lied to, though every fact he had been given would prove true. He had a plausible story, and if he were inclined to stop investigating, they had given him a reason. If, on the other hand, he continued, there was little he had been told, except the answer to this question, that he could not have found out himself. Both men recognized it as a trustbreaker.

Haight waited, every sense alert for the falsehood he knew was bound to come. Finally, Anglesey laughed hollowly, saying, "You seem to be in possession of all sorts of odds and ends, Jack. Where did you get that information? This is America, for God's sake, not some third-world country."

Haight nodded slowly, answering, "You're right. And yet, I can't help thinking of McKinley, Lincoln, and Kennedy."

The words hung between them. The names of the three murdered presidents were like a gauntlet, and Haight was immediately sorry he had thrown it.

Knowing he had changed the nature of the conversation, Haight asked, "So, Colin, what is it you want of me?"

The slim, aristocratic man chuckled quietly, replying, "Why, to save you from yourself, Jack. There's no point in pursuing this illusion."

He paused, then added, "We are aware of your interest in expanding into Latin America. That effort can be facilitated."

Haight smiled thinly.

"Facilitated by Centron?"

Anglesey gave that eloquent shrug again, replying, "Facilitated by many elements, Jack. There are a number of intersecting interests here, and they all want your cooperation."

The man waited, the cigarette now ignored, its smoke trickling into the clear spring air. Haight knew this was a one-time offer. He would not be threatened. If he did not accept the peace pipe being offered, he would be eliminated. He had access to some pretty high-powered people, and he had resources, but nothing that would match what Centron could command. In any case, much of his access had been eliminated since he did not know what elements in the government were supporting Centron. Anglesey had given him a sketch of the circumstances but had not given a single name. Without this, there was no way to approach anyone since he could be talking to a member of the cabal. This may not be a third-world country, as Anglesey had indicated, but it was made up of determined men who had held power for so long they did not know how to be denied. Haight had to get out of Anglesey House and figure out his next move. He knew no more than when he had arrived, but the cover story would be close enough to the truth to give him a way of proceeding.

To stall for time, he asked, "How much access are we talking about?"

Again, the shrug, then, "How much do you want, Jack? You've done well, but we own Latin America. It could be yours. At least, a substantial part of it. We could also help in Africa. And when China opens up, as it will sooner or later, we would help there as well."

Haight, impressed, said, "That's a lot of access just to avoid losing control of shipping and to prevent embarrassment."

Anglesey shrugged again.

"'A lot' is a matter of perspective, don't you agree? Anyway, what is your answer?"

Haight laughed outright.

"What do you think is going to be my answer?"

Anglesey joined him in the laughter and stood as he reached for another cigarette. Haight stood as well, recognizing the meeting was over.

As he turned, Anglesey said, "Of course, we will need a token of your cooperation."

Haight felt something tighten inside him, guessing what was coming.

"What do you have in mind?"

"Oh, I am sure you've guessed. We'll need any additional letters and anything else you may have that relates to this."

It was Haight's turn to shrug. Again, as he was turning, the other man interrupted his movement.

"One other thing."

Haight waited, the tension in his stomach now almost unbearable.

"The boy. He knows too much about us. It is regrettable, I know, but quite necessary, I assure you."

This time, Haight took a little longer, but finally he nodded again.

As Jack Haight drove away from the house, his stomach growled. He would eat on the plane. In the meatime, he needed to relax and think through what he knew. Today's information was perplexing, but there was a curious logic to it. No doubt Colin Anglesey was a mouthpiece for someone who lived in the shadows and pulled the strings. Anglesey had given him a number of warnings, and he would be expected to heed them. They would not be fooled by his acquiescence to their attempt to buy him off, but he needed time, and, apparently, they did, too. That was the only way he could explain this approach. Where was Romulus? Haight had not seen him since Panama, but something in the way things were playing out seemed to suggest Romulus' hand. Haight knew Romulus' style, and this cat-and-mouse game that turned lethal without warning was exactly what made the man so feared in the dark world where he lived. Haight wondered when he would show up again.

CHAPTER THIRTY-FOUR

FAIRFAX COUNTY, VIRGINIA 1976

At that moment, the man who occupied Haight's thoughts was rewinding the tape of the conversation he had listened to only a little while ago. Romulus did not turn as Anglesey entered the room nor did he immediately respond when the man cleared his throat, but when he did turn, his face was dark with anger.

"You should learn to keep your bloody mouth shut."

Anglesey recoiled as if he had been slapped, and his face turned red. Romulus walked across the paisley carpet until he was standing almost nose to nose with the other man.

"You, Anglesey, are remarkably incompetent. Do you think you told him enough? What did you learn from him? Nothing."

Romulus turned away in disgust. Colin Anglesey's eyes hardened, the natural blue shading into gray. He was not accustomed to being addressed in this way and chafed under the tongue-lashing.

Finally, he said, "It was not I who botched the job at the boy's apartment. It was not I who somehow managed to kill an innocent girl. It was not I who, with this action, brought

Haight into the hunt. And I am not the one who seems incapable of anticipating what he is going to do. You have been following him around as he has been gradually unraveling what others have put together. Please, do not speak to me of incompetence."

Romulus was looking at him with eyes that seemed distant, lost in themselves, and then he said, "Some day, I shall kill you."

"I hope that it is to better effect than the other deaths you have caused already in this matter. Enough of this. What did you make of Haight's response?"

"Haight's playing for time. He thinks if he has enough time, he'll be able to figure this out. It is what any analyst would do. Haight has no stomach for action, but he'll work this out now that you have provided him these tidbits of information."

"But will he accept the offer? And if he does not, how will he hope to keep us from finding out?"

"Haight won't accept the offer. He will try to protect the boy, but he is too late for that."

Anglesey looked up sharply, asking, "What have you done?"

"It's really very simple. Besides Haight, the boy is the only one who knows enough about this to be a problem. Haight won't give him up. But what if the boy is already dead?"

Romulus' voice trailed off at the end of the sentence, and Anglesey stared at him, a peculiar look on his face.

"Is there any solution of yours that does not involve death? Don't you think killing the boy will force Haight to come after us?"

"No. Once the boy is dead, Haight will come to see where his interest lies."

Anglesey was uncomfortable with the reasoning but said nothing. He was not afraid of Romulus, but the old man's protection kept Romulus inviolate. One day, though, the old man would die, and Romulus would be alone. Indeed, if he was right, it might not even take the old man's death. Something had changed about Romulus in the last few weeks. He was more assertive, and if he was already counting the old man out, then Romulus would not last long. The thought pleased Anglesey, and he smiled before saying, "Fine. If you think that is the way to handle Haight, go ahead. I think you are wrong, and I will communicate that to the old man."

Romulus shrugged his shoulders in a conscious parody of Anglesey's habitual response and walked out of the room. Anglesey watched as the incredibly broad shoulders disappeared down the carpeted stairs, and, in spite of himself, he breathed a sigh of relief. He was a brave man and had confronted danger in the field many times, but this man, Romulus, was different from anyone he had met. In a world where danger was constant, Romulus walked alone, a nominal extension of the government but really a free agent whose only loyalty was to the dying man in Long Island. Now, even that seemed to be changing. Anglesey was sure Romulus was working on his own, and he would wait and see where that led. Maybe he would not have to risk anything to get rid of Romulus.

Colin Anglesey picked up the telephone. A moment later, a strong, authoritative voice came on the line.

"Hello, Senator. Haight won't take the offer. I believe we should meet to determine what to do."

He listened for a moment, then hung up and walked down the long stairway. Reaching the bottom, he called for the black man who had answered the door earlier.

"Harold, would you prepare the Anjou room for company tonight? Prepare for six people. And the staff can have the night off."

The middle-aged black man answered politely and walked away. Anglesey looked around the room, staring at the eighteenth-century model ships he collected, as had his father before him. Near the window, the sunlight played around the H.M.S. Victory, Lord Nelson's ship that had saved the Caribbean from the French, and he wondered what it must have been like to be on board that ship. In many ways, he felt the world's great feats had ended in the eighteenth century, the mechanical revolution of the nineteenth being simply an extension of the order the eighteenth had imposed on Europe and America. The one great act of the first half of the twentieth century, an act that surpassed anything achieved in the eighteenth century, was the building of the Panama Canal. It was America's triumph, and they would hang on to it, no matter what the fool in the White House was saying. Haight was getting in the way, and though he had nothing against the man personally, Haight could not be allowed to disrupt their plans. He, too, would have to be eliminated, if necessary. The group had wanted this from the start, but he had argued for the offer to be made to Haight, hoping the man would back off. Still, he believed Romulus. Haight would try to string them along, and this could not be tolerated. Tonight, he would make a different recommendation. Haight would have to be stopped.

CHAPTER THIRTY-FIVE

Rupert Barnes sat quietly overlooking the canal, which wound away from him in both directions, a silver snake gliding between two restraining walls. The sun was high in the sky, and the brightness hurt his eyes. In the distance to his left, a large ship was coming around the bend of Gold Hill. Tugs guided the huge bulk of the tanker away from the wall of the canal, pointing it squarely down the waterway, heading east toward Gatun Lake and the Atlantic. It was humid, but he had thrown a blanket across his legs and shoulders.

The ship was now closer, and Barnes could make out the little figures who stood on the deck watching the work of the tugs. Once in the canal, the seamen had little to do, all of the traffic being controlled by the Canal Authority's pilots. This was a delicate job, since the walls could beach a ship in a moment of carelessness or indecision. Barnes felt a wave of pride as the ship glided down the waterway approaching where he sat in his wheelchair on the hill overlooking Culebra Cut.

He had watched the raising of the ship about an hour ago at the locks at Pedro Miguel, and though he had seen the first ship through the canal almost sixty years ago, Barnes felt the same pride now as then. Sitting in the small visitors' stand, he had watched as the TIROGA was brought into the lower lock some fifty-six feet below. The giant gates, thirty feet high, were slowly closed and locked behind the ship. In front of the ship, another huge gate stood closed, locking in the water that was trapped twenty-eight feet above. With gradually increasing rapidity, the water had flooded the lock.

Slowly, as the thirty million gallons of water rushed in at a rate of three million gallons per minute, the huge ship was lifted from the bottom, floating as lightly as cork up to the next lock. When the lower lock had achieved the same water height as the upper one, the gates of the upper lock were opened, allowing the ship to be pulled forward by the electric trains. The operation was delicate. It was also serene, almost noiseless among the yells of the schoolchildren who had come to watch. There had been something mythic about the gradual appearance of the ship from the depths of the sea. First, the very tip of the spar, the huge bridge, the decks, and finally the whole ship in view, sprung from the deep like some prehistoric monster. Now, as the ship slowly approached, he stared at the green, still mysterious rain forest where the remains of the other Culebra lay, drowned by this canal, and there was a sadness in his soul. Barnes raised a hand to his watery eyes and rubbed the wetness away.

Vegetation covered the sharp escarpment of Culebra Cut, giving it an innocence he did not remember. Filled with water, the Cut gave no indication of its horror, the lives it had taken, or the fear that had been ever present. Barnes looked to the left, at the old wooden bridge into Gamboa, and marveled at the expanse of water that was so still now. Far away, next to the bridge, two ships with Russian registry lay anchored in the roads, connected by two lines of chains. The bridge shook uncertainly as a large bus, alive with schoolchildren, came slowly across. The children waved at a figure who waved back energetically.

In spite of the vegetation, the severe slope of the Cut was still noticeable. That slope had been the result of the landslides. Even now, the thought of the hill sliding into the gullet of the Cut caused a shiver. The flatness of Gamboa gave no indication of the sharp incline that was to follow as the land climbed to the peak of the Continental Divide. It had been foggy earlier, but not even the mist could disguise the sheer bulk of Culebra. The water appeared a dull silver as it lost itself in the mists of Gatun Lake. In the distance, behind the TIROGA, three other ships were coming into view.

"So many secrets," he whispered.

Squinting against the glare, he watched the majestic approach of the TIROGA. The size of the ship was amplified by the narrowness of the channel along which it glided silently. The little blue-and-white tugboat that had pushed and guided it through the locks was now being pulled behind the ship. In the background, the mysterious dark green, lightened by the blue haze that hung perpetually over the mountains, stretched toward the sky, ending in the peaks that split the country.

He thought of the deaths and wondered about the cost. At night, he could still hear the screams of hurt men and the even louder silence of the dead ones. Still, something magnificent had been accomplished here. As the ship slipped past him, the little tugboats steaming back and forth like flies around an elephant, he could not find it in himself to condemn the actions that had constructed such beauty. Sitting between the two points of Culebra Cut and Gold Hill, he admired the precision of the idea. This was the stretch that had defined the canal, and in it still lay the true beauty of the cut. The confrontation of man and nature had been most fierce here, and man had won. The Continental Divide, the malaria, and the yellow fever had been defeated, and this single ship gliding serenely past, almost no sound from its engines, was the proof.

As the ship slid by, obscuring the view of the water for a moment, Barnes' eyes shifted to the deep jungle that stretched away in the distance, and he again shook his head. Through an intermediary, he had spoken to the old man in Long Island, and, tonight, he was meeting with his representative. It was important for the man in Long Island to know Barnes had nothing to do with Culebra coming back from the grave. Barnes was not interested in the politics of the Canal's return to Panama. As long as it was managed effectively, he did not care about its ownership. For him, the pride came not from the ownership but the achievement, and that was undeniably American. Nothing could take that away.

The switch in ownership, however, was not simply a matter of pride. He knew what was buried in the jungle to the north. That had caused the fear in Long Island and in Washington. The extraction of the gold from Panamanian territory would be embarrassing, but it would be infinitely more dangerous if the massacre came to light. That was the only word for it. He had participated in it; indeed, it could even be said he had led it. Fifteen thousand had died. The water came to his eyes, and the jungle blurred, turning into a film of mist that shut off his memories as well. This time, he did not wipe his eyes, and a single tear slid down his sun-reddened face. In the haze, he felt cut off from the universe, alone on this hill overlooking the sharp descent into the water below.

He knew now that his letters had started the nightmare again. How many had he betrayed? Whom had he not betrayed? Almost everyone with whom he had then been in contact was dead, many because of him. Now, there was to be more death, and he knew the man coming tonight would bring that message. The voice on the phone had made it clear Barnes' life was at stake and could be saved only by sacrifice. Who would it be this time? Barnes was tired and found himself wishing for death, wishing for something to stop the fear that still sat on his shoulders like a vulture. Worse, he knew that, just as so many years ago, he would do as Octavius Bryant, the Captain, commanded. His shoulders slumped as he thought of the world he had destroyed.

CHAPTER THIRTY-SIX

PANAMA 1976

Later that day, from the thirtieth floor of the Miramar Intercontinental, Barnes observed the ships in the bay awaiting passage through the canal. They looked disordered and purposeless in the light haze that lay over the Bay of Balboa. Below, the marina was in shadow, and he counted thirty clusters of light on the water. Off to the left, the harbor lay under the impartial eye of the Bridge of the Americas, and high on top, the lights of the vehicles moved with a slow dignity, going north and south. Waiting for the mysterious man who had called on Bryant's behalf, he glanced toward Ancon Hill, which stood like a brooding sentinel overlooking the harbor and the city. Laden now with radio and satellite antennae, it was a far cry from the rough, inhospitable promontory he had climbed more than sixty years before. Having sneaked out of the jungle, determined to expose the secret hidden there, he had climbed the hill that night but, defeated by his fear and indecision, had crept back into the jungle a broken man. How many lives had his fear cost?

But I was afraid of what the Captain would do to Richards, he thought.

Instantly, the lie rose up in his conscience, and he wheeled slowly over to the other side of the suite. Through the glass walls of the room he could see the accusatory finger of the imposing Banco Continental blocking out the eastern sky. Panama was a jumble. This quality it had not lost, though now, unlike when he had first come, the confusion was man-made. Several blocks away, the gingerbread church, La Iglesia de Carmen, with its two abbreviated steeples crowned by crosses, faced the Via España. The church had not been there when he had lived in the city, but he remembered the spot. He had sat there after crawling down the darkness of Ancon Hill that fateful night. After that, he had written the last letter to Audrey. In that letter, he had poured out his torment.

By the latter part of 1911, the gold was exhausted, and the camp had changed. The men had lost whatever ease had existed in the early days, and as there was nothing to spend their money on, the discontent had grown. In every respect, the camp became a slave plantation. No longer was the labor of the men encouraged; instead, they were *driven*. In the years following Barnes' promise to the Captain, he became the second in command, and the Captain seemed to trust him—as much as he trusted anyone. Barnes came and went as he pleased, and the men separated themselves from him. Eventually, he found himself isolated, with only the Captain's ironic, laughing voice for company, and this had driven him to the village on the beach for solace.

After four years of visits, Leila was still an enigma. She seemed so complete, so much a part of her surroundings, that he could not get beyond her exterior. Because she seemed almost never to speak to anyone else, he told her everything. That night, after failing to speak to Colonel Lemieux, Barnes headed directly to the village. The villagers along the way now knew him. The silent Spaniard seemed to know exactly when he was coming, for he was always there, ready to take "the white man who spoke like a black man" to the village at the edge of the beyond.

Entering the village, he noticed something different. The men were not in their customary circle, and the village seemed agitated. With the men absent, the women were straggling about the clearing, performing tasks the nature of which he could not determine. Leila sat inside the hut, her delicate body wrapped in the soft cotton the Kuni women wore. She was making molas, brightly colored designs of forest animals stitched on cloth backgrounds. Barnes stood admiring the beauty of the guinii, the colored beads covering her lower legs.

She had not turned her head, though she was aware he had entered the hut, and he watched as she threaded the needle through the soft cloth, waiting for the pattern of natural colors to emerge. Her face seemed normal, like an olive that had been left in the sun too long, brown and pointed toward the chin. She looked alive only to the work, black hair hanging neck-length, straight and shining, feet resting on a wooden bench into which slots had been cut to fit her heels. Barnes tried, unsuccessfully, not to think of the other side of her face. He had by then developed a love relationship with the woman. The men had, for a while, gotten him into that intoxicated state before he went to her, but he resisted one night and after that had no longer taken the drug.

They might have considered them married, but he knew too little of their customs to be sure. They were secretive about their beliefs, and Leila would look at him with her almond eyes, silent, whenever he asked for an explanation. He had never been around people who seemed so intent on separation yet never objected to an outsider's presence. He could bring no gifts. Whenever he brought something from the camp, they would make a big fuss about accepting it, but the next morning he would find it on the path just outside the clearing. Once, thinking he had broken some custom, he asked Leila why. They had just made love, and he had chosen the moment carefully, thinking she would be vulnerable. Leila rose and walked to the door, her naked body outlined against the light from the moon outside. Just as he was about to get up, she turned, something in the texture of her movement stopping him, and said, "You bring things you not want. Things change us."

Barnes was offended, and his first instinct was to deny this, but gradually, the meaning came to him. They preserved their way of life not by excluding people, but by excluding the things they brought. He often wondered why a beach people such as they spoke no Spanish. They should have been among the first people in contact with the Spaniards. Something else surprised him. These were a sea-dwelling people who did not fish. The canoes on the beach were not serviceable, and most lay half rotted on the sand.

He remained silent for a long time, watching the delicate woman who had become his partner, but whom he still did not know, thread the needle she was using. He did not concern himself with members of the tribe. Except for Leila, he knew no one in the village and had trouble with most of their names. They showed no interest in him beyond sharing the drug at night, and once he had forsaken that, there was nothing to hold him in the group.

In four years, nothing seemed to have changed in the village. Once, he asked Leila where they buried their dead, but she had simply looked at him, her almond-shaped eyes a silent rebuke. He had been surprised that night when she had answered him.

What he understood amazed him, for it gave evidence of a most extraordinary exercise of the will. They preserved themselves through the simple act of determining not to accept the cultural elements of the outside. That raised the question of his function in the village. Whenever he left after the sun came up, the men were gone, and the women moved about silently. There were few children, and Barnes had no clear sense of anyone having grown up here. Once, he thought of staying awake all night and following the men when they left, but he never had the opportunity. As he had lain in the night, the luminous eyes of the woman held him, and when the first stirrings had come from outside, she moved toward him, holding him between her legs. He had never sought to find out where the men went after that.

Worried she would not answer, he now asked Leila what she meant when she said that he brought things he did not want. The serenity of the woman's neck never changed, and he watched the small, even pulse beating just under her jawline as he waited for her response.

After a while, she said, "Forest changing. It reject you."
"What do you mean?"
Again, the long silence, then the response.
"You hurt forest."
"I have? Or all of us?"
She looked at him, and, for the first time, Barnes saw what looked like affection in her eyes. He melted before the gaze, wanting the warmth to continue. The horrible scar no longer made him want to turn away his gaze because there was a beauty to Leila that seemed to absorb it. He had become used to the sharp contrast between her right side and her left and had learned to see selectively, to position himself so that what he thought of as her good side would be visible. Certain she understood this, he often felt ashamed and would self-consciously touch the burnt flesh. Now, her luminous eyes seemed to take up her whole face, and though he could see the scar, it did not matter. As she looked at him with almost beatific warmth, he understood that his question made no sense. Something dulled in him. To Leila, he was no different from the rest. He belonged to the group from the outside, the group that would change them. He

wanted to ask why her people did not fight back but could not frame the question. Instead, he asked, "Why is it important to keep the jungle unchanged? What are we doing to it that is so bad?"

Again, he waited a long time for the answer, but when it came, he was no wiser.

"Shape of rivers change. Life divided."

Perplexed, he asked, "We are killing something? What are we killing? And what do you mean by 'life divided?'"

But Leila turned back to her molas, carefully stitching the soft animals on to the cotton background. Barnes felt frustrated, even angry. He did not understand. For him, change was important. All life changed. How could anyone construct a culture on the belief that things would not change? It made no sense. Yet, as he looked at the woman's neck, with its perfect arch of serenity, and the sure swiftness of her nimble fingers as she stitched the molas, Barnes felt sure he was looking at something that had not changed for centuries. That something produced the beauty and the art Leila was creating, and he wondered about the certainty of his claim. Thinking of the men who sat in the circle at night, complete in themselves, serene in the certainty of their world, he wondered. Most of all, as he looked at Leila, bent over the cloth, the perfection of her relationship to the molas evident in the very curvature of her body, the swift certainty of her hands and the sureness of her eye, he wondered.

Out there in the distant jungle, he, too, was striving to create. Thousands of men were digging into the belly of the earth, seeking the means to reshape the world. The gold was a trickle now, but it had always had one purpose: to recreate the world, to change it. Leila was right. The jungle was changing, but she had no idea how much nor for what purpose.

The focus of the work shifted during 1911. Even before the father, Edward Bryant, came to the site, the nature of the work had changed. The men were forced to dig further and further into the earth. The grumbling began when the gold showed signs of being exhausted, and it quickly became obvious that the Captain was building a series of tunnels underground. These were huge pathways that, as far as the men could tell, led nowhere. To them, the extraction of the gold had a purpose. The Captain did not explain the reason for the change, and, as the death toll grew, the grumbling intensified. Slowly, the number of guards increased, and they became more remote from the men. In the first year of the change, the fever struck, and the death toll was prodigious. The work practically ended, and the survivors developed a fear of the place. At one point, the dead piled up so quickly they had to take the bodies out of the camp into the deep forest, where they were burned. Barnes thought of the sharp, crackling sound of the bodies and the powerful roar of the flames that formed the background to what many swore had been the screams of the dead men. Leila was right. The forest had lost its innocence, torn apart by the huge fires that raged within it, consuming the death that the earth had given forth. It had taken eight weeks to find the right doctor, and by then, the camp was decimated. The survivors had a haunted look, almost as if they were ashamed of their lives. Seven hundred men had died in fewer than two months, and it had sapped the energy of the place.

It was then he saw the will of the Captain, Octavius Bryant. He would not allow the project to stop and immediately imported more men from the West Indies. Barnes was still not sure how he had done it so quickly, but the men came. At the same time, the kidnappings increased, and more men from the canal were brought to the site in the jungle. Something changed, and, though Barnes was not sure what it was, their relationship to the canal subtly shifted. The project in the jungle now sought more of its laborers from the Canal Zone, and, as this happened, the camp changed. There was little laughter, and the work, always hard, became brutal. A timetable somewhere drove the work, but Barnes did not know what exactly it was. He only knew that it was his job to keep to the timetable. They had four years to finish the project in the jungle. Somehow, the year 1915 was now the deadline, and if they were to make that deadline, then the pace of the work had to be brutal. There had never been much consideration of the men's feelings, but now, any semblance of concern disappeared. In the early years, the work had started at sun up and ended just before the light disappeared. Now, the work was organized into shifts so that it never stopped, the men disappearing into the ground every seven hours.

Richards had not changed. He still did prodigious amounts of work, and he kept his distance from Barnes. Barnes had never forgotten Richards' face on the day of his second confrontation with the Captain. He had expected a show of gratitude, but all he had gotten from Richards was silence and that one look of hatred. In spite of this, feeling responsible for the man, he still tried to protect him from the worst excesses of the work. Richards understood what Barnes was doing but wanted no part of it, and he continued to work the killing hours, showing no effects of the labor. He became something of a leader to the men, who respected both his strength and his independence. It was, therefore, no surprise that when the confrontation with the men occurred, Richards was at the head of it.

The day started out calmly enough. The eleven o'clock night-shift crew came out of the ground just as he awoke, and he looked out of the open window to see them congregating in the clearing rather than heading off to bed, as was their custom. There was a good deal of whispering, and something curdled in his stomach as he recognized what was happening. Taking the rifle, he walked out into the chill of the morning, struck by the sense of unreality in the place. It was the normality, much more than the threat of the men, that was eerie. Yet, his senses were preternaturally clear. His mind registered the fact that some of the men must still be sleeping or not involved in this, because only about two hundred were in the clearing. Barnes felt the anger rise in him. Everything about Richards' posture told Barnes he was behind this. The Captain came from his hut and lounged against the doorway, a secret smile on his face. That smile changed something inside Barnes.

The milling around stopped as the men stood phalanx-like behind Richards, their faces stern but showing the ragged edges of fear. Barnes experienced an odd sense of fatefulness as he walked across the clearing toward the men, their black skin gray in the early morning light. There was something familiar about the confrontation, and he felt lost in time. The men appeared to be in a mist, and he felt his difference from them more profoundly than ever. A sense of timelessness encased the scene, and he thought, somewhat irrationally, that this was a tableau, not at all real.

Still, something protruded into this sense of unreality with a discomforting poignancy. It was the silent bodies surrounding the men. The circle of guards had closed, and Barnes was sure the Captain would give the order. The man leaned against the doorway of the hut, and, as Barnes' eyes met his, the Captain nodded millimetrically, an ironic smile on his face. The nod confirmed Barnes' suspicion. The Captain was not worried about killing off his workforce. They could be replaced easily enough.

Barnes turned back to the men, the sense of unreality returning with his change of perspective. Close up, they appeared much more threatening, with Richards' giant frame dominating the group. Barnes held the rifle casually in both hands.

"Well, what is it, Richards?"

The big man looked at him closely, contempt clear in his eyes.

"We wanta talk wid somebody who can mek decisions, Barnes. Him over dere."

This last was said with a nudge of his head toward Octavius Bryant.

"You deal with me, Richards. I handle personnel."

Richards' face broke up into little pieces as he laughed softly. As the sun slid from behind the distant mountains, although the direct light had not yet come, the strands of luminescence gave his face the shape and texture of a mask. Barnes almost took a step backward, and a certain rigidity came into his body.

"Personnel? Dat is w'at wunna call slave labor now?"

The word shortened the distance between Barnes and Richards, so that Barnes felt as if the man was up against him. There was a profound discomfort in this juxtaposition, and, in spite of the coolness of the morning, he felt the heat in his body.

"There is no slavery here, Richards. You are well paid for your work. You did volunteer to come here."

"True, Barnes. I come 'pon my own accord. But wha 'bout dese men here? Dem come to Panama as free men, but dey di'nt come out here in de middle uh dis jungle by choice. Wunna bring dem here. If dem aint slave, den dey want to leave now, and go back to de worl'."

Barnes felt trapped. He heard the truth of Richards' statement, but it was too different from how he had constructed his world. They were making more money than ever, so they could not be slaves. He had known men like these all his life, had seen the struggle of their lives in the makeshift societies they inhabited, with their disease, poverty, and premature death. They had been freed from all that by this enterprise, so how could they talk of slavery? Still, one irreducible fact remained. He could not allow them to leave, and that fact ate at his conception of the universe he had created, giving the lie to his next statement.

"You will leave when the job is complete. That was the agreement when we started, Richards."

"Wid me, yes. But not dese men. Dey di'nt sign no agreemunt wid Bryant. It is dem dat I talkin' for."

Barnes had a difficult time with this. Richards had no responsibility to the men, so why was he risking so much for them? Even as he thought about Richards' words, a soft, mocking voice came from behind him.

"I wonder what Ruby would do?"

Barnes tensed, struggling not to turn as the words sliced through him, making a mockery of his indecision. His eyes hardened, and Richards, seeing this, changed too. He tried to walk around Barnes, heading in the general direction of the Captain, but Barnes moved to his right, blocking the huge man's path. The sense of inevitability returned, and inside the anger, there burned a core of sorrow. Richards must have sensed it too, because just before he grabbed at Barnes' shoulder, something like pity showed briefly on his face.

Barnes would never be sure how the rifle came up, but an explosion of sound broke the silence, and the huge man stood straight up, a strange look on his face. There was no surprise there, but something else that frightened Barnes. It was a look of contentment. The body struck the ground like a half-ripe fruit falling prematurely. The guards' guns were pointed at the crowd, but there was no fight left in the men. There was something both obscene and vulnerable in the exposure of the dead body that seemed so artificial. Barnes was not sure what to do next. The guards saved him because they came rushing up, intent on taking the body.

Before they could touch it, Bryant's voice, sharp and commanding, ordered, "No. Let it lie."

The guards jogged back to their slots in the circle, and Barnes walked slowly away toward his hut, glad of the dusk that prevailed there. Some time later, the Captain came, his voice mocking.

"I would have thought with your background, you would know better how to take care of your property."

Barnes' anger choked him, and he pressed his forehead into the rough surface of the table. His anger was useless. Having killed for the second time, he struggled to place this fact within his conception of himself. He had not changed, yet, something was different, and this frightened him.

Behind him, Octavius Bryant waited for a response, but Barnes wished only that the man would go away.

"How easily you have sacrificed my gift to you. Any regrets, Barnes? Of course, this does not in any way negate your vow of loyalty to me, does it?"

This last was said with a brief chuckle, and Barnes turned slowly, the deep imprints evident in his forehead.

"A human being is dead, Bryant. Doesn't that mean anything to you?"

The man lifted his eyebrows and tilted his head to the side.

"Yes, it does. You have just destroyed a good worker, Barnes. He was worth two of the others. More importantly, you've destroyed the model of the worker we need to complete this project on time. And most importantly, you've sworn yourself to me to save the life of a man you've killed. Ironic, isn't it?"

Barnes turned away, not wanting to see Bryant. Ignoring the man, he walked out of the hut, striding past the body that had fallen with its arms outstretched, making what looked at first glance like a rough cross. He plowed into the forest, not certain where he was headed but not caring much either.

The snarl brought him up short.

The deep jungle surrounded him. The area was unfamiliar, and, though not far from the camp, he felt isolated. Yet, in the jungle, you were never alone. He heard the soft padding moving all around him, and his heart beat loudly in his ears as he tried vainly to control his breathing. Having stormed off without the rifle, he stood frozen, every sense alert to the possibility of attack.

Then, he saw it. Like magic, it appeared ahead of him, and, even in his fear, Barnes noticed how magnificent a beast it was. The jaguar stood with its head raised, the yellow, enigmatic eyes fixed on him. Not knowing what to do, he simply stood his ground. There was nothing aggressive about the posture of the animal, but when it tossed its head, he jumped.

Then, the creature moved toward him.

As he looked into its eyes, trying to will it away, Barnes noticed a wound near the left eye and felt an overwhelming sorrow. The whole world seemed to be in pain, and he accepted the rightness of his death. There was nothing he could do to prevent it, and his shoulders slumped.

Suddenly, the beast jumped, landing within three feet of him. Its snarl filled the jungle. He had closed his eyes when the creature leapt, and when he opened them, surprised to be alive and unhurt, the lithe creature had disappeared. Three feet away, though, there was a smattering of blood. Walking cautiously toward it, he thought the creature had hurt itself. Then, he noticed the snake chopped into two even halves by the powerful jaw of the jaguar. Barnes stared at the dead snake, aware of the returning silence of the jungle.

CHAPTER THIRTY-SEVEN

PANAMA 1976

In the dull light of the room high above Panama City, Barnes wrapped his arms around his body. He was always cold now. Across the distance, the steeples of the church pointed to the sky. It was ironic the man had asked to meet there, as if he knew the spot had some significance for Barnes. Through the open window, the sounds of the city climbed to him. The crystal face of the clock showed it was minutes after seven. The man had said he would call at seven. Barnes worried about a rendezvous so close to his hotel, but the man had insisted on the banking district and, specifically, the parking lot of the church. Now, across from the church, the parking lot of the Colegio International Oxford contained a single car. Barnes could not remember whether it had been there when he had first sat down. Further back from the street, the empty school buses sat, a natural cover for anyone who wanted to hide. To the left, the massive buildings of the commercial district, bracketed by the silhouettes of the Banco Continental and the Banco Exterior, obstructed his view, slicing the magnificent sweep of the Bay of Balboa into pieces through which it was possible to catch glimpses of the southern mountains that swept up to Darien. He trained the night binoculars past the Clinica Metropolis at the dark shadows of the churchyard, but there was nothing to be seen.

Barnes was nervous. He sat in the darkness of the room, aware of how little he had wanted to feel for the past fifty years. Maybe that was why he had headed back to Panama when the summons had come from the man in Long Island. Maybe, even then, he had known the story had to be completed here in the land whose name meant "abundance of fish, flowers, and butterflies." The memory of how he found that out came unbidden, and Barnes' eyes misted over as the past reached for him.

CHAPTER THIRTY-EIGHT

PANAMA 1911

He awoke late the day after his abortive attempt to see the Colonel on Ancon Hill. The sun was high in the sky, and the sultry heat crept into his skin. The hut contained a couple of clay pots, some wood Leila had collected for making her fire, two full-length dresses, and a wooden stool. In the other corner was the footstool Leila used when making molas. The hut was not square and boxy like the others because a narrow section had been added to the traditional rectangle. Leila kept it dark, the entrance covered with a heavy cloth, and he had never felt any curiosity about the space. Now, the cloth beckoned.

He entered the space. It was dimly illumined by sunlight entering close to the ground at the far end of the room. Bent at the waist, he waited for his eyes to adjust to the darkness. The room in which he stood was bare except for some bowls containing a clay-like mixture. Barnes picked one up and held it to his nose, but the smell was unremarkable. Bowl in his hand, he admired a long robe that hung on a peg near the dim light at the end of the room. The robe, when he ran his hand over it, was surprisingly soft, and Barnes was reaching down to move aside the cloth that blocked the light when the hair on the back of his neck stood up.

Something else was in the room.

Before he had time to think, there was a flash of light as the cloth was pushed aside by a creature that disappeared into the sunlight. It was all very quick, but he had seen enough to know it was the jaguar. Trembling, Barnes wondered how long it would be before this creature attacked him. The contents of the bowl were scattered all over the ground, and he was about to clean the mess up when the cloth parted, and Leila stood in the doorway.

The open door threw enough light into the room for him to see the robe. It was made of feathers and stitched to it were the most beautiful molas he had ever seen. Unlike normal molas, however, there was only one creature represented. It was the jaguar, depicted in a thousand positions, and, from time to time, its features became interwoven with those of the women.

Barnes was on the verge of touching it when Leila said, "Come."

They walked from the room. She brought bananas, soft jelly from the coconut and papaya, and in a clay jug was coconut milk. He sat on the floor wolfing down the food, still curious about the jaguar and the robe. Finally, he asked her timidly, "Why was there a jaguar in the room?"

"Room is forest. Jaguar live in forest."

"I understand that," he responded irritably. "But why here? It almost seems as if the hole in the wall is designed to allow it to come in."

He stopped, finally understanding the enormity of what he was saying.

"Leila, have I been sleeping with a jaguar in the next room all this time?"

There was no change in her face, but her serenity seemed magnified, and the burn receded, subsumed by the peace she now exuded.

Then, she said, "Jaguar all around. It belong to forest. Forest belong to it."

Barnes lay back, thinking how different their points of view were. He had been saved by the jaguar only a little while ago, but it had never occurred to him that the jaguar could be a friend. If he had had his rifle that day, it would be dead. Men still disappeared in the jungle, and it was generally believed the jaguars took them. No one who worked in the jungle was inclined to wait and find out the disposition of the animal, and the walls of the huts in the camp were full of the black skins, that lost their luster within days.

Leila was looking at him as if reading his thoughts, and he asked softly, "Your people don't kill the jaguar, do they?"

Smiling, she shook her head, and the light changed the color of her eyes, making them golden. He wanted to ask about the robe in the next room but did not. Finally, he asked, "Do you kill any animals at all?"

Again, she gave the little smile but did not answer. Instead, she said, "Panama mean 'land of abundance of fish, flowers, and butterflies.' Before we came, there many more. Stories say butterflies cover earth. Sun was angry because butterflies hide beauty of Panama, and he send jaguar to frighten them away. Jaguar did as great sun want, but jaguar fall in love with beauty of butterflies and not want to frighten them away from Panama. So, sun angry with jaguar and left him in Panama to guard forest and, if he want to return to sky, to keep balance between things."

She stopped, but Barnes felt she had more to say.

"What a beautiful story. But how did you come to be here?"

She hesitated for a while, then said, "Jaguar never make balance. He fall in love too easy. Other animals take advantage of him. When great sun see, he send Kuni to help jaguar. That Kuni work."

Barnes liked the story. He liked even more that Leila was talking so openly to him, so he ventured a question.

"Do you worship the jaguar, then?"

Again, she smiled, and his heart leapt. She was truly beautiful. The sunlight was coming into the hut now, and there was a penumbra around her head. The details of her face were hidden in the light and darkness, but her beauty emanated like a beam. The slightly crooked teeth showed as she spoke.

"Jaguar brother, not god."

"And the robe with the jaguars on it in the next room?"

But she smiled and encouraged him to eat.

He lazed around as the women went about their business. With nothing to do, he walked down to the sea, which rolled in to the beach in slow, ponderous waves that died as they reached the sand. Further out, the water was flat, and he wondered about the islands out there, hidden in the watery distance. He had not seen Barbados for six years, and now, thinking of the island brought his mind to his sister, Ruby. She did not write often, and, truth was, neither did he. The plantations had been losing money, but he could not bring himself to care about that. 'There is nothing more important than the land, my boy," had been his father's mantra, but he felt remote from it, though still attached to Ruby, whom he found overbearing. She still made him nervous, even now that she was far away and no longer in control of his life.

Something unformed still beat in his heart for Audrey, and in his last letter, he had asked if she thought one's first love ever dies. Except for one period when illness sapped his strength, he had written to the girl almost every month for the past six years; and though no response ever came, the letters connected him with something that approximated his old self, a self he knew was dying.

Sitting on the warm sand, watching the waves, Barnes wondered whether he had become a better man. He was certainly wealthier. The last four years had seen his fortune grow and, though there was little use for the money in the jungle, it provided him with a powerful sense of accomplishment. He would return to Barbados a success. Still, he had no urge to return now. In fact, with the exception of the trips to Panama City to see the broken madman and the nightly trips down the river to the village, he felt little urge to leave the camp.

"I couldn't be becoming comfortable here, could I?"

His voice surprised him, and he stood, skimming a flat stone across the water. It skidded along for six hops, and, intrigued by his success, he searched for other stones, casually flicking them across the water. He found himself thinking of Audrey, wondering whether she had married. He had never asked Ruby, for fear of her contempt. Ruby had no time for the people in the village. She had inherited their father's genes and gave evidence of the same contempt his brothers had. He had always been the odd one. The youngest, he had not grown up with the same passion for control the others had. His two brothers and his sister had always fought for leadership of the brood, and, too young to compete, he had become the rebel. In a sense, he was still doing the same thing. This sojourn in Panama was no different from his fights with Ruby at home. His life had changed though. He could command men now and no longer doubted his ability to lead. He had money and confidence.

"So why don't I go home?"

The question, however, was meaningless. Before he had left, Archie, his schoolmate, had said Barnes would be building a civilization in Panama, and something of this vision still drove him. This thought, however, exposed the falsehood, for what he was doing had nothing to do with civilization. Sitting again, leaning his head on arms that rested across his knees, Barnes knew he was being foolish. The choice had already been made, and there was nothing to be done now.

Still, he could save the men—if he had the nerve.

Three weeks before, he and the Captain had sat on top of the hill and talked of the project. Richards had been dead for three months, buried in some unmarked grave in the jungle, and during that time, Barnes and Bryant had spoken little. Barnes still felt he had been manipulated into killing Richards, although there was nothing to justify this belief.

He stayed away from Bryant unless he had no choice. It was, therefore, a surprise when the man invited him to the hilltop. Barnes thought of declining but recognized the silliness of this.

Bryant started the conversation, saying, "Don't you think it's time to forgive yourself?"

Barnes listened for insincerity in the voice but could find none.

"How do you forgive yourself, Bryant? I thought that belonged to a power outside of yourself."

The man chuckled, but his eyes did not join in the laughter.

"I once had to ask myself that question. I answered it in a way convenient for me. I have no regrets."

He paused, then added, a note of sadness in his voice, "Family is always a burden, Barnes. It's true you can't choose your family, but I'm not convinced it would make any difference if you could. Humans have a common genesis, so our family is everywhere. Take your sister, for instance. Ruby, isn't it? She seems closer to me than to you from what I've seen. Maybe we're related, Barnes."

Angry at the intrusion, Barnes said nothing. Ruby had nothing to do with this, and her name spoken in this place felt like a violation. Bryant added, "Richards had to die. He would have eventually torn control from you. Every man in this camp understood that, Barnes. Except you. There is one thing about leadership you do not yet understand. Don't ever seem to act because you have to, only because you want to. The men know you were reluctant to kill Richards. You wanted it forced on you. That has not earned their respect, whatever you may think. That is dangerous, Barnes. The only real control we have is fear and the illusion of invulnerability. Once remove that…well, who knows?"

Barnes waited, knowing Bryant would explain himself. He was surprised, therefore, when the man asked, "What did you think of my father?"

"Your father? Why, he seemed a nice enough man."

Bryant laughed, shoulders shaking.

"'A nice enough man.' That is priceless. And it's just what he would like to be, too. Do you know who he is?"

"No."

Bryant continued to chuckle, twisting a large ring. Barnes had never noticed it before. It was solid gold, with a large red stone.

"He created a whole world fifty years ago. Out of the chaos of the West, he made order with his railroads. It was a monumental task, but he conquered the mountains, the blizzards, and the beasts—both human and animal—out there. It was a hard land—still is, in many ways—almost without form, but he saw the possibilities in it and shaped it to his purpose. He made lots of money doing it, but that was never what drove him."

The man stopped, and Barnes, intrigued, asked, "What did?"

"The construction of something bigger than he was; the taming of that wild, unmanageable land; the fulfillment of his ego; the definition of his fate: Choose what you will. I choose to believe he had no choice, Barnes, that the universe spoke to him, he answered, and the result was magnificence. In a very real sense, the states are united because of his answer to the universe when it called."

Barnes shrugged his shoulders, wondering what this was about. Bryant must have read his mind because he said, "It's about you, Barnes. Look at those men. That is the result of purposelessness. The only result is thralldom. They are from an old but tired race that has lost its purpose, Barnes. We cannot afford to be like that."

Looking out over the clearing where the black-skinned men worked, Barnes did not see thralldom but, rather, the results of a desperate attempt to escape exactly that in their own islands. For most of them, the act of uprooting themselves would have been a difficult one. Laden with their fears, the act of moving from the islands to the unknown land to the west must have been frightening. Still, they had come. Barnes felt pride in their actions.

"I think you misjudge them, Bryant. They are not long removed from the worst form of thralldom imaginable: slavery. In a very real sense, Panama is the first movement of these people since they were brought to those islands. Imagine the psychological import of that. This is, in many respects, their first coordinated, voluntary action. It has to be seen for what it is, an act of liberation."

Bryant smiled without much mirth, turning in the wooden seat to look at the white West Indian.

"You really believe that, don't you? That this movement is a conscious act of liberation? How naïve, Barnes. You must see the world as it really is, not simply how you wish it to be. A dissipated people will seek masters, as these people have. Their being here suggests something different to me. It suggests that your class has lost its ability to rule. These men are here, Barnes, not as any profound act of freedom but because you have lost control and cannot keep them there. Any subject people develops an extraordinary perspicacity, as these people have. They have found you out, Barnes, and they have found you wanting."

The argument was useless. Bryant was not listening to him, and he felt certain the conversation was a sideshow. The Captain wanted to tell him something else.

Suddenly, the man asked, "What was your father like, Barnes?"

Barnes stopped for a moment, thinking. How could he describe his father, a man he remembered as a giant figure who was at times cruel, at times kind? How could he explain the complex emotions he had felt toward the man who ran the household, as he did the politics of the country, with such power and ease? Most of all, how could he explain the tremendous sense of inadequacy he felt when he thought of him, the sense that he had never been good enough, never quite measured up? Nothing in his father's behavior had created this sense of inferiority, but it was there as surely as if the man had assured him of his uselessness. He almost never thought of his father. When he thought of anyone in the family, it was more likely to be Ruby. Not that thinking of her made for any greater comfort, but she was more manageable somehow.

He had not answered, and Bryant continued, "He dwarfs you, doesn't he?"

Then, Bryant, something like a catch in his voice, added softly, "Every son must destroy the father. Only in this way is he ever free."

Barnes looked around sharply at Bryant, knowing this was the point of the conversation.

"Ruby is stronger than you because she has slain the father. You, on the other hand, have kept him alive. You cannot see the dissipation in those men down there because the rot has set in within you too. You have not yet lived, yet you are dying, Barnes. All because the father still lives."

The glimmer of something monstrous and frightening occurring to him, Barnes asked, "Where is your father, Bryant?"

The small man smiled, the eyes opaque.

"Who knows. Somewhere in the universe. When he came here, he was tired, had ceased to strive. He wanted to end this project. We disagreed. He left. I don't think I will see him again."

Barnes realized he was afraid of this man.

"Then what are we doing here? You've never explained the purpose of this infernal digging into the ground, but you've led us to believe your father is the driving spirit. If he is not, then what are we doing? "

Bryant laughed before saying, "He and I disagreed as to ends. He is no longer associated with the project."

This was said with a finality intended to preclude additional questions, but Barnes asked, "So what is the project's purpose?"

"It is about destiny, about purpose. Mostly about control over contingency."

Barnes raised his eyebrows, thinking Bryant would be laughable if he were not so deadly.

After a while, Bryant said, almost to himself, "I wonder what your soul is worth. But then, to you, it is worth nothing since you have already given it to me."

Barnes laughed uneasily, replying, "Not my soul, Bryant. All I promised was my loyalty."

"Is there a difference, Barnes?"

Barnes could not answer the question, and later that night, lying on the hard bunk in his hut, alive to the sounds of the jungle, staring into the solid darkness, he was afraid. Not simply for himself but for the men who were digging into the bedrock beneath the jungle. The Captain had given him a vision of the future that he found stifling, and, as he laid, his throat felt dry.

The Captain had taken Barnes down into the ground, and they had traversed the full extent of the tunnels. The mine-shafts had been widened, and the walls were a solid, shiny rock. The bottom of the tunnels were flat, unlike when they were seriously mining the gold, and wide enough to accommodate a truck. Barnes was surprised at the depth of the tunnels, and as he and the Captain trundled slowly along on a makeshift flatbed, a picture emerged. They were eight tunnels that started from a point near the entrance. From that common entrance, eight ramps, spread roughly in the shape of a sea fan, had been dug to a depth of close to two hundred feet. Then, at that depth, the eight tunnels had been dug horizontally. Barnes could only guess at the distance underground, but it was considerable, and the arc of the half circle made by the eight tunnels covered a distance of more than three miles. It had taken them all afternoon to work their way through the tunnels.

At one point, they reached a section far from the horde of men who were digging, and Bryant stopped and turned the lamp off. Fear crawled into Barnes' belly as the darkness closed in on him. Bryant was beside him, but it was impossible to see. The darkness came alive with little white specks that, though visible, carried no light. His imagination, starved for stimuli, constructed images to give it perspective, but this knowledge did not eliminate the fear—nor did the preternatural silence of the man next to him.

Then, the man's amused voice came out of the blackness.

"Impressive, isn't it? This is the only place I am truly at home."

"Then you are a very strange man, Bryant. There is nothing here except blackness."

The man chuckled, replying, "Precisely. It is possible to construct a world here. All you need is imagination, don't you think?"

The white spots disappeared at the sound of voices, as if his mind, with something real to attend to, had lost interest in creating. He felt that some part of what the man said was true. When he asked about the project, Bryant's answer surprised him.

"Do you think there needs to be a purpose? If there were no purpose, would the accomplishment be any less?"

"But there is a purpose, is there not? Tell me these men are not digging up the whole of Panama for nothing. To hell with that. Tell me I am not wasting my time in this disease-ridden place for some crazy fantasy of yours."

A hollow, mirthless chuckle came from all sides of him in the uncertain geography of the absolute blackness.

"What do you believe in, Barnes? You have lost faith in the world your forefathers created, but you have replaced it with nothing. You have sought purpose in another man's dream. You've hoped Panama would provide the certainty your little island did not. You desire greatness, but you have no conception of what it is. Is not that the reason you are here, why you came to Panama? It is more honorable what those black men are doing than what you do. They, at least, have extracted something from the country. Their purpose is ignoble but singular and understandable. You, on the other hand, have no idea of your purpose. To what will you be loyal, Barnes? It is difficult to be unattached for your whole life."

"And you would give me purpose. Is that it?"

"I already have. I am simply waiting for your acknowledgment."

The light suddenly came back on, and, within its circle, Barnes saw the small, gnome-like face of the Captain peering urgently at him.

"You swore loyalty under duress, Barnes. If we are to go any further then you must decide where you stand."

For a moment, Barnes was uncertain if the man was talking about going farther into the tunnels. The thought of being left behind frightened him.

The shadows on the walls crawled in the lamplight as he said, "I am with you."

Bryant's face crinkled in a smile that resembled a grimace, and worry crawled in Barnes' mind when Bryant said, "Careful. That is a second promise."

"Yes. And you have promised nothing."

The man chuckled, answering impishly, "But I have already given much."

"There is one thing you have not given. I need to know why we are here, digging under the forest. There seems to be no purpose anymore. The gold is almost gone. It would help if I could give the men a reason for their work."

The Captain's eyes burned deeply into Barnes'. Finally, Bryant said, "I can give you the reason, but you cannot tell the men."

"Why not?"

"Because they cannot ever know the purpose. It does not concern them."

In the darkness of the underground, the Captain confided in him, and Barnes felt both horror and admiration. Without his father's wealth, the purpose of the construction had indeed changed. Edward Bryant, the Captain's father, had dreamed of constructing a new city in the jungle. From what the son said, the man wanted to experiment with a world in which the search for wealth would be eliminated since he would have created a society in which all men would be wealthy. Edward Bryant had been curious about what would happen in such a society, what would motivate men, how they would compete. The Captain had changed the focus of the project and, remote from his father, sent him reports of a city he had no intention of building. Instead, he mined the gold, and this had kept his father happy for the first few years.

Then, Colonel Lemieux persuaded the White House that the Panama Canal could be completed in considerably less time. This did not bother the Captain since the tunnels would be completed long before the expected time. Edward Bryant, however, had been terribly angry about the changed timeline because the Panama Canal was the perfect cover for what he was attempting. Without the activity of the Canal, with its constant importation of men and materials, its occupation of the Panamanian landscape and the fury of the construction, his efforts would soon have been discovered.

The changed timeline brought Edward Bryant to Panama. Once there, the deception became obvious, and he cut off support, not realizing his son was no longer dependent on him for financing. Barnes interrupted at this point, asking what Edward Bryant would do now that he had been betrayed, and the Captain said in response that his father was no longer of any concern. Barnes was not satisfied with the answer and, intrigued, waited for the Captain to continue.

The Captain, it turned out, had always been in the employ of the group of men who opposed the Panama Canal. These men were powerful, and Barnes was nervous because he was sure this knowledge committed him in some way.

When he asked why the tunnels were being built, the answer shocked him.

The men who financed the Captain had lost their opportunity at a Nicaraguan canal seven years before, after wasting a fortune preparing for it. Their original reaction had been to destroy the Panamanian endeavor, or at least to make it so expensive the project would be abandoned. Because of Edward Bryant's influence, this had not happened. In any case, the Captain, while accepting payments, had not worked too hard at it since he thought the plan silly. If the Panama route failed, there would not be enough political will to make an attempt in Nicaragua for a generation. So he took their money while ignoring their directives, creating enough of a stir in Washington, from time to time, to keep them happy. The Southern senators could constantly point out the cost, the delays, and the broken promises. All of this meant nothing when the Captain's father had been supporting the project. The original intention had been to dig a single tunnel under the forest to within a mile of the canal. At that point, the eight tunnels would have been constructed in the same fan-like shape Barnes had seen. When Washington, under the urging of Colonel Lemieux, changed the plan from a sea-level canal to a lock canal, it actually made their work much easier. That change would create an artificial lake from the redirected waters of the Chagres

River. That lake came to the very edge of the jungle. The tunnels would not have to be dug all the way to the Canal Zone, several miles away.

Barnes impressed, had asked, "What are the tunnels for?"

An intense look came into the Captain's eyes as he responded, "Contingency, Barnes. Someday, we may need to close down the canal. The men who are financing this would do it now, but that makes no sense. The canal will make a fortune for whoever controls it, and I intend for that to be Bryant's Shipping. Why waste that fortune because a bunch of fools are angry and creating plans that will never come to fruition?"

"But why would we need to close it down at any time?"

Bryant stared for a while, then said, "Because one day someone will question the validity of our ownership of the canal.When that happens, we will destroy it."

The words were said in such a matter-of-fact way that it had taken a while for the meaning to sink in.

"Why would we need to destroy it?" Barnes asked incredulously.

"It all comes down to purpose, which, as I have explained, you do not understand. The canal will be ours or it will not be."

"Who would challenge the United States for the canal? You are not making any sense."

The Captain laughed quietly again, his shoulders shaking.

"You are like a politician, Barnes. You cannot see past tomorrow. National pride is a strange thing. Columbia is weak now, but we should not expect that it will remain so. Sooner or later, its national instinct will be to regain Panama, and the prize will be the canal. The idiots in Washington do not see this. All they see is the might of their navy and the ease with which Columbia capitulated seven years ago. No one should be fooled by this. There will come a time when we will have to fight for the southern continent, and I fear the canal will be the cause. Like I said, Barnes, it's a contingency."

That day, sitting on the deserted beach, his mind reaching out for something that made sense in all he had been told by the Captain, Barnes came to three conclusions. First, the Captain's father was indeed somewhere in the universe, but it was probably not a place of his choosing. Second, he was now, whether he wanted to be or not, irrevocably committed to the Captain. Third, the men who toiled in the belly of the continent would never be allowed to leave. The enormity of that thought numbed him. He was at a crossroads. He had killed, but this was different, and the scale of it created a numbness in the core of his soul. There were now close to fifteen thousand men in the camp. Could he just do nothing? He also thought of his situation. The Captain had confided in him, and Barnes had given his pledge of loyalty, but to what had he pledged himself? With what enormity had he allied himself?

Before him, the sea became still, and his heart pounded with terror. Then, in the silence, came the sharp, short snarl of a jaguar, and he shivered. It sounded very close.

CHAPTER THIRTY-NINE

PANAMA 1976

Leila had been right. The jungle had been changing, the deaths having infected it in some incomprehensible way. Barnes looked down at the churchyard again. The shadows had changed. Cars rushed past on Avenida Espana, creating the illusion of a line, but the lights never penetrated the darkness of the churchyard. Whoever had chosen the spot was familiar with the city. Barnes was becoming impatient. It was well after ten. The man was late, or maybe he was not coming. Barnes was no longer sure how he felt about the meeting. He had not thought about his earlier days in Panama for many years, having, it seemed, detached that time and placed it in a secret compartment. Ruby's death sixteen years ago had been his last connection to that period. Now, the letters brought back the pain and the horror, and Barnes felt an undercurrent of anger at whoever had raised this ghost again. In this respect, he was sympathetic to Octavius Bryant, the man he once called the Captain. He, too, must have tried to forget that time. He, too, would be loathe to be reminded of a past that had destroyed them both. Yet, Barnes knew he and Bryant were different and would always be so.

Sitting in the wheelchair, he thought of the man who had turned him into a monster. Maybe it was time to bury the hatchet. His pain had, after all, occurred a long time ago. Even as he thought this, though, Barnes knew that Bryant had ripped his life apart in too many ways for him to forgive. Barnes might have forgiven him the taking of his innocence. At least in that he had been a partner, more or less willing, but he could not forgive him for Leila. That had been vicious, and, worse, it had been gratuitous.

This thought was, however, interrupted by the soft purring of the telephone, and soon, he heard the light step of his bodyguard/nurse. It was time to go.

As soon as Barnes saw the big man who emerged from the shadows cast by the church, he recognized something about him. It was in the ease with which he moved, the confidence that the space he occupied was his. This, more than anything, assured him the man had come from Octavius Bryant.

Barnes sensed his bodyguard becoming more alert and said softly, "Easy, Hu. Nothing's going to happen here."

By this time, the man had reached them, and he stood above Barnes, blotting out the sky.

After a moment, he said, "Good evening, Mr. Barnes. Mr. Bryant was quite relieved to hear from you."

Before Barnes could respond, a large van pulled into the parking lot, and his bodyguard moved between Barnes and the man. Barnes reached out, and the bodyguard stopped. The big man had not moved when Hu started toward him, but Barnes felt certain he was prepared.

As if to acknowledge this, he said, "Thank you, Mr. Barnes. There really is no need for unpleasantries. I would like to speak with you in private. The van is fully equipped to accommodate your chair."

Barnes made a quick calculation and arrived at the conclusion that this was not the way he would be killed if they wanted him dead. In any case, it was a little late to worry about death now. With this, he asked Hu to return to the hotel. The van was soon headed down Balboa Avenue toward the Altos de Oro section of town. After a while, they pulled into a spacious driveway, and two men carefully helped Barnes from the van. The iron gates closed silently behind him as he was pushed into the house. Once inside, the big man brought him a cup of tea and then sat down.

"Mr. Bryant sends his regards. He is anxious to be rid of this problem."

Barnes laughed softly at the formality of the speech. He was trying to remember something he had heard several years ago about Bryant adopting a kid from Europe, and he wondered if this was the one.

"He won't have any problems in a little while. We are both too old for this world. We should leave it to you younger people," he responded somewhat irreverently.

Barnes thought he saw the hint of a smile flicker across the big man's face.

"Perhaps, Mr. Barnes, but I assure you he is well in charge of his business. In any case, you wanted to see him. He is quite ill, as you probably know, and has very few visitors. He was, however, glad to hear from you. Your disappearance immediately after the information came out about the canal placed you in rather an awkward position."

"He should've known better."

The big man shrugged and added, "He doesn't. There is too much at stake to be anything but careful, Mr. Barnes. He asked me to ask you if you remember your vow. I am not sure what he means, but I suppose you do."

Barnes nodded, a frown on his face.

"He asked that I remind you of it. He also asked after the health of your sons."

Barnes tensed. It was not like Bryant to inquire about his children, and Barnes recognized the statement for the threat it was. He looked at the big man who sat across from him, and, in the eyes, he noticed the blankness, the disinterest that the cultured voice belied. This man was a killer, no matter how well he dressed or how solicitous he was. Barnes had seen eyes like that too many times in his life, had made use of men with exactly that look too often, to be fooled by this man's manners. The anger he thought had died rose in him. He had come to make peace with Octavius Bryant, but the first thing the man had done was threaten him. It was just like Bryant. He was aiming his poisonous eye at Barnes' sons. The old man struggled to control his face.

"My sons are fine. Doing quite well, as a matter of fact. Will I get to tell him how well they are doing in person?"

"Perhaps, Mr. Barnes. As I said, he sees few people these days. He is, however, most anxious to find out where you stand in this affair."

"Is he worried I might be inclined to tell someone what I know? Why would I do that after all these years?"

"Meaning no disrespect, but he fears your growing awareness of your mortality may induce remorse. That has been known to encourage changes in lifelong behavior."

The man was looking at him speculatively, and Barnes knew he was once again being judged. Something inside him revolted against this, something he thought had died a long time ago, but which, with the emergence of Culebra over the last few weeks, had come back with all the power it had had in his youth.

"Young man," he said now, "what we all did is so long past that it should be forgotten, not repeated. If I had any intention of trying to destroy Bryant, I would hardly wait until now."

"As I said, the thought of one's death makes for the most unusual changes of heart."

Barnes nodded, asking, "Why is he so worried, anyway? He owns everyone. He has always been untouchable. So why is he worried?"

"It does not matter, does it?"

"The hell it doesn't. Young man, Octavius Bryant and I were in hell together for a long time. He is not the kind to worry, so why is he running around after this information? And why did he have the others killed? Don't bother to deny it. I recognized his work from the moment the names of the other five appeared in the paper. Did he worry I would seek revenge? Is that why he sought me out? If that is the case, then tell him I am too old. All I want is to be left alone."

"We all wish that, Mr. Barnes. It is not always possible, however."

"What does that mean?"

"Well, whether you intended it or not, you are the cause of this particular problem. It is, after all, your letters that have caused this. He wishes for you to make amends."

Barnes looked the big man over carefully, then said, "You never did tell me your name, young man."

"I am called Romulus."

"The son of the she-wolf. The brother of Remus. The reputed founder of Rome."

"I am impressed, Mr. Barnes. I did not know you were a Latin scholar."

"Not much of a scholar, son, but I did suffer through it a long time ago. Anyway, Romulus, what do you mean by 'amends'?"

"Mr. Barnes, we have a problem. We have retrieved the copies of the letters. In a short while, we will have the originals. There is only one source of the information left."

"The boy?"

The big man nodded, and, for a long time, they looked at each other. Barnes knew what was being asked of him, and he hated the man who was asking. He also knew that his choice was no longer free. The reference to his sons was pointed, and he was expected to understand. The Captain had not changed. Barnes wondered for a moment if the man would ever die, if he could die.

"Doesn't he think I have given enough?"

"A question best asked of him, sir. I could not answer that."

"Is it necessary to kill the boy?"

"It has been decided. There is no other certainty, Mr. Barnes."

"And this is my assurance that I have nothing to do with all this?"

"Let's just say Mr. Bryant wants your help."

Barnes was tired. It was unusual for him to stay up this late. Also, the room was cold.

Hating himself for what he was about to agree to, Barnes said, "You may tell Bryant that the boy can be handled."

The big man nodded, but before he could complete the action of rising, Barnes continued.

"Just one moment, young man. Before I order this boy's death, I need to hear this from Bryant himself. Meaning no disrespect, Romulus."

The big man sat again, staring at Barnes. He seemed amused.

"Mr. Barnes, I did not intend this to be a negotiation. The Captain, as I believe you call him, will decide when he wants to see you."

Barnes smiled, replying, "Maybe you should check with him, son. He will want to see me."

"He does, Mr. Barnes, but all in good time. First, you demonstrate your loyalty, then we'll see about the meeting."

"Then maybe you can tell me this. Why is this so important? I thought it was over. We failed, after all the time and the work."

Barnes stopped for a moment, then added almost to himself, "And the lives."

He did not see the look of contempt that flashed across Romulus' face, for it was instantly gone, and the voice was emotionless when Romulus said, "I cannot make that decision, Mr. Barnes."

"Then call Bryant and let me know. I am not as young as I used to be, so please take me back to the hotel."

Romulus nodded.

CHAPTER FORTY

PANAMA 1976

As soon as Barnes left, Romulus was on the phone. It was late, but he knew the old man in Long Island would be awake. The conversation was brief, but at the end, Romulus breathed a little more easily. He still did not understand the relationship between Barnes and the old man, but, once again, Mr. Bryant had overridden his recommendation to be rid of Barnes. It was not squeamishness that held the old man back; Romulus had been the instrument of too many deaths to believe this. He could not understand this hesitation. Still, the old man was dying, so he had only to be patient.

Bryant had not found out about Romulus' independent action with Hanscom. The ex-agent had not known much, but, between his screams, he had given enough information to narrow down the possibilities for Romulus, who had not known about the old man's involvement in the construction of the canal. He had also not known about the relationship between the government and the old man in this connection, but Hanscom had given him enough of a link, and it had been relatively easy to track the story down after that.

They had identified the boy's computer signature—not difficult since he was so clumsy in his pursuit of information on Centron—and Romulus had duplicated the signature so that his own investigation had become indistinguishable from the boy's. This served two purposes: It covered his tracks and heaped more blame on the boy whom the old man had finally been persuaded to eliminate. Instead of having it done quickly and efficiently, though, he had constructed this elaborate game of having both Haight and Barnes kill the boy. It was silly but consistent with what was becoming a pattern of erratic behavior.

Still, Romulus was not sure. The old man was devious. What if an action he took on his own upset some delicately balanced plan the old man had made? Romulus was also worried about the people who were associated with this project. He hated men like Anglesey, living fictions that existed as icons to be respected, but whose lives were so debased they simply extracted the vitality from the world. Men like Anglesey should be eliminated, and when he took over Centron, they would be.

He wondered why the old man had not told him about the extent of Centron's involvement in Central America. If the region was so intricately involved in the past of the organization, and the old man's associates were even now constructing a new level of involvement, why was he, the heir apparent to Centron, kept out of the planning? Romulus had no answer to this question, and it bothered him.

After the confrontation at Anglesey's home, Romulus had not left the area. Later that night, wanting to know who was behind the plot, he had crept back to Anglesey House. The estate was protected, but it had been easy enough to obtain the plans to the security system and to bypass it. The men had arrived in limousines with darkened windows, and the cars had driven directly into the large garage. Romulus, anticipating this, positioned himself outside the house. The servants were gone, and Anglesey, having an unwarranted faith in the electronics that protected his home, had no dogs. It was an easy climb to the roof of the connecting garage and through the half-opened bedroom window. From there, he crept down the stairway until he heard voices in the sitting room. Slipping into an adjacent room, he stood in the dark.

As his eyes became accustomed to the darkness, he moved toward the door and opened it slightly. He knew most of the men. Senators Harvey and McConnell, both from Southern states, he expected to be there. They still had dreams of a resurgence of the South. Anglesey sat in a large horsehide chair that was clearly not of American origin. Sipping a clear drink was someone with whom Romulus was very familiar. It was the Deputy Director of the CIA, Lance Morton, and next to him was Robert Clement, Special Assistant to the Vice President. Romulus' lips had parted in a smile. So this was the hub of the conspiracy. The other two men in the room were Latin. One Romulus knew. His name was Amador, a wealthy newspaperman who was more dilettante than journalist. The other man sat next to him and was obviously not part of the circle. Romulus recognized the look, though. He was the dangerous one.

He listened through the cracked door, hearing why the conspiracy had been hatched. Everyone had an interest. They could not allow the return of the canal because too much money would be lost. Centron was affected in two ways. First, it stood to lose control of the canal. This meant that its ships, which had traversed the canal at nominal fees, would suddenly incur millions of dollars in additional costs. Secondly, and just as important, there was the fear that, given the rising nationalism of the Panamanians, the canal could be overtaken by hordes of nationalists who would shut it down. This would be a disaster second in scale only to the cutting off of oil from the Middle East. The men in the room were still reeling from the effects of the oil embargo only a few years before, and Centron was in no mood to have another dislocation.

Amador said little, and Romulus wondered why he was there until Anglesey turned to him and asked, "And how is our campaign going in the press?"

The fat man with the clipped moustache looked uncomfortable.

"Not well, Colin. It is impossible to make any headway against the feelings in the country. The publishers, whatever their beliefs, are seeing the mood of the people, and the editorial positions are almost uniformly in favor of the return of the canal to what is being described as 'its rightful owners.'"

"That's horseshit, Amador, and you know it. We built that canal. If we hadn't come there, the place would still be a cesspool with death in every corner. You people would still be in the condition we found you in almost a hundred years ago."

This angry outburst came from Senator McConnell, and as the Panamanian flushed angrily, Robert Clement, the assistant to the Vice President, moved smoothly to intervene.

"There's no need for that, Senator. We knew it would be difficult to control editorial opinion. Señor Amador has been steadfast, though not very successful."

This last Clement added with a charming smile that did not disguise the dig, and Senator McConnell, recognizing he was not quite outside the pale, shouted, "Then why're we paying the fat fuck millions of dollars? We need results not reassurances."

Amador had risen, his face jiggling, and Anglesey moved quickly over to him, speaking softly. Whatever he said evidently mollified the man because, after a while, he smiled tightly and sat again.

Robert Clement was continuing, however.

"It is true that if we can turn the editorial positions against the return of the canal then the President, actually both Presidents, would have a more difficult time continuing the talks on the treaty. I should point out, though, that Señor Amador's failure is not the only one in the room. The CIA has not been notably effective in mobilizing a contrary opinion either."

The Deputy Director looked distinctly uncomfortable. When he responded, it was almost self-defensively.

"Well, we did find the entrance to the tunnels. If we have to go to plan B, then they'll be indispensable."

"True," Clement responded. "I would hope, however, that we don't have to go to that extreme, don't you? I was speaking about your inability to mold public opinion in Panama in spite of the untold millions we seem to be pouring into that country. I have no desire to destroy the canal. That's a last resort. I would like to head the thing off short of that, if you don't mind."

"What about the President? Any chance of changing his mind?"

This came from Senator Harvey, a quiet, white-haired man from Louisiana who had the reputation of being a deal-maker. Clement shook his head.

"That'd be the best of all possible worlds, but he's so taken by the naïve notion of reducing injustice in the world that he sees nothing beyond that. And, unfortunately, his naivete is dangerous. His excursions in Africa are becoming an embarrassment to everyone, but they can be overlooked. This cannot. With the proposed signing in less than four months, we have to act."

"And what does 'act' mean, Robert?" asked Colin Anglesey, who sat with the long-stemmed crystal glass poised near his lips.

The room seemed to close in on itself. Each man looked at Robert Clement, who sat back in the chair, a hint of regret on his handsome face. When he spoke, there was a great reluctance in his voice.

"That, of course, is Bryant's decision. We have not heard from him directly in several days, but we had agreed that the elimination of both Presidents would completely destroy the talks. No American or Panamanian president would touch this issue for a century. There is still, however, the problem of the Partido Radical. And how are we doing with them, Nieves?"

As if he had been expecting the question, the quiet man who sat next to Amador turned his head to look at Robert Clement.

"The radicals are not a problem, Mr. Clement."

When he did not continue, Senator McConnell leaned forward and snarled, "And what the hell does that mean, Nieves? We can't afford to have this thing blow up into another one of your people's rebellions."

Nieves did not respond, instead turning to Clement with a silent appeal in his eyes. A sharp look silenced the Senator.

"There will be no rebellion. The Partido Radical is not motivated to protect the canal. Their interest is more mystical than political."

McConnell could not control himself and asked quickly, "Mystical? What does that mean?"

"Well, Señor McConnell, you probably would not understand. The Partido Radical is largely composed of the remnants of several Indian groups from the area around where the tunnels are located. They were opposed to the canal when it was being built because they believed it would destroy the spirit of the country by slicing it in two."

"You mean they are willing to destroy the canal because of some mumbo-jumbo about the spirit of the country?"

"We all have our mumbo-jumbo, Señor McConnell."

A short silence ensued, only to be broken by McConnell again.

"What about Haight? That is why we came here anyway. What are we going to do about him?"

Anglesey placed the glass delicately down on the oak table before he responded.

"Haight will, I have on good authority, not comply. He will stall for time, though. I did offer to help him gain access to Latin America. Haight is no knight. He is involved because we attacked him. If that jackass who works for Bryant did not botch the job at the apartment and end up killing the girl, Haight would not be involved at all. Now, he feels he has to protect the boy. The best we can hope for is that he will hesitate for a few days. In any case, he will not be an ally."

Romulus, in the room next door, made a mental note to make Anglesey's death particularly nasty.

"Why're we fooling around with Haight? Why not just eliminate him, too? It's going to be too dangerous to leave him alive, anyway."

"All in good time, Senator," Robert Clement replied. "Haight is too visible, too important, to have something happen to him so close to our action. More importantly, we have not been able to find out if he has any of the information salted away for someone else to get hold of it. There is no point eliminating him if what he knows is then to become public knowledge."

"But how much does he know?"

Everyone looked at Nieves since he had been the one Haight contacted. The small Latin American raised his hands, indicating he did not know.

"Haight is an analyst. It is difficult with them to say what they know. Their job is to take information and make sense of the patterns. He may know nothing, or he may know exactly what we are doing. The question is whether he has passed information on to someone else."

"So what do we do in the meantime?" Senator McConnell asked, ignoring Nieves.

"We proceed as before. Anglesey, will you pass this on to Mr. Bryant? We place the explosives in four days as planned.

Nieves, you will return to Panama and make sure that Partido Radical does not change its mind."

He then turned to the Deputy Director of the CIA.

"Lance, it all depends on you. Are your assets in place?"

The Deputy Director nodded, and the Vice President's assistant stood up, signaling that the meeting was over.

Romulus stood very quietly as the men trooped past where he hid, then quickly ascended the stairs, making his way back to the roof, where he watched as they drove off. Minutes later, he reactivated the alarm and, within half an hour, was on his way back to Washington.

Now, sitting in Altos de Oro, surrounded by the gentle hills of Panama City, he wondered how all of this could be turned to his advantage. He worried about the old man's weakness now. Centron was still held together by the old man's will and his willingness to act quickly, harshly, and without remorse. That is why this hesitation with Barnes worried Romulus. The conspirators at Anglesey House did not know who he was. Even Anglesey thought of him only as Bryant's glorified messenger. He had always been in the shadows, a man with many faces and names, but he understood Centron better than anyone alive, with one exception. Still, he knew his ascendancy to the leadership of the organization would not be unchallenged unless Bryant made an unequivocal statement. So far, this had not come, and Romulus was torn. Bryant would not last much longer. Now, he had agreed to see Barnes, whom he wanted to kill the boy. He had also ordered that Haight be required to kill the boy, but when he had told Romulus to have Barnes do the same thing, it was as if he had forgotten the other order. Romulus had experienced a contradictory set of emotions. He supposed he loved the old man, who was the closest thing to a father he had had for most of his life and to whom he owed everything. Yet, that very man had taught him the danger of sentimentality, had drilled this lesson into him from his youth. Strength must win out, and the old man was weak now. He would expect no less from Romulus.

He picked up the phone and said, "Would you tell Mr. Barnes that his request has been granted? I shall fetch him in two days, upon completion of his task."

CHAPTER FORTY-ONE

The boy was gone!

Haight stood with Antonio Peques, looking down at the path where the tracks had disappeared. Around them, the slight swishing of the long pines made a mockery of their worry. The scene was peaceful, the sunlight bright, and the sky a translucent blue. None of them noticed the slight chill in the air as they stared at the footprints, the evidence that Dean Greaves had been there. He had been running quickly but not flat out, as would have been the case if he had been chased. That much was evident from the depth of the imprint the shoes had made. After he had not come back for lunch, they had followed the route he normally ran and now stared in frustration and bewilderment at the footprints. He had disappeared!

Returning from Anglesey House the day before, Haight had said nothing to Dean about the danger he was in, only asking the chief of security to keep an eye on the boy. Haight rotated his gaze slowly around the valley. The meadow was at least a mile across, and he moved his eyes along the edge of the pine trees that bordered it. The scene remained peaceful, and no one spoke until Haight said, "Let's get the John Deere. I want these woods combed."

Antonio nodded but did not turn. Instead, he headed off into the woods, his huge body surprisingly quiet. Haight walked rapidly toward the house, castigating himself for his stupidity. He had been foolish to think they would believe he would get rid of the boy. He had been complacent, assuming he had the upper hand since he had the originals of the letters. They had lulled him into carelessness. There was no doubt Romulus was behind this. Haight felt the rising anger, and he stopped, bending over and breathing quickly. He straightened up after a while, breathing the cool, pine-filled air deeply into his lungs. Romulus!

The man stood like an avatar, a reminder of Haight's failure in Vietnam. Haight had ordered many deaths, but Romulus' escape into Cambodia had been like a dark stain on his conscience. War was not supposed to be conducted like that. Romulus was not a soldier; he was unlike anything in Haight's experience. He was a killer, without remorse and totally immune to human suggestion. Haight was not proud of Vietnam, but he knew the war had to be fought. He could accept the damage it had done, the deaths it had caused, but there was still a boundary across which man should never trespass because, if he did, then all that separated him from the beasts in the woods would disintegrate, and civilization would no longer be possible. Romulus' actions in Cambodia had shown Haight the other side of the political restraint that had characterized this war, a restraint that, until Romulus' escape into Cambodia, he had chafed against. The line of terror and murder the man had created in a few short weeks had sickened Haight, and, to this day, he believed it had brought on his mental breakdown. The mind will only accept so much that deviates from the norm, and Romulus had been the limit of that acceptable deviation. Now, he had kidnapped, perhaps killed, the boy Haight had taken under his wing. Haight felt a deep core of anger at this.

Upon reaching the mansion, Haight quickly jumped into the vehicle, heading back down the path. They had seen no blood, so maybe there was some reason to hope. He wondered why he had allowed himself to be drawn into this battle that was not his. The boy, until a few weeks ago, had meant nothing to him. Still, he had invited Dean into his home, and they had violated that. Haight's anger burned, and it was in this haze he saw Antonio Peques emerge from the woods several yards in front of him. He was holding something in his hands.

"I found his tracksuit and running things. They were over by the path on the other side of the hill."

Haight stepped out and headed into the woods. He was soon at the site Antonio pointed out. It was immediately obvious that a car had been parked there for some time. Haight walked around the spot, trying to figure out how this had been done. Whoever had the boy had taken the time to change his clothes. They had also felt comfortable enough to park in broad daylight on his estate, not quite two miles from the house. That suggested confidence. Something else nagged him, but he could not quite put his finger on it. The tire tracks from the car were clearly visible on the dirt road, and Haight followed them until they disappeared at the wooden gate that allowed entrance from the secondary road bordering the estate. There was nothing on the road.

Back at the house, Haight sat in front of the boy's neatly stacked papers. He had liked Dean from the beginning and had not thought much about his race. Now, he wondered why that had been the case. Haight did not consider himself a liberal and had paid little attention to the struggles that had ignited the country in the last ten years. His energies had been turned elsewhere, and only when Martin Luther King had begun to speak about the struggle in Vietnam had he caught Haight's attention. He knew that, sooner or later—more likely later—the races would have to work things out between them, but it did not seem such a pressing problem. These things took time, and it was foolish, he knew, to hurry history. Things were difficult for the blacks, but they would have to wait for history to catch up with their aspirations. Dean, however, had seemed somehow different. It may have been the assurance he showed from the beginning by never raising the issue of his color. In fact, he seemed immune to the possibilities inherent in it, and it was probably this that Haight had noticed. The boy's competence had quickly muted any noise of race, and Haight had come to depend on him for the information he had been gathering on Centron.

A huge pile of computer cards contained the data the boy had collected. Dean had tracked the information back to the early part of the century, discovering that all of the major corporations making up the conglomerate were founded between 1906 and 1921. Since most of these were originally transportation companies, Dean had guessed they were related. It had been difficult because the records were old, and some had been destroyed, but once Dean had given him the name, Haight had been able to ascertain that Edward Bryant had formed the original companies—at least until 1911. After that, the man had disappeared somewhere in South America in some vain attempt to build a city. Haight had read the story in the *Post* of October 18, 1911 and found it interesting that Bryant's companies had been created at the same rate after 1911 as before. It was almost as if the great man's death had made no difference. Haight understood that corporations are not run on any single man's personality, but, with a figure as large as Bryant, it was not unreasonable to expect some slowdown. There had been none. More remarkably, there had been no dominant figure identified after Bryant's death. It was as if the corporations were spawning themselves. Yet, he knew this was not possible. It had taken a tremendous amount of capital and will (maybe more of the latter) to create what had become Centron. Yet whoever had done it remained faceless.

He and Dean had been puzzling over this the night before. The boy had suggested, somewhat facetiously, that Edward Bryant's spirit had probably survived and carried on. They had both laughed, but, now, Haight was not so sure there was not something in what the boy had said. Someone had known exactly what Edward Bryant's plans were and had carried them out flawlessly. Haight leafed through the stack of typed sheets, not sure what he was looking for but needing something to do while he put the information together. Still, he knew he was trying too hard, so he sat, allowing his mind to go calm. Dean had been trying to identify new names that seemed to be dominant in any of the new corporations. There was evidence of interlocking directorships, but Haight did not find this particularly ominous. The circles within which the rich traveled were rather small, so it was not surprising that the same people showed up on different boards.

Suddenly, he stopped and shuffled back to the front of the stack. Something had been nagging him. Now, he knew what it was. Wetting his finger, he quickly rifled through the stack of reports on Centron, dividing them into two piles and noting the corporations' names. Soon, he was erecting the two piles more quickly. The pattern he had dimly noticed was correct. The purpose of the corporations had not changed. By 1929, they had created a virtual monopoly over transportation, and most of that trade was by then going through the Panama Canal. As he stared at the corporations' officers' reports, he saw what had been bothering him. While before 1911, Bryant's name had appeared as E. BRYANT, after 1911, it simply appeared as BRYANT. There was no initial. Haight knew it was not unusual to carry the name of a dead corporate partner, but it was highly unlikely that someone would casually make the change he had just noticed. There was something else. In the 1950s, the name disappeared altogether. This, in itself, was not suspicious. Maybe the corporation had finally changed hands internally, and the decision had been made to eliminate the identification with the founder. Still, he was alert to the possibilities now.

From inside the desk, Haight pulled out the letters he had retrieved from Dean's mother. She was a gracious lady with a deep Southern accent, and he wondered what he would say to her if her son was dead. He laid the letters down between the two piles of corporate reports, trying to unravel the connection he suspected existed between the two sets of documents. He had read the letters looking for information supporting Dean's thesis that the canal was much deeper than appeared to be the case from the official documents. Evidently, the boy had misinterpreted the numbers, which had combined the excavation in both the jungle and the canal proper. Still, though Dean's original assumption had been proven incorrect, he had found out something much more important. Something evil had happened in that jungle, something so bad it had driven the author of the letters to write it out in code to a woman he had loved all those years. It could not be the stolen gold since the man had written somewhat matter of factly about that. Something else had haunted this man, so that, after the last letter in 1912, he had disappeared, his haunted voice shut down midsentence. Haight wondered what this man had been like. From the letters, it was clear he had become a jailer of sorts, and it was equally clear he had been in great conflict about this. What had happened in that jungle to cause a literate, cultured man to become frightened and inarticulate? Haight reached to the bottom of the pile of letters and pulled out the last one, dated September 30, 1912.

Dearest Audrey, it has been some time since I have written, and about that I am not only sorry but also somewhat distraught. I hope this finds you well and your family in good health. I think often of your mother and the day I spoke to her as she left the Great House. I had not until then realized you resembled her so closely. When she looked at me that day, I could not help but see the same spirit and fire in her I have always seen in you. This is not in itself strange, but I found it unsettling that I had missed it before. And today, as I struggle to make some sense of my existence, I wonder again what else I have missed. I sometimes feel as if I have lived in this world without eyes, and now I seem to be moving in a mist that threatens to lift but, in fact, only allows me to see that I was completely blind before.

This land has become darker, and I cannot see my way out of it. I have sold my soul for something that is worthless, something I did not need. Why, I cannot explain, nor do I understand. In this land, the extraordinary has become commonplace, and I feel as if I am living at the bottom of a hole that is curved at the top, and so, I cannot see the sky. We are not building a civilization here but constructing a hell that consumes life at an unbelievable rate. I have come to believe we were all condemned to die before we came here, and we simply live out the sentence for a short time before our consciousness leaves us. None of us will leave here alive. Even if our bodies are allowed to go back to the world, we are all dead already. I have tried to find a morality to make this bearable, but it is impossible now. My soul, if I have one, is so corrupted by this land that nothing, absolutely nothing I pray for finds its way beyond my hole.

Yesterday, I buried seventeen men. The soldiers—that is all these guards are—shot them when they tried to break out from the camp. This is not the place I came to six years ago. Has it only been six years? Something of the life we brought has gone. This is no longer a place of free labor. Now, the men are afraid, and they are constantly plotting. We are losing men each day, and we have had to replace them more quickly. We have seven thousand men in the camp now, and the work is furious. We are also using thousands of Indians. The floor must be completed before the canal is functional, and that has forced the Captain to bring in more men. They have no idea what they are building, and that has robbed them of the normal incentives. The Captain has instituted a system of incentives himself. He is offering more money to the men. This works for a little while with the newest recruits–more like kidnapped victims, really—but they soon realize that money does not buy them anything. No one has left the camp in the last five years, and though he reminds them every day of the wealth they are accumulating, no one believes anymore. The men suspect they are being lied to, and, to tell you the truth, I do not know if they are wrong.

Fear drives the camp now. Many of the men have come from Barbados. I no longer get close to them. Not that they wish to get close to me, anyway. They know I dictate the pace of their lives, and you should see the looks in their eyes, Audrey. I used to believe that when men are worked like this, they became deadened. These men do not. There is a fire behind their eyes that almost illuminates the night. I used to think it was hatred, but it is not. It is a determination not to die in this place. I have forgotten that, Audrey. I am not sure I would understand the expectations of the world anymore. Something vital has left me, and I fear that if I walked among men again, they would see that something, a soul perhaps, is missing. I used to think of the jungle as a place of power and peace. There is a sibilance to the wind that sounds like the voice of God, and when the rain storms come rushing up, you can hear it from a distance like the earth welcoming, with a scream of pleasure, the pounding of the falling water. But there is no God here, and there is no welcome. What I mistook for a welcome was really the scream of fear as the world cowers beneath the onslaught of the floods that descend. There is no love in the jungle, and where it springs, it soon becomes perverted, twisted into something that is unrecognizable. Death soon follows—or worse.

I am constantly afraid, Audrey, of the looks of the men, the insanity of the Captain, and the guns of the guards. Most of all, I am afraid of myself. I am afraid of what I have become and what I have become capable of. I am afraid that I can now see what is wrong and do it anyway. I know I will soon be asked to commit some indescribable wrong. The work here will soon be complete, and there is a strange feeling creeping into the place. The sounds of men's silent voices are frightening, Audrey, and when that disappears, there is the whispering. It is a whisper unlike anything you have heard. It fills the jungle with its noise. Only the Captain seems unaware of it. Even the guards, those gryphons with guns, are tense. They have made a new perimeter, and their huts are not part of the camp anymore but now sit in a huge circle around the workers' huts. We have cut a huge hole in the heart of the jungle to accommodate the numbers we have brought in to do the work.

Last month, a friend died. He had lost his mind a long time ago, but I used to go into the city to see him, and, despite his insanity, he would come to the bay each month at the right time on the right day. While we talked, Audrey, he would from time to time make sense. I believe he must have been a teacher at one of the schools in Barbados because he would occasionally make references to classes, and he seemed aware of literature and some history. He was mad, but he seemed so much a part of the world that I needed the contact. He did not understand me, and so I could talk to him. His insanity was like a protection against something he feared. He was horribly broken from one of the landslides that occur so often in this place. I do not know how he died, although from the inquiries I made, he seemed to have died peacefully in an alley somewhere in the city. Still, no man should live or die like that. In many ways, he was my last contact with this land, and when he died, something seemed to fly away from here. I know I am not making sense. I don't understand it either, but you are the only person to whom I can say these things that are bursting my heart.

I believe that, since you have not written to me, you are not able to read my letters. I hope they bring you some happiness, though. God knows that writing them is the only source of pleasure I have in this world now. It is also the only relief I have. I struggle from time to time to think of a God who would allow this place to exist, who would allow these things to happen, and I have a difficult time understanding Him. I sometimes feel we are lost here, hidden away from the eyes of the universe, left to create this hell that consumes us. A year ago, I lost a friend. I am not sure if she died, but whatever happened to her was because of the Captain's cruelty. She had said to me once that the world had been created here in this jungle, and that all things lived in peace until the sun became angry at the butterflies, whose number and beauty blocked his view. He sent the jaguar to get rid of the butterflies, but the jaguar fell in love, so the sun sent man to help him. I sometimes feel we are again hidden away from the view of whatever looks down on us, and though the jaguar is here, man cannot help him as my friend said they did before. We are now the ones sending up the mist through our acts of evil. I wonder what will be sent to cleanse this place of us. Who will be sent to help us, Audrey?

Outside, as I write, I can hear the sound of the jungle. It is as if it never sleeps. The animals have adjusted to each other's habits, and the natural enemies avoid each other when possible. So, as the day animals go to sleep, the night ones come to life, and through it all, I hear even now the sound of the jaguar. He now comes closer to the camp than in the early days. We have lost men to the beast, and the Captain has sent hunting parties after him, but to no avail so far. In fact, protecting the men from the attacks of the jaguar was the reason given for moving the guards' huts out to the circular perimeter. They have not been able to stop the beast though. It seems able to move right past them without being seen. No one is sure what to think, and I know the men are saying the jaguar is not really an animal. That is nonsense, of course, but one can't help but wonder.

I have not slept all night, and it will be dawn soon. I can hear the sounds changing in the jungle, and soon I will hear the men as they change shifts. I have not been underground since a year ago, but judging from the rock and dirt we have carted away, we must be halfway to hell by now.

Forgive me for dumping all of this on you, but I need to say something or I will die from what is being held inside me. I miss you, and I still remember the nights spent in the darkness on the hill. Do you ever think of those nights? I often wonder if you have forgotten what they meant. I was too young to understand what love meant then, but now I understand that what we call salvation is dependent on love, and I have always needed that from you. Do you remember the first time we made love? I think of that frequently now. Do you remember the laugh we had when I discovered I had burned the skin off my tail-bone because I had been laying on a rock and the movement had taken off the skin so that I was bleeding, as were you, when we were done? We joked about both of us losing our virginity at the same time. I want those to be my memories and my thoughts, Audrey, not these shapes and undefined faces I see when I close my eyes. There is a face that comes back all the time. It should not haunt me because the face carries the most inexplicable look of forgiveness, but I cannot accept it, and it rips at my heart. Faces seem to haunt me now. Except yours and your mother's. There was something I saw in your mother's eyes that day she came to the house that said I was tied to her and to you. I have never understood that look, but I have felt encouraged by it. Maybe in that look there is the possibility of salvation. I don't know what I am talking about, but that look has stayed with me. What do you think it means?

This may sound strange, but I wish you would pray for me. I cannot pray for myself. I do not believe my prayers would rise very high. Maybe yours would. Or maybe it is too late for all that. I don't know. I am not asking you to wait for me or anything like that. I know that would be unfair since I am not sure what I am anymore. I only ask that you love me as I love you. I must go now. The light is coming, and I must see that everything is set for the day. I hope you stay in good health and you prosper. Love, Rupert.

Haight put the letter down on the table and sat back, staring at the ceiling. He felt very uncomfortable reading the letter but was drawn to it, wondering about the man who had written it. It was a look not only into the past but into the man's soul. What had happened to cause the despair so evident in the letters after 1911? Before that, there had been the usual complaints about the weather, the work, and the strangeness of the place. In fact, the letters could be divided into three categories. The early ones spoke with a good deal of excitement about Panama. He seemed to be enjoying the labor and the learning he was engaged in. He also seemed to have formed some friendships. This tone lasted for only the first year or so. Then, he had evidently been sent into the deep jungle, and although the tone changed, he still seemed to think he was engaged in something important and useful. The letters written in late 1908 had begun the change, talking more of the relationships in the camp and how they seemed to be breaking down. The excitement had given way to complaint and then to a kind of muted fear that was never fully explained. After 1911, though, the letters were full of despair. Why had this man changed so much and so quickly? Reading all the letters together, it was easy to see the change, and it was shocking. In a mere six years he had gone from a young, somewhat naïve boy to a very disillusioned man who feared for the loss of his soul. What could have caused that, Haight wondered. What had happened to the man in 1911?

Suddenly, Haight sat up straight. 1911! He rifled through the sheaf of officers' reports, checking the dates again. Yes. He was right. The changes in the corporation's board had taken place in 1911. Edward Bryant had also disappeared in South America in 1911. Now, Barnes' letters were clearly identifying 1911 as the year when something bad happened to him in the jungle as well. Haight rested his head in his hands, trying to clear his mind, to see the patterns that were sure to be there if he could find the right orientation. Impatience was the enemy now; and though his every instinct pressed for action, the worst thing to do would be to run off in some uncertain direction just to satisfy the urge toward movement. He had to think.

Something was in the details, and he knew from experience that perspective determines vision. The dates, he was sure, had to be more than coincidence. Not quite a pattern, they formed a network of possible lines of investigation, and he would have to follow each one to see where it led. He was certain one of those strands would lead to the boy.

What did he know for certain? Something was going on in the heart of the government that was counter to where the foreign policy of the President was taking the country. Powerful men, including some in the CIA, were involved. These men were tied to the shadowy corporation Centron, which controlled much of the world's shipping and apparently controlled the Panama Canal itself. There was some concern about the return of the canal to Panama. The reasons here were less clear but amounted to a combination of nationalism, economic control, and fear of the Panamanians having control of one of the world's major waterways. Then, there was something more ominous that had led men to kill because Dean speculated that the canal was deeper than was officially thought. Dean had misunderstood the meaning of the difference in the statistics, but, clearly, something was wrong with the official record. It was not that the canal was deeper, but something had been constructed in the jungle north of the canal. It had involved lots of tunneling, and the disposal numbers had caught Dean's eye. Still, the fact that the secret project and the canal used the same disposal sites suggested cooperation or, at the very least, the turning of a blind eye. If that were true, then it meant the government, or at least some representative of the government, had been involved from the beginning, and if that was the case, then he needed to look for elements of continuity. If he could find someone who had been involved between 1904 and 1915 or so, then he could talk to that person. Any of these people would have to be close to a hundred years old now, if they were alive at all, but it was possible someone had survived. If he could find such a person then he might be able to make some sense of this. Haight knew he did not have enough information, and it was silly to torture himself searching for patterns that would only become clear with more data.

Outside, the valley was bathed in sunlight. No sound came from the house. This room had been soundproofed a few years ago, and he had installed the computer that took up a full side of the room. After he had taken over Haight's Plastics and Paints, the value of the huge machine had increased as the business of the world became more complex. He thought again of the boy who had proved to be a wizard with the computer, but quickly turned his mind back to the information he needed.

Sooner or later, he would have to get this information to the President, but while there were several acquaintances who could arrange this, Haight was no longer sure whom he could trust. Also, he did not want to endanger anyone else. Still, to find Dean—assuming the boy was still alive—he would have to move quickly. He had to figure out the significance of the year 1911. That, he felt certain, was the key to understanding what had happened to Dean. Haight could not bring himself to think of the boy being dead, and as his hand closed into a fist at the possibility, he turned from the window, stalking through the door, which closed quietly behind him.

His wife was coming in from the patio and waved at him, but there was no smile.

"Have you found out anything about Dean?" she asked.

Haight shook his head, following her into the study. He was on pins and needles, his impulses driving him to do something, his mind cautioning against precipitous action.

"He'll be all right, Jack. I'm sure of it," Madeline said, looking at him with some concern.

Grateful for the reassurance, he reached out, covering her hand, and she smiled, accepting the caress. Haight's mind drifted back to the boy. He did not have a plan, and there was no one else to approach. Antonio Peques was checking discreetly, through the police, for any report on the boy, and was also checking the airlines to see if his name turned up on a ticket. Haight was not optimistic that these investigations would lead anywhere, but they had to be done. Eliminate the obvious, and that defines the problem. The old mantra of the analyst.

He was not aware Madeline was speaking until she pinched his hand. He looked at her, surprised.

"Boy, you are lost. I asked if there was any way I can help."

"I don't see how, darling. I'm stuck on a date. A number of things seemed to have happened in 1911, but they don't connect—at least, I can't find the connection."

She looked at him quizzically, and he explained what he had found in the letters and the official reports of the corporation. She thought for a moment, then said, "Clearly, something Bryant did in Panama started the whole thing."

"But he'd been dead since 1908."

"You don't know that. All you know is he disappeared in 1908. No one ever found Bryant's body, did they?"

"No. But it's well documented he disappeared in South America, not in Panama."

"I don't know much about Bryant, Jack, but it just seems to me it's too close not to check it out. For most of us, Panama is in South America."

Haight thought for a moment, then walked to the telephone. He spoke only a short while. When he returned, he said, "That was Harry Downes at commerce. I don't know why I didn't think of him before. He was a labor historian at Princeton before coming to Washington. You were right. He's sure no one ever really knew where Bryant died. The South America story just became the accepted history. I asked him if he knew of any event around 1911 that is related to the Panama Canal and may have something to do with Bryant, but he couldn't think of anything. He did promise to make some discreet inquiries though."

"I do hope he's careful, Jack."

She did not have to say what she meant, and Haight nodded grimly.

Three hours later, the man from Commerce called back.

"Hi, Jack. I couldn't find anything important. The only thing that seems to have happened was the creation of the giant lake that forms the middle of the canal."

"What do you mean, Harry?"

"Well, apparently, once the decision to make the canal rise over the mountains was made, they had to solve the problem of some river that flowed into the canal area. I can't remember the name, but they actually dammed the river and made it into a lake or something like that. It was pretty important at the time. I couldn't find any relationship with Bryant though. In any case, he had been dead for three years by then."

Haight thanked the man and hung up. Something else of importance had occurred in Panama in the vicinity of the canal and the secret project in the jungle. He would wait to hear from Antonio, and if his report led nowhere, as he expected it to, then he would be going to Panama. He was no longer worried about being followed. Whoever had taken the boy would expect Haight to look for him, so there was little need for secrecy.

Fifteen minutes later, he had heard from Antonio. As expected, Antonio had found out nothing, and Haight asked him to get the plane ready. Haight was packing a light bag when the phone rang.

"Jack Haight here."

"Hello, Jack. I think we should meet."

Haight did not respond immediately, but his heart was beating faster. It was Nieves, the man from the CIA.

CHAPTER FORTY-TWO

PANAMA CITY 1976

Rupert Barnes sat in the dark room thinking of what he had set in motion and trying to convince himself he had done the right thing. Hu was gone, having left two nights before on his way back to the United States to find the boy. Barnes had agreed to rid the man in Long Island and himself of the threat to the secret in the jungle. In return, the man had agreed to let Barnes know what was being planned in Panama and, more importantly, to avoid any contact with Barnes' two sons in Philadelphia. In some ways, they had returned to their old relationship, with the man offering something undefined for something tangible that Barnes would give. The difference was that he now intended to kill Bryant. In the circumstances, the boy's life seemed a small price to pay for the chance to destroy the man whose life had haunted his for almost seventy years. Barnes adjusted the blanket across his legs, feeling a coldness that had nothing to do with the air conditioning, which had been turned off for some time now. This was the final price he had to pay for the life he had led.

Sitting high above the city, staring down at the snake-like traffic below, Barnes felt that something vital had gone out of him. He did not have long to live and would have to atone for his actions, although it was really his lack of action that had proved deadly. The world should be rid of the Captain. There was something ancient and evil about him that Barnes had always recognized but had learned how to explain away or to ignore. In the jungle, he had allowed Bryant's brilliance to blind him to the evil that Bryant embodied, and he had been seduced by the possibilities the man had created. He still liked to think that Bryant had corrupted him, and, for this, Barnes hated him.

Now, watching Panama City spread out beneath him like a Roman candle, the fiery edges of which ended abruptly when the mountains intervened, he knew what he had to do. One thing would scrub the guilt and the contamination from his soul: the death of the man in Long Island. Seventy years ago, he had been there at the creation of the monster that was Bryant. He had helped him protect the evil in the jungle and had stood by, in fear and impotence, while the man committed the act Barnes felt had condemned them both to hell. Long before that happened, however, he had seen the emptiness of Bryant's soul.

He had been living in the village by the sea for a week when it happened. Though he was determined not to go back to the camp, the thought of the men haunted him. Yet, Leila had the capacity to take this guilt away, to make him forget. As he sat on the beach, watching the tranquil sea send its gentle waves toward the shore, it was hard to believe that, at his back, only a few miles away, there was this world that seemed the antithesis of the village. He had become consumed by Leila's body, as if it could destroy the fears that held him captive. As the days passed, he came to believe that, in her body, he could find the salvation he craved, and, as time went by, the inside of the jungle receded somewhat. The women were shy of his presence, so he spent most of his time alone while Leila was off in the jungle. She did not leave with the men but was gone soon after he awoke and she had fed him. It was then he realized that the women treated Leila with a deference he had not noticed before, and he wondered at this.

One night, he asked her about her role in the village, and she looked at him uncomprehendingly, saying nothing. He repeated the question.

"Why do the women act so restrained when they are around you?"

She did not understand the word "restrained," so he explained, and she answered, "Maybe you reason."

Barnes thought about this for a moment. Then, seeing the amused look on her face, he realized she was teasing him.

Frowning playfully at her, he arranged his face into a question. Instead of answering, she asked, "How long you come?"

"About five years. Why?"

"Why now notice?"

Barnes thought for a while, recognizing the rebuke, and then shrugged.

"Not important then. Not important now."

"I just didn't notice, Leila. That doesn't mean it wasn't important. I just never thought to ask before."

The burned side of her face stretched a little as she laughed at him. Rising from the pallet and taking his hand, she walked into the small room in which he had seen the jaguar. She took the robe down and placed it in his hand. It was warm, as if alive. Barnes ran his hand over the beautiful feathers, looking for the means by which the molas were attached but could find none.

Finally, he looked at her, a question in his eyes.

"That why women respect."

Barnes did not understand, and she added, "Leila protect robe."

"But what is the robe? Is it important? Valuable?"

"It robe of butterflies."

"Butterflies?"

Leila nodded, and, upon looking more closely at the garment, Barnes was surprised to find that the fabric was of butterfly wings. He had assumed they were feathers.

"So does that mean you are a queen or something?"

"No queen. Cacique leader of village."

"Then what does the robe mean?"

"Robe unity of all things, Rupert Barnes. Sun. Jaguar. Jungle. Kuni. Robe hold together."

"And what does that make you?"

"Servant."

Still not sure what she meant, Barnes walked back with her to the main section of the hut. Lying on the pallet, she said, "Rupert Barnes, what you build in forest?"

Barnes did not immediately answer, realizing that the momentary hesitation made his answer suspect.

"The truth is, I don't know. We are extracting something from the ground."

"Gold?"

He was, at first, surprised. Though the Captain had been using Indians as guards for some time now, Barnes was not sure if Leila's was the group being used. Still, the gold was taken out of the camp through the jungle, and the Indians probably monitored that movement. In any case, Indian workers in the tunnels now outnumbered the West Indians.

"Yes. We have taken gold from the ground."

Then, in a fit of relief, he poured out his heart to the gentle woman. She listened, her face serene, the scar receding into the relief of the night. Barnes emptied his soul and felt the freedom that came with his speech. He had not realized how much he had held things in, and as he poured his pain into the woman, she came close to him. When he reached for her, however, she gently pulled away and walked out of the hut. Returning with the potent drug the men smoked, she handed him the pipe. Leila soon lost consistency, her face bending into the shapes of their early days together. Her cries filled a space within him, pushing out the fear, the pain, and the guilt. Clutching at her, the depth of her answering, he felt the tingling along his nerve endings and reached across the spaces he was desperately trying to eliminate with this contact. Leila writhed around him, bringing the secret sounds of the night. In a distance he could not measure, Barnes felt himself uncoil, stretching out in directions his mind told him were impossible. And then, in the depths of him, he felt the tightness, the ball of heat that held the cold at its center, and his mind left him. A snake streaked out of him, leaving his mind behind.

Inside Leila, the extension of himself flexed, pouring his self into the woman who held him, crying things he did not understand. They held each other for a long time, and Barnes felt certain that something vital had left him and attached itself to the woman. He rubbed his face against hers, feeling the scar of her burn scratch him. He did not pull back as he ordinarily would but held the slender woman closer, feeling the wetness between them. He pushed futilely to prevent his shrinking self from slipping from her, feeling her move to meet him, but he was falling, and when she accommodated him, his body squeezed right through her and disappeared on the other side. His mind was lost in some place that was quiet, warm, and wet without being annoying, and sleep came quickly.

The groan brought him back from a place that was dark and inviting with a dim light burning in the center.

He could not bring his eyes into focus, and his muscles bent at odd angles. The hut lost its shape and undulated in waves among the colors of the butterflies. At the center of that unstable universe was the groan that inflicted itself on his mind from time to time. He could not locate the source, but the inside of his brain ached without any clear point of pain. Then, the mist cleared, and he groaned. Two figures were writhing–no, not that, but Leila was on her knees, and, behind her, the Captain had injected himself in an obscene gesture of callousness. Barnes saw the woman's face contort in agony and tried to push himself up, but his arms had turned to rubber. The horrendous thrusting of the man behind the woman tore at Barnes' soul, and he screamed at Bryant to stop. Leila's face kept bending out of shape, but the scar glistened in the nightlight. Her eyes asked him to stop this assault, but he could not move. He tried to turn his eyes away from the coupling of the two, but his attention was drawn to the point of their contact, where the woman was stretched in impossible ways to accommodate the thrusting of the man. A sob tearing out of him, Barnes tried to rise again but fell into the blackness.

The last sound he heard was the thin scream coming from the woman, a scream that signaled not so much fear but a contained hatred, and he looked up to see the twisted smile on the man's face as he stood high above, holding the woman's hair and emptying himself into her. Barnes fell asleep.

The sun was high in the sky when his eyes opened, and he closed them again as the glare burned. The images of the night came back in a rush, and he sat up, looking for the woman. She was not in the hut, and Barnes walked unsteadily into the clearing. Leila stood at the water's edge. Hurrying to her, he placed his arm on her shoulder. He could not meet her eye, but as she turned to stare at him, something indefinable passed between them, and he touched the burnt face. Then, he headed back to the camp, the anger a tight, deep burn in him. He had always known a time would come for the confrontation with the Captain, and, as he sat in the skiff, Barnes composed himself into a single will: revenge for what had been done to the woman.

The camp was quiet when he entered the gates, guarded as always now by the hard-faced men who surrounded the ever-widening area. He walked briskly to the hut that served as the headquarters and looked inside. The uncontrollable anger that had consumed him when he left the village was gone, replaced by a cool sense of what he had to do. It was clear Bryant respected nothing, particularly not Barnes, and he would have to be stopped. Bryant, however, was not in the building, and Barnes jogged over to his hut. This, too, was empty. He came out, looking to the hilltop where the man frequently sat, but, again, there was no one there. Barnes, feeling the core of hatred cooling as he was forced to speak, asked one of the managers where the man was.

"Mr. Bryant left two days ago for the United States."

"But...that...the States, you say?"

The man looked at Barnes strangely, then said, "He left something for you."

Reaching into a desk drawer, he handed Barnes a note. The message was short and innocuous, except for one statement. Bryant had been called back to the United States, and, in his absence, Barnes would be in charge of the compound. The last sentence read, "I know you are having second thoughts, but things are working out fine."

Barnes walked back to his hut, confused and weary. Could he have imagined the rape? He couldn't have. It had been too real, too clear in his mind, and Leila's odd behavior had confirmed that something had happened. The Captain must not have left for the United States but had come to the village and demonstrated his superiority in the most degrading way. He had taken Barnes' woman in front of his face. That thought made him feel guilty. After all, it was Leila who had been violated, but he could not get out of his mind the challenge inherent in the act. If it had occurred.

Barnes, confused, did not visit the village until the Captain returned from the United States. Three months had passed, and he felt stupid when the man approached him with unaccustomed joviality, apparently refreshed by his time away from the jungle. That night, Barnes, freed of his responsibility, headed back to the village, a raging need in his soul. The men had not yet joined each other in the circle, but Leila showed no surprise at seeing him. Taking him into the hut, she pressed his hand to her stomach.

Barnes frowned, then asked, "Are you pregnant, Leila?"

The woman nodded, looking at him urgently, waiting for his response.

"When did you find out?"

Tension had crept into his voice, and she continued to look closely at him, the clear, dark eyes that could become opaque in an instant searching for something. Barnes struggled to find a way to be happy but was uncomfortable. Marriage he dismissed as impractical because he could not take this woman from her place in the jungle. Even as he thought this, the lie beat against his conscience, forcing him to investigate his feelings. He had no intention of staying in the jungle. What was his relationship to Leila? Had he always assumed he would leave her? How would he go? What would she feel when he did? Realizing he had never thought of this before, Barnes stood rooted to the ground, a smile on his face.

Finally, rubbing her stomach with one hand and her destroyed face with the other, he said, "I am very happy."

Leila turned away, going into the back of the hut where the jaguar sometimes slept, and Barnes stood, thinking of his life and how it seemed constantly to be determined by events he did not want. Most of all, he thought of the Captain astride the woman. He and Leila made love later that night, clear-eyed this time, and he lingered over her as she opened to him in a way that he thought of as more possessive. For the first time, as they found each other, she talked in a soft, sibilant language that sounded like the trees addressing the wind. He did not understand a word, but the sounds soothed his tortured soul.

"I never really knew," he now mumbled to himself, watching the lights far below him slither past the hotel.

Now, thinking of his impending death, Barnes wondered how his life would be measured. Until the last few weeks, he had given little thought to what would happen to him after his death, but digging into his past forced him to confront what he had done or allowed to be done so many years ago. So many deaths—intentional and otherwise. Now, he was contemplating two more. There was no salvation for him, and if that was true, then he might as well make peace with himself. Barnes wondered whether it was possible for evil to exist without good. He had seen little that was good in his life and had done even less. Yet, by any measure, he had prospered. What accounted for that? Was there no balance to the universe? Did not God measure things out according to the worth of the individual? Or was it that since man's actions could not save him, so, too, they could not damn him? Was it all a lottery, then? God's joke? To have man strive for a salvation that would simply be determined by the luck of the draw?

Barnes snorted, saying under his breath, "What a crock! I must really be getting ready for the grave."

At this, he laughed silently, then quickly turned serious again. He would rid himself and the Captain of the boy, and then he would have the opportunity to get close to Bryant. Given the hell that Bryant had put him through, it was only fitting that he be the one to end the tyrant's earthly existence. With this thought, he sat back in the chair, staring at the dark mountains that covered so much from history's sight, remembering.

For weeks after being told of Leila's pregnancy, Barnes was ambivalent but not unhappy. He went to the village every night during that period, trying to get used to the idea of fatherhood. He had never really understood the relationship between Leila and the village. The men did not pay any attention to her. In fact, none of them came close to her. The women, on the other hand, were becoming increasingly deferential, and this perplexed him. For nights after learning of her pregnancy, Barnes was haunted by the image of the engorged Captain spreading Leila open, and he could neither excise the image from his mind nor be certain the act actually happened. Leila had not raised it, and he could not ask her if it had occurred. Yet, the thought that she might be carrying a child that was not his was never far from his thoughts. Once, he broached the subject, laughing and suggesting that he had had a dream in which she had been made love to by a devil, but her eyes turned opaque, and she stared at him until he turned away in shame.

To avoid the thought of the Captain and the woman, one night, he asked about Leila's role in the village.

"But you never seem to talk to the men. Why is that?"

"Talk with you."

The hint of a smile told him she was teasing.

"Yes. But you don't talk to anyone else. The other women are always teasing their men. No one ever seems to approach you. Why?"

"You want them to, Rupert Barnes?"

Exasperated, he shouted, "Why the hell can't you just answer the question?"

Immediately, her eyes turned inward.

"Men not talk to me. I belong to you," she answered softly.

Barnes was perplexed. The other women were not restrained around the men. Then, pointing to her scarred face, she added, "And this."

Barnes' heart went out to her, and he gently caressed the corrugated cheek. Careful to avoid the subject so as not to hurt her feelings, he had never asked her how she had been burnt. Now he did.

"Sacrifice for guardian of robe."

"What do you mean?"

"Face, body belong to jaguar. Burnt so no man will see me."

Having always assumed the scar was the result of an accident, Barnes was horrified to find out she had been deliberately burned. He started up, swearing, but her gentle laughter quickly restrained him.

"Rupert Barnes, this important?"

"Damned right it is. What right have they to scar your face like that?"

She shrugged, replying, "Honor to be guardian. One who can change."

"What do you mean 'change'?"

"I choose you. Other women cannot."

Barnes understood her to be saying that other women had their partners chosen for them, but she was able to make her own choice.

"What does the robe do? Is it supposed to protect the village?"

"Protect Kuni."

"But what do you do with the robe?"

"I keep," she said as if talking to an idiot.

"Will the robe protect you from what we are doing in the forest?"

Her answer was instantaneous.

"No. You destroy Kuni and robe. You divide life, and Kuni die."

She had, once before, mentioned the dividing of life, but he was not sure what she meant. When he asked if her pregnancy would affect her role as guardian, she said, "Not guardian."

"What do you mean?" he asked, surprised.

"Child is," she replied, pride and wistfulness in her voice.

Before he could ask her to explain, she turned to him, her body open and inviting, and he lost himself in her.

The next night, the village disappeared.

CHAPTER FORTY-TWO

PANAMA 1912

Charles Lemieux stood, hands rigid behind his back, looking at the giant structure that was nearing completion. Gatun Lock was the first of the giant locks that would move ships from one ocean to the other. The size was awe-inspiring. Black figures moved about at the top, where they had been working for the four years since the decision had been made to build a lock canal. Lemieux remembered the interminable rows of cars that had taken the dirt away from the cut. Even today, with most of the excavation now complete, he still marveled at those early days. Much had changed since then. They were now at the final stage: the construction of the locks. Then, the canal would be ready. A powerful feeling of pride ran through Lemieux. He had sacrificed much for this victory. At this thought, his face turned dark, and he braced against the onslaught of emotion that threatened to over-power him.

"Claudette," he said in a strangled voice.

Lemieux tightened his grip on his hand, and the pain brought some semblance of order back to his face. Still, the pounding in his head continued, and he thought of the sweet-faced woman who had never lost faith in him. Claudette Lemieux had died the year before, on the eve of their triumph. For, indeed, it was as much hers as his. She had been steadfast always, showing him the way out of the multitude of struggles he had faced in this land. When he buried her, the rain had fallen all day, and he and the other pallbearers stumbled and slid as she had been lowered into the grave.

Watching the lock being finalized, Lemieux thought of the orders he had finally received. He would be leaving in two weeks, his wish to be free of the place finally granted one year after he had requested it. He had already decided to resign his commission in the Army, having been offered a position with a shipping company. Lemieux was not sure he would fit into any civilian enterprise, but the offer was lucrative and the cost minimal. In fact, there had been no cost at all. A year ago, one month after his wife died, he had simply been asked to build a dam to block the river at Madden's. This was not his original intent, the plan having been to build further to the west. When the request had come, brought by the white fellow from Barbados, he had at first ignored it.

A week later, the fellow returned, this time bringing the name that changed Lemieux's mind. He brought a message from Bryant. Lemieux was surprised because he had heard that Bryant was dead, but the man convinced Lemieux that his erstwhile benefactor was alive and well, though he wished this information to be kept secret. Lemieux asked a thousand questions, but the fellow provided no answers. Bryant wanted the dam to be built at Madden's, and Barnes had plans with him to show the effects of the change in location. Lemieux, impressed with the schematics, agreed that the slightly changed location improved the water flow through the middle part of the canal. An engineer reviewed the schematics, but Lemieux's decision was already made. He owed Edward Bryant too much not to grant him this favor, particularly since there were no negative effects.

Until then, he had not heard from Bryant since his last visit to Washington and, for a year after that, had received no support from the man. Yet, when his difficulties with the disappearing men had become most acute, Bryant's ships returned, bringing him an ever-increasing supply of men from the West Indies. Men continued to disappear, but word came that they would be replaced as long as he did not investigate too closely. He did exactly that, and the canal had been built. In this country, Lemieux had lost two persons who were very close to him, and he suspected that one of them was a victim of whatever Bryant was doing in the jungle. He had no proof, just a feeling he was increasingly reluctant to pursue as the difficulties mounted and his problems were solved only by the presence of Bryant's ships.

Lemieux could see the miter gates of the lock; behind them, the great cliff stood like a battlement, a castle wall high above the bottom. Thousands of men were pouring the concrete that would be the floor of the lock, which looked like an enormous flywheel. His eyes settled on the black figures who moved about the unfinished lock. Two of them carried a length of chain over their shoulders, moving carefully on the train tracks along the top. The skeleton of the lock was in place. In the distance, the six-inch thick pine planks that made up the foundation looked insubstantial. Yet, the structure itself was frightening, and Lemieux could not help but feel some sense of satisfaction at this wonder he had created. All along the cut, the terraces stood, illuminated by the sunlight against the red clays that had threatened the project in the early days. From the bottom to the top of the cut, there were seven terraces, making the top of the canal several times the width at the bottom. It was a simple solution that had been expensively learned.

Lemieux turned away from the enormous hole before him and walked toward the truck, sad because he would not see the end of this marvel. He was going home. At least, he was going away from Panama, for he was no longer sure that any home existed. The last year had been hell as he had tried to bury his mind and his feelings in the work of keeping the canal on track. Many marveled because, when Claudette died, he had not taken even a day off. He could not. Thinking would have brought madness. No one had approached him, understanding that it would take him a lifetime to adjust to the loss of the woman who had made him believe in himself. He had pushed on, gradually losing sight of himself in the blur of the work. Though white suits had replaced the uniform of the earlier days, he still had a military bearing. One sensed, however, a stiffness that was not entirely natural, as if he were holding himself against some blow that might fall. His hair was entirely white, and, having lost its earlier luster, now appeared limp. It had thinned, and as he pulled the strands across the balding crown, the attempt seemed pathetic when contrasted with the power of his pugnacious jaw. The strength he had exuded in his youth had slowly been sucked out of him, and Lemieux's eyes were moist when he turned his back to the canal.

For several months, none of the men had disappeared, and Lemieux was relieved. Three years ago, he had sought to find out what was going on in the jungle. That night at Bryant's home, staring at the extraordinarily detailed map, one name had surprised him. Culebra. It was considerably further north than the Culebra he knew, and after checking every available map, the only place the name had shown up was in the heart of the canal. Assuming Bryant's map to be in error, he had forgotten about it. Then, a year ago, he had been approached by that white islander on Bryant's behalf and, while calculating the overflow that would occur if he changed the location of the dam, had found some old French survey maps. On those maps, there was another Culebra to the north. Lemieux knew he would have to move all of the Indian tribes out of the area to be flooded and was grateful to have found the place. Still, something told him to be careful. He had not discussed his findings with anyone.

When Barnes returned to get the final estimates from him as to the water flow when the dam was built, he had asked about the villages in the area. Barnes had become un-readable. Lemieux remembered thinking how like the black fellows Barnes was, having the same ability to disappear right in front of you, to close off some part of himself so that you thought you were looking at a piece of wood. Yet, the very change in the man confirmed Lemieux's suspicions. Barnes indicated that "we" would take care of the tribes to the north. In any case, he pointed out, Lemieux had no ju-risdiction beyond the Zone, and so he could not officially be involved in relocating the tribes. Lemieux noted that Culebra would also be flooded, but Barnes had not reacted except to shrug his shoulders. The man was either a terrific actor or Lemieux's assumptions about the relationship be-tween Bryant and Culebra were wrong. There was one thing, however, he could not deceive himself about. In changing the dam's location, he had changed masters. The lake would now flood more territory in Panama not ac-counted for in the treaty giving the Canal Zone to the Americans. Worse, he had abdicated his responsibility.

It was not the kind of thing that would go unnoticed, and this had been particularly so when the level of the lake had risen much more quickly than expected, threatening to overrun the dam. It was clear the engineers had miscalcu-lated the width of the flood plain over which the lake would be created, and they had wanted to go into the jungle to seek out the obstruction. Lemieux was in a panic and somewhat distracted at that time because it was only weeks after Claudette's death. The white islander had come in the night, telling him not to worry because they were working on the obstruction. The water would stop rising soon. For three days, Lemieux endured the questioning looks of the engineers. Then, the level dropped precipitously, and he found himself again grateful to Bryant.

This act, however, convinced him he should leave Panama. He had lost something vital: the complete faith necessary to impose his will on a challenge and tear it apart. He had not simply given way to Bryant's will on the relocation of the dam, accepting an intermediary's assurance about the lack of danger posed by the rising waters. Something worse had happened. He had been glad to have someone else make the decision for him, and that had never been his way. Furthermore, it was not the way to complete the canal. Too much depended on leadership, and having lost the passion, he should be gone from this place. It had taken too much.

Lemieux continued to stare at the lock, no longer seeing anything but Claudette's image in his mind. She had weakened after his return from Washington four years ago, but he had been too consumed by the excavation and the labor problems to confront her over her refusal to return to the United States. He had watched as she thinned and lost energy, never admitting she was dying.

By then, the worst of the epidemic was over, and the work in the hospital was less strenuous, but just watching her deny the weakness in her body had been horrible. At first, he encouraged her to stay home and rest, but as the disease ate through her body, the conspiracy of denial was established, and everyone pretended she was all right. Torn with the pain of her effort to appear normal, he was almost glad when she was unable to make the trek to the hospital anymore. As she laid in bed, the protective layer overhanging it, he had come each day, knowing she would never leave. She never changed, and everyone admired the spirit of the frail woman who seemed neither to accept nor fear death. Lemieux thought of his last conversation with her.

By then, Claudette had lost most of her color, and the darkness under her eyes seemed a permanent scar.

He looked at her, unsuccessfully trying to hide the hurt that was tearing him apart. She tried to smile, but her face was a mere rictus, and he watched from behind the protective net, unable to touch the woman who had shared his life for so long. She continued to look at him, that strange smile ripping her face apart and his heart along with it. When she began to speak, he rested his head tentatively against the netting. A nurse rushed over, warning him against the contact, but he irritably ordered her away, eventually resting his head against the bed near his wife's mouth. Her voice was hoarse, but Lemieux could still hear something of her playfulness.

"You...look...like...hell," she whispered.

He moved his head against the bed, and she touched it through the netting.

"I love you. I love you so much, Claudette."

"I...know. Love...you...too. Wish...I...could...touch... you."

He broke then, the tears running down his cheeks, but she did not allow him to fall into depression.

"Some...soldier. Crying...in...public. What...ever... will...the...men...think... Colonel?"

Her smile widened, and he guessed she was laughing, but no sound came from her. She stared at him, the fondness he had taken so much for granted now a source of consolation.

Finally, she gasped, "You have succeeded, Charles. You have given too much to this place. Don't... let...it... take...your...soul."

Relaxing after that, eyes closed, she breathed shallowly. Lemieux watched her for a while, waiting for her composure to return. He had heard that, at these times, men became numb, and he found himself wishing for numbness, but a lump in his chest hurt as if someone had pushed a hot poker inside him. Feeling useless, he watched the woman who had given texture to his life lay on the white sheets, a slight dampness on the pillow around her head. Her hair, stringy now, was spread untidily over the pillow, but this was not what he saw. It was the face that, though bloodless, still held his attention. The delicate bones of her brow were more prominent, but, to his mind, they simply emphasized the best feature of her face. When she again opened her eyes, there was a sparkle in them. Not sure if she was crying, he reached out through the netting to touch her, not caring that the yellow fever was contagious. Only her touch mattered, and, were it not for the presence of the ever-vigilant nurses, he would have climbed beneath the covers. Understanding this, she smiled, and the light brightened in her eyes.

"You have to…go…on, Charles. But…not…here."

"What do you mean, 'Dette?"

She waited a while, then added, "Panama…is…already…yours. You…can't…give…anymore. Go home."

The last words came more forcefully, and then she closed her eyes again, seeming to sink further into the mattress. When she fell asleep, he left, leaving instructions that he was to be informed if her condition changed. When they came early in the morning, Lemieux knew she was dead. He did not go to the hospital immediately but stood on the veranda watching the sluicing rain pour down, scraping away the topsoil and carrying it inevitably to the sea.

Now, as he stared at the giant hole, the two feelings of pride and pain conjoined in him. If all went as planned, in fewer than three years, the locks would be complete, and there would be water in them. Still, Claudette had been right. He could give no more.

Later, sitting in the front car of the train as it moved slowly along the edge of the canal, heading west to Panama City, he passed the section where the new lake had been created. Far to the north, the tree line obstructed his view, as the silver gray of the water gave way to the deep green of the jungle. It was an illusion, this ending of the water, for it penetrated far into the jungle, and, not for the first time, Lemieux wondered what he had buried under the redirected waters of the Chagres River. He sighed. It was no longer his concern. He had spent too much time pursuing this dream, and it was time to go. In his pocket was a letter authorizing his resignation, and Lemieux felt relief at the leave-taking. Still, beneath the pain of his loss and the relief at his going, something nagged him. Not only would someone else get the credit for completing the canal, but more important was the sense that he had lost something indefinable in this place, something that had made him, in spite of his success, less than when he had arrived.

When the train left him at the terminal, Lemieux stood for a moment, looking up at the house on Ancon Hill. He would be glad to give that up. It contained too many ghosts, and he had never wanted it in the first place. It had been Claudette's dream house and now seemed more like a tomb than a home. Resolutely, he strode up the path, waving the waiting driver away. At his back, the furious labor of the canal continued, but Charles Lemieux would never return to the cut.

Even two weeks later, when he traveled east to the city of Colon on his way to Washington, he stared straight ahead, determinedly ignoring the work that had brought him fame if not fortune. There had been no ceremony to celebrate his leaving. In fact, for quite some time, few knew he had gone. Stepping aboard the Bryant ship that would take him north, he was directed by the captain to a first class berth, and Lemieux, observing the plush surroundings, wondered what he had lost in Panama. He did not settle in his cabin until the green of the Panamanian jungle disappeared into the mist, and when he did begin to unpack, it was with a heavy heart.

CHAPTER FORTY-FOUR

PANAMA 1976

Haight braced himself as the company jet came to an abrupt halt. Across the aisle, Antonio Peques sat stoically, his bulk all but obscuring the light from the small window. Haight felt comfortable knowing he was there. Nieves had insisted Haight come to Panama, promising to explain Centron and Panama. Haight had not needed too much persuading since he believed that Dean's disappearance was related to whatever Nieves had to tell him. In any case, he was in no position to negotiate and had flown through the night to reach Panama City. It was close to midnight, but, though tired, he was alert.

Antonio turned to him, saying, "I still think it's a bad idea to see this guy on your own. You don't know what's out there, sir."

They had had this argument earlier. Nieves had insisted Haight bring no one with him. Haight folded up the desk and replied, "It's been decided, Antonio. He wants to see me alone, and I have few options. You'll stay at the Miramar Intercontinental until you hear from me."

"Do you even know where you're going, sir?"

"Now that'd be silly, don't you think? To ask me to meet him in secret and then tell where he is." Then, relenting, he added, "Sorry, Antonio. I guess I'm a little tense."

It took no time at all to get past the sleepy customs guard, and soon Haight was met by two men, both with a distinctly Indian look. They were expensively dressed and filled out their jackets quite adequately. They headed outside to where two large cars waited. Antonio was invited in to one that would take him to the hotel. Haight entered the other, in which sat two other men of the same general build and look as the others.

Soon, Haight was rocketing westward toward the Bridge of the Americas and then north toward the darkness of the central country. The men were silent, but Haight sensed no hostility in the silence, and he relaxed, watching as the place names flitted by. Just after they passed the residential district of Vista de Vacamonte, one of the men said something quietly to the driver, who suddenly floored the accelerator. The oversized American engine bellowed as the car leapt forward in the darkness.

The man who had met him in the airport said, "Sorry, Señor Haight, but this is a precaution. Señor Nieves believes you have been followed for several days, and he does not wish to have any prying eyes following where we are going."

For a long time the powerful throb of the engine was the only sound that could be heard. Then, the car slowed and turned at a sign that said Las Uvas. He could no longer see beyond the lights of the car, which now seemed to slice into the darkness, creating a twin funnel within which the motes appeared to be swimming. He had noted the villages as they passed. El Espino. Los Llanitos. Villa Rosario. Ludice. At El Epave, the car slowed to a stop, and the driver turned the engine off. They sat in the darkness, and Haight knew they were waiting to see if a car was following.

After a while, the man said, "You will forgive me, Señor Haight, but we were instructed to blindfold you at this point. It will be a while, so you will have to trust us."

His eyes were covered, and the car again tore into the night. It went around in circles, and, after a couple of turns, Haight had no idea in which direction they were going. Once they were sure he was completely confused, the car settled onto a bumpy road. After an hour or so, they stopped, and the man led Haight outside. Water was falling heavily somewhere.

Then, the man next to him said, "Be careful now. We are going to be descending. Just hold on to me, and you'll be fine. We have quite a walk ahead of us, but we'll soon take the blindfold off. Just bear with us, please."

Haight grunted, and then they were moving carefully down a slope, heading toward the sound of the water. They crossed a log bridge, and, after a while, there was spray as the water thundered close by. Then, they were climbing, and after about an hour, the blindfold was removed. Haight blinked, thinking the cloth had blinded him, but soon realized it was just the darkness. The climbing resumed, and the air cooled considerably. He was breathing quite hard, and soon asked the men to stop.

"Can you tell me where we are headed? Okay, forget that. At least tell me your name."

"Sorry, Señor Haight. I am Emiliano. The others are José and Martin. And now, we must keep going. We have quite a way to go yet."

They resumed walking, and Haight found himself wondering about these big, silent men who were leading him up the mountain. Why was Nieves bringing him so far away from the city for this meeting? He was certain the men with him were not from the Agency, and, if they were not, then that raised some interesting questions. What was Nieves doing up here in the mountains? What did he know about what was going on in the country? Haight hoped to learn something useful tonight, something that would give him some clue as to what had happened to Dean.

When the men stopped for a short break, he asked, "How much further, Emiliano?"

"Maybe another half hour, Señor Haight."

It was more like an hour and a half later that the hill flattened out, and Haight sensed more than saw a large house silhouetted against the skylight. Dead on his feet, he was happy when Emiliano showed him to a room. He did not undress but fell across the bed and was instantly asleep.

The dawn had not quite arrived when Haight awoke, and he knew immediately he was not alone. Not moving, he opened his eyes cautiously, but it was unnecessary since Emiliano's voice came from the darkness.

"Sorry to wake you, Señor Haight, but the Jefe awaits you."

Haight was instantly on his feet and, quickly taking his toilet, followed Emiliano down the hall. They took a staircase into a basement that expanded into what was apparently an underground meeting place, and, as Haight walked into the room, he was quickly and somewhat apologetically checked for weapons.

José Nieves sat in a large chair that dominated the room, flaring at the top like a fan. Behind him was a magnificent painting of a jaguar, and draped over his shoulders was a robe that appeared to be made of feathers. Haight stopped, on the verge of smiling, but something in the way Nieves sat and the way the four guards hovered around him froze the thought in his mind. In the ensuing silence, Haight looked around the room, quickly noting that there were no chairs. The older men sat on pillows. In the shadows around the perimeter of the space, many men stood. Haight was perplexed, and he now looked back at Nieves, who finally said, "Hello, Jack. Welcome to Panama."

From the intonation, it was not clear whether he meant the country or this place where they now stood.

"Thank you, José. I wondered where you'd gotten to."

Nieves stood, and two men moved almost unobtrusively toward him, taking the long robe from his shoulders. In spite of the dim light, Haight could see that it was beautiful, with what looked like the flowered patches he saw the native women making in the city.

Nieves must have noticed him looking at it because he said, "It's beautiful, no? It's also very old. There's a story attached to it as well, but it would mean nothing to you."

"Actually, I'm not so sure. Try me."

"Well, my people, the Kuni, believe it was shaped by the sun itself and given to the people for their protection. There is always someone in the village who guards it, and it passes through to the firstborn of that person. We believe the robe makes the guardian one with the jaguar and the forest. Also, it is the embodiment of all the Kuni."

Nieves looked at Haight closely as he spoke, and, after a while, Haight asked, "Am I to understand you are the current guardian?"

Nieves nodded.

"What has all this to do with what's going on with the canal? And the boy? You intimated you knew something about him."

"All in good time, Jack. Come. Let's watch the sun rise."

He stepped down from the slightly raised dais, and instantly the four guards moved with him. With a slight smile, he asked, "Jack, you have no intention of harming me, do you?"

He waved his hand, and the guards stepped back. Emiliano, however, followed Nieves.

Outside, dawn was being manufactured, and golden striations streaked the eastern sky, breaking the dark clouds into angry but impotent trolls who were being whisked away. Night still contested the right of way but was clearly losing the battle, and Haight felt something he was not aware his soul was capable of: awe. While the sky was lightening, the land itself was dark, but, in the west, he could see the giant tip of a mountain. It was not sufficiently high to catch the rays from the dawn, but, illuminated by the lightening morning, its dark bulk was imposing.

Haight was anxious to talk, but Nieves was in no hurry. There was something religious in Nieves' worship of the dawn. There was much Haight did not understand, and he would have to be patient. Nieves seemed inclined to be helpful, but Haight had no idea what sort of organization Nieves controlled, although it was clearly military.

As the light gradually brightened, Haight gave himself up, as best he could, to the dawn and found, much to his surprise, that he was soon less tired. The sounds of the day had begun. Monkeys chattered nearby in the bush. Then, in the midst of the sounds, came the sharp scream of a larger animal, and Haight jumped.

Nieves laughed softly, saying, "Don't worry. It is just my brother making your acquaintance."

"What was that?"

"A jaguar. There are several on the mountain. They protect us as we protect them."

Finally, after several false starts, the sun broke through the restraining clouds, and Haight was bathed in the glow. Nieves closed his eyes, holding his head back, and Haight, on a whim, did the same. As he stood there, feeling the warmth surge through his body, for the first time in years, his mind was clear. Nieves' voice forced him to open his eyes.

"It is the most beautiful spot on earth. If you hold very still and listen, you can actually hear the pulse of the world."

"Yes. It makes no sense, but you are right."

"However, you wish to speak of this world not the next."

Haight was a little worried. This place was pleasant enough, but he was uncomfortable. As if in reply to his unspoken question, Nieves said, "I know this is not what you expected, Jack, but the relationship between this and what you want to know is important. I thought it best that you see what is here before you hear the rest. I suppose one could say this story begins in what you would call myth and what we call our tapestry. According to that tapestry, we, the Kuni, were sent by the sun to protect the unity of all things when the jaguar, who had been sent before us, failed. The jaguar, you see, fell in love with the butterflies and lost his reason. We were sent to restore it. For many years, the Kuni kept the balance between the forest, the butterflies, and the jaguar, but then the Spanish came. As the Kuni fell back before them, the land bent to the will of the Spanish. The sun became angry and left the Kuni because, like the jaguar before them, they, too, had failed to ensure the unity of all things. Before the sun left, however, he gave the Kuni magic to make the robe of the butterflies, and as long as the robe exists and the Kuni protect it, there is hope of the eventual reunification of all things. Are you bored, Jack?"

"No. Actually, it's quite interesting. I assume it has something to do with what's going on now."

Nieves nodded, and then continued.

"The Kuni have always lived in the forest, but when the Spanish began to change the land and to press into the forest, it was decided that one group of the nation should go to the edge of the land and study the Spanish. Since the Spaniards were more trusting of Kuni women than Kuni men, it was decided that a woman should appear to lead them. She would be the go-between for the Kuni and the Spanish. They did not trust the woman, however, and to make sure she remained Kuni and would not be tempted to go off with the Spanish, they burnt one side of her face, disfiguring it so that her beauty would be lost. This became the practice of those Kuni who lived on the edge of the forest near the sea. After many years, having striven to remain unchanged, they became hardly recognizable as Kuni, for the main body of the Kuni had changed over time, and the group at the sea had not. An oddity at first, they later came to be admired as the original people and were given the task of forever bearing the robe of the butterflies."

"But I thought you said only women were guardians of the robe. Why are you in that role now?"

Haight was not insensitive to the fact that the way he had phrased the question suggested acceptance of the myth, and Nieves smiled.

"It was so until my grandmother's time, as was the scarification. She changed both things. She was a remarkable woman, Jack. Actually, quite enlightened in many ways. She was also the first of the guardians to go over to the Spaniards, although he was not really Spanish."

Then, he added almost apologetically, "My people do not distinguish among the whites. Anyway, she fell in love with a man from the outside, and she bore a child for him. My mother."

"So you are half Spanish?"

"Actually, no. Part Kuni and part Barbadian. The white man was from Barbados. You have his letters."

"Barnes is your grandfather?"

Nieves nodded, a wistful look on his face. Haight frowned. Nieves was related to Barnes, and Dean was somehow connected as well. Then, Nieves said, "Come. I want to show you something."

They walked to the other end of the hill, and then, with the rising sun at their backs, Nieves pointed across the valley to the next mountain. On the slope, Haight could see the long, white stalks of the cuipo tree with its bald trunk and the branches sitting at the top like an inverted mop. There was something vaguely familiar about the mountain, but Haight was not sure what he was expected to see.

"Look at the outline, Jack. Does it remind you of anything?"

Haight studied the mountain and, after a while, asked uncertainly, "Is it the outline of a woman?"

"Very good. That is Anajansi. Our stories say that after her lover was killed by a Spaniard, she ran into the woods and died of grief. There, the woods grew over her, and now she resides in the mountain. My people believe she returns in the shape of our guardians from time to time and that my grandmother was another one of her visits to the group."

Haight's impatience must have showed because Nieves said, "I'm sorry, Jack. I sometimes become lost in the stories of my people, but I'm not being entirely irrelevant. Your dilemma is related. You see, something happened in the forest out there a long time ago, something that is still having an impact on your world today."

"What happened? The letters indicate that someone was extracting gold from the land. Barnes was involved in that. The letters also imply that something horrible happened out there, but they don't say what it was."

"Yes. Something happened. Our stories say that thousands perished under the water. No one has been able to prove it though, and many have dismissed it as legend."

"Do you mean the water that created the canal?"

Nieves nodded, and Haight continued, a strained note in his voice, "But if the people in the area died under the water, how did your people survive? Didn't you live in the area, too?"

"That's the mystery. Our stories say that, weeks before the floods came, my grandmother led her village and the jaguars out of the forest and took them to the mountain. When the waters came, they were gone. It is said she was told by the sun."

"Interesting. Do you believe the story?"

Nieves laughed.

"Well, the group survived. We are here."

Then, the smile faded from his face, and Haight had the distinct impression of the man changing, becoming somehow different. When he resumed speaking, the humor was gone from his voice.

"My country has been split in half, Haight, and the life has been drained from it. We need to take it back. That is why the canal must return to us."

"But isn't that on the verge of happening? The President seems determined."

"Your President is naïve. He doesn't understand what is arrayed against him. The group of which I spoke when we met in Washington is powerful, and it contains many who are close to the President. They intend to destroy the canal."

Haight looked at him as if he were crazy.

"What do you mean 'destroy'? It'd take a nuclear bomb to destroy the canal."

Nieves smiled grimly.

"No. Not really. There was a faction that never wanted the canal to be in Panama, and while most of the individuals are dead, the purpose has remained. They're prepared to destroy the canal rather than have it returned to Panama."

"But how?"

"That's a long story, so we'd better sit down."

They walked back to the east of the house and sat in the sunlight. Someone brought glasses of mango juice, and they both sipped.

"When the canal started, Edward Bryant, who I'm sure you know, supported the construction in a variety of ways, but he withdrew his support around 1908, shortly before his death. No one's sure what caused the change of heart. Bryant had been removing gold from the forest, but that was never his main purpose. The gold was intended to finance some silly idea he had of building a city in the jungle. Then, he died— or, at least, he disappeared. His son, who had taken over the project, had no intention of building the city. He'd been in the employ of the faction that wanted to end the canal project. He took their money, but he had his own purposes."

Haight, intrigued, asked, "What was it he wanted?"

"Good question. When his father died, he inherited the Bryant empire, so he had little need for money or power. Seventy years ago, he built the means to destroy the canal. Now, the faction opposing the President has employed him to do just that if the treaty is concluded."

Haight wondered at the casual nature of Nieves' description.

"How's this to be done, Nieves?"

"The younger Bryant built a series of tunnels in the forest. They go deep under the ground and now lay under the northern end of Gatun Lake."

Haight shrugged, a question in the gesture.

"There are eight tunnels, covering an area of close to four miles, and they have been laden with explosives."

"Jesus Christ," Haight breathed, his mind now alive with the images of what Nieves was saying. Then, he said, "But if he built tunnels miles away from the canal, how can exploding them make any difference? They'd need to have an atomic bomb."

Nieves did not answer, and Haight, feeling the silence, turned to him.

"No. You're fucking kidding me, right?"

"I never kid, Haight."

"When is all this going to happen?"

"As soon as the treaty is signed. They had lost the exact location of the tunnels, as the forest has changed quite a bit in the years since they were dug. The CIA located them for the group."

"Nieves, how do you know all this? And who else have you told?" Haight asked quietly.

Nieves looked directly at Haight, then said, "I know, Haight, because I am a member of the group."

Haight's eyes narrowed as he waited for the explanation.

"I've been part of the group for three years. They are very concerned about the 'revolutionary element' in the country, so I was recruited to infiltrate the 'revolutionaries'."

"These men here?"

Nieves nodded, and Haight looked at him with new respect.

Haight said, "You said this group has hired Bryant. Are you suggesting he is still alive?"

Nieves nodded slowly, and Haight responded.

"Christ, he must be...what? A hundred?"

There was an odd tone in Nieves' voice when he said, "Sometimes, Haight, I think he is much older than that."

The silence that ensued changed the atmosphere of the morning. Suddenly, Nieves turned to him.

"I need your help, Haight. This whole thing turns on Bryant. If we can get rid of him, then the whole group will be thrown into confusion. These are powerful men, but, in many respects, they are amateurs. They have big dreams about the United States and an overblown sense of its importance. They are dangerous, it is true, but without Bryant's leadership, they would be useless. Ironically, they believe they have bought his services. I can't believe he is interested in them or their purposes. It is the same today as when he built the tunnels. He had his own purposes then, and he has them now. I'm not sure what he wants, but I feel certain it involves the destruction of the canal. We cannot allow that. The division of the land tore the heart out of the Kuni. In cutting the land in two, the Americans destroyed the unity the robe sought to provide my people. We have become reconciled to that fact. We would not be allowed to replace the land that was taken, and this is the only way to rejoin the spirit that was torn apart by the canal. The world depends too much on the canal, and it is doubtful if even Panamanians would stand for it."

"But I don't understand, Nieves. If you want to have the canal shut down, and this group is going to do it, why are you upset? It would seem their purpose and yours coincide."

Nieves nodded, but his answer contradicted the gesture.

"Not quite. My people have changed since the early part of the century, due in large part to my mother's influence and, I dare say, mine as well. We recognize that there may be ways of benefiting without destroying the canal. If the canal is returned to us, then our people will benefit again, and maybe some of the profits of the canal will stay in Panama instead of disappearing into the coffers of those who now control us."

"The United States?"

"In a way. I was thinking of Centron, however."

"Centron? How exactly are they involved in this?"

"Bryant is Centron. They control everything on this continent, Haight, and probably on yours, too."

"Yes. I've had some dealings with them. Do you know a fellow called Romulus?"

"Yes. Bryant's heir apparent. He's a killer of the first magnitude. He's smart, too. He's been the conduit to Bryant for a long time. No one has seen Bryant for the last ten years, but Centron has not slowed in that time. In fact, its influence has extended since the old man disappeared."

"There's something I don't understand, Nieves. If Centron controls the revenues from the canal and uses its control to reduce its own costs, why would it want to destroy the canal? Wouldn't that be defeating its own purpose?"

"No. Centron is actually much less dependent on the canal now than it has been in the past. Its shipping companies have been building giant cargo ships, and these cannot pass through the canal. Because of the volume of cargo, it's actually becoming cheaper for them to sail around the continent than to pay even the reduced rates they enjoy at the canal."

Haight had read about this in the last few weeks but had not seen the connection between the growth in the number of superships and what was going on. Still, it all made sense.

"One last question. How can Bryant or this group possibly destroy the canal with explosives that are miles away? I wouldn't think that an explosion such as you describe would be very effective."

Nieves nodded slowly.

"They won't have to. Come with me."

Haight followed Nieves into the house. Downstairs, they came to a locked door, and Nieves punched in a combination. Inside, three men sat before glowing screens. Nieves walked up to one and said, "Carlos, bring up the picture of the forest."

While the man was fiddling with the machine, Nieves pulled Haight over to a geological map.

"Look at that. Notice anything?"

Haight stared for a while, then shook his head. Nieves pointed at a red line on the map.

"That's a major fault line. It runs northeast to southwest across the forty-five miles of the isthmus at this point. Some time in the past, it must have been volcanic, but it's not been active for centuries. Somewhere along this line is the series of tunnels Bryant built. Are you getting it, Haight?"

"No. What's the point you're making?"

In response, Nieves asked, "Carlos, you ready?"

He walked over to where the small Indian sat manipulating some pictures.

"There. These are the projections Carlos has made based on different blast strengths and various locations along the fault line. Look at this. If we use this location and assume that each of the eight tunnels is packed with some form of high-grade explosive, this is what happens."

Carlos manipulated the images, and a blast balloon appeared. Another picture came up on the screen, and Haight saw rocks falling in the caves. He looked at Nieves, who touched Carlos on the shoulder. The images shifted. It was clear he had changed both the location of the tunnels and the blast strength. Again, the balloon appeared, and then, as

Haight watched, the fault line moved. It continued to move. It took a little while for Haight to realize what was happening, but then, to his horror, the top of the land slipped away. Carlos had provided color to the images, and Haight saw the blue flow of water as it fell with the tilted land. He stood watching the disaster in miniature, a sudden coldness settling in the pit of his stomach. Something told him this was not a fabrication.

"They're going to drain the lake," Haight said, his voice strained, and Nieves nodded.

"Do you know this for a fact, Nieves, or is this speculation?"

"Some of it is projection, but there is no other way it can be done that gives the illusion of a natural disaster. I'm convinced they will not do something that's immediately noticeable as man-made."

"What do you mean, you are convinced? I thought you said you were part of this group. Don't you know when or where this will happen?"

"Everything's told on a need-to-know basis. It was not thought that I needed to know."

"So you really don't know anything. We are just guessing here."

"It is a very educated guess, Haight."

Haight was silent for a while, then he asked, "What do you want from me?"

"You have the resources to get to Bryant. We don't. We need you to get rid of him."

"You must have forgotten who I am, Nieves. You live in that world, not me. Even when I was in the business, I was never a field agent. What makes you think I can pull something like this off?"

When Nieves spoke, the friendliness was gone.

"You'll have to find a way, Haight."

Nieves started to walk out of the room, and Haight followed.

"Look, Nieves. This is really not my affair."

"I was afraid you'd say that."

He walked over to a phone and dialed. After a while, he said, "Say hello."

Haight took the phone. The voice on the other end said, "Hello," and then the phone was taken away. Haight took a sharp breath and turned to Nieves, his eyes burning.

"Now you understand why you will help us."

Haight knew he would because the voice on the other end had been Dean's.

CHAPTER FORTY-FIVE

Rupert Barnes sat in the car, aware of the imposing bulk of Romulus beside him. He was calm, calmer than he had been in half a century. Feeling the throb that was always present in his lower back, he stretched unobtrusively to ease the pain. Soon, this would all be over, and the pain would be gone. Barnes felt relief more than remorse at the thought. The early dusk of the Long Island evening sat gently on the Atlantic as the car moved gracefully in and out of the heavy traffic on the Belt Parkway. The day before, Barnes had called Romulus after receiving the package. Inside had been a tracksuit that he had immediately guessed, even before reading the note, was the boy's. It had been bloody, and on the jacket were the initials DG. The letter confirmed that these stood for Dean Greaves. If he had any doubt about the boy's fate, the finger in the bottom of the package with the ring still attached convinced him. The ring had the same initials. The call to Romulus had completed the transaction.

Now, on his way to see Bryant, Barnes searched within himself to see what he felt about the man. He had expected hatred, but, to his surprise, upon deciding to end this, a calm had come. When Romulus picked him up at Kennedy Airport, he had looked at Barnes curiously. Both of his nurses/bodyguards had been left in New York City, and Romulus had frisked him quickly and unobtrusively. There had been a question on Romulus' face when he felt the syringe, and Barnes explained that he needed to take an insulin shot every six hours. This could be easily checked, and Romulus probably knew it anyway. Since his nurse would not be around, Barnes indicated he would need someone to administer the insulin later. Romulus had continued to look at him, a curious smile on his face, but he had agreed.

Now, Barnes allowed his hand to fall to the coat pocket where the covered syringe lay. He would end this thing with Bryant, no matter the cost to himself. He was not sure how Bryant's people would react once he was killed, but Barnes had done all he could to protect against a reprisal. His sons' homes were under constant surveillance now, and Hu, his bodyguard, had arranged for more protection. In any case, there was no point worrying about it. He had decided. The living would have to take care of themselves. Truth be told, he was counting on Bryant's death appearing natural, so there should be no threat to his sons. Not for the first time, Barnes wondered why he had never brought his boys into his businesses. He had helped them with the establishment of their practices but had not allowed them even to represent him. It was as if he wanted to keep them insulated from the past that had created the wealth. Somehow, it had never affected their relationship. After his wife died and their careers had taken off, he had seen less of them, but their relationship remained affectionate. The boys had done well and were close. Both international lawyers, they frequently collaborated on cases, and he felt a special pride in the fact that they were upholding the law.

He would not live much longer but had had a long life. Given the opportunity, there was much he would have done differently, but he was not going to lament. He had lived more fully than most men, and if hell beckoned, then so be it. In any case, he had protected his children from his past, and there was something to be said for that.

Barnes was tired, the trip from Panama having drained him, although the Lear 31A jet that had brought them back provided a smooth ride at 47,000 feet. In spite of the comfort of the plane, the altitude had been hard on his semi-crippled body. Now, feeling tension in his back and lower legs, Barnes squirmed in the seat, seeking a comfortable spot.

What would it be like to see Bryant after so many years? How would he feel? Their last few months together had been tension-filled. Though never able to prove it, he was certain Bryant was responsible for the disappearance of the Indian village, and, for days, Barnes had walked with thunderclouds around his head. He thought again of going to Colonel Lemieux, but something stopped him. He remembered Bryant's note: "I know you are having second thoughts," and though nothing was said, Barnes was certain the disappeared village had been held hostage against his obedience. Barnes had almost gone mad. Leila had been the small area of sanity in this place of madness, and, without her, in the following months, a darkness descended.

When the men began to build the giant gates, he did not ask why. Bryant ordered him to change the shifts, and at some times, five thousand men were below ground at the same time. The work became furious. The dirt came out of the ground at a prodigious rate and was carted away by the non-stop trains of donkeys. Barnes did not know where all the extract from the ground went, and he wondered. He also wondered about his failing will, aware that he no longer fought the Captain.

Several weeks after the village disappeared, Bryant broached the subject with him, and the man seemed sympathetic. Barnes recognized Bryant's deceit, always most evident when he seemed most sympathetic. Thinking of the conversation in which Bryant had said that the son must kill the father, he now wondered about Bryant's own father.

Without Leila, his life turned into one long round of work. After Richards' death, there were no large-scale confrontations, but the small rebellions continued, as did the attempts to escape. With the furious pace of the work, there were more incidents, and he was kept busy controlling the men's anger. When the gates were designed, he inquired about their purpose, but Bryant was non-committal. Still, Barnes wondered. The doors were to be watertight, and, as the steel took form, Barnes was consumed with a sense of foreboding. He had not been underground since the trip with Bryant and frequently found himself wondering how far the tunnels extended.

Bryant and Barnes now walked around each other, avoiding conversation, so when Bryant addressed him one morning, he expected some order about the work. Instead, Bryant invited him to the hill. Once seated, sipping a cup of very strong cocoa, Bryant was silent for a while. Barnes waited.

"I heard the villagers at the shore have moved," Bryant finally said.

Barnes did not respond, and Bryant continued.

"I know of your interest in the Indian woman there, but it is for the best you know."

Barnes silently appraised him.

"You insist on your own dissipation, Barnes. It is almost as if you have no sense of who you are or what you are capable of. Your liaisons with these women will do you no good, you know. It really is best that the woman is gone."

"Did you have anything to do with that, Bryant?"

The man chuckled softly, his spare shoulders shaking.

"Why do you make me into a monster, Barnes? We're no different, you know. We want the same thing, though you do not yet know it."

"And what is it we both want?"

"Clearer definitions of the world. A return to a time when purposes were clear and our positions were assured. There is too much confusion now, too many possibilities. We can't afford the confusion."

"What are you talking about? I don't understand a thing you're saying."

"Of course you don't," Bryant replied, laughing.

The sun caught Barnes' eyes at an angle, and for a moment, he saw nothing.

"Your problem is that you really believe in progress, that somehow we are, as a species, improving. What if the reverse were true, Barnes? How would you explain that? What if we have moved from a perfected state to this?"

Bryant pointed to the disorderly camp below, with the black men working at their tasks. Barnes could think of no perfected state he had left, and said so. Bryant snorted, replying with something like anger in his voice, "You are being obtuse. It is remarkable that in almost seven years—a lifetime in this place—you have come no closer to defining your purpose for being here, yet you resist the purpose provided for you, the purpose I give. Why is that, Barnes?"

"Maybe it's because I see no purpose. You are pursuing wealth, Bryant. Pure and simple. That is purpose enough for you, I guess. I suppose it's not enough for me. I had hoped for something else, something more internal, more useful. And whatever you may think, I have found that."

"The exorcism of Ruby," Bryant replied mockingly. "You think that a sufficient purpose?"

Barnes did not reply immediately, and Bryant continued.

"Or did you build the civilization you intended?"

"No. I have not done that, but, then, neither have you. Somehow, you have perverted your father's purpose here, and, in doing so, you've constructed nothing. The only value that has come out of this place has been the gold, and he discovered that, not you. Everything else you have done is an exercise in futility. This infernal digging against an eventuality is pure insanity, and the men realize that. It's why we are having such a difficult time with them. You have built nothing here, Bryant. And what are the gates for? To hide your madness? It's a little too late for that, don't you think?"

Barnes was surprised at his outburst, but once started, he could not stop.

"You have failed here as much as I have, Bryant."

Even as he said this, though, he knew it was not true. Bryant was right. There was no purpose to his being in the jungle. He had lost interest in the money, carrying inside him a weight that could not be lifted.

When Bryant responded, his voice was quiet.

"Sometimes, chaos is creation."

Barnes did not understand.

In the weeks that followed, the digging continued, and the gates were built. The air in the camp was torn apart by the sound of hammering and the flaring of the welding torches. In the night, the fire burned, creating day. The noise was overpowering, and Barnes had no time to think. This was like work on the canal, one constant assault on the eardrums. Barnes began to walk away from the camp in the evenings to escape the pounding in his head, but through it all, there was the picture of the woman who had disappeared. His every contact with Bryant reminded him that she was gone, and he could not rid himself of the thought that Bryant was responsible.

One evening, feeling particularly lonely, he found himself walking in the direction of the river, going to the landing place, but the Spaniard had disappeared. Barnes paid for a boat, rowed himself down to the entrance to the village, and stood in the middle of the clearing, looking about him as if he expected the woman to appear. In the dusk, the sand showed no evidence of the village. It was smooth and pure white. There was no sign of the blackened stones on which the villagers had cooked nor the stakes that had been the anchor for their huts. Everything had changed. The coconut trees whispered to him a familiar song, but his ears could no longer hear it, and the voice of the jungle escaped to the sky unnoticed. Barnes sat on the cool sand all night, and, as the watery moon rose, he thought, in a confusion of images, of two women, so different and yet the same.

Sitting there, near the sea, with the ocean whispering in his ears, he thought of Audrey's innocence. Her trusting eyes had been so alive with hope that he had been reluctant to look back, afraid she would see into his soul and find his uncertainty. She had loved him, and now, in his loss, he thought of her and what she had meant to him. Audrey had defined his possibilities for love, for in giving so much without any demand, she had confirmed something in him. His innate sense of self had been bolstered by the girl's love, and he had been made more certain of his maleness. In this way, she had shaped him and, in some ways, spoiled him, for he was made confident of his charm, and this had led to his selfishness. Audrey had been shy, restrained in the gift of her love, but that restraint had been a dam that held behind it the might of a river. He had never understood that, content to accept the girl's gift as his due. He had no idea what happened to her after he left Barbados, and while writing to her out of a sense of duty and guilt, he had never embraced the thought of a return to her.

Somehow, Leila's disappearance made this clearer to him. Now lonely, he understood for the first time what his leaving must have meant.

The place became a solace for him, and he returned frequently to sit in the space, thinking about the woman he craved, seeking in the very air some relief from the pain in his soul. Sometimes, it seemed he could almost hear the voices, subdued and speaking words he did not understand, close by, and he would turn sharply, seeking Leila's face.

Resistance gone, he supervised the work like an automaton. The men were changing as well. With the building of the gates, recognizing that the project was coming to an end, they began to anticipate the escape from the jungle. Resistance declined. There was a new vigor in the work, and, for the first time in a long while, Barnes heard laughter in the camp. In this atmosphere, the number of guards was being reduced, and this, too, was seen as a hopeful sign. On the day the doors were put in place, the men were assembled. When the huge gates closed with a pneumatic hiss that shut out the sounds of the jungle, there was a short silence. Then the men exploded with hand clapping and back slapping. Barnes, too, felt pride in the completion of the project, and he laughed until he saw the face of the man who stood beside him. Bryant's face was twisted into a smile of such malevolence that Barnes could have sworn the bones beneath the flesh were visible. Something stopped in his heart, and his fears for the men returned.

"I need you to see Lemieux in the city."

Barnes nodded, distracted, and Bryant smiled at him.

"Well, it's almost over now. Soon, you will be free."

"Will I?"

Bryant laughed, nodding, and Barnes added, "So much has changed in these few years. I feel like a different person, almost as if I don't know myself."

Bryant's chuckle contained a tinge of irony.

"That last part is true, but it is no change. You have never known yourself. With you, I feel as old as a father."

Then, looking around him at the now dispersing men, he said, with something like whimsy in his voice, "You will be defined by this experience."

"What do you mean?"

"Oh, nothing. I'm just talking."

That night, Barnes told Lemieux not to worry about the rise in the dam. On his return, Bryant frightened him by stepping from behind a tree. In the night, the moon cast evanescent shadows, and the man seemed insubstantial yet frighteningly real. Barnes reported that Lemieux would co-operate, and Bryant, pleased, gave Barnes orders to go to New York. With the completion of the work in Panama, Bryant was moving his operation to Cuba and wanted Barnes to meet someone in New York to negotiate the terms of his entry into that country. Barnes was happy to leave Panama for a while. After seven years, and now prosperous beyond expectations, he wanted something more than the primitive conditions of the camp.

He laughed at the thought of clean sheets and warm water, and Bryant said, "Thinking of escape, Barnes?"

"After a fashion," he answered, realizing he had not once thought of escape. Yet, Bryant's question raised an interesting possibility. Before he could formulate the thought, however, the man responded, "Put the thought from your mind. There is nowhere to go. Every possible means of travel you could use, I control. I would find you. In any case, you are being made wealthy beyond your meager imagination, so why run away like a spoiled child?"

And, like that, the pleasure of the trip to New York dissipated, replaced by a nagging ache. He went to New York, and after a month, he received a telegram instructing him not to return since the project was so close to completion. Something inside him tightening in that instant, he made reservations on the next ship back to Panama. Gatun Lake had been created while he was away, and he was driven by some proud worker to see the new, man-made lake that stretched away in the silvery distance, far north of where he stood. With a deep sense of foreboding, he took the first train to Panama City, waiting until dark before plunging into the jungle.

The first sign of water came within an hour. It squelched underfoot, and soon it was too deep and muddy. He tried going around it, but the water was everywhere. After trying for hours to find another way, he dejectedly returned to Panama City. Next morning, he took a train back to Colon. There, he rented a fisherman's boat and sailed up the coast to where the village of the Kuni had been. He walked into the jungle, heading for the river on which he used to sail to see the woman, but, before he reached it, the water appeared again. Tied to a tree, however, was a skiff. This he appropriated and soon was furiously rowing up the river. On all sides was the dark silver of the water, and, without the familiar markers, he was soon hopelessly lost. Still, he continued until, quite by accident, he found a huddle of huts. It was the village where the Spaniard used to meet him. There was no one in sight, and the huts closest to the river were submerged. He sailed around a bit, but saw no one.

Pointing the skiff into the forest, he tried to find the old route, but he was not sure of anything. Drowned animals were everywhere. In the stillness of the forest, his breathing was labored. After a while, the trees began to look like sentinels, and the silence hurt his ears. Suddenly, Barnes shouted into the silence, trying to convince himself he was alive. Contemptuously, the silent world did not return his voice, and, as the silence absorbed his sound, he was left feeling more alone and lost. After sailing around for a long time, convinced he had reached the camp, he sought some marker to tell him he had arrived. There was nothing.

When the body floated from behind a tree, he jumped so hard the boat almost capsized. It slid by, partially decomposed, and bumped into a tree, where it hung up for a moment before slipping from sight under the water. Barnes sat, his body trembling violently, staring down into the water for other bodies. The water, dark after the first few inches, simply reflected his face, broken and shaking, with the tears running down. There was nothing he could do, and, pointing the skiff south, he headed toward the shore.

Now, sitting in the car with the powerful man beside him, he felt again the fear and the anger of that moment in the forest when he had known what had happened. At least fifteen thousand workers had been buried by the water. At first, he could not understand why they had not just gotten out of the way as the water had risen, but, since then, he had spent a fortune investigating this and had a pretty good picture. The message taken to Lemieux sealed everyone's fate. He knew now that the extract from the tunnels had been strategically deposited at the mouth of the Chagres River, partially blocking this exit, and when Madden's dam, built by Lemieux outside of Gatun, was fully in place, this caused the rapid rise in the lake. Bryant had been able to assure Lemieux that everything would be all right because Bryant controlled the blockage at the river's mouth. When, as Barnes surmised, that block was suddenly blown apart, the water had rushed across the area, sweeping all before it in an avalanche rather than the gradual rise that Lemieux in the Canal Zone assumed. It was the only way that Bryant could wipe out all traces of what had gone on in the forest, and he had been successful. There was never an investigation, never any outcry. Somehow, fifteen thousand people had disappeared, and no one had noticed.

The car turned into a secondary road and moved swiftly along the quiet backwoods of Long Island. Soon, they swung into a long driveway, at the end of which, hidden in the darkness and the trees, was the house.

It will end here, Barnes thought, as the car braked gently.

Two men came from the house and helped him into his wheelchair. The first thing Barnes noticed was the cold of the house, and his body, already chilly, seemed to shrink. Romulus wheeled him into a room where a small bundle lay.

It was still, and in the darkness, he was not sure if it faced him. The smell of death pervaded the room. Romulus pushed the chair close to the bed and left. It was some time before the bundle stirred, and then only to push the blanket down from its face. He did not at first recognize Bryant. The face was gone, at least the flesh was, and a skull stared back at him. The eyes had sunken into the man's head, and the prominent cheek and forehead bones dominated the space, appearing monstrous. It was the eyes that Barnes concentrated on, though, for they were anything but dead. They glowed in the subdued light with a ferocity that tugged at his soul. Barnes knew Bryant was seeking dominance, weak as he was, and Barnes fought against the tug of the man's will.

After a while, Bryant laughed, a surprisingly gay sound coming from that grave of a body.

"You have changed. Not in any way that is useful, but you have changed. Have you come to put me out of your misery?"

This was followed by a chuckle, and, when Barnes did not answer, Bryant continued in a slightly chastising tone, "Come now. We will not speak again. You may as well say what you have to say. You are a little too old to be bashful. Romulus tells me you have gotten rid of the boy. How wonderfully ironic."

"What happened in the forest, Bryant?"

Again, there was the little laugh.

"All this time to ask a question to which you already know the answer. How disappointing. Are you, perhaps, expecting remorse? There is none, you know."

Barnes was being sucked into the voice, which was so confusing since it did not seem possible it could be coming from the death's head. He was frightened, something of the superstition he had grown up with in the island now tugging at the back of his consciousness. This was a dying man, and yet he could feel the power of his voice. The last time he had heard the man speak like this was the week before the village disappeared.

The jaguar had been regularly dragging men off, and Bryant ordered Barnes to find it and kill it. Standing at the edge of a clearing in the forest, the sunlight emphasizing the darkness of the trees beyond, Barnes felt the same ancient superstition rising in him. He had had several encounters with the jaguar and, knowing Leila's bond with the creatures, wondered how he would do this thing. Men were being dragged off, but, after a while, he had felt no personal threat. Still, there was a tension as he watched, from the protection of the trees, the magnificent creature that had come from the darkness to drink. When he aimed the rifle, something stopped him. Barnes would never be sure, but, for a moment, Leila was so clear in his mind that he saw her across the clearing.

As his hand trembled, the voice came from behind him, saying gently, but with powerful suggestiveness, "Now would be a good time, Barnes."

He shot the beast. His aim was less than perfect, and while the blood spurted from the animal's shoulder, it disappeared into the forest.

Now, Bryant, even in his weakened state, was attempting the same thing.

"Why did they have to die?"

"Pragmatism. It was useless to risk the project. But you know all this. Why are you asking the silly questions? Nothing that went on in the jungle is of any interest to us now. You really want to ask about the woman, don't you?"

Knowing he was being taunted, Barnes felt the hatred well up in him.

"You have spent a lifetime living between dream and reality. Now, you want to know what it is you have missed. It is too late, you know. Poor Rupert. All this movement and still not sure of your creation. I know this will disappoint you, but I cannot help you."

Barnes felt the question choking him, but he still could not frame it after all these years, so he asked instead, "The village by the sea. Did you have anything to do with its disappearance?"

The bundle on the bed shifted, and a strange smell escaped, a sour smell that combined medicines, age, and something else that was just beyond consciousness, and, for a moment, Barnes was not sure if the smell came from the bed or from himself. Then, the man said, "Given what you think you know of what happened in the jungle, shouldn't you thank me if I did?"

"That depends."

"Yes. It does, doesn't it? Well, yes, I had something to do with their moving, but it was really Leila who organized the trek into the mountains."

"She knew what was going to happen and moved her people out of harm's way?"

Bryant laughed, a dry sound.

"You will never be anything but a romantic, Barnes. It was rather more prosaic than that. I told her what was going to happen and allowed them to leave."

Barnes paused before he asked the question.

"Why them, Bryant? Why that group and not the other tribes?"

"You are asking for confessionals again, Barnes. We are beyond that."

Barnes, watching the outline of the skeleton under the sheets as it shifted again, thought, *There is almost nothing to him.*

Then, looking down at his own body, he noted ruefully that he was much the same. Not even the blanket over his legs could disguise the thinness of his shanks, and, suddenly, he felt weak, not sure why he had wanted to see this man. Bryant had no power over him anymore. They were both headed for the grave, and there was no point in having another death on his conscience. He held his head down, and the mocking voice came to him from what seemed like a fog.

"Wavering again, Barnes? You really must show more resolve. Your accidents destroy people, and you agonize, thinking that is enough for your salvation. Your pursuit of salvation is an act of futility. Our acts have no value beyond themselves, and there is no scale on which they are weighed. You create your own evil, and you can forgive yourself. The problem is, you don't even know what your sins are."

The skeleton rearranged itself, and now it lay on its side, staring at Barnes, who felt the truth of the words like a boulder on his shoulders.

Suddenly, Bryant said, "Like your accident with Audrey."

"Audrey? What about Audrey? What do you know about her?"

"I have found out everything about you, Barnes. Did you know she had a child?"

Barnes looked up, something tickling the edges of his mind.

"I didn't know, but that is hardly surprising, is it?"

"Not at all. But did you know she had that child nine months after you left Barbados?"

Something struggled inside Barnes. He did not want to believe what this man was saying. Yet, something did not allow him to deny it. Still, if it were true, why had no one told him? Why had Ruby not said anything? Why would not Audrey herself? Bryant must be lying.

"Audrey could not have a child that was mine."

"Poor Barnes. Such a complicated past. Audrey's mother–Ruthie, I believe her name was–do you have any idea who she was? And why do you think your sister, Ruby, hated the village so much? Any ideas, Barnes?"

Barnes was shaking. Something was lodged in his stomach. He did not know what Bryant knew about him, but whatever it was would be painful.

He braced himself before he asked, "What are you getting at?"

"Actually, I am getting at your family relations, Barnes. I warned you about your cavorting with the exhausted stock, but you thought me—what would they call it today? Racist? What a silly word. In any case, I am saying that Ruby and Audrey's mother are sisters."

Bryant watched, a slight smile on his face, as Barnes collapsed. His already bent body folded forward as the import of Bryant's statement hit him.

When he responded, his voice was weak.

"You're lying. Tell me you're lying."

The sheets moved.

"I could, but I'd be lying. Your son came from your niece, Barnes. The wages of sin, so to speak," he finished with a laugh.

Barnes held his face in his hands, trying to convince himself that Bryant was lying but failing miserably. He could see Audrey's face in his mind, the innocence combined with the trust and the passion that his mind now shied away from in shame. A small sound, animal-like, escaped him, and he thought of the syringe in his pocket. He hesitated now. What had Bryant to do with his depravity? His fall had occurred long before he met the man. He would leave this place, let Bryant die in his own time.

Then, Bryant said calmly, "Wavering again, I see. Actually, it gets worse. You should have checked on your progeny, Barnes. They are all around you, you know."

"What do you mean?"

"Well, let's see. Take the box you have there. I understand you have brought me a souvenir. It really does not become you. Somewhat ghoulish, don't you think? In any case, what you have in the box is also related to you—your Audrey's grandson, as fate would have it. But it is best, don't you agree? You created the abomination, and now you have ended it. Fitting, I think."

Barnes could not think. He was not aware that his hand had reached for the syringe, nor that he had plunged it into the skeleton's arm. The man looked without much interest toward the wall, as if he expected someone, but no one was there. Barnes watched as the man continued to look at him, a slight froth forming at the corner of his mouth. Then, his eyes died.

CHAPTER FORTY-SIX

NEW YORK 1976

Behind the hidden glass, Romulus surprised himself by making the sign of the cross as the old man expired. There was no remorse, only a sense of arrival and fulfillment. He would be in charge of Centron now. Inside the room, the other old man slowly recapped the syringe and placed it in his pocket. Romulus waited as the man turned his chair laboriously around and started to move toward the door.

When Romulus opened it, Barnes said, without much intonation, "He just died."

Romulus pushed the chair out of the dark room where the skeleton seemed to have shrunk even more. He thought of killing the man in the chair but quickly dismissed it. *Let him live with his knowledge. It is what Mr. Bryant would have done.* Romulus shook his head in admiration of the dead man. Even in his death, he had taught Romulus something, and when he had looked over to the hidden glass, it was as if to say, "Do you see how it's done?" Something deep inside Romulus responded, and, as he pushed the wheelchair out to the van that would take the old man to the airport, he thought, for the last time, of the dead man inside.

There was work to be done. This would be his first leadership decision as the head of Centron. The explosion would rip out the basin of the lake, and the water would drain away, into the ground, eventually slipping into the sea. Without Gatun Lake, the canal would be destroyed, twenty-seven of its forty miles soon turned to dried mud under the brutal Panamanian sun. Centron's investment in the superships would be paid back in only months, as other shipping lines watched their costs escalate because they would have to take their smaller ships around the tip of South America. As he saw it, in four months, most of those lines would be bankrupt, and then Centron would move in. They already controlled the majority of the world's shipping. This act would give them the rest. In this respect, nothing had changed since the sixteenth century. Whoever controlled the world's shipping effectively controlled the world. Centron would do this under his leadership. He would take care of the old man's burial, and then head to Panama to supervise the destruction of the canal.

No, he thought with a tight smile, he would supervise the coronation of Centron.

CHAPTER FORTY-SEVEN

NEW YORK 1976

Barnes' mind was in turmoil. He was not sure what to do, and try as he might not to think of what Bryant had said, it was impossible. In his mind's eye, he saw the girl, whom he was sure was dead by now, with her shiny body glistening in the moonlight, holding on to him, saying things he wanted to hear. He shook his head, trying to clear the thought from his mind, but time betrayed him, and the past thrust itself into his present with a painful insistence. Outside, the night looked ordinary, the cars flitting by with monotonous regularity, but inside the car, time had changed for him, and he was again in the island, a boy learning, as he thought, the nature of life. What should he do now? There was no way to make up for what had been done. Ruby was the one to blame. Or his father. No one had told him. Another one of those secrets the family hid so well, even from itself. He felt the old resentment of Ruby come up hard inside him. She had always kept things from him, always treated him as if he were less than she. He had never understood why she despised the village so much, but it made sense. She had known of their father's relationship with Audrey's mother, and this would have offended her. No one, especially Ruby, would have wanted to tell him.

Barnes could not, however, avoid his participation in his downfall. The girl had been innocent, and he had pursued her. He hugged himself, pulling his frail arms around his body in a gesture that lacked all deception. What had become of the child? He whimpered. Had he just killed his grandchild? At this thought, he straightened up, pressing into the back of the seat. He had been so anxious to find and destroy Bryant that he had not thought too much about the boy. Now, someone had killed his grandson, and Barnes felt renewed anger flow through him, a hot stream in the cold of his body.

Someone had killed his grandchild!

It was true he had not known about this grandchild until an hour ago, but it was his blood nevertheless. There was so much he did not understand, but he did know that whoever had sent him the finger and the tracksuit could not be unaware of his relationship to the boy. He had to find out who that was.

Bryant had not had the opportunity to tell him why the Panamanian jungle was so important again. Even in death, Bryant had outsmarted him. Barnes still did not have the information he sought.

The tiredness descended upon him, and, for a moment, the lights dimmed. He would go to Panama for the last time. This whole mystery would end there.

The big man, when told that Bryant was dead, had shown no surprise and no remorse, and Barnes found himself wondering whether it would be the same for him when he died. Would those around him, like Hu, whom he had nurtured for so long, simply pick up with another employer? His sons would care. He thought of them now with an affection he had not felt for some time. Once this was over, he would have to spend more time with them, if they wanted it. Barnes hoped they would. Still, he could not get the thought of the dead grandson out of his mind and found it frustrating not to have an image of the boy. This further angered him. No one had the right to keep the fact of his child from him. His mother, his father, and Ruby had conspired to keep from him his relationship to Audrey, and then Audrey, her mother, and Ruby had done the same with the child. There was a pounding in his skull, and the ache in his back was like a knife pressing into him. There was no order. Somehow, his life had lost its pattern. The logic of his existence had faltered, and he sat, alone in this moment, perplexed and angry. His grandson's killer gave a point to his anger, and on this he now concentrated. He would find whoever was responsible and repay them the favor of his destruction. This decision made, Barnes closed his eyes, the pain in his back subsiding somewhat. Outside, the lights of the city glowed, making a mockery of the night.

CHAPTER FORTY-EIGHT

PANAMA 1976

Haight was nervous. He was not accustomed to the jungle, particularly one that was silent and watery. He had heard some of the Southeast Asia veterans talk of the jungle in Vietnam, with its heat and danger at every turn. He had never been to Vietnam, though he had directed that theater for five years. Now, he was in another jungle, moving slowly toward the middle of the bush. Occasionally, something splashed in the water, and he worried about what caused the sound. They had been on the water for hours, and he wondered if Nieves knew what he was doing. Nieves did not trust him. In fact, now that he had been with the group a few days, it was clear Nieves trusted no one, not even Emiliano, who revered him. Haight glanced at the six men who sat stoically in the boat that was being rowed to avoid the sound of an engine carrying in the stillness of the night.

It had been a hectic eight days since the meeting on the mountain. Haight had agreed to help, although it was still not clear what he had gotten himself into. He did believe the canal was in danger, and the picture of the bottom dropping out of the lake was frightening. He thought of the ships that would be traversing the canal at the moment when the lake disappeared and felt a frightening anger at the callousness of the men who ran Centron and who would destroy the lives of so many. Also, he did feel that the canal was an American creation and should not be destroyed, whether in the interest of some misguided nationalism or for someone's gain.

Nieves' group was apparently made up of the remnants of a tribe that had been displaced from the region some time ago. They wanted to protect the land. That did not really interest Haight, but they had the boy, and, in any case, he could not ignore the threat to the canal. Haight had finally gone to the President, using his Senator as the contact. The gentle man who now occupied the White House seemed out of place in the severe dignity of the mansion, but Haight had found him intelligent and quick to understand the situation. He had shown neither surprise nor outrage but had listened quietly as Haight outlined the plot. The President had from time to time asked a question, and he had frequently looked over to his National Security Advisor. Haight had the distinct impression that neither man was entirely surprised by the news. The National Security Advisor, whom Haight knew from his days in the State Department, had asked only one question and that had been whether their response should be overt or covert. The President had replied that it had to be off the record. That left Haight squarely in the middle. He would have to provide cover for the assault on the place in the jungle. There must be nothing to trace this back to the White House given the involvement of so many in the President's orbit. Nieves had given him a list of those involved, and these men were now watched around the clock.

Nieves had visited Anglesey, and it had not taken long to find out that the assault had begun. Centron's ships had already transported the equipment necessary to pump out the water from the area. Haight had wondered about this until he realized that not much water would have to be pumped. All they needed was access to the gates. While the jungle floor was flooded, it would not be a difficult task to clear a small section of the water. They also knew that the means of destroying the lake floor had been transported only days before. Haight had taken four days to put a team together using his most trusted contacts, and Nieves had insisted that his men be part of the operation. Haight had no objections as the agents he had pulled together were accustomed to working with all sorts of groups.

One problem they faced had been solved by the presence of Nieves' men, anyway. Because of the infection of the Agency, they had decided not to use anyone from the Latin American theater of operations. Most of the men with him now had been recalled from Southeast Asia, and many of them had had little sleep in the last four days. They were hard, silent men with whom Haight had dealt over the last decade, and, though they were not personally known to him nor would he have recognized any of them on the street, he was intimately familiar with their records. Two things worried him. He did not know the timetable for the destruction of the lake nor the location of the old camp.

Haight slapped irritably at something that landed on his neck as the leading boat moved easily in the darkness, and his boat, second in line, followed. Haight continued to worry. They were unprepared for this, his every instinct told him. He would have preferred more time to plan, to work out the details of the assault. They did not even know the strength of the enemy, although, as Nieves had rightly pointed out, it was unlikely too many men would have been brought into Panama for this operation. In spite of the magnitude of the act, the mechanics were actually rather simple. The tunnels ran along the fault line of the isthmus. It was only necessary that explosives of sufficient magnitude be placed at strategic points along each tunnel. The explosion would shear off the connecting rock that held the fault together, creating the effect of an earthquake and breaking off the northern bottom of the lake. The water would rush out like that in a sink from which the plug had been removed, and anything on the lake, including the many ships anchored there, would be sucked along with the drainage.

Suddenly, the small light on the lead boat went out, and he immediately killed his light as well. The other boats did the same. Soon, a hand touched him, and Nieves' whisper came from the darkness.

"We are here."

Haight stared into the luminous darkness of the jungle but could see nothing.

"How do you know?"

"Listen."

Haight held his breath and at first heard nothing. Then, just as he was about to exhale, a low hum came to his ear. It was a generator. Not wanting to risk any noise, he squeezed Nieves' arm in confirmation, then quickly tugged on the rope that connected his boat to the one behind him. Soon, the six boats were in a rough circle, their bows pointing inward. It had been decided that, once contact was made, Nieves' boat, laden with the six Indians, would scout around. The other five now lay silent in the water as Nieves slipped into the night. While he waited, Haight listened to the sounds of the jungle, trying to imagine this place before the water had come and chased everything up into the trees. Something was fluttering close by, and he wondered if it was an owl. There was a restlessness to the night, and it increased his nervousness. He pulled back the dark cover and looked at the luminous face of his watch. It was just after one in the morning.

We are running out of time, he noted impatiently.

Without any knowledge of when the blast would take place, he was also not sure if they were safe. Maybe the generator was a good sign. Presumably, if the intruders were still there, then the explosion was not imminent. Although, with Centron's record, he could not be sure. They had used disasters before to cover up their acts and would not hesitate to do it again.

Just as he was beginning to fidget, Nieves' voice whispered in his ear.

"There are four men guarding the gates. They are Indians. Not from our group. The pump you hear is keeping the water out. There are three boats tied up outside the dry area, so I am assuming twelve men. That means eight are inside."

Haight grunted and thought furiously. Eight men inside suggested one was in each tunnel.

He was about to ask Nieves about the possibility of disabling the guards when the man, as if reading his mind, said, "The water is being held back by a semi-circular berm. The guards are in the dry space in front of the gates. We won't be able to approach them without being seen."

Something in Nieves' tone warned Haight that the man had a solution, and he waited.

"We will eliminate them from the boats."

"How? We can't use guns."

"With arrows."

Haight almost laughed. He was going into this confrontation with bows and arrows. Still, any weapon killed with equal finality. This decided, Nieves set off again. The noises in the jungle stopped, as if nature itself was listening. Again, a long time passed, and his tension rose as he strained to hear any sound suggesting that men had died. There was nothing. Then, a boat materialized out of the darkness again, and Nieves said, "Let's go."

They moved carefully now and soon came to the berm. The men quickly scampered down the sides, using the crude steps made by the sandbags heaped one on the other. They were soon inside the giant gates that had been built into the hill, and Haight stood outside as the others disappeared, three to a tunnel, hurrying to find whatever had been placed there to destroy the lake. Standing in the eerie light of the night, he marveled at the size of the gates.

They must be thirty feet high, he thought, touching them. Pure steel. How did they manage to manufacture this in the jungle seventy years ago?

In spite of himself, Haight felt some admiration for the men who had built the gates, but he quickly squelched the thought. The same man who had built these gates had also murdered the workers. Somewhere out on Long Island, according to Nieves, he lived, almost dead himself but still causing other men's deaths. Haight felt a strong urge to confront this man, to tear from him the explanations he gave himself for his acts. Haight understood cruelty. He had seen it too many times, had himself acted cruelly on too many occasions, to be surprised by it. He had seen evil only infrequently, but he recognized its presence, and this was it. There was no place for Bryant in this world. Once this was done, someone would pay him a visit. This would force the confrontation between himself and Romulus, and at this thought, something pounded in his ears, almost shutting out the sounds of the night.

Suddenly, two of the men came rushing from the gates.

"They are all over," one gasped.

"What are you talking about?" Haight asked, but the man simply pointed to the tunnels. Haight jogged to the entrance and descended into the darkness that was relieved by a string of lights. At the bottom, he stepped off the crude elevator and walked carefully toward the mouth of a tunnel. As he approached, Nieves came from a second. Even in the dim light, Haight could see Nieves looked pasty.

"What is it?" Haight asked urgently, and the man stared at him, an odd, questioning look on his face.

Nieves grabbed his shoulders and hissed, "Why?"

Haight extricated himself from Nieves' grasp and walked swiftly in the direction from which the other man had come. Within seconds, he stopped, gasping for breath.

Skeletons were everywhere.

They were piled on top of each other as if the men had been trying to get to an exit. Haight felt weak and leaned against the cold wall of the tunnel. His mind seemed to be swimming in a dream, but something still had to be done.

He ran back to Nieves, shouting, "The explosives. Have we found them?"

The man, looking stunned, nodded, and Haight breathed a sigh of relief. They walked slowly back to the bottom of the elevator shaft, and there Haight found seven men he did not recognize guarded by some of the men he had brought. Seeing the glassy-eyed stares, he knew each of the tunnels contained more skeletons.

"Where is the eighth?"

Nieves nodded in the direction of the most distant tunnel, saying, "Emiliano went in after him. He's not back yet."

Haight took the gun from Nieves and walked off to the dark mouth. Inside, a string of lights gave a dim luminescence to the place, and, hugging the wall, he moved swiftly along, surprised at the size of the tunnel. His shoes rang on the stone floor, the only sound he could hear. He was, therefore, unprepared when a figure appeared, a small gun pointing directly at Haight's heart. The man was clearly frightened, and Haight stood very still.

"Get out of the way," the man croaked.

He had blood on his jacket, and Haight wondered if it was Emiliano's.

"Not much point in it. There are twenty odd men out there. Half of them would kill you without thinking for desecrating their forest. You're better off turning yourself over to me."

The man swore viciously at him, and the gun trembled, causing Haight to hold his breath. Then, the man brought the other hand from behind his back. In it, he held a small box with a single button. Haight knew immediately what it was. His face must have changed because the man laughed harshly. Haight's mind spun as he tried to stay calm.

"Do you know what exploding that device will do? Don't be foolish, man. You will kill yourself if you press that. My way, you get to live."

Fear was all over the man's face when he answered.

"If I fail, I die anyway."

Haight stood quietly, mesmerized by the man's thumb on the button, aware he was too afraid to be reasoned with. In the man's dilated eyes, Haight saw the resolve growing, the grip tightening on the box. Haight's body tensed. Then, the shadows shifted. Emiliano rose slowly, noiselessly, and as the man's thumb started to press down, his hand flashed. Haight heard the man cry out, but his eyes had involuntarily closed in anticipation of the explosion. He opened them when he heard the shot. The man, already dead from the knife protruding from his neck, pulled the trigger a second time. Then, there was silence. Haight rushed over to Emiliano, and the oversized Indian smiled wanly before losing consciousness. As Haight eased him to the ground that bore so many skeletons, there were shouts in the distance and the sound of running feet. By the time Nieves reached him, Emiliano had stopped breathing, his life taken by the bullet that had torn away half his throat. Nieves gently touched the giant. He was crying.

"I know it's no consolation, but we did prevent a disaster tonight," Haight said.

Nieves nodded, something dark at the back of his eyes.

"We have to destroy this."

Haight nodded. Nieves gave orders to his men quietly, and they moved the recovered explosives to new locations. They would blow up the berm and allow the water to return. This would flood the tunnels, and when far enough away, they would explode the gates. Then, the whole sorry episode would be over. Except for Romulus and the old man who had created this monstrosity.

As he sailed away, Haight did not look back. Not even when, almost an hour later, he heard the muted roar of the explosives and, after a while, felt the tug as the boats shook on the water. The danger was over, but something hard and cold burned in his heart. In the silent darkness, they headed east. They were to be met in Colon and then whisked by helicopter to Nieves' camp in the mountains. There, the boy would be returned to him, and then he would be on his way to the States to find two men.

CHAPTER FORTY-NINE

PANAMA 1976

In Panama City, Romulus sat with his night glasses trained north. Something was wrong. There had been no call. His fingers tapped anxiously on the window. He knew intuitively that Haight was involved in whatever had gone wrong. Hours ago, before he had dispatched Anglesey to his maker, he had been told that Nieves had asked about the timetable for the destruction of the canal. Nieves must have been desperate because he had been careless. He was not supposed to know anything about that aspect of the operation, and his questions would have raised the suspicion of anyone with any intelligence. Anglesey, the jackass, had cooperated, anxious to show he was on the inside. Fortunately, he had not known the location of the tunnels, and Romulus now swore angrily at himself for having assumed Haight would not be able to find the place.

Romulus was angry but not distraught. He did not want his first operation as the head of Centron to end in failure, but this had never been his operation. The people who dealt with Centron would not be much interested in the distinction, but he was not too worried. Busy protecting their own hides, they would not be able to touch him. Still, failure could become a habit, and, in his world, that always led to the grave. He would have to send a message. Haight would have to be killed, and in the most brutal fashion.

When the clock in the hotel room showed three, he stood and walked to a small suitcase. From it, he picked up what looked like a gun, checking the chamber to be certain it contained fourteen darts. Tonight demanded silent work, and the darts were as effective as bullets. He knew where Haight was headed. His informants at the airport had confirmed that Nieves' men had picked Haight up several days before. No one had seen him since, and that meant he would be at Nieves' hideaway in the mountains. Nieves foolishly believed this was a secret, but Romulus knew where the camp was, and that is where he was headed.

Dawn was breaking when Romulus moved into position on a small knoll overlooking the camp. The place was quiet but well guarded, and he lay silent, swivelling his head slowly from side to side in an effort to identify any unusual movement. The Centron helicopter had dropped him off three miles away, and he had been on a forced march to reach the camp. Below him were three guards at different locations on the hill. They would be easy enough to take care of. He wanted Haight. Nieves could wait.

Romulus lay on his stomach, watching, and it was while in this position he heard the low voices coming up behind him. He quickly ran his hand over the ground on both sides of his body to see if there was a path. There was not, and he pressed himself into the ground, fading into the darkness of the grass. As the men passed, he recognized Haight's voice, and something inside him relaxed. There is a state that Zen masters achieve just before action, in which the pace of the universe slows, and life is lived out between the moments. This is the state Romulus now sought, and as he lay, his breathing slowed, and his body lost its rigidity. He was transforming himself into something many said was not quite human, for he had been known to walk into places from which escape was said to be impossible and had walked out again. Always, there would be death. Now, he was seeking that state. These men would be tired, and, feeling protected, they would fall asleep quickly and sleep deeply.

Twenty minutes later, Romulus moved, and it was as if the wind moved. He knew the exact positions of the three guards, and four minutes and three darts later, the camp's main house was unprotected. This was always the most dangerous part, moving from full darkness to partial light, and he approached the house slowly, giving his eyes time to adjust. As he was approaching the gallery, using the side of the house as cover, someone stepped out from the door. Romulus froze, exhaling slowly and with barely a sound. He watched the silhouette and soon relaxed.

The gods are on my side, he thought, as he recognized Haight's lanky figure.

Romulus knew he should simply fire the dart and be gone. It would be a while before anyone knew the four men were dead, and he would be out of the country by then, but he wanted to see this man's face as he died.

As Haight walked down the steps and stood in the clearing, staring up at the sky, Romulus moved swiftly behind him and, placing the dart gun against his back, said quietly, "Come."

Soon, the two men had disappeared into the trees that bordered the clearing. Haight did not resist, for he knew Romulus' skill. This was not his strength, and so he walked where Romulus directed, deep into the forest that surrounded the camp on the hill. When the man told him to stop, he did, not turning around. Haight was interested in his emotions. He felt fear, but it was remote, placed at a distance. Accepting that he was going to die, Haight was determined not to beg for his life.

Facing Romulus, Haight felt the malevolence emanating from the man. Then, the cultured, slightly accented voice asked, "Well, Haight, any last words?"

"None I can think of."

Haight, conscious of the gun, was surprised at the steadiness of his voice. Then, he said, "Actually, I do have one question. What interests of Centron were to be served by destroying the canal?"

Romulus breathed heavily and replied, "Mr. Bryant had his reasons, and I have mine. His were about honor, and mine are about power. Of course, it's all over now. I am aware the authorities have been alerted, and there is a good deal of military traffic about the area, so it will not be possible to complete this assignment. No matter. The canal's destruction was useful and opportune but hardly imperative."

"Then why?" Haight asked exasperatedly, and Romulus chuckled.

"Foolish men who dream of dominating the world, Haight. They pay well to sustain that dream, not realizing the world is already dominated. Centron controls a good deal of it. Perhaps it would be more accurate to say that it influences the world. Foolish men still think of nations and their honor, unaware that these have become irrelevancies. I know the men who are at the heart of this plot will die. Your President will be reluctant, but even he will recognize the exigencies. There can be no trial. It would damage your public image too much. So the Americans will take care of Centron's problem."

Haight listened to the cultured voice, the slight mid-European accent more pronounced as Romulus spoke, and he knew the killer was right. There would be no trial. Once the threat was over, the six men at the heart of the plot would die. Haight could not bring himself to feel sorry about this, but he was tired of the killing. Something inside him seemed to give up, and his shoulders slumped. Romulus must have noticed because he said, "Goodbye, Haight. I never did say thank you for staying with me on that adventure in Cambodia, so here is your reward: a painless death."

Romulus raised the gun. Haight felt nothing, accepting his death with a stoicism that surprised him. He kept his eyes open, serene and waiting. Then, the forest moved. Haight jerked his head up, staring at something that his mind did not quite comprehend. Romulus saw the frightened look, and, in spite of a lifetime of training, the terror was so clear on Haight's face that he turned.

Then, the forest leapt.

Haight saw the monstrous animal, and, as it moved, the sky disappeared for a moment, the stars blotted out by its giant frame. There was no sound as it brushed by Romulus, and he fell, knocked down by the weight. Haight stood petrified as the beast stopped at the edge of the woods, staring at him. In the lightening sky, he saw what appeared to be a scar next to its eye, and, as the giant animal turned, he noticed that it limped. There was a slight rustle, and then it was gone, the dawn closing around it like a shroud. He was not sure how long he stood there, his heart pounding. He walked to where Romulus lay. At first, he thought the man was still alive because there was no blood. Then, he noticed the unnatural angle of Romulus' neck. When Haight tried to lift Romulus, the head lolled to the side. Aware he was not alone, Haight stood. Nieves, his shoulders draped in the robe of the butterflies, watched. The two men stared at each other until Nieves said, "Her thanks to you."

Haight nodded, knowing he was hearing nonsense but believing it anyway, and, with a deep breath, he walked past Nieves and out of the forest.

CHAPTER FIFTY

CHARLESTON, SOUTH CAROLINA 1976

Three weeks later, Jack Haight stood looking down from the thirty-first floor of the Haight Building in Charleston. He was on his way to Washington to meet with the Secretary of State. There had been a whole spate of resignations in the services, and he was being invited back into the fold, probably at the President's request. At this thought, he felt a slight nervousness, having left Panama with the distinct impression he had missed something.

Nieves had been gone when Haight awoke the morning after Romulus' death. At breakfast, they brought Dean in. The kidnapping had all been a charade, but Haight was not able to question Nieves about it. The man had again gone underground and would not be found unless he wanted to be.

Later that day, the headline of *La Prenza* had read "AMADOR DEAD," and Haight's mind immediately turned to Nieves, though the paper indicated the publisher had died of natural causes. In the plane, looking down on the mysterious land that showed its green, encouraging face from the air, he had wondered where, in all that greenery, laid the camp they had destroyed. When the plane banked right, bringing the sea into view and blotting out the land from his sight, he had not been entirely uncomfortable.

On the pavement below was an old man who had been taking his breakfast there for the last few weeks. An attentive Asian nurse reached over and wiped something from the man's mouth. When the security cameras picked up the two men for several days in a row, Antonio Peques had reported it to Haight. He now knew that it was Barnes, but, though curious, he had dug no further, not even when he received the large check he had been asked to handle for the boy. The note had indicated that no further contact was necessary, and Haight respected that. Now, he watched as the man's head jerked sharply to the right and then turned slowly, apparently following the movement of someone on the sidewalk. Haight knew that Dean had arrived for work since this was the man's pattern every day.

Sighing softly, Haight turned away from the window, walked to his desk, and called down for Antonio to get his bags. He was on his way to Washington.

CHAPTER FIFTY-ONE

Charleston, South Carolina 1976

Rupert Barnes sat in his wheelchair outside the small café across the street from the headquarters of Haight's Plastics and Paints. The café opened at six, and Barnes was brought by every morning at seven, about fifteen minutes before the boy arrived. At first, it was to convince himself the boy was indeed alive, but now something else drew him. He was not sure how to phrase it, but it could be love, pride in the boy, or perhaps a vague sense he had found something that completed him.

Barnes still felt the shame of his discovery, but that had lessened as the days had passed, and he now accepted that his indiscretion, as he thought of it, was not intentional. He had not known. His first instinct had been to go to Barbados, to find out the truth of what Bryant had said, but this would do no good. He had checked, fully expecting to find that Audrey was dead, but, to his surprise, she was still alive, still in the island and, most surprising, living in one of the Barnes' old houses. He did not know what to make of that. He still felt no blood relationship to Audrey, even though he now knew the truth of her descent. In his mind's eye, she remained as he had last seen her, a little shy, a little spunky, and deeply passionate. This image sustained him now, and he fancied he could see this in his grandson, who walked with such confidence into the building across the street. Barnes still did not know what danger faced the boy, but Dean was protected.

Three weeks ago, his men had scoured Panama, seeking to learn who had killed the boy. He rented a villa in Altos de Oro, and, on the second night, a man brought a message that the boy was all right but Barnes' inquiries were endangering him. The note also promised that the boy would be returned as soon as the danger was past.

The note had been signed "Leila."

Barnes had been torn but called his men back, trusting the name. Obviously, the woman was dead, but someone clearly knew of his relationship to her. However, the clincher was the offer the note made to have the bearer remain with Barnes as a hostage of sorts until the boy was returned. It had been eight days before he heard anything, and then he was told to be at the airport at a certain time. There, he had seen the boy and the tall man he later learned was Jack Haight board a private plane.

Relieved, Barnes returned to the villa, and only then had he turned his attention to the note that was signed in the name of the long-dead woman. Hu had gone into the dark world of Panama City to find a man who knew of these things, and a meeting had been arranged.

The man who had come introduced himself oddly.

"I am the son of Leila's daughter."

Barnes felt the import of those words and had stared at the man, trying to see in him some resemblance to the woman who had consumed him almost a century ago, but he could not. His memory was too dim and, feeling the pain of his loss, Barnes fought to ask the question that had haunted him for so long.

As if the man knew of his uncertainty, he had said, "I am only sure she is my grandmother, but the legends say that all of the protectors come from many sources. What does it matter who our fathers are?"

Barnes felt the shame burn in him, shame for his cowardice so many years ago and shame for his need now. Worse, he knew no relationship was possible with this man who seemed capable of shading his face even in the light. This grandson would disappear once the conversation was done, and clearly he wanted Barnes to disappear, too. Barnes agreed.

Now, each day, he sat in the wheelchair, waiting for the boy to come by so he could see him. In the last few weeks, his American life had seemed a shadow, a substitute for something real and vital he had sacrificed in his youth. Were it not for his sons in Philadelphia, he would be adrift without moorings. Looking across the busy street where the boy was walking with that loose, athletic stride, something inside him thrilled at the sight, for, in him, he could see Audrey. The boy had the same subtle shading of the skin and the visible bones across which it seemed to be stretched.

As Dean disappeared into the tall glass building, Barnes closed his eyes, and, for a moment, he was back on a hill, in the darkness, feeling the power of the young girl beneath him, and something like a terrified sob escaped him.

CHAPTER FIFTY-TWO

BARBADOS 1976

Antoinette sat, as she always did, at the foot of the steps, reading from the newspaper. The old woman shuffled irritably as the St. Lucian woman stumbled over a word.

"Dem don't teach wunna nuttin in dat lil islan' you come from? Spit out de word, girl."

Antoinette sucked her teeth and continued to decipher the word. The old lady reclined on an ottoman, her head tied with a cloth of uncertain color. She occasionally rubbed her knees where the throbbing pain of her arthritis sometimes made her close her eyes, but she was not unhappy today. Two days ago, her letters had been returned, and with them had come a check and an explanation from her grandson. He still referred to her as his aunt, and this sometimes made her sad. She had never gotten over the pain of giving her son up to her mother, and these events of the last few weeks had brought it all back with a poignancy she had thought impossible after all this time. It was strange how Panama still seemed to be bothering people's lives.

As the younger woman continued to read, the old woman closed her unseeing eyes again, and, soothed by the lilting voice, she drifted away, the world dissolving inside her head. She occasionally whispered something the younger woman could not hear, but Antoinette was accustomed to this and simply continued reading to herself. Sooner or later, the woman would wake up and ask about what was in the newspaper, swearing she had not fallen asleep. The younger woman smiled.

The old woman, however, was not asleep.

Her mother had never been the same after Miriam's death. Audrey did not attend the funeral, but she heard Ruby Barnes had come to the gravesite late, just when they were lowering the dead woman's casket into the ground.

Ruthie walked toward Ruby, and the place became still. Even the men lowering the casket stopped, the ropes taut in their hands. The two women approached each other, and, though no one could hear what was being said, the conversation was clearly heated. Eventually, the white woman turned away. Ruthie returned to the gravesite. For days, the village was abuzz with the confrontation, and the details of the conversation, which no one had heard, were created and repeated as fact.

A week later, Ruby Barnes summoned Ruthie to the plantation house. This was now a considerable walk since they lived on the western end of the island, and Ruthie sent a message back to that effect. The next day, a horse and cart came for her, and she told Audrey to get dressed.

It was with some fear that the girl ascended the front steps of the plantation house, although that fear was reduced when Miss Kirton, the cook, appeared to answer the door. They were taken through the house to the eastern verandah, and Audrey stopped when she saw the gardens. These stretched away in the distance, eventually disappearing under the brow of the hill that began the second terrace of the island. She had never seen anything like this, and, as she stood staring, something moved in her heart. Immediately, she imagined

Rupert walking with her through those gardens, but, just as quickly, the image faded, for she knew this would never be her world, though its beauty penetrated her very soul.

The image was completely shattered when Ruby Barnes' sharp voice said, "What is she doing here? I asked you to come."

Her mother, not flustered by the woman, calmly responded, "Wha'evuh affec' me, affec' she."

The tension between the two women was obvious, and Audrey was proud of her mother because she did not appear to be afraid of the white woman. Ruby Barnes looked angry for a moment, then uncertain, but, eventually, she asked them to sit down.

"I did not want to confront you the other day in the graveyard, but I want you to understand that if you ever speak to me like that again, I will have you—"

"What? Have me what? Whipped?"

Ruthie's eyes narrowed to slits, and her whole body inclined forward as if she was about to spring. Ruby pulled back but did not answer the question. Instead, she said, "I know what has been said in the village about my being responsible for Miriam's death. I wanted you to know I had nothing to do with it. Her husband was killed in Panama, and I heard about it. I told her, that's all."

Ruthie looked at the woman who sat squarely in the wooden chair, her face averted to the east. She did not speak for a long time, but when she did, her voice, though quiet, had a hard edge to it.

"How he get kill, Miss Barnes?"

The question hung between them, and Audrey suddenly felt she was involved in the drama somehow. Something was dawning in her mind, and she was afraid of it.

"And why you feel dat you had to tell Miriam? Why?"

The woman continued to stare at the eastern horizon, and her mother asked angrily, "It is dat no-good brother of yours, ain't it? He kill she husband, right?"

Ruby Barnes looked around at this, some kind of struggle going on inside her. Audrey could see that she wanted to be angry, but something sapped her will as she both nodded and shook her head in response to Ruthie's question.

"When you Barneses goin' stop destroyin' people life? You don't feel dat you do enuff? Wunna got to go on killin' an' killin', mashing up everyt'ing dat wunna come in contact wid. Sometimes I does feel dat wunna is pure devil people. Whe' wunna come from? Wunna aint got nuh mercy and nuh feelin'."

Audrey watched as the white woman turned red, her eyes narrowing, and again she got the feeling that something was left unsaid. Still, she was afraid her mother would get into trouble for talking back to the white woman, so she said, "Ma. Stop."

Her mother's eyes turned on her. Audrey's heart quailed, for there was something in those eyes she had never seen before. There was fear, pain, and a fierce protectiveness, and her mouth snapped shut before that look.

"You, shut up," came the harsh reply, and Audrey subsided.

To her surprise, Ruby Barnes' voice was uncertain and almost apologetic when she answered.

"It was an accident, Ruthie."

"It always is wid wunna Barneses. Wunna just ain't nuh good," her mother responded resignedly, and Audrey wondered what accounted for the note of familiarity that had crept into the conversation.

"And you, Ruthie? You think what you are doing is any better?"

Her mother stood up and, looking down on the woman, said, "Doan start wid dat foolishness. We aint had nuh choice. This worl' doan forgive dem t'ings. Not atall, and you know dat. I aint had nuh choice."

Her voice had taken on something of a pleading note, and Audrey sat watching these two women, so alike yet so different, struggle to reach some understanding of their situation but finding it impossible. Both were afraid of something, but neither could say what it was. When her mother glanced at her, Audrey became convinced she was somehow involved in it. Audrey knew they had been given the house on the western side of the island because her mother told Ruby Barnes about her pregnancy. Why she would have done that, Audrey could not guess. No one in the village had known of Audrey's pregnancy, so why would her mother tell Ruby Barnes, and why would she expect the white woman to keep her secret?

The three women sat in this tight circle of discomfort until the silence became a force that ate into their souls. To the east, the long cane blades waved magnificently in the strong breeze that carried in it the smell of the sea, and Audrey marveled at how the land looked now that the rain was falling again. It had come with Miriam's death, and the drought had gradually retreated.

Still, the village was no longer the same. With the men gone or returning home broken in body and spirit from the foreign land that took their lives with such casual ease, the women too were leaving. They headed for different parts of the island or, more and more often, were leaving the island itself.

She had gone to visit her friend Angela, and the girl was pregnant again. Angela still had no children but seemed always on the threshold of giving birth. The village was dying, and this she saw as she had driven through on the cart with her mother.

Now, sitting with Ruby Barnes on the verandah at the Great House, she was aware of something else. From the driveway, the house seemed solid, immovable, but now she could see the little flakes in the paint where it had dried and broken. The drought had been hard on the Barnes plantation too, and, for a moment, she felt sorry for the woman who ran it.

That was the last time she had spoken to Ruby Barnes. As the years passed, she became more convinced that something stood between her family and the Barneses, besides the child she could not own. Her mother did not mention the family again until she was on her deathbed. Then, she had sent Audrey to the cellar to fetch a packet, and there Audrey found the profusion of letters Rupert had written to her over a period of eight years. Audrey had been torn between instinctive resentment of her mother for keeping Rupert's letters from her and sympathy for the old woman's condition. She had thought that, even in death, her mother did not allow her to feel any emotion uncomplicated by contradiction. That same night, with her mother's labored breathing coming to her from the next room, she had written to Rupert, pouring out her soul to the man she thought had deserted her. It was the only letter she wrote, for there had been no reply. By then, she assumed, he had left, having given up finally, thinking her uncaring.

Still, the letters had sustained her, had blotted out her husband's fierce thrusting and his calls for her. In the letters, she had found solace and something of the beauty contained in the books she had long ago read in school.

Audrey opened her unseeing eyes and said roughly to the woman who was still reading aloud.

"Look, girl, you goin' have to read it ovuh ag'in. You read it so bad dat I miss de sense of it. De Americans give back de canal, you say?"

The young woman smiled and said yes. She started from the top again, this time raising her voice so the old woman would be sure to hear.

THE END

Also by Ronald A. Williams

FOUR SAINTS AND AN ANGEL

Estelle first laid eyes on Mark St. Auburn when she was only eleven years old. She was St. Euribius' rich plantation girl, and he was a well-known but troubled villager. The attraction was instantaneous and strong enough that their lives remain intertwined despite infidelity, emotional breakdowns and violence. Mark disappears, and Estelle moves on, taking refuge in the love of her lifelong friends.

When Mark resurfaces after twenty years, bringing violence and fear into their lives, they are forced to come to terms with the impact this charismatic but insular man has had on them. As they discover more about Mark's past, not only their future but the nation itself is threatened.